WATERFORCE

A novel by

Jack Bell Stewart

A Response to the Threat of Terrorism in the
New York City Water Supply

Copyright 2018 by Jack Bell Stewart

This is a work of fiction. Names, characters, places and incidents within are the product of the author's imagination or are used fictitiously... Locations and basic information about the New York City Water Supply and its nineteen reservoirs have been resourced at the DEP website, books in print, news agencies, and personal visits. The methods used by terrorists depicted in this novel are completely fictional, as are some of the more vulnerable locations. This novel is a wakeup call to real possibilities, however flawed it may be when applied to actual conditions. Water terrorism can happen in ANY city in the world. Names of elected and appointed officials have been changed. Any similarity to real people is unintentional.

PUBLISHED IN THE UNITED STATES OF AMERICA
v. 7.1

ACKNOWLEGEMENTS

It took me years to write a novel. Along the way I moved twice, from New Hope PA to the Catskills, and—eight years later—to, Florida. That means three writer's groups! Bucks County Writers, Writers in the Mountains, and Sarasota County Writers Meetup. Members of all three groups contributed valuable lessons on my journey as a writer. Special thanks go out to Don Swaim, Barbara Apoian, Ev Ellsworth, Ann Epner, Phil Potak, Cliff Miller, Jim Tuggle, Jim Hannah, Philip Mygatt, Glenna Blomquist, Sheri Lasker, Gretchen Meyer, Antaeus Belevre, Lyn Blume, Chris Angermann, Bill Stewart, Bet Stewart, Emily Stewart, and so many unnamed friends who listened to me recite chapters and offered helpful suggestions to keep me from falling off the inevitable literary cliff.

Special thanks to Bill Enslen and to John Mickelbank for extensive proof reading.

WaterForce is dedicated to the memory
of my dear friend and mentor,
Donald H. McGee

FACTS: The New York City Water Supply System
The Delaware and Catskill Watersheds supply over 97 % of NYC water through a system of reservoirs, streams, lakes, aqueducts, and tunnels. The Croton Watershed supplies about 3% of the total. Nine million people are served by the system, which provides 1.1 billion gallons of fresh unfiltered water per day. The largest reservoir in the system is the Pepacton Reservoir, which holds about 140 billion gallons, and was completed in 1955. The combined watershed region is 1972 square miles. The New York City Water Supply System is the largest in the world, and includes nineteen reservoirs and three controlled lakes.

https://nyc.gov/dep

https://www.nycwatershed.org/

Chapter 1

August 1954—Shavertown, NY

A rnold Van Rosendael sat on his front porch with his shotgun in his lap, waiting for daybreak, and the arrival of demolition crews. Someone was going to die today.

My great-great grandfather looked at the ruins in what once was a peaceful small-town neighborhood. Ornate Victorian homes lay in forlorn piles, waiting for trucks to carry the refuse away to distant landfills. Broken windows and porch railings formed their own weird skyline and conspired together to remember the laughter of children and the beauty they had once provided the people of Shavertown, New York. The East Branch of the Delaware delivered a steady supply of water to three other river communities in the Catskills, all victims of the march of the new reservoir to come.

Officials would soon convey an order to vacate Arnold's condemned property, and a bevy of officers would arrive to halt his protests and cart him kicking and screaming away to jail. There was not a lawyer who could win his case, not even the renowned Herman Gottfried, who had finally been beaten by big city lawyers advocating the "better good" and "future welfare" of the people of New York City. They promised that "you mountain people will enjoy the preservation of the rural character" of the Catskills. That comment did not sit well with 'we mountain people'.

Arnold opened another Genesee. Not because he normally had a beer at seven in the morning, but because it was the last of his drinkable liquids. The bastards had fractured his well yesterday when they bulldozed the house next door. In frustration, he raised his gun, aimed into the pile of rubble, and pulled the trigger. His disheveled white hair collected shards of flying wood.

He'd been up since three, finishing a codicil to his will that he hoped would rectify the injustice of today with seed money for...someone, sometime. No current relatives were to receive a dime. Only a special family member in the future, motivated by worthy issues of the watershed, would be funded, that is IF the person was living by Arnold's standards. The money would need the benefit of decades of growth to do what needed to be done. But it was the only plan he could offer.

The grubbing crews dynamiting stumps along the river set off the next explosion, and interrupted his thoughts. Another century-old oak or chestnut blown from its home in the valley sent birds into a panic. A bulldozer started its engine, and the air smelled of swirling demolition dust, fresh mountain dirt, and foul diesel smoke in the August heat. Shards of mud followed an air-born training wheel from a child's bicycle, whirling in the air like a clay pigeon, and nearly hitting the windshield of a green and white fifty-two Pontiac making its way through the obstacle course that used to be Main Street.

Another blast of dynamite felled a tree that split apart behind the dusty car, which swerved at the sound of TNT sending football sized rocks flying into the air. The grimy auto stopped in front of Arnie's house. He watched his son Charlie get out of the car and waddle through the rubble in the yard. Like his dad, he wore enormous overalls with a burn hole in the breast pocket where he kept his pipe. A stained plaid shirt was rolled to his elbows. His graying hair stuck out of a hole in his straw hat, and a pin that said "Ike in '52" sat precariously beside one that hoped for the "Brooklyn Dodgers in '53." Like father like son, Charlie's gray beard captured remnants of yesterday's lunch.

The passenger door opened, and the legendary Attorney Gottfried emerged. He wore his usual three-piece navy pinstriped lawyer's suit with an immaculate white shirt and no tie. He emerged from the rider's seat with a leather brief case and a dour look on his face.

"You been awake all night, Pops...with your shotgun and all?" Charlie sat down on the rusty metal porch swing, straining its remaining strength.

"Hell no...for a little while, I guess. What's the difference how early I get out o' bed? D-Day—Delaware River Day—has arrived."

Charlie looked down at the fist-sized rocks piled like a pyramid next to a box of twelve-gauge shells on the deck beside him. "A poor man's arsenal, Dad. If ya run out of shells you can throw rocks." He picked up a fist-sized stone to admire it.

"Hey, Counselor Gott, ya bring my papers?"

"Good morning to you too," Gottfried said. "Jeez! Place looks like Korea back in fifty-one." When nobody laughed, he brushed the dust off his sleeve. "Look, why don't we go to breakfast, and talk about all this out of range of the dynamite? It'll do you good to get away. Say, the Bun N' Cone up in Margaretville." He offered a hand to Arnie, and was promptly greeted with a slap on his arm.

"Screw you, Gott. I ain't moving. I can't leave. The water Nazis will be here any minute. Let's get down to it, right now. You do what I asked?" One hand on his gun, he

8

reached out the other to receive a manila folder Herman offered from his briefcase.

"Yes, your majesty royal pain-in-the-ass. I did what you asked. But I'm telling you, as your lawyer...this will destroy your legacy. It'll prevent all of your heirs from getting one dime after you've left the planet. Probate will laugh their ass off. Please, Arnie, let's talk about this."

"You know what? Once I sign this, and it's legal, I don't care what you have to do to get this done. It's my stuff, my money, and I get to say what happens." He stopped to read, scowling after absorbing the first several pages. "I knew you'd water this down, so I went ahead and drafted my own version that gets it right, the way I want it." He drew thick black lines through Gottlieb's version on the second and third page.

"Hey! That's an original, typed nice. Gladys worked hard on that!" Gott protested.

Charlie sighed and handed him a pen. "Calm down, Pops. I don't know why you need a damn lawyer if you're just gonna write it yourself. You know I don't agree with you ...but, they're your wishes, and—"

"You're damn right they're mine. I'll tell you both, I'm not such an old fool that I think you're not going to try to block this after I'm gone. But maybe somebody down the line will need money to prevent another damn lake for New York *City*." Another dynamite blast, closer now, seemed to fire his temper. He raised his gun and peered through the sights at the bulldozer. "I ought to...I mean, what the hell do they need eighteen huge lakes for, and this one, twenty-two miles long with over a hundred billion gallons, ruining four historical towns? You could water every garden in the state for a century with that much water."

Out of breath, his heart pounded so hard he could feel his shirt throbbing. A tear escaped and dropped into his beard, hydrating a dried hunk of macaroni.

"Easy, Pops. It's too late. It's a done deal. And you're acting like a stubborn old stump. Martha and I tried our best to help, signed your petitions, and testified in court. I even bought the shells for ya, even though it scares me to death what you might do. And the money..."

"You got it made already, kid. Besides they didn't offer me enough for a pot to piss in for this house." He flipped through the document until the signature page appeared. He pounded his fist on the document to emphasize his words. "Get out your notary stamp, counselor. Get ready to include MY codicil in MY words. I'm givin' it all to the cause."

Charlie placed a gentle hand on his father's shoulder.

"What cause'? Pops, you know it's a lost battle."

"Yes, but the war is not lost, son. You're just too lazy to fight it. The nine thousand I have goes in a trust fund for a family member in the future who has the balls to do something about this fiasco. Who knows? Might be worth quite a bit down the line. Just remember, counselor, I am of sound mind right now. Where do I sign this bore-ass piece of paper?" He added his hand-written notes to the document, the promises for the future he couldn't trust his lawyer to compose. Gottfried squeezed the notary stamp to imprint the will and the new codicil. Arnie scratched out several signatures with an angry flourish. "Now you keep this safe until the time comes. I want this invested for the future in something that'll grow. If you ever die, which I doubt, you old coot—you got to pass this on to the next legal genius. Promise?"

Attorney Gottfried nodded reluctantly.

A huge bulldozer lumbered into his front yard from the street to allow a black and white patrol car access to the driveway. As Arnie contemplated the trigger of his shotgun, Constable Dibble sauntered over to the porch with handcuffs dangling in his left hand and official papers in his right. His six and half foot beanpole stature towered over the men seated on the porch. He watched Gottfried stuff the document back into his briefcase and paused for a diplomatic minute before delivering his news, twitching his bushy mustache as if it was spring loaded.

"Arnold Van Rosendael, I'm sorry about this, but I got me your third order to vacate, an order of eminent domain, two appeals denied, and a warrant to take you downtown, lock y'up. The wreckers are already waiting. You're the last one within the take-line between Margaretville and Downsville, and if you try to stay here, the water's coming soon, and you'll just get to watch your own house burn and drown. Burn and drown...burn an'—"

Arnie raised his hand in a gesture of peace. He opened and unloaded his shotgun to show he was no threat and pointed it to the deck. He was suddenly too tired to care. Years of letters to Mayor Wagner, Governor Dewey, even President Eisenhower, endless double talk, expensive legal battles, worthless press releases, diminishing attendance at nonstop rallies, and harsh arguments with his own neighbors had left him practically standing alone against the power of New York City's thirst for another reservoir.

He felt like a small abused child. "I knew you'd be coming. Please, please don't make me watch my house burn."

"I won't, Mr. Van Rosendael. But I got to take ya downtown if ya won't leave." Constable Dibble fingered his handcuffs in a not-so-subtle gesture. "Oh, by the way, here's

11

your check for the property, the one you refused last week. Just sign here that you received fair compensation for the house and the land."

Arnie looked at the check. "Nine-hundred twenty-nine dollars? Are you shitin' me?" He spit on the ground, hitting Dibble's boot. "This is the nineteen fifties, not the Civil War! The house down the street, by the same builder, sold for eight thousand two years ago. And you call this 'fair compensation?'" He sat on the front step and nodded as he glanced at the briefcase Attorney Gottfried held in his lap. Without warning, his eyes clouded, and tears streamed down his face. His whole body shook like a crumpled bush in a windstorm.

It was Gottfried who broke the awkward silence, and finally spoke out as his advocate. "Come on, Constable. Give him a break. He's already got his things packed. Charlie and me are here to load things up in the car, take him up to Margaretville. No reason to arrest him now. The man just lost his family home, and his whole town is gone. All for nine hundred bucks?"

"Sorry, counselor, but the project is already several months behind, no thanks to Arnold Van Rosendael. I got to do what I got to do." He opened the folder with the warrant inside.

Charlie said, "No need for handcuffs. I'll help him move, myself. I promise."

Constable Dibble scratched his head, shifted on his feet, and scowled. "It's against my orders...but...if you promise he goes peacefully...but he's gotta leave *today*, in fact—*now*."

Wasn't that just the worst? Talking to him as if he was already dead! He kicked the can of Genesee off the porch, slung his empty gun over his shoulder, and opened the front door. Suddenly, his eyes widened like he'd thought of a wild idea. "Okay, guys, knock it off. Let me get rid of my gun and go get my wallet. Let's go have some breakfast before Dibble has me in the clink." They didn't look convinced until he announced, "Tell you what, I'll buy."

As the screen door slammed, Gottfried said, "Well, I'll be a monkey's uncle! He's finally got some sense about him. Did you see the look on his face? He's suddenly become a good citizen. And I've never seen him pick up a check in a diner in all the years I've known him."

Inside his house, he paced the floor. He no longer cared to hear how New York's largest reservoir would provide another hundred-some billion gallons of water for the CITY, how great the fishing would be in the new reservoir built for the CITY, and how the area would benefit economically by sending *his* water to the damn CITY. The CITY had consumed his entire town, and left him with nothing. He had exhausted all of his resources.

They waited patiently for Arnie to say goodbye to his home. They could see him through the front window, strolling through his living room for the last time. He picked up a picture of his departed wife, dressed in a flapper gown in the 20s. He walked through the dining room into the kitchen and peered through the back window into what was once her prize hollyhock garden. The glass eyes of the eight-point buck over the fireplace seemed to plead with him to save their home. But the men on the porch felt like they were violating his privacy, and one by one they faced the street to let the old man have his last moment with a home that had been in his family for five generations.

A hundred feet away, near the old 1877 Shavertown covered bridge, another blast shook the earth and splattered chestnut roots and pristine Delaware River water high in the air, no surprise when the sound cracked the glass in the front window and shook the boards under their feet.

Constable Dibble said, "This damn town is starting to sound like target practice for Sherman tanks." A momentary silence seemed to permeate the dust in the air.

After a long moment, the sound of worried birds started up again. Gottfried said, "What the hell is he doing in there? Maybe we better go on in and see what's keeping him." He looked through the front window, seeing only a shadow against the glass.

Suddenly, another detonation rocked their ears, the distinctive blast of a twelve-gauge...from inside the house. The explosion overpowered echoes in the valley, followed by a spray of blood and fleshy parts against the breaking window. The men on the porch dove for cover, covered in glass and airborne blood.

"HOLY MOTHER OF...Dad, what the HELL!?" Charlie cried.

Covered with blood and glass, Gottfried was too shocked to move. Arnie's dentures flew through the glass and landed at his feet, blown out of his mouth half intact, with blood dribbling out of the front teeth, poised as if they could utter his last argument. Dibble threw up over the railing. Charlie took off in a run and dove into the front seat of his Pontiac while he frantically searched for his keys.

The driver of the bulldozer revved his engine and tilted the front-end loader into position. He looked at his list. One more house to go, and only two months behind schedule.

Chapter 2

Present day, The Pepacton Reservoir

The old Ford pickup turned from the main State Highway 28 onto the reservoir road. It crossed the new Shavertown Bridge, and cut its lights before it slowed down to a crawl. The road was desolate, and seldom had much traffic at two in the morning, but the driver was careful anyway. After a mile or so, the rusty pickup pulled into a small clearing, protected from sight only by a thin grove of white birch saplings and some overgrown snakeberry bushes. Two men dressed in black opened the doors cautiously and struggled to lift a heavy wooden half-barrel planter out of the back without spilling its contents.

"Careful, damn it," Michael whispered. He flipped his hoodie over his head, in case anyone was watching. He was dressed in tattered black jeans and a sweatshirt that said, "Rebel Yell," unshaven and unwashed for several days. Clean him up and he'd make the football team if he'd wanted that.

"I can't see with this ski mask." Bro pulled the mask off. "And the gloves don't give me any grip."

"I'm tired of your whining. We've got to be careful!"

"Couldn't we have gotten a full barrel, so we could just roll the damn thing down the embankment?"

"Do you ever stop? Next time, you do the shopping."

"I'm just saying. It's only a half-barrel tub, not easy to drag. This thing don't hold that much. And look at the tracks we're leaving," Bro said. After minutes of struggling, they were still less than ten feet from the back of the pickup.

"Yeah, right. Next time I'll bring a sled."

"When we do the Schoharie?"

"Not yet. Let's just do what we're supposed to do. One target at a time."

"You're the man, boss. But this thing is heavy. Shit. Knocked over my beer." Bro kicked the empty can into the bushes.

"I've got an idea. We'll strap it on my skis to make it easier." After locating a rope, they dragged the barrel onto a pair of cross-country skis and tied it on top of the bindings, creating two runners. Another rope served as a dragline, and they hauled it through the snow, over rocks and tree roots, down a steep embankment to the water.

At the water's edge, the gloves came off.

"What the hell are you doing?" Michael said.

"I can't dump it if I can't keep a grip on it."

"And with your prints all over it now, we'll have to lug the it back to the car after we dump it. Freakin' pinhead. Let's go...on three. One, two...three." The dirty white powder spilled out of the half-barrel and mostly into the water. It looked like a huge pile of flour, coagulating as it mixed with the cold water, and bubbling as it slowly sank.

"Help me with the barrel."

"*You* take it back to the truck. They're your prints."

"Come on, Michael, give me a hand."

Michael pulled out his Buck knife, cut some branches. He dragged them behind as they struggled up the embankment, scrambling the footprints on the way. After he pulled the truck back out into the road, he covered the tire tracks with snow, and dragged the branches over the top.

They loaded the barrel and the skis back in the bed of the pickup. Michael muttered, "Looks pretty good, but we gotta cover our prints a little better…"

Suddenly a flash of distant headlights filtered across the reservoir and through the wintered trees bare of leaves. They looked at each other in panic, using hand signals as if they could be heard. The approaching car was still more than a mile away, but it was traveling fast over the bridge, and soon the road would curve to a place where the headlights would illuminate them. They dove into the cab and skidded as they took off to avoid discovery. They rode in silence for several minutes. Once they were safely out of range, they could finally let off a little steam.

"I can't believe we did it!" Michael turned on the radio. On the Walton station, the only one they could get, Liza Minnelli sang about New York City to them. *My little town blues…are melting away…*

"After all that talk, we finally did it. And got away clean!" High fives and knuckle bumps were exchanged. Time to gloat. Time to celebrate.

"New York City'll never know what hit 'em!"

"Bout time."

Michael turned up the volume. As he brushed white powder off his pants, he crowed his own version of Liza's familiar tune. *"…If we can send it there, no one will ever dare, to mess with us, New York, New York…"*

"Let's celebrate." He opened the last beer and handed it across the front seat after he took a hit for himself. He reached into his pocket, feeling for his gloves, and slipped the left one on to his hand. He checked all around for the other glove, trying every pocket. "Oh crap!"

"What? What's up?" He threw a hard look at the passenger beside him.

"Nothin', Michael."

"Nothin'? Something wrong?"

"Can't find my other glove." He opened his jacket to search the inner pockets.

"You didn't drop it back there, did ya?" Michael looked worried and slowed the car as if to turn around.

"Nah. Probably dropped it in the truck bed. It was full of that powder."

"You stupid dweeb. If they find it..."

"I'll try it on. Be like O.J. 'If it doesn't fit, you must acquit.' Besides, we can't go back now. That car on the bridge...could be..."

"You can be such a dumb turd sometimes."

"Forget about it. Let's go home, get some beer. Like I said, time to celebrate."

They headed back to Margaretville on the other side of the reservoir. They passed Summerfield's, with shadows of waiters inside setting tables after closing. A man cleaned the grill in the Chinese carryout joint, and a dog shivered as he peed on the entrance step to the Cheese Barrel. They parked the truck across from the old Galli-Curci Theater on Main Street and walked a few steps to their apartment over a shop on the road. It was a desolate street at night, with most buildings still under renovation after Hurricane Irene's floods had all but destroyed them in 2011. A light went on nearby, across the street on the second floor. But they paid no attention. They were ready for a victory beer.

Inside, the place had the disheveled look of two twenty-something men who called the small apartment home. A stained second-hand mattress hugged the living room floor, without sheets, a dirty blanket providing its only promise of warmth. Dishes piled high in the sink, an old fifties couch rescued from the trash, and the prize possession, a new sixty-inch HDTV, paid for with a stolen credit card.

As he peeled off his black turtleneck and popped open a beer, Bro said, "That was fun. And so easy. I can't believe how vulnerable these reservoirs are."

"Yeah. You'd think they'd have more patrols out. Or sensors, cameras, whatever."

"They've got cameras near the dam. But the lake is twenty-two miles long, with dozens of inlets and streams and hidden shoreline. How could they possibly guard all that?"

"No way, they can't. Must be at least eighty miles around the edge."

"Do you think we had enough powder?"

"I don't know. We used what they gave us. I'm no chemist, and not a doctor. We're just the delivery boys."

"Got that right. I think we did a damn good job, for sure."

"Gonna be a city in trouble! Serve the bastards right, for what they done. Can't wait! Turn on the news. Maybe we can watch the show."

"Won't be on yet."

"Maybe by tomorrow?"

"Well, maybe not, but like soon enough. Couple of days at least. It's a hundred forty miles to the City."

He turned on the TV, and soon they were mesmerized by two phony wrestlers putting on a show of macho theatricality with each other. The Latino guy was obviously going to be the winner. So predictable, like the turmoil they had just created.

Chapter 3

Kingston, NY

I'm Titus Rose. Our family shortened its name from Van Rosendael after the scandal of my great-great grandfather's suicide back in the fifties. After four generations, the boys in the Rose family were destined for notoriety. I couldn't have been more different from my older brother. While he was climbing the academic ladder in grad school down the city at NYU, I took pride in sleeping through my senior year at Margaretville Central School. Two years later I managed to be the youngest sophomore at SUNY Delhi, first in my class, and every teacher's protégé. Dad wanted me to be more like my brother Parker and stop wasting my time writing, but people seemed to like my work, and some even said I was smarter than Parker. My politics, if you could call them that, were full of small town bull. The people who made fun of my last name called me names like 'Rosy Ass' or 'Rose Blossom', and they had to answer to my brother in the years before he left for the Big Apple. Now, I was alone to fight the mountain idiots left behind.

Parker, on the other hand, excelled at being the perfect grad student and reading everything he could get his hands on. He graduated second in his class of seventeen seniors and won a scholarship to Columbia for undergrad and NYU for grad school, where he took up environmental studies. He'd always been a bit of a rebel. At twenty-six, he was a perfect fit for the brainiacs at NYU and easily found friends among the liberal activists in the East Village he called home. He'd already racked up an impressive list of protests from environmental issues to Occupying Wall Street. Bottom line, Parker got all the attention. But I knew I was at least as smart as he was.

I was driving too fast along Highway 28 to the Kingston bus terminal to pick up Parker for a few days of skiing on his three-day President's Day recess. Even though we had our differences we had that blood-brother communication that came from sharing the woes of our parents' broken marriage and a vicious custody battle. In that as in most other things regarding us, our father had used *his* superior intelligence for a crafty winning strategy. Dad was a patrolman for the Department of Environmental Protection—the DEP—and we were his sons there to do his bidding and totally within his strict definition of the world.

No surprise that I was running late, but I knew I'd find Parker inside the Dietz Stadium Diner next to the bus terminal. From the front door Parker's shiny grey skinny jeans, collarless purple shirt, black hoodie, and high-top laced Skecher boots looked out of place in this tired Hudson River town. Sliding into the booth my brother had chosen near the back, we greeted with the customary handshake known only between brothers and the standard greeting that really meant almost nothing. "Hey bro...got a smoke?" "Yeah, but ya can't smoke in here." "Really? Bummer." "How's Tina?" "Good—still screwin' like bunnies." "She's hot!" "Watch it there, little brother. She's *my* squeeze." "You sure?" Blatant chauvinism and meaningless brother-talk just like old times.

Parker brought me up to date about his environmental studies at NYU, getting very excited and emotional as he spoke of irrefutable proof of global warming, deforestation of wetlands and jungles, the world's overpopulation now soaring over seven billion, the futile frustrations of recycling, and corporate America's attempts to deny the simple recognition that there are imminent problems the world must face immediately.

"...It's past the 'concern' stage, Titus. It's time for environmental action, and I mean widespread protests, like the Vietnam era, like way past the Greenpeace movement. I mean, like, something that will keep the world alert."

I said, "Hold a sec. You're talking serious action here. I thought you were happy just being a member, getting the magazines, the coffee mug and that rad tee shirt."

"I am sort of. The tee shirt is cool. But like, we sent twelve thousand e-mails to the CEO of Costco about protecting the oceans. But do you think for one minute he did anything about it except call his techie guys to clear out his in-box? We're all getting frustrated. Al Gore was right back then. The earth is a living being, and we're killing it. It's not enough to intercept a fleet of whaling boats in Japan or picket BP. Or follow oil tycoons around–like David Koch, who could give a rat's ass about our planet."

A waitress delivered our midnight breakfasts and smiled at Parker like he was some sexy exotic creature from a Broadway musical. I looked forward to seeing my brother on our home turf, unlike my last visit down the city, where I felt intimidated, out-reasoned, and out-done among Parker's intellectual friends. Besides, skiing was one of the few things I was good at, and I was looking forward to surpassing a bro who was losing his ski-legs from being away in the big city for most of the past five years. These mountains feel like my own, and I would make skiing at Belleayre my ticket to dominance in the game of sibling rivalry.

"So, you're not happy just being a peaceful activist? I can't even..." I said, slurping my cup of jo.

"I'm saying that we need to redefine the word 'activist.'" He leaned over the table, and looked intently into my eyes, like he was holding a dark secret. "Do you realize how much money they've spent trying to confuse the scientific realities of climate change, hide the real facts, and stall legislative bills to curb climate pollution? We've got to bring these bastards *down*." His fist slammed the table, raising the toast off his plate.

"Dude, you're like, going berserk on me. I mean, I thought we were going to have a fun skiing-thing going on. I'm not like, ready to listen to this all weekend. I mean, we're in the Catskills, Parker-boy! Like, forget the world. Nobody cares about anything but fishing, hunting, and skiing up here." I slumped back, threw some shade by crossing my arms.

Parker set his coffee mug down hard. "*That's. Why. I'm. Talking* to you about this! Right! We're in the beautiful Catskills—our *home*—where people are at least ten years behind the dinosaur age. Even Anthony's mom, the old hippie activist, can't even decide whether to let them put more cell phone towers up around here so we can talk to each other." Parker stopped to drag his toast through the egg yolk on his plate.

"Ti, do you realize the Catskills could be a major political battleground? And it's complicated. They've got nineteen reservoirs for New York City spread around north of the city. We're in a prime area for confrontation on a major issue!"

"I don't get why it's such an issue. We get to fish, and they get—"

"They get OUR WATER." He tried a simpler approach. I hated it when he talked down to me. "Did you ever think to ask, 'Who owns the water around here, anyway?'"

"Well, I guess the city does," I replied, but there was a question already written on my face.

"Look at it again. The water comes down off the mountain, through our property in a fair-sized tributary, and then it empties into the East Branch of the Delaware. Let me ask you: we own the water on our land, right?"

"Well, yaass! It's *our* water. We drink it, fish in it, swim in it, dig our wells."

We both took a drink of water, and then he unloaded the trick question. "The New York City limits are a hundred and forty miles away. So why does the city get to dictate what happens to the water when it flows from our land into a river that dumps into a public reservoir?"

"Damn, I never thought of it that way," I admitted. I was beginning to see what grad school had done for him. I had to learn how to think on his level even though it was clear he'd progressed a lot further at Columbia and NYU than I had at SUNY State College at Delhi.

"This is the fundamental question behind all the other issues."

"'Fundamental,' eh?" I thought, trying to come up with something intellectual like my brother did. "Yeah, but the good thing is that it protects the land from development and we've got clean water. And so does New York City." Good one, but his answer put me in my place.

"Always the fisherman talking. 'Don't mess up my trout stream.'"

Now he'd struck a nerve, and I had to respond. "Sure, the reservoirs and the streams are great...for fishing. We've got the Pepacton, Cannonsville, Ashokan, Schoharie...yada yada...and the Esopus Creek has the best fly-fishing in the country. I happen to *like* fly fishing—the way it is." My eggs were getting cold.

"See, it's a difficult issue," Parker said. "The land is protected, but it mostly benefits the New York watershed. They never asked us if they could take the water from *our* land and then *sell* it to New Yorkers. They steal over a billion gallons from us every day. Meantime, they're buying up all the vacant land to prevent people from building homes. Dad says that policy has depressed our local economy for over sixty years."

"Dad *says* it depresses the economy, but he *works* for the DEP, which is *owned* by New York City. And when New York spends money on land deals, they pay taxes, and build water treatment plants, all of which helps the economy and preserves the watershed," I argued.

"That's a good boy. You've been trained well with the same bull they've been feeding us for over a hundred years," Parker said. "Let's start with the economy." He cut his egg whites into little islands and moved them one at a time across his plate, saying, "The land is sold to the City, for the same reduced price per acre as in years past. No growth in value there." He moved the egg pieces across the plate. "But can anybody live on that land? No! Does anybody spend money in the economy, build homes, and help support the grocery stores, the shops and the ski slopes? Double no. The damn bears don't buy groceries. The coyotes don't build homes and buy cars. Dad protects the land, but there is zero money coming *into* the economy. So, no growth means...no new jobs and permanent recession." He crushed the egg whites with his fork and broke a yoke to demonstrate his point.

"You're right. You know, Dad...he's always been on both sides of the issue. He gets paid to protect the water supply, but it was his great grandfather that committed suicide trying to save his home in—what was it called?"

"Shavertown. And Dad hasn't gotten over that. The DEP. The Department of Environmental Prostitution, he calls it, in private," Parker said.

I laughed at the old family joke. "*Protection,* dufus. Environmental *Protection.*"

Parker paused to pay the waitress, buying my meal like a big shot from New York City. "I know. It's been a family grudge ever since they took the house and great-*really*-great Grandpa blew himself up. But it's true. No growth means no economy can ever be healthy up here. And when one of our brilliant governors decided to close Belleayre Mountain to save his budget, it depresses everything in the region. Motels, inns, restaurants—everything depends on the success of Belleayre, Plattekill, Windham, and Hunter ski resorts."

"But didn't they just approve a huge project to expand Belleayre?"

"Sort of. But we haven't seen the money yet. Been contested in the courts since 1999. It'll take years."

"Parker, my man, this is too confusing. First you want to protect the planet, now you're saying that if New York preserves the rural countryside in the Catskills, it's bad because our economy is strangled." Now it was my turn to lean across the table. "Which is it, Parker? Whose side are you on? At least Grandpa Van Rosendael knew where he stood."

Parker threw up his hands in frustration. "It's the same down in the jungles of Nicaragua. The locals depend on deforesting to make a living, but it's an ecological disaster when they cut *too many* trees. There has to be a balance or the whole planet tanks."

"But nobody can agree how to balance it. Man, you've got to decide what you're so hot about. Trees or paper? Water for New York, or fish for dinner? Houses or nature? You're the NYU genius. Choose your battle, bro." Maybe I'd finally gotten under his skin.

"You're right, Titus. I get all excited, but then I can't even understand all of it."

"Let's go skiing. I don't want to think about this. You need to figure this out."

"Right. Got a smoke? I'm out."

"Don't be a derp. Can't smoke in here."

"Really? Balls. If I'm going to be an environmentalist, I should quit."

"Trouble is, you never will quit, like Tina did. Say 'hey' to her for me."

"I will, but *you'll* never get near her! She's my main."

Same old Parker.

Chapter 4

Belleayre Mountain

It was the last run of the day, and we were tired from too many black diamond trails, too many beers at lunch, and six hours of trying to outdo each other pounding through the moguls. Parker and I had a few moments of rest as we rode up the lift that would take us to the double-black diamond runs we lived for, the run that would start at Dot Nebel with its bumpy moguls near the top, then carry us into the intermediate blue trail called Cayuga, off the trail for a mile through the woods, and finally down the bunny trail on Deer Run.

"Not too many people on this side," I said, relaxing on the lift.

"This is my favorite run. This and Winnisook on the other side." Parker looked behind us across the valleys to the snow covered peaks, dotted randomly with winter chalets and permanent homes. "Look behind you. We can see the backside of Hunter Mountain, the North Dome and Westkill over there. And across the valley, the trails on Plattekill way to the north."

"There's nothing like flying down a trail at a million miles an hour..."

"...and yelling 'CA-*YUUU*-GA!' But I'm glad this is the last run. I'm beat," Parker said.

"You spend too much time plotting demonstrations and sitting on your butt," I teased. "Let's call up Anthony. Maybe we can have dinner in Woodstock tonight." Before Parker could answer, I'd dialed Anthony's number. By the time we reached the top of the lift, we had an invitation to share dinner at Anthony's.

We slid off the lift chair, turned a sharp right, and took Dot Nebel by surprise, leaving sprays of powder as we wove through a minefield of moguls, yelling "CA-*YUUU*-GA!" The four o'clock sun dipped lower towards the west, sending a golden glow over the ridges protecting the bluish winter mist in the valley below. Fresh snow crystals reflected low sparkles of sunlight like glitter in a disco. At the bottom, it was sad to loosen our boots and load the car for the trip to Woodstock.

****

"Damn! We're snagged behind a DEP car," Parker said as we passed through Pine Hill.

"At least it's not Dad."

"Yeah, that would be a riot. We should probably have dinner with him instead of going to Woodstock," Parker said.

"He'll get over it. We already made plans with Anthony."

"Hey, let's follow this cop, see where he goes. I'm just, like—curious."

"After growing up with Dad, you don't know where a DEP car goes yet?"

"I've got my reasons. Besides, we never followed Dad when he was on one of his 'missions.'"

"Okay. Let's party."

We dropped back a half mile and followed the white car with the green Department of Environmental Protection logo. After crossing my favorite trout stream two or three times on Highway 28, the DEP car turned away from the Esopus Creek towards the far side of the Ashokan Reservoir at Boiceville, following the reservoir road for a few miles. We slowed to a crawl when the officer pulled over to inspect a set of car tracks where the road passed close to the water. He got out and crouched down to inspect the area closely.

Parker whispered as if the DEP officer could hear, "Jeez! You can't even stop and make yellow snow without the water-Nazis close behind."

"But I suppose Dad is just 'Dad,' and of course he's no 'water-Nazi.'"

"Look. Dad is no dummy. He collects his check, but he's never forgotten what happened to great-awesomely-great-grandpa," Parker reminded me. "I'm sure it still bugs him after so many years."

"Why don't we ask him?"

"That's lame, Titus. Get him all riled up again. Make him fight with his own conscience. Let him question why the hell he works for the DEP after our family got evicted from their home before the Van Rosendaels had to become the Rose family. And I thought you were just into fishing and skiing."

"I *do* listen to your rants and raves, you know."

The DEP car turned back on the road, and turned onto a narrow two-lane in Shokan, then cruised down Peekamoose Road and veered off at the tiny town of Sundown. We followed him for miles through beautiful wooded mountains on roads and fresh snow on the slopes. When the officer reached the Rondout Reservoir, he pulled into a parking lot next to a bunker-type concrete and stone building with a high barbed wire fence surrounding the perimeter.

"I can't imagine what that structure could be," I said.

Parker said, "Whatever it is, they sure do protect it. Look, there's another DEP car pulling up next to him.

"You know what's weird? There's hundreds of miles of unprotected shoreline, but we're looking at two DEP cars huddled together to guard a fortified bunker that's already got a barbed wire fence."

"You'd think we were in Pakistan," I said.

"Dad always talked about that huge underground aqueduct connecting the Pepacton to the Rondout. I'll bet this is the outlet, where it empties into the reservoir, and flows through to the city."

"Yep. But their job is to protect the vulnerable junctions."

"I guess. But why leave all that shoreline exposed, and then only guard a couple of fenced-in concrete buildings? Kind of like protecting all the bank branches with two guards at an ATM."

"Right. But they can't build a fence around every reservoir? NOT!"

"Yeah. THAT'S not going to happen."

Suddenly a third DEP car, from nowhere, pulled up behind us, red lights flashing. "Hurry, get your seatbelt on. I can't afford another ticket. Cost me over a hundred bucks last time," I said. Quickly I rolled down the driver's side window, turned on the interior lights, and placed my hands high on the steering wheel, like Dad taught us.

"License and registration, please." I handed him the papers, saying nothing. After the officer strolled back to his car, we could see him in the rear-view mirror talking on the phone. As we waited nearly ten minutes, it became evident that seat belts were not his main interest.

"You really think Dad is that tortured about working for the DEP?" I asked.

"Usually he's sort of in denial." Parker shifted in his seat to look me straight in the eyes. "A few years ago, he told me about Grandpa Van Rosendael. He was the last holdout in Shavertown before they filled the reservoir. He had appealed to everyone, all the way up to President Eisenhower. Dad says it was a shock to everyone when he strolled back inside his house for the last time and shot himself before the city could take his house."

"He was stubborn. Kinda like you, wasn't he?"

"I guess, maybe. But something else is really interesting. Triple-great grandpa left a trust fund to finance a blood relative who would fight the city on any contemporary watershed issue. And it's grown since nineteen fifty-four."

"You're kidding!" I replied. "But...why didn't Dad tap into that money?"

"He said he's thought about it, but it would jeopardize his job if he joined the 'other side', as he says. Like, I guess he feels the family pain even now. We'd be a lot better off if Grandpa van Rosendael had gotten what the house was worth, and if the money had stayed in the family. It's a really thorny issue with Dad. Whenever we discuss it, he like, breathes heavy, and his neck gets all red, and I can tell there's a lot of anger he tries to hide."

"He's never mentioned a word to me."

"I know. He doesn't see you as a political type." Parker rested his feet on the dashboard.

"Right. I'm just the youngster, the family nobody 'cause I didn't make it into a New York City big-time university," I whined like a six-year-old.

"Come on! With that photographic brain, you're smarter than I am!" Parker turned to look at the DEP officer in the patrol car. "He sure is taking his time with that phone call."

I had to ask, "Okay. So what about this trust fund? How much is in it?"

"You wouldn't't believe. It started with about nine thousand dollars."

I clapped my hands together. "Wow. That's a chunk of change!"

"Yeah, well, like sixty-some years later, it's grown."

"How much, Parker?" I leaned forward and cocked my head sideways, like what's-his-name on *Law and Order.*

"A lot. It was invested in IBM and Kodak, and later Apple, Microsoft, and Dell."

"Come on. I'm your brother. You can trust me." This was getting ridiculous.

"Yeah, well, I don't have my hands on it yet. But Dad says he's going to make it happen."

"Come on, Parker-boy. Spill."

"You've got to keep this secret. I mean, don't tell ANYONE. And don't tell Dad you know about this. Like, I haven't even told Tina..." Sometimes Parker could drum up more drama than a Broadway play. He took his feet off the dash so he could stare at me.

"Okay. My word of honor. You're in charge. How MUCH? Details."

"Over four and a half mil, after it grew for sixty-some years. It lost a lot during the recession. Used to be over five."

"Mil, as in 'million?'" I was just about to yell out a "holy shit," but a knock on the top of the car stopped the conversation abruptly. The officer had returned and handed my license and registration through the window. After hearing the amount, I felt guilty, like we'd just been caught in a bank heist. I started shaking, and I was so stunned I dropped my license through the window. The officer groaned and stooped to pick it up. "Sorry, Sir."

But Parker kept his cool. "If you don't mind my asking, officer, why did you stop us?"

"Just a routine check. The power plant is here, and the intake to the aqueducts. We like to know who's hanging around."

"Our father's a DEP, you know…"

"Yep, I just talked to him. He owns the car you're driving."

"Yeah…right, he does own the car. We were just, like, curious, you know…"

"But you followed Officer Ramone for fifteen miles. Maybe you should ask your Dad next time you want a tour. Without him along, you guys were getting a little too close. Here's your license. Be careful on the way back."

As the cop walked back to his car, Parker said, "Well, I guess that took the air out of our balloon, didn't it!"

I turned the car around. The drama was still in the air. "Four and a half mil! So, we're like, rich! Four and a half mil! Holy balls."

"No, no, it's not for us, Titus. But we can finance one hell of a good organization to fight the issues. It'd be nice if you and I did it together. You up here in the mountains, and me down the city. It's the perfect team."

"Sounds…I guess." It was intriguing, but I had a lot to learn. I should have listened better when Parker had spouted off about the issues. It suddenly dawned on me the advantage we would have with me in Margaretville and Parker down in New York. There was something very intriguing about having plenty of money to back an important political movement and running it from both ends: people at the source of the water, and the big city that depended on it. All my life I'd only cared about cruising through school, never choosing a major at SUNY Delhi, and mounting all the girls I could get my paws on. But this was different. Following my hormones had no real purpose, but suddenly there was a worthwhile cause I could take part in. I felt the excitement of something important for the first time in my life. If only I really understood it. "Parker, don't we need to figure out what the issues are before we act?"

"Sure. We've got to sort it all out. It's not all that clear, even after I've studied environmental issues for my whole college career. And Dad sort of muddies the whole thing."

"You said that before...I don't know if I understand." Damn. This was like two blind guys wading across the Delaware. Two *well-funded* blind guys. "So...talk to me."

"First of all, we have to admit that the DEP-controlled watershed delivers a lot of benefits. With the watershed stretching through two thousand square miles of mountains, the entire area is protected with strictly controlled development, and there are laws concerning septic systems, wells, and pesticides that help it stay healthy."

I turned off the engine again and stretched back in my seat. "That's the positive side," I observed.

"But there are big-time side effects that are negative. You see, we're in a permanent recession up here. If the city buys up most of the land, there can't possibly be a normal economy because there is no growth, and that is a recipe for permanent economic hardship. There are only small businesses in Margaretville. When the City buys most of the land, fewer people can move here, build houses, buy necessities that support local businesses, and work locally.

The economy is permanently screwed." No doubt about it, Parker was smart.

I turned to look him in the eye. "Dad talks about this sometimes, when he gets hammered."

"Yes, I've heard him. We were a boom town when the reservoirs were being built in the fifties, with construction companies, hotels, resorts, restaurants—we had more of everything. Since then, the whole area has slowly gone downhill, into permanent recession. Margaretville Central School graduates less than twenty seniors each year, but it was built to hold almost seven hundred. And our dairy farming has *really* suffered."

"You were first in a class of—"

"Sixteen," he answered. "Delaware County used to supply the majority of the milk for New York City. We could *sell* the milk back then, but we don't make a dime from the water that we give freely for New York to sell to its citizens. What a crock!"

I said, "You're right. They take the water for free, then sell it down the city."

"Right, and none of this creates real commerce for our stores. It's not all one sided. There are agreements they've made. We get sewage treatment plants and water systems in almost every town, and the reservoirs for fishing.

I was catching on. "The city's motivation is to protect *their* water. But it's only been recently that you could take a sailboat, a kayak, or a canoe on most of the reservoirs."

"Right. But never a motor boat—only the DEP is allowed to pollute a reservoir with a gasoline motor! Back in the fifties, they promised the people of Shavertown there would be recreation and summer tourism on the reservoirs. But *that* promise has taken over sixty years..."

"I see now. They've screwed our whole economy," I said.

Parker continued, "When you add a *real* recession and seasons with little or no snow to what we already have, we're *really* down and out. Think about how many small businesses have failed up here in the last few years. Course, if they had a strong spokesman up here...somebody with some financial backing...you know, working with a team..."

I smiled. I knew my brother well. "You knew I'd sign up, didn't you?"

"I was hoping. Maybe it'll give you something you can believe in, besides college women and fishing."

"Don't forget skiing."

"I'd just as soon forget how you skied my ass off on the mountain today."

The car lurched forward, exploring the upper region of the speed limit. An incredible feeling of strength permeated the air, far beyond the brotherly bond we'd always felt. Parker's shaggy curly hair seemed to glow in the low sunlight blasting through the windshield. I had to admit, I really loved my brother. I'd follow him to the depths of any reservoir in the Catskills.

"Come on, let's get to Woodstock before we miss dinner. Maybe we can get Anthony to see the light."

"That'll be the day," I said.

I nodded forcefully, and we looked at each other, smiling. We bumped knuckles, did the brother handshake, and yelled simultaneously, "CA-*YUUU*-GA!" A contract had been made.

Chapter 5

The Crime Scene

Herb Rose drove slowly along the reservoir road in his DEP patrol car. It was a beautiful winter day, showing off the Pepacton in strong reflections of late winter light glancing off melting ice and water. The road wound for miles along the meandering path of the reservoir made from the East Branch of the Delaware. The largest in the system, the Pepacton supplied nearly half of the total water needed by New York City each day. Completed in 1954, and over sixty years later, the wreckage left after its creation had grown into what now was a beautiful mountain lake over twenty-two miles long and lined with mature trees blending with the natural environment.

Herb's muted green uniform was different from the NYC regulation blue police attire, and his Smokey-the-Bear hat sat on the driver's seat next to him. He had been with the Department of Environmental Protection for his entire career, and was looking to retire soon, after his son Titus got through SUNY Delhi. Following in the footsteps of his older brother Parker, Titus was still full of surplus teenage angst and anger that could stop his progress cold if he got sidelined into something weird. But Herb felt he still had a chance of influencing his youngest rabble-rouser to avoid disaster. He pulled over to send a text message to make sure Titus was still in class. His new phone could reach the classroom, even though the professor might disapprove of texting during class.

Hey, Ti. Howz yer day? What's Miss P wearing 2day? U R in algebra now I hope.

Soon the answer came back. *Well yeah, Dad. OMG. Miss P is HOT 2day. Lo cut top, lots o legs. I LUV numbers. al-ge-BRA!.*

Herb laughed and answered the text. *Don't wet y self. Eyes on the math bk. Pick u up @ 3?*

And Ti's answer. *Cool. C ya.*

****

I closed my phone quietly under the desk. I should be listening to what Miss Proust was saying about formulas, linear and quadratic equations, and other nonsense I would never use, especially here in the Catskills. I strained to see if her dress might be the least bit hot but turned away when she glared at me with knowing eyes. My mind wandered back to the discussion yesterday with Anthony and Parker. Parker was so bright, incredibly opinionated, and seemed to know how to use his New York trained gifts. But me? I'm still stuck in algebra with a beautiful but ornery teacher at the front of a required class. But I would ace it anyway, if I could just keep my horny eyes off her body.

Anthony said the city had five hundred forty million dollars each year to buy land in the Catskills. Okay, at six thousand an acre…I'm in a math class, for God's sake…that would be about ninety thousand acres they could buy! Now, if the average plot of land is, say fifteen acres, that's six thousand lots they buy every year! All in the name of preventing the public from buying the land. And that means over six thousand fewer people to buy groceries, cars, lumber, and ski tickets…each year. Don't forget skiing. And fishing…

I got so caught up with the meaning of the DEP land grabbing that I completely zoned out of Algebra class. Miss Proust stopped my daydream like a highway wreck.

"Mr. Rose." She walked down the aisle to the last few seats, where I was hiding behind Jeffrey, my football buddy from Margaretville. "Mr. Rose, if I can interrupt your daydream for a moment, can you tell me the correct equation?"

Even though I should have remembered the equation from last night's glance at the textbook, I stammered, "Uhhh, that would be six thousand lots, Miss Proust. Fifteen acres each." The class broke out laughing, and hands shot up with the correct answer. Miss Proust called upon Angela, who had just arrived from the City with her haughty attitude that just about made me sick, every time.

"2x minus 2y divided by the square root of z," she answered, looking straight at me with a smirk. That little pretentious city-babe probably studied college algebra back in sixth grade in Manhattan. Made me even more determined never to use algebra again, especially when I could figure out how many acres the DEP could buy in my own head. I wonder how in the hell her parents bought the land for *her* brand new five-bedroom log home, anyway?

****

Herb turned back onto the road. Fresh tracks displayed evidence of a pair of deer searching for food. Edible food was scarce in mid-winter with still more than a foot of melting snow on the ground, and no spring greenery yet. He crossed the reservoir at the Shavertown Bridge, with views three-quarters of a mile in both directions on either side of a waterway looking much like a major river—perhaps the Hudson River would look like this, if it flowed through the mountains. He waved at the driver of a pickup truck, a local man who worked near the DEP office in Downsville, at the west end of the reservoir. Like any rural community, people knew each other at least by face, or by the make of their truck. It was rare to see another vehicle on this stretch of road, even in the middle of the day. He slowed around a hairpin curve where the road ran close to the water.

His car wheels nearly ran over something on the road. He backed up and slowed to a stop to investigate. As he leaned down to pick up the snow-dusted object, he also noticed the black marks of a vehicle that had peeled rubber as it squealed onto the highway. Not there yesterday, he remembered. His hand stopped inches from the black glove. It wasn't snow on the fingers. A white powder had spilled over most of the fabric. Maybe he should bag it, not touch it. Looked like cocaine. But what was it doing out here in the wild?

He walked back to his cruiser to get a plastic bag from his crime kit. He glanced towards the water. The snow had been disturbed in a path leading from the road to the water and got his attention. He could tell the path was fresh, not there yesterday. He crouched down to examine the scene without disturbing the tracks. Long ski tracks, and the messy footprints of...probably two men. For a moment, thoughts of his sons, skiing around the reservoir, came to his mind. He took a closer look through his binoculars, a powerful set that could provide details from the top of the fifty-foot trail to the water's edge. Looked like narrow cross-country skis, leaving tracks poorly erased by branches dragged behind them. The suspects had dragged something heavy down the embankment. And the ski tracks were not the typical pattern of cross-country skis, with a back and forth "walking" pattern. Instead, the tracks were constant, more like a sled, and sunk deep in the snow like they had weight on them. No sign of poles. Something heavy went downhill and was lighter coming back up. But what, and why? He thought of the possibilities. Hunters dragging a deer? But why heavier going downhill on the skis? He ruled out a canoe launch. Wrong season, still too much ice to launch a boat. Again, he recalled, the only people he knew who skied around the reservoir in winter were his own two sons, Parker and Titus. Surely it couldn't be...they'd be hot-dogging on downhill runs at Belleayre, not struggling on wet snow through the woods on the reservoir. But the ski tracks and two sets of footprints went straight to the water and returned. It didn't look like marks from dragging a body...or a deer. It couldn't be his sons...

His binoculars stopped on a large boulder on the shore that was partially in the water. A streak of white across the rock looked like spilled flour or powdered sugar. The reservoir was beginning to melt along the warm shallow water near the shore. There was a pool of cloudy white gook on the surface, clinging to the shoreline like a massive bubbly detergent spill. He studied it for a minute until he thought of the white stuff on the glove. Cocaine? No. Why dump valuable drugs?

Suddenly the whole scene clicked together. This was what he'd been trained for, to protect the water supply. This could be the real thing. Most of the time, he patrolled the reservoirs in his car, inspected private septic sites, monitored fishermen and hunters for licenses, and tested the water for pesticides and fertilizer run-off. But this was a real security alert. Returning to his patrol car, he pulled on his HAZMAT suit, and grabbed his crime kit and a camera.

The strong morning sun was melting the snow quickly. But he managed to shoot some photos of the tracks with high contrast to show the shadows and details. He got close-ups of boot prints, ski tracks, the spill on the boulder, the soapy slime patch clotting together on the surface, and the tire tracks from the pavement next to a tape measure he laid down to record the size and pattern of the treads.

Satisfied with the thoroughness of the initial investigation, he radioed back to the Downsville DEP office. Describing the incident as a "possible crime" he said, "Mo, I got a ten-ten I need to discuss. Switch to the secure channel." There were few people he trusted more than Mo, a longtime chemist with a PhD who could answer just about any question about toxins in or out of the water.

"Ten-four." They both switched to Channel 9, listened for the arrival of the other. "What's going down, Herb?"

"There's been a dump of white powder in the water, Mo. I took initial photos on a snow trail to the water and tire tracks on the road. Probably happened last night."

"Sounds like coke or heroin."

"Dumping drugs doesn't make sense. Looks more like a toxin or a detergent."

"Better get your HAZMAT suit on, Herb."

"I'm way ahead of you. Got evidence of powder on a glove in the road, and the same white stuff on a boulder partially in the water. But the test kit didn't confirm a much— except that it's definitely an organic substance."

"What's your twenty?"

"About a mile past the bridge on Reservoir Road. I'll clock it on the return."

"Roger that. Should...we kick this upstairs right away?"

"Where's Tom? Is he in? I'm hoping not. Are you reading my mind, Mo?"

"He's in a meeting with the shirts from the big A."

"Maybe that's lucky. Let's wait before we invite the big-wigs."

"Ten-four. What's the water looking like?"

"Soapy, coagulated white slimy residue floating on a melted patch of water near the shore, hemmed in by soft melting ice on the surface. There's powder on the boulder next to the water. The dumpsite is deep in an inlet, and the stuff is sort of clotting like it can't dissolve. Not much current to mix it or move it."

"How much powder?"

"Can't tell. Could be quite a lot. The tracks are deep. Something heavy went down there. Some of it sank, and the rest is stuck on the surface over an area about forty feet along the shore."

"I guess you'll bag the glove. And see if you can get a sample from the water. But don't touch the stuff. Bring it back here so we can get it to the lab."

"Done."

"Might just be somebody dumping trash. Be sure to keep your HAZMAT gloves on."

"It's not trash. It was transported in something big and heavy. Maybe a hundred pounds or more—the tracks are deep. But why would they cart it all the way to the water if it were trash? This doesn't sit well with me. Whoever brought this here wanted it in the water."

"I agree. You taped off the perimeter? What charges do you think we're talking?"

"Reckless Endangerment, Risking a Catastrophe, Plotting a Terrorist Act, and any of the DEP or DEC Conservation statutes. Could be any of 'em, State or Federal."

"We'll get a cleanup team down there right away. You'd better stay with it until they get there."

"Ten-four."

Herb texted his son with regrets. He hated it when he couldn't live up to his promises as a father, often more of a habit than an exception. Last week it was the threat of floods, then an unscheduled release of water into the Esopus Creek, and now, a strange white powder. No wonder Titus Rose was so messed up, an authentic rebel without a clue.

****

I 'd made it out of algebra without a second embarrassment when I got Dad's text message. *T.— Sorry. Something's going down. Can't make it. Call a friend for a ride. Dad.* I sent back my message with a vengeance. *No big surprise, Always my part-time dad— T.* Sticking another needle in the divorce issues would make his red neck turn neon.

Chapter 6

Woodstock

Bonnie Guarini tasted the sauce that had simmered for three hours. It was an old recipe, one she'd perfected and expanded from her mother's original Sicilian ingredients when she grew up in Brooklyn. Through the years, she'd added a little more garlic, a touch more Italian seasoning, a spicy special-order sausage, definitely more red wine, and her secret ingredients, a dab of wasabi mustard mixed with a generous sprinkling of whatever dynamite weed she had in the drawer...for luck, of course.

Long known as an eccentric gourmet nut-case, Anthony's mom settled in Woodstock in 1969 and never gave up her liberal causes and her free hippie lifestyle, with touches of witch's sorcery, freestyle religion, and leftwing action politics. Her curly hair had gone gray, and splayed out in twisted disarray. Her bulbous nose showcased a wart the size of a black-eyed pea, and her wide smile displayed teeth ready to cause eyes to light up on the face of a lucky dentist. While some of her friends abandoned the sixties revolution and became corporate clones, she stayed true to her beliefs, still busy protesting, signing petitions, marching off to Washington for the umpteenth worthwhile cause. When she wasn't raising hell about global warming, the continuous onslaught of capitalist wars, the shameful control that corporate America had over the government, or the harmful preservatives in the food supply, she took solace in tending her massive organic garden, with her prized dinner-plate dahlias and variegated roses edging a myriad of herbs and tall vegetables covering three prize specimens of cannabis sativa gargantuan.

The strident electric sounds of Jimi Hendrix, The Doors, Pink Floyd, and Cream from the Woodstock concert were long since gone, and the magic mushroom hill at nearby Yasgur's Farm was peaceful now. But at the summit, a $100 million Tanglewood-style concert pavilion and museum tells the story of the 60s with exhibits such as "The Hippies" and "Three Days of Peace, Love and Music." A younger Bonnie was photographed leading a group of Viet Nam protesters, preserved on a wall mural for all eternity in the museum. She had that youthful idealism in her eyes, even then. But the town of Woodstock, an icon of the 60s revolution, had drastically changed. She scowled at the idea of the unwanted transformation.

As she peered out the window on Tinker Street, past the tourist traps and tongue-in-cheek signs warning *Hippies use the side entrance*, she saw her son Anthony removing the cross-country skis from the back of his old pickup truck. Though she was used to it, she couldn't help but think what a shame it was that the whole sixties movement was encased in Woodstock commercialism, as if the town was some strange museum dedicated to hippies like they were mannequins sporting period costumes at Macy's. Woodstock was like the cute little ugly duckling that became a billion-dollar Donald. But there were still people with principles, friends who helped her to remind the nation that peace was still the best choice over getting involved in endless Near-East wars.

Woodstock and the Catskill Mountains was her home, and the bumper stickers on her little '68 Beetle read like a history book of liberal causes through the years, starting with all the local issues:

No Cell Towers!

No Wind Turbines!

No Guns!

No More Reservoirs!

No Fracking Way!

Also prominent was a less political collection on the side windows:

Potheads Against Drunk Driving.

Woodstock—Gateway to...uh...uh...

Please Don't Squeeze the Shaman.

Legalize It!

Woodstock—Still no McDonald's

And her personal favorite, *Woodstock—Land of the Freak, Home of the Vague.* Also present were remnants of every war protest since Viet Nam, and an *Occupy Wall Street* sticker.

She smiled at the history of issues displayed on every rusted surface of her old ramshackle wreck. She looked at her flickering seventeen-inch eighties TV, with blue haze and red outlines the only colors left, precariously hanging under the cabinet next to the stove. One of these days she'd have to get one of those fancy flat-screen HDTVs. Maybe next year, after the old one fell off its rusty bracket.

The talking head on CNN returned after she applauded for a commercial for the new Prius.

New methods of terrorism are thought to be in the works from ISIS-inspired terrorist training camps in countries in the Near East and Africa. Fears of targeted attacks on New York include violence and assassination directed at specific officials, hit and run urban assaults, food source poisoning, cyber-terrorism, nuclear or bioterrorism tactics, and threats to the water supply. CNN will focus on each of these in special broadcasts every night this week and next...

Bonnie turned the volume down when Anthony arrived with his imitation of Kramer skidding into Seinfeld's apartment. "Hey Ma, dude, we got guests for dinner." He dumped his cross-country skis against the coat rack and tossed his boots on the floor. "I'll get two more plates. Parker and Titus'll be here, right behind me."

"I'm making some sauce. There's plenty for everybody, sweet cheeks. Oh yes, your dad called. Says he's got a present for you. I hope it isn't another rifle."

"He's a hunter, mom, not a bank robber. Guns have their place. I'm nineteen, for god's sake! Like, I can handle it."

"You know how I feel about guns. I don't care if it's a rat in the alley. We don't kill living things!"

"Yeah, yeah." His hand formed the peace sign. "Mom, you've got to let me form my own opinions about these things."

"And don't be mocking the peace sign. It's a serious symbol."

"...that you can buy in every fucking souvenir shop in Woodstock."

"And don't say that word."

"What...peace? Only problem with peace is that it never fucking works. But I thought you liked peace."

Bonnie gave up, smiling. "Fuck yes, I like peace. Without the *fucking* guns, or the *fucking* souvenirs." She pulled her snakehead hash pipe from her flannel shirt pocket and poised it for some fire.

"Mom! You said 'fuck.' Again and again. Two bucks in the jar! I'm way shocked. Pay up."

****

We overheard the end of their discussion as we walked up on the porch and burst through the screen door. Parker imitated Anthony's imitation of Kramer, but he crashed into the center island cabinet, knocking a bottle of St. John's Wort on the floor. "Dude, brought some beer. What's for dinner?"

"Mom's sauce on linguine." Anthony cracked open a beer. "Outside for a toke?"

"Thought you'd never ask."

"Mom?"

"Thanks Little Green-weed, but I already did a number. And it's in the sauce. So don't over-indulge." She raised a ladle full from the pot, letting it splash back into the sauce.

The three of us exited outside to the porch. She yelled after us, "One too many cocktails makes a drunk. Same with Mary Jane...did you *hear* me?"

No one "heard" her. But I had to say, "Your mom is so cool."

Anthony grimaced, but I could tell he was proud of his mom. "She's hip, and she's still totally into politics. Last week she got all riled up about New York City buying all the land in the watershed."

"What's to worry? Keeps the mountains from becoming a crowded suburb," I said, baiting him just for the fun of it.

"You can't believe that," Parker said.

Anthony said, "Sure. Mom says, last month New York City got five-hundred forty million dollars to buy more land up here."

Parker said, "So what did she do this time?"

"Went to about six of the land parcels, and posted big signs that said, *NYC—STAY IN YOUR OWN BACK YARD.*"

"She's so cool."

"She's possessed. She says, in the old days, everybody in town would be out there protesting." Anthony packed a pipe, handing it to me as he lit his lighter. "At least she let's me toke."

"Wish my dad wasn't such a dick about it." I took a long drag and handed it to Parker.

Parker said, "I can't quite picture dad toking in his DEP uniform. Does she ever get you involved in one of her causes?"

Anthony answered, "Yeah, especially the watershed business. But I've got my own opinions, you know."

I said, "You're becoming a mountain redneck. You're damn lucky to have a mother who believes in good causes, Anthony. Those signs she put up are way cool. The DEP is allowed to buy entirely too much land, and so far, everyone just lets it pass." I surprised even myself. I sounded like I had an opinion that counted. Parker chimed in, and the argument got interesting with a lot more facts and figures. I guess both Anthony and I learned a lot out on that porch while Bonnie cooked pasta-con-ganga. Maybe, the next time she organized a protest, Anthony would join in. But when he did, he turned out to be much more of a loose cannon than I ever imagined.

Chapter 7
High-tech Decisions

Herb and Mo huddled together in the water-testing lab in the Downsville lab at the west end of the Pepacton Reservoir. Test tubes and beakers, filter flasks and glass funnels, racks of Petri dishes, and a refrigerator populated the room. The shelves above were filled with gauges and instruments, an idle Bunsen burner, bookmarked manuals on toxins and pollutants, and a rack of water sample bottles labeled and organized by date and location. Each of three stainless steel lab tables was equipped with its own sink; water, gas, and vacuum sources; a fume hood; spectrophotometer, rotary evaporator, and a computer keyboard and screen. The door to a fireproof cabinet for flammables, acids, and other liquids lay open and accessible.

Mo had worked for the DEP for many years and was proud of his laboratory and its accomplishments to monitor fourteen of the nineteen reservoirs in the New York City water supply. Officially, he reported to Officer Herb Rose, but his education as a biochemist and expert on toxins overshadowed Herb's scope of experience and education. The two men made an efficient team with complementary skills in the field and in the lab. Through the years, they had bonded as friends in addition to a long history of professional trust.

"I suspected that the organic substance is a potent bacterium from the field test," said Mo. "It has eaten or paralyzed all available organic microbes in seven Petri dishes with a voracious appetite."

Herb looked through the microscope on the lab table. "Look at this! It looks like tiny wiggling hot dogs in an insatiable orgy of reproduction," said Herb.

Mo opened the Lateral Flow Testing Device that would give him a toxin result in minutes. It included over a dozen tests. He started testing for the most dangerous toxins and analyzed individual samples for the presence of ricin, anthrax, cholera, staph enterotoxin, tularemia, Y pestis, and six strains of botulism. "If any of these test positive," he said, "we'll have to send a sample to a lab in the City to verify the results."

"How long will that take?" Herb asked.

"A minimum seven days," said Mo.

"Crap! Seven days we don't have when the mystery substance could reach the City in less than forty-eight hours. Isn't there any other test that we can use?" Herb's hand was starting to shake in sync with his fear of the answer.

"The first six tests were negative. The last test was developed during Desert Storm for field-testing in the Army. Even though the toxin was only partially dissolved in the frigid Pepacton, I chose the liquid collection field kit to conduct the chemical assay."

Herb was becoming impatient at the slow process and even slower answers from Mo. He watched as Mo diluted the sample in a tube of sterile saline and carefully added three drops to the lateral flow testing device. After three minutes, the liquid began to turn colors. He used a bio-luminometer to crosscheck the results. After repeating the test with a fresh sample, he recorded the readings on a form he would send to the lab in New York.

He removed his gloves, carefully washed his hands, and turned to Herb. "I don't have the ability to test this irrefutably. But these results point to Onabotulinum toxin A., a gram-positive anaerobic bacterium. I think you had best run this down to the lab in the City immediately."

"I agree. But what the...?"

Mo looked at Herb like a child needing an explanation. His complexion and bushy eyebrows pointed to his foreign roots; there was still a slightly different inflection in his words after three decades in the US and a Harvard Ph.D. in biochemistry. "It's the cosmetic form of botulism, the kind used to treat facial wrinkles. The name comes from the Latin for sausage, because of its sausage shaped molecule. It cures all sorts of things when used in very tiny doses."

Herb asked, "But the amount dumped in the water— would it be enough to poison the water in all of New York?"

"Well! It would be enough to smooth the faces of a large city full of extremely vain women." He laughed at his own joke. Herb noticed the inappropriate joke, always shocked at Mo's strange sense of humor.

"So, we can only assume that someone raided a Botox supplier and dumped it in the reservoir."

"Could be. Probably. Almost certainly." Mo said, as he raised those eyebrows.

"But I thought Botox had to be injected under the skin."

"Yes, that's how a doctor administers it. However, in this case, they chose an inefficient method of delivery. An aerosol delivery method would be the preferred method of delivery, highly toxic and fatal in very small doses." A look of superiority lay etched in his face.

"But this wasn't aerosol...it was dissolved in the water."

"Yes, but no matter. A toxin is a toxin. It's lethal no matter how it gets into the body."

"How does it work?" Herb asked.

Mo crossed his arms and sat on the lab stool. "It's basically a nerve reactor. It binds to the synapse of the nerve endings and decreases or even prevents the release of acetylcholine in the body. I don't think anyone knows how an unknown amount will affect the city or how fast it would achieve maximum toxicity."

"Come on, Mo. Speak English. I'm not a biochemist," Herb said with his hands on his hips.

"Sorry. Okay, in English...it's strong stuff, really, really bad." He smiled cryptically. "I'll make it simple. Medically, and properly applied locally, it can help involuntary muscular spasms like tics, cramps, and tremors in the eyes, the hands, the face, even the back...and they're discovering many other incredible applications, like pain management and treatment of certain kinds of stroke. It's a miracle substance if you know how to use it."

"A miracle, eh? And I thought it was just for wrinkles. But what is the effect on the body if it's an overdose—the toxic downside of the stuff?" Herb tapped a pencil rapidly on the table.

"Effects from overdose include flu-like symptoms, an increase in pain and, with a really high dose, permanent atrophy and paralysis of muscles, usually the lungs. And that causes mind-boggling pain and suffocation when the lungs can no longer work. You've seen women who have had too many facelifts and treatments—their faces are almost paralyzed. No expression, just like stone. Imagine that kind of paralysis happening in the lungs. Trust me. Botulism is one of the most potent bioterrorism weapons known to man." This time, he did not smile.

Herb sat hard on a lab chair, shocked to the core. "Damn. Why do you suppose they chose to dump powder in the water if the most lethal method is airborne delivery?" Herb asked. He was used to it, but Mo's peculiar sense of superiority was irritating, especially since Herb was the boss, not Mo.

Mo's face showed his sarcasm. "I don't think they knew what they were doing. If they were able to obtain that much powder, they probably didn't know how to convert it to aerosol, and they obviously intended to pollute the water, not spray it as they could have for better results. I don't think they realized it might not easily dissolve in frigid water. These are amateurs, not real chemists. These guys would no more get through Harvard than a Rhesus monkey."

Herb continued, "And look at all the other things they left for us to find. Tracks in the snow, a glove and a boulder with toxin all over them, a beer can with DNA and fingerprints, and tire tracks on the pavement."

"And they just dumped it, no mixing, no dilution first. The best delivery methods were ignored. Definitely amateurs."

"Still, this could be serious."

"Yes, kind of like playing with nitroglycerine with a lit candle." Mo flicked his lighter to demonstrate.

Herb said, "Okay, enough with the flames! So...what about the effects of dumping it in the water supply? Must be different from injecting it under the skin."

"I'm not entirely sure. By the time it's diluted in a couple of billion gallons of water, there might be very little effect on the population in New York City. It has to pass through the new UV filtration plant and the chlorination process. The ultraviolet treatment is new, not really tested on massive quantities of toxin. But there's still a valid concern. If it survives through the entire system, we might still see outbreaks of horrible flu-like symptoms. At the worst exposure, paralysis of the lungs, and a painful death for—who knows how many people?"

Herb shook his head. "The UV treatment plant was just recently opened, but would the UV and the normal dose of chlorine kill the bacteria?"

"In a laboratory situation, yes...perhaps..."

"Given the volume, it's not proven yet."

"And what about how fast it multiplies. Look at these Petri dishes!"

"Again, in a laboratory situation, it reproduces faster than a field full of horny mice." Mo smiled, but restrained himself from enjoying his own joke.

"You medical geeks have a sick sense of humor. Can't you take any of this seriously?"

"Sorry, Chief." He put his head down.

Herb looked at a gauge in the array of testing equipment attached to the ongoing experiment. "How would temperature make a difference?"

Mo admitted, "Here in the lab, the temperature is controlled at sixty-five degrees. In the reservoir, it's near freezing, and it wouldn't reproduce that quickly. But, you see, we would have to wait a long time for this experiment to work if we reduced the temperature to thirty-four degrees, like the reservoir. Maybe we wouldn't even see the effects until spring. And by summer, it would be reproducing like those mice."

Could Mo ever give him a straight answer? Herb said, "One thing in our favor is that the water next to the shore seemed to be surrounded by thick ice on the surface, and it was dumped in an inlet, in a spot with very little current to pull it under. The big question in my mind is whether this was the only dumpsite. Did we discover the only one, or is this one of many? And how long does it take to work? How much time have we got before somebody gets sick? Are you with me, Mo?"

Mo looked through a reference book on toxins and poisons, flipping familiar pages. Herb looked over his shoulder.

"In Sittig's *Handbook of Toxins and Hazardous Chemicals and Carcinogens,* it says that after exposure, it works very quickly, from less than eight hours to several days."

"So, we have less than eight hours from the time it is ingested, plus the time it takes to reach the city." Herb said.

"Yes. If it takes several days to reach the city, then who knows? But don't forget the volume issue. The amount it would take to pollute a reservoir a hundred and forty miles upstream from New York City is almost immeasurable. It might take a hundred tanker trucks or more, not the hundred pounds that you found. And if chlorine kills it, the amount of chlorine would also have to be strong. There are a hundred and forty billion gallons in the Pepacton, delivering one point four billion gallons to New York every day, and mixing with several billion gallons from other reservoirs long before it hits New York," Mo said. "And, by the way, I *am* taking you seriously." Mo began pacing the room, following Herb around the perimeters of the lab.

"I'm sorry to offend, my friend. Okay, so the volume of water is in our favor. But what about the pools of concentrate? I know damn well it didn't all dissolve. There was no one there to stir it into the water."

"You said the HAZMAT team was able to collect most of the globs of partially dissolved powder, right?"

"Yeah, that's if we were right about how much was actually dumped. But what if there were tons of it in different locations, and we only saw the last hundred pounds?" Herb replied.

"The pressure of all that water going quickly downhill through the aqueduct tunnels would surely dissipate any undissolved pools of powder."

"But what if it arrives in small globs of concentrated toxin?"

"We don't really know how long it will take to reach the City. Or...we may know in a matter of a few days or less."

"When I talked to the lab in the City, they don't seem all that concerned."

Mo answered, "They're not thinking right. Especially if it doesn't really dissolve and travels in concentrated globs through the system. That translates into serious problems in isolated areas in the City. Anyone could become sick, or die."

"And what if you and I are already exposed?"

Mo looked at his watch. "Well then, we'll know about that in a few hours. I would think."

"What constitutes a lethal dose for one person?"

Mo removed another manual from the shelf and looked for the statistic to answer the question. "This is unbelievable. It says...about three one-hundredths of a milliliter."

"So...only a few grains of powder?" Herb wiped his hands on his shirt, as if that might help.

"Just about." Mo washed his hands again in the lab sink.

"There's one more thing that might help us. The Stanford Sensors installed in all the spillways and aqueducts. You've heard about them. But only you can explain how they work."

"They're disposable chips embedded in tiny plastic sheets that are linked to a semiconducting network-transistor embedded in a carbon nanotube. These chemical sensors are indestructible in water, only one atom thick and can detect the presence of TNT, Sarin, and a number of other toxins."

"Let's hope that botulism is on the list. I heard of that in a seminar last year. Professor LeMieux at Stanford developed that, yes? We'd better check with him."

An eerie silence filled the room. Both men watched the Petri dishes with bacteria multiplying rampantly. Neither wanted to speak for an eternity of minutes. Suddenly, the sound of squealing brakes tore through the silence, revealing an eighteen-wheeler skidding on the highway after a very close encounter. There was no crash, just a return to silence. Prophetic perhaps, as both men seemed to wake up and come to the same conclusion.

Herb said, "I'm hoping this is the only incident. Maybe the HAZMATs got most of it out, and the chlorine and UV will kill the rest of it down in the Bronx."

"We need seven days to verify the field test. You think we need a press release and an official warning before we verify the results?" Mo asked.

"There'll be a lot of public panic if we do that. Remember the last time. Tom didn't want it made public, and it turned out to be nothing."

"Maybe that's what the terrorists want. Widespread panic is even better than a few dozen deaths. If we go public, we're playing into their thirst for public alarm."

"Do you realize the reprimand if we're wrong?"

"Tom can be brutal. It could end our careers." The pacing began again as both men tried to reason beyond all reason.

"I don't think either of us wants to make that decision. Tom won't want to make the decision either, and he'll blame us for bringing him a problem like this."

"You're right. His reactions are always unpredictable. I sure as hell don't want to face him. I think...we should wait for the results from the lab," Herb decided.

"Right. I think we should wait. Too many questions, not enough is certain."

"Maybe you can call your lab buddies and ask if they can speed up the results."

"Not likely. It has to grow in a Petri dish, just like here. Takes seven days to verify our own tests, no less."

"So, you're saying it could take only a few days to kill someone, but it takes seven days for us to find out if it *could* kill someone."

After a long silence, Mo said, "I've been here almost twenty years. I think."

"Thirty-four for me," said Herb.

"This is...really...very risky for us." Mo said. "I couldn't take it if you and I were blamed for this. Unemployment in Downsville, New York is not a pretty situation for either of us."

"Okay then. We wait." Herb said. Their eyes met in silent complicity. Herb zipped his jacket, placed his DEP hat on his head, and checked his holster. The door was only a few steps away from the Petri dishes on the lab table. Once he was outside, the threat to his career felt a lot less imminent.

Chapter 8

Father & Son

Dad still hadn't told me what was the big deal about not picking me up after my algebra class yesterday. With my truck in the shop and all, I was stranded no matter what until they found a used transmission for the old wreck. But it was my wreck, and I loved that old '99 Dodge. But Dad was in one of his funky moods, blaming it on "the pressure at work", like he had something more important than driving around the reservoir and giving tickets to New York City flat-landers speeding through the mountains. And the embarrassment in Miss Proust's class was still with me, making me permanently not give a rat's ass whether I graduated or not. The only hope I had was the mission that Parker and I had taken on...but I had to be careful around Dad. We'd been driving for several minutes before Dad made a pathetic attempt at conversation.

"At least if I have to drive you to Delhi, I get to see you," said Dad.

"Whatever."

"You're in a mood today." He looked at me like I was in a mood nearly every day. "Did you have fun skiing with your brother?"

"Yeah. What-ever, Dad."

"You're lucky to have any skiing this year. There hasn't been a lot of snow. The governor almost closed down Belleayre to save on his budget."

"That's what Anthony's mom said. There was a big protest she organized, with petitions to the legislature and hundreds of letters. I guess it did some good. They laid off a third of the permanent employees in December, but at least Belleayre stays open for another season."

"Do you realize what would happen if Belleayre really closed down? That place is the lynchpin for the entire economy up here. If they closed, the bed and breakfasts, motels, all the restaurants, and half the businesses in every small town would close in an eighty-mile radius."

I was surprised. For once, Dad seemed to be taking the same argument that Parker spouted off about just last week. This was getting more interesting. "See! Skiing isn't all bad. It brings lots of money in." Adults can always agree if you talk money.

"Damn right it does. And we need it," Dad said. We traveled peacefully for a few minutes. "Look I'm sorry I couldn't pick you up on Friday. Something serious happened at the reservoir." He looked at me as if he wondered if he should say any more. "We've got a little time. Let's drive up there and let me show you. It's a real crime scene. You know that shoreline. Maybe you can help me with this."

At first, I thought it would be a wasted sightseeing trip. What the hell was he up to? I was curious, but I still responded, "What-*everrr.*"

Dad turned on Highway 28 south and took the turnoff towards the reservoir. Soon we crossed the New Shavertown Bridge and slowed down near a yellow crime tape along the edge of the reservoir.

Dad looked at me with his inscrutable cop mask. "Son, you see that boulder near the water?"

"I've got two eyes."

"Try to hold back on the sarcasm," he said. "See, down there by the water. That's not snow. It was deliberately dumped in the reservoir. We got most of it but there's still some powder clinging to the boulder. We're trying to figure out what happened."

"Looks like some kind of detergent."

"Exactly."

"But...what is it?" *WHY all the drama, Dad?* But suddenly, I was in total shock by what I saw. "Hold on. See that deer? He's like, staggering like he's drunk."

Dad added, "And he wasn't even scared by the sound of my patrol car." He turned off the engine and reached for his binoculars.

The young four-point buck cocked his head to one side, then went down on one front knee, and kicked with his other front foot to right himself. He dug his antlers into the snow as if to attack the ground. After struggling to get up he banged his snout hard into a rock.

"That's got to hurt," I whispered. "What the hell is wrong with him?"

"I never saw a deer act like that. Looks like he's trying to get something out of his nose, or his mouth."

"You already put down crime tape. But deer don't know that."

"Yep." Dad gripped the steering wheel and looked at me suspiciously. "Do you know anyone who cross-country skis around here besides you and your brother?"

"Not really. It's not that great for cross-country here. Parker hasn't done anything but downhill when he comes home from NYU. And I don't usually come down here in February."

"I know. This is the season for downhill. There's usually no one here at all."

"Look...the deer. He's like, shaking."

Dad said, "He's having trouble breathing."

"He's in a convulsion. I've got my video cam. We should record this."

"Good idea, son. This is important."

I started shooting video. The deer seemed to lurch forward on his knees. He quivered and dug his snout hard into the ground. His back legs seemed to shake with the rest of his body in a violent uncontrolled convulsion. His tongue hung out of one side of his mouth and his eyes showed nothing but pain and panic. His stomach was bloated, and blood spewed from his mouth as he struggled for breath. He stood up, ran straight into a tree, and collapsed on his side in the snow. He choked on the blood and made a loud braying sound of distress.

I couldn't take much more. "He's in terrible pain. Should we put him out of his misery?"

Dad was focused on the struggling buck as the convulsion got even worse, but he managed to say, "Titus, give me the camera. And get my Glock out of the holster. You're much spryer on this steep slope. Go down there closer to him, but be careful—he might charge you. I'll record it from here." He focused on the buck down below.

I couldn't believe that the man with the DEP badge wanted me to do the deed. Suddenly I felt queasy, like I was going to spew. I'd never felt this way when I'd been hunting a deer. But this was different. Was I an agent of mercy or was I the murderer of this poor creature? Was he braying to scare us off or was he in terrible pain? "What could have caused this?" I asked.

"I can't...say. But believe me this wasn't his fault." The camera was glued on the tragedy unfolding.

The buck stood up choking violently. His eyes were blood red and he seemed too weak to keep up the shaking. I slid down the embankment with Dad's sidearm. When I got within ten feet of the buck I looked back. Dad nodded, while still keeping the video on. In a final act of self-defense, the buck pawed at the ground and lowered his head, gasping for breath with bloody phlegm drooling out of his mouth. His antlers dug into the snow and his head turned violently to one side while his eyes bulged out in despair as he brayed like an animal hit by a car. When I was about six feet from him, I took aim carefully and squeezed the trigger. The explosion echoed across the lake after hitting the young buck in his left temple. He looked shocked as he slid to his knees, gratefully relieved and lifeless.

I struggled up the slippery embankment. By the time I reached Dad I couldn't handle it any more. "I've...never seen a deer that looked so...so helpless and in pain." Head down, I handed the gun handle-first back to my father. We'd been hunting many times before and taken down many deer in the woods. Would he think I was less of a man because I cried? I prepared myself for his manly rebuke. Instead, there was a different shock. Dad was the one who was close to losing it.

"Titus, I need to tell you something. That deer. He was poisoned. Someone dumped a horrible toxin in the water. Probably he drank the water near the boulder. Please don't tell a soul. But I'm sure of it now. This is bioterrorism. We've confirmed the results in the lab. And now I see how powerful it is." Herb holstered the gun and took his hat off. "That poor beast. We'll have to get the HAZMATs to take him back to the lab." He looked at the blood running out of its mouth. "God, am I in deep shit!"

I turned to face him. I didn't expect this. "But...why, Dad?"

Herb sat on a boulder, his head down between his knees. "Because I...I should have reported this two days ago. I'm really screwed."

"So is the water, I guess."

"You. Have. NO idea."

Chapter 9

Coming Clean

As we returned to the car, a change came over my dad that I had never known possible. I could see how upset my father was by the way he was driving, by the tears he tried to hold back, and by the sweat erupting from his face. He kept mumbling to himself.

"I never realized it was so..." He also didn't realize he was accelerating the DEP car.

"If they'd trained us so we'd know..." He slowed around a sharp curve, but the car swerved, and I realized Dad wasn't focused on the road at all.

"Too late. Too damn late to..." As he rounded another curve a porcupine crossed the road. Herb slammed on the brakes, but he hit the poor animal and it slid under the engine block. We stopped to see if it was still alive. Dozens of porcupine quills were stuck in the front grill, and the bald injured animal struggled to crawl through the ditch and up the embankment by the road.

Dad stopped the car and got out, but he seemed to collapse in the middle of the road. "I could have stopped this...the people down the city..."

"Dad, at least he's still alive."

"No, son, I don't mean the porcupine. I could have stopped this toxin dump from getting so out of control. I just don't know what I was thinking." He shook his head sadly.

I insisted on taking the wheel, with Dad secured in the rider's seat. He'd never let me drive his patrol car before, but under these conditions it really was no big thrill. I had never seen him so down and out. What did he mean by what he said? I had to get him to open up and tell me what was going on. "So, Dad, you can't blame yourself for this. It's not your fault."

"No. I didn't poison the water. But my job is to prevent something like this, or to clean it up immediately. You don't realize how serious this is. A deadly poison has been released in the Pepacton. We know what it is, but we don't know how much, or even how many places it was dumped. We took over a hundred pounds out of the water where that deer died. I should have reported this immediately, before it spread and starting killing. That deer proves what it can do."

"But look at the size of the reservoirs. There's no way the DEP could protect it all effectively."

"It's still my job. I...I should have...done...more." He looked across the car at me helplessly. I had to try to help him sort through this.

"I just don't get it, Dad. Your job is almost impossible. But...your priorities are even more confusing. They hire you to protect the watershed for New York City. But you just signed over a trust fund so Parker could *fight* New York City's control over the watershed."

"Parker told you about that?" Now he looked even worse.

"That's right, Dad. I wasn't supposed to tell you. But, at this point...he wants me to join him." I gripped the wheel as if it could protect me from his mood.

He waited a full minute before answering, "Well, I'm glad, actually. But Titus, please. You've got to keep this money absolutely secret. And keep it legal. No one can ever know where it came from."

"I realize that. But the deer...Dad, this could be important proof!"

"Son, I've told you about Great-Great-Grandpa Van Rosendael. How he struggled to stop them from taking his home. How he lost the battle in the court and the press...and how he killed himself rather than to see them take his house the day before the water was released." He hesitated for a moment, looking like a felon on the stand. "I know this doesn't make much sense. But I have to have a job. The DEP has been my life. I love these mountains, and my job is to protect the water. Sixty-five years later, it's a different world. It sure doesn't help that an old family feud with New York put me in this position. It tears me apart. Our family history is full of resentment for what they did to us back then, and I should probably hate these reservoirs and use the money to fight it all. But my job is to protect it and allow the water system to expand and develop."

"So...you get to keep your job, and let Parker and me lead the fight? I guess that's...but if you're financing him and me, doesn't that make you sort of a terr—?

"A *terrorist*? No, Titus. Far from it! The issues are different today. Terrorism was what happened a few days ago when the water was poisoned. We're not even close."

"And me and Parker...what will we be?"

"There's a hell of difference between an activist and a terrorist, although sometimes the law can't seem to see it." Dad sighed, and I stopped the car for a minute for him to collect his thoughts. He seemed more in control, more resolved now that we'd come clean with each other.

"Dad...all these secrets. I'm not supposed to mention the money. I can't tell anyone about the deer, even though it is positive proof that backs up what we need to do. This is like, lame."

Dad said, "Here's why I 'm backing Parker. He's getting a degree in environmental science, and I think he'll go to law school after. I trust him, and I'm damn proud of him. He's got good ethics. He'll be able to decide who's right and wrong, and how to use the money to fight the right issues. And with the right methods. None of us are terrorists, son. Whoever put that stuff in the water has a whole different agenda, and some very lethal tactics. You saw that buck dying. This is dangerous. You get it."

"I couldn't stand to watch that."

"I didn't think you were mature enough to take up this battle with Parker. But I guess he has a better read on you than I did. I know you'll both make me proud."

"Damn. I think I understand you, Dad. Maybe for the first time ever. I...we can do this!"

"Poisoning the water was wrong, Titus. Wrong on a lot of levels. And since Parker got you involved in the issues, I'm giving you a cardinal rule. Don't ever cross that line between activism and terrorism. Don't get so angry and so desperate that you lower yourself to tactics like that. Otherwise, I'll have to take action to—"

"You'll have to stop us, I know, Dad. I love the mountains. And the reservoirs. I'll never harm them. Not for any reason."

"And if they let me keep my job I'll be a secret ally."

"They will, Dad. Once they know what really happened..."

"Don't go there. They can never, *ever* know. See, I made a big mistake. I should have told someone two days ago."

"And created widespread panic down the city?"

"Panic is not the only threat. It's not an easy call. You don't know my boss."

"Actually, I've heard. You just protect yourself, Dad. We'll do the rest."

I'd never seen him look so despondent. This time, it was Dad who borrowed my response, "Whatever."

Chapter 10

The Protesters

Bonnie's house in Woodstock was filled with hand-painted signs and banners. Volunteers helped paint slogans with wide tip markers and paintbrushes. Bonnie Guarini roamed through the crowd of thirty and growing. "Put your name and info on the sign-up sheet. And sign the petition—it's going to the governor."

She had put out pizza and pretzels with beer and box wine on the dining room table. Anthony mesmerized a small crowd, presenting the tactics they might use for the cause. It wasn't a typical group of youthful protesters: not just college-age rebels ready to jump on any bandwagon that appealed to their senses. These people were a mixture of veteran Woodstock protestors with common causes through the years and folks bound together by various important issues, all for slightly different reasons. Young skiers from New York and from over a dozen Catskills communities mixed with Hudson Valley businessmen who recognized an important controversial issue. Familiar faces from contemporary movements had found a fresh worthy cause.

"Only a few years back, this same group was galvanized by the governor's annual strategy to single out Belleayre Ski Resort for budget cuts and the threat of closing," said Anthony. "Even after the protests, nearly one third of the jobs at the resort were lost before new management took over. And recently we've been devastated by extremely cold winters with little or no snow."

After a fifteen-year delay, a massive new expansion program for Belleayre was finally approved in 2016, but it would be years before the region felt the impact of new job opportunities. But today, the people were the same, but the cause was more immediate.

A woman asked Titus to talk about the new issue. He answered, "The DEP has been dumping five hundred and eighty million gallons of muddy water from the over-flowing Schoharie Reservoir into the Esopus Creek. It happens every single day, not just for one day, but now for over a hundred consecutive days. No one knows exactly why."

"Okay, but what damage has it done?" she asked. Her long hair flipped from one side to the other when she talked.

"There is evidence of damage to private septic systems, decimation of fish spawning grounds, destruction of rich farmland, erosion of fragile stream banks, and damage to municipal water systems farther south along the Hudson Valley. Just look at the newspaper last Sunday."

The news in print was incriminating. Representatives from the DEP and New York City had refused to reverse their decision. A costly lawsuit was filed by Ulster and Delaware Counties against the DEP and the City. Photos of dead fish and flooded farmland graced the front page.

A man with furry muttonchops and a handlebar mustache said, "The city will win this battle. Mountain residents simply don't have the monetary strength to fight."

Bonnie answered, "It's time for local opinions to become known. It is time to voice strong opposition. This is an important issue that will harm the wellbeing of all of us. Haven't we paid enough of a price through the years for the sake of the City? "

After distributing copious amounts of pretzels, beer, wine and pizza, Bonnie was on her soapbox today. "The DEP is charged with the responsibility of *protecting* the watershed, not destroying it with fifty-eight *billion* gallons of muddy water in less than four months. This deliberate flooding action amounts to nothing but planned and premeditated destruction. How can we *ever* trust the DEP again?"

Anthony started the crowd chanting, "Water Nazis! Traitors! Water Nazis! Traitors..." The volume increased. Finished signs were stapled to poles for demonstrations in Woodstock, all four ski resorts, the state capital in Albany, and the mayor's office down the city.

Anthony was excited. For the first time ever, he'd been put in charge of deciding who would carry the signs, a job that inflated his youthful ego. He strutted back and forth, making sure that every rabble-rouser in the room was armed with a slogan, and the bigger signs given to people who looked like they were energetic enough to raise the signs higher and yell the loudest. He played the role well, stopping to chat with each person and arm him or her with facts, figures, and emotion to keep them well fueled for serious protest.

Anthony worked the room with an armful of signs to distribute. Suddenly disaster struck. "Damn it!" he exclaimed as he stepped in a bucket of red paint. His foot immediately stuck in the two-gallon pail and splashed onto the carpet and Bonnie's favorite recliner. This would be the last straw for Bonnie's forty-year-old living room. Instead of screaming for help—a mop, a sponge, anything to prevent the dreaded spread of red—he pawed at his lower leg with his hand, and only managed to splash it on his shirt, his hair, his face, and his black beret. He hobbled across the room and through the kitchen to the back door, dragging the half-filled bucket and spreading disaster along the way.

Bonnie screamed, "Stop! Anthony, you're making it worse." But the energy for protest only increased from there, and Anthony was not about to let a little red paint put a damper on his enthusiasm for leadership. Soon, almost fifty enraged citizens emerged from Bonnie's tiny cottage onto Tinker Street in a spontaneous protest parade through Woodstock, an impulsive rehearsal for activities the next day. Anthony limped ahead like an injured one-legged vampire, now covered with revolutionary red, spread from head to toe. His trail of paint would lead tomorrow's protesters down a historic path of protest.

Instead of a thoughtful demonstration, the event elevated peaceful dissent into a thunderous faction of disgruntled radicals, spurned on by the stubborn traitorous actions of the agency charged with protecting the watershed. The DEP had their hands full.

Most residents of Woodstock were glad to see the fires of protest awakened once again to validate their liberal legend on the map. But conservatives didn't like this disturbance of the peace. Certain citizens called the DEP, and the local police. Word of the protest spread quickly on Twitter, Facebook, and local networks with frantic phone calls for a call to action, or a plea for peace and reason.

****

By the following morning, a tangled traffic jam on Highway 28 spontaneously developed. Somehow, Anthony's blood-red symbolism translated photographically to images of violent rage, and a color photo of Anthony appeared the on the front page of the *New York Times*, the Albany *Times Union,* the *Kingston Daily Freeman*, and the *Catskill Mountain News*.

Citizens for and against the issues descended on Woodstock, from upstream and downstream along the Esopus Creek in nearly fifteen thousand square miles of the Catskill region, and from communities along the Hudson valley from Albany to New York City. Environmental groups such as Greenpeace and Riverkeeper sent representatives. Police from Albany, Schenectady, Kingston, Margaretville and Oneonta joined the Woodstock contingent to keep the peace. When the New York State troopers joined the ruckus, it was painfully evident that this was no second coming of the famous 60s Woodstock concert. This was the definition of protest.

The Arab Spring of 2011 proved how quickly and effectively social networks could mobilize disparate groups of citizens. Woodstock in the twenty-first century was no different. Liberal groups seemingly appeared out of nowhere and gathered for the cause. But the right-wing Hudson Valley Patriot Militia also arrived on a fleet of motorcycles with clubs, tear gas grenades, and stun guns to "help the overwhelmed local police." Sarah Palin issued an absentee opinion on Fox News from a distant speaking engagement in Arizona. Donald Trump added his own twisted commentary to help true Americans understand the issues that placed blame on the "ignorant mountain hippies". By eleven that morning, Woodstock was as crowded as a miniature Times Square. Politicians called for reason and calm on CNN. But who listened to them?

Chapter 11

Opinions

I was in another part of the Catskills last night, so I missed Anthony's red paint revolt. I arrived in the morning before they closed off the main roads into Woodstock. I walked the streets in amazement, recognizing friends from all over the Catskills who had answered the leaderless call to action. Strangely enough, opinions on the right and the left seemed to divide every group. I stopped near the main intersection in town, where musicians and street performers often entertained tourists for dollar tips tossed into a tattered guitar case. Factions from the Patriot Militia were busy arguing among themselves, uncertain as to which side they should support, and how they could stir the soup. The length of their hair strangely had nothing to do with which side was chosen. After all, was not "The Donald" among the shaggiest in the Glidden Revolution?

"Damned if I'm going to let the DEP ruin my fishing stream," commented a gnarly middle-aged man in a musty thirty-year-old leather jacket, decorated with large red stars on the shoulders.

A woman with entirely too many male hormones seemed to agree. "It's the best damn fly fishing in America. And now it's a muddy torrent...the bastards."

A man sitting on his Harley with the Rolling Stones tongue-logo on his back, commented, "You people don't understand. This water came from the Schoharie Reservoir way up stream. It overwhelmed the aqueduct connecting to the Ashokan. You can tell it was the Schoharie...the mud in the water is rust red."

His motorcycle women added support for her man. "Idiots! The water has to go somewhere! Downstream is the only choice. By fishing season, it'll all clear up again."

A young student with buttons *against* the war in Iraq, *against* the Afghanistan and Iraqi wars, *for* the 99%, *for* the Occupy Wall Street struggle, *for* a rent strike somewhere else, *for* the Arab Spring, *against* the DEP, and *for* a half dozen peace symbols in every color, jumped up and down, and argued, "You've got your head in a very dark place...you are SO totally wrong, like *totally!*"

"Right on, brother!" shouted Anthony, using vernacular borrowed from Bonnie's Nam era.

A lawyer from Margaretville stood on a park bench reciting a well-prepared statement through a bullhorn. "We're gathered here today to try to impress on the DEP that there are alternatives to uncontrolled dumping from the reservoir into the lower Esopus Creek. No one invited local residents to the table for intelligent debate or consideration of alternate plans. No one asked us. The DEP is flooding the creek simply because it CAN." The crowd responded enthusiastically with shouts and cheers. Signs were raised. The group across the street repeatedly chanted, "What do we want? Clear Water! When do want it? NOW!"

A man named Michael was having the time of his life watching the controversy. He and his friend Bro stood near the middle of the group, smiling as if they had created the argument. "This is tailor made for us, Bro. All this energy, and they don't have a clue what we did!"

"Ya think anyone's discovered the shit we put in the Pepacton?" he asked, looking to make sure nobody heard.

"No way. Not yet. It'll take a few days to reach the City," Michael said with confidence. This is like a beautiful revenge. And we didn't even have to stir up the crowd here. I love it!"

"Look at these idiots! They're all arguing about the creek, and nobody realizes what we did!"

Michael replied "Careful. Someone will hear us."

"They'll know, soon enough."

"Yeah. Wait 'til they have a real reason!" He turned to soak up the energy of the crowd.

This was the most exciting thing to happen in all the Catskills in a long time. I listened for a while to the famed lawyer. Soon a familiar figure bumped my elbow and joined me. I was shocked at Anthony's appearance. "What the hell happened to you?"

Anthony replied, "I had a spontaneous meeting with a can of Glidden 'Smoldering Red' last night. This is so awesome! I made the cover of the *New York Times* this morning. They all think I'm the one who started all this. Even my mom loves it, though she won't admit it. She says I inflamed the crowd on purpose, looking like a bloody refugee from the war in Syria."

"'Smoldering Red', eh? You could have taken a shower last night!"

"Yeah, I guess I'm kind of getting off on the notoriety. They showed my picture on the *Today Show* this morning," Anthony laughed. "So—totally cool!"

"You're a fool. And you're no revolutionary leader. With that beret, and the red paint, you look like those posters of Che Guevara from the sixties."

"A little red goes a powerful long way. I'll wash it off later when things settle down around here. I think...I think I make a pretty good impression, don't you?"

"Cool move, *Che*. You're more hippie than your mom, and more theatrical than Lady Gaga." Although I razzed him real hard, in truth I really admired his spirit of revolt. And could Glidden pick a name for the occasion? Wow!

Anthony said, "This has got me thinking. Wearing red paint is a great way to..."

I interrupted, "...but it's not a terrific way to stir up real action."

"Mom used to be a Weatherman in the sixties. I've learned a lot from her stories. We're going to need to go underground soon, where we can do something that really counts."

"And what would *that* be?" I asked. There he goes again, making trouble. Mountains of it.

"I'm not sure. But it needs to be something drastic, something no one will forget. We need to blow up something, fuck up the water for the city..." He was puffed up like a red bull.

"You're over the top, Anthony. This will pass in a few days. There are already too many people over-reacting here. THINK about this!" I wished I could tell him what I knew had to be kept secret: he didn't know that an overwrought radical had already poisoned the Pepacton. How could I stop myself from telling him that the issue of flushing out the Esopus Creek wasn't half as serious as some unknown terrorist poisoning the water supply? Oh god! How to stop a raving lunatic before somebody gets hurt?

"No. I'm *not* 'over the top.'" He grabbed my sleeve and looked straight into my eyes to emphasize an important point. "It's time we taught New York City a lesson they can't ignore. You *know* I'm right about this. Call your brother. I know you'll do anything he tells you. Parker will support this."

"I will call him. But there's a lot you don't understand about what's going on, and even more you don't understand about Parker. He's not ready to start a war."

"Okay. So, tell me. What does it take? Sixty years ago, they forced your family out of their homes, and your Great friggin' great grandpa blew his brains out. Then your dad spends half his life trying to justify the reason he's working for the City's interests instead of what local residents need around here. The reservoirs bring us great fishing, free waste treatment, and pure water. But at what cost, Titus? You and Parker were the ones who told me the Catskills are in permanent recession. And all of a sudden, the DEP is sponsoring wholesale destruction of the Esopus. Ask your own father! He works for the City. He must have a hell of a time with his own conscience. Titus, for god's sake, what does it take to get your attention?"

He was right, even with that red face. I was mortified. I looked down at my shoes. For the next few minutes, there was complete silence between us. I watched the protesters with signs, wondering what really set them off? How far would they go? Is this a good thing or not? What part should we take in this? Look at all the anger about flushing out a reservoir through their favorite fishing stream. I mean, shouldn't we take advantage of all this energy, now that hundreds of people were all worked up? Didn't the people have a right to know about the toxin in the reservoir? But then, proof like the poisoned deer, how could we ever stay in control? It was a polarized group. How could everyone be so inconsistent, so confused, and so divided on issues that now seemed so obvious to me?

And I had made a promise when I signed up to join my big brother. Even with the help of four and a half million from the Trust Fund, I had no simple answer to Anthony's challenge.

"Anthony, just trust me. I'll join in this battle. *My* way." That seemed pretty lame, noncommittal, and so, like Sinatra. I had so much to learn about leadership. Especially while the cannonballs were flying every which way with no definitive target.

Almost in defiance of the police presence, a confrontation broke out between several people arguing.

A local businessman argued with a seasoned hippie. "What's wrong with a temporary release of a little water? It settles before it gets to New York. It won't harm a thing."

Looking like the second coming of Steven Tyler, a young man said, "The turbidity is not caused by melting snow. It's caused by the alum they dumped in the Schoharie aqueduct."

A woman in a green and yellow fluorescent silk dress joined in. "Alum? ALUM? Are you crazy? We had over eighty-five inches of snow this winter. Where do you expect all that water to go? Downhill, that's where. Through the Esopus, into the Hudson, and downstream. Idiot!"

A crowd gathered like magnets in a steel mill. A man in art studio paint-spattered jeans said, "We've had plenty of severe winters. But the Schoharie intake pipe got buried in mountains of mud, and now the water's like, totally muddy. *That's* why!"

Steven Tyler said, "That started years ago. So why can't they fix it?"

Mr. Business replied, "I heard they need to build a multi-level intake, like in all the rest of the reservoirs."

Harley-man countered, "What a smart ass! Water is water. If it's good enough to drink in the city, it's good enough for the friggin' fish."

"You've obviously never fished for trout, and all you care about is New York CITY!" said a man in a rainbow trout shirt and a hat with fishing lures attached all the way around the brim. He looked like if he yelled too loud, he'd be using his own tongue for bait.

"I fish all the time," said Harley-man. "But not in the Esopus. There are plenty of other streams up here. Why get all upset over one little crick?"

"Obviously you are happy drinking filthy disgusting mud water," Anthony shouted.

Suddenly we could hear his mom from across the street. "Way to go! Give 'em hell, son!" Bonnie shouted as she lit her corncob hash pipe.

"Be a man! Drink beer. Who the hell cares?" Harley-man puffed up his chest and clenched his fists.

Neon silk-lady said, "You don't need to go fishing to see the mud in the Esopus. It used to be clear, so pure. And now it stinks like Flint, Michigan."

"The DEP doesn't care what we think." Even his voice sounded like the real Steven Tyler.

Painter-man could still argue, in spite of what he'd smoked for breakfast. "I don't get it. I heard the City was fined over five million dollars for this. But they won't stop. They've ruined one of the most famous trout streams in the world."

Harley-man was clearly bigger than anyone else, though he seemed to match his aggressiveness with extreme stupidity. But that didn't stop him from arguing both sides just to piss everybody off. "They don't ask fishermen. Nobody *cares* about fishermen. All they care about is shipping our water to the frigging city."

Fisher-man said, with his hat lures jangling as he got more animated, "And what are they supposed to do, call *you*? You stock shelves at a grocery store. What the hell would you know about it?"

"So you want to get personal? I'll show you *personal.*" And Harley-man knocked Fisher-man's hat off his head. Vintage fishing lures scattered across the pavement like runaway minnows. Finally, the hat hooked itself to Neon lady's silk dress. She squealed like a wounded pig and ran in circles as if she could shake off the attack of the onerous fish-hat.

Soon a shoving match erupted, and police moved in to stop the demonstrators from hurting each other. The DEP had sent in a riot squad, and they soon had seven people in handcuffs. A woman with a yard of grey hair screamed, "Fucking water Nazis! You have no authority here."

A man in horn-rimmed glasses and a brown corduroy jacket with elbow patches answered, "Are you kidding? These guys haven't had a damn raise—not one red nickel—for seven years! And they're still doing the best they can to protect idiots like you."

"Screw you, buddy! We don't *need* an occupying army. We don't *need* some guy with a badge from the City telling us we can't go near our water. We don't *need* any more broken promises." Silk dress lady got into his face, only three inches from touching him nose to nose, and shook her finger angrily into his eyes.

A DEP officer pulled her back, and pinned her arms behind her back, followed with the zip of a nylon band that handcuffed her wrists together. She screamed, "Damn you, pigs! You're *hurting* me. I'll sue you until you don't have a frigging penny! I think you broke my arm. Let me go! Raymond go get my dogs! I'm warning you, I have four pit bulls...you'll be sorry." The rest of her tirade was cut off when they shoved her into a police van and locked the back doors.

Me and Anthony were mesmerized, watching from a nearby corner. Anthony kept repeating, "This is awesome! Like, totally, like *awesome.*" I had my video camera rolling in order to show Parker how this was going down. Parker was in New York, doing environmental studies, and missing all the real action. But I could witness it from the where I stood, and it was all on video. When we got together in New York City next week, I could show my smart-ass brother plenty of motivation to put Great-really-awesomely-great grandpa's secret endowment fund to work.

Michael said slyly to Bro, "This is like readymade for us. Yes!"

Chapter 12

New York State of Mind

A fter a crowded transfer from the bus gate to the subway through the bowels of Port Authority, I waited for the A-Train to roll into the express platform at the West 34th Street station. I stopped to buy a magazine at the newsstand on the platform. Almost everyone in line bought a bottle of water and a newspaper. New Yorkers are weird that way. They'd prefer to buy a bottle of water from Maine than drink from their own Catskill water supply, a source that was just as pure, or probably more so, than any bottle with a "natural spring water" label and a three and a half buck price tag. Like, if it's that expensive, it *must* be better than the stuff they get out of the tap. And that's *if* they knew that a lot of bottled water comes from a source that isn't that special. Minutes later, New Yorkers, in their normal mode of *hurry*, exchanged places between the platform and the train. I joined the ant scrimmage, toting a backpack with a thermos full of *real* Catskill water, my video cam and a change of clothes.

I had over three hours to think about the meeting with Parker. It wasn't that I'd changed his opinion about everything. If anything, the events over the past week had solidified my views so much that there was no turning back. I no longer saw myself as the apathetic mountain boy who cared about nothing but women and weed, fishing and skiing, and sleeping most of the way through college. Now, with my new mission, I needed advice in areas I had never even considered. I'd learned about the issues from the protesters, at least, as far as they understood them. And most of them were just as confused as I was. They knew how to get all worked up, but ask any one of them to explain why, and they'd be so confused they'd have to change the subject to another issue they knew even less about. I needed somebody who'd give me an angle that exceeded the mentality of the emotional protesters in Woodstock. And graduate-level wisdom that would guide me to a strategy on a dangerous toxin that was working its way closer to the city every hour. Parker would know what's happening. The only thing I was damn sure of was that Anthony's reckless ideas would lead to nothing but trouble. Dad made me promise to rise above that. I owed that much to that poor poisoned deer, if not my confused father.

Lost in these thoughts, before I knew it, the A-Train had pulled into the 72nd Street Station. I'd gone the wrong way, north toward the Upper West Side instead of south to the Village. Like I needed another reminder I was not a real New Yorker. I asked a young man for directions, and he was helpful and nice, not at all like the legendary New York City rudeness. But without thinking, I flew through the exit turnstile instead of crossing over the stairs to the downtown side and ran up the stairs to the street. I would have been embarrassed if Parker was with me. But I had time. Why not explore a little?

Maybe I'd hike over to Central Park for a rare opportunity to take a stroll through the world's most famous planned recreational area. As I hiked eastward along 72nd Street, I remembered the visit I'd taken through the Catskill Watershed museum back home, where I picked up a map of the reservoirs and the complex system of aqueducts feeding the City. The map showed that the Catskill, Delaware, and

Croton systems merged in the Kensico and Hillview reservoirs near the north border of the Bronx, and continued to Central Park before distribution to the boroughs of Manhattan and Brooklyn. I tried to imagine finding some trace of the underground system within walking distance. Surely there would be a structure covering a pumping station, a control valve, or part of the underground distribution network. Where would it be? And why did I need to find it?

As I entered Central Park, I recalled that there was still some sort of old reservoir deep beneath the meadow where thousands gathered in the summer to enjoy Shakespeare performances and rock concerts. Constructed during the Civil War, Lake Manhatta had started as an aboveground lake, and had been the only major reservoir inside city limits. Union soldiers defended against a Confederate plot to blow up the High Bridge Aqueduct over the Harlem River in what might have been the first act of terrorism against the New York City water supply. Underneath the Great Lawn a system of underground distribution valves and connecting pipes were built in 1906 and later modernized to quench the thirst of the growing borough of Manhattan. At the north end of Central Park, there was still a small lake renamed the Jacqueline Kennedy Onassis Reservoir.

I strolled north through the park, zipping my hoodie against the February winds. I dodged discarded syringes and wine bottles in a tunnel under the road that reeked of urine and human feces and avoided some nasty looking homeless characters who actually looked quite at home in their cardboard boxes and third-hand tattered blankets. I looked for signs of the water distribution system, perhaps a manhole cover, an entrance to a shaft, or a pump house.

Meanwhile, I realized I still barely understood what position I wanted to take. With the video I held in my backpack, I had a lot of potential power to influence. But influence whom? How and why?

When I crossed the 79th Street Transverse Road that crossed Central Park, I came upon a medieval looking structure, a small castle built of stone that rose up out of the granite knoll. This had to be the old gothic style Belvedere Castle, built in 1867 as an observation tower at the north end of Lake Manhatta, the highest point in the park. I recalled that it now housed a weather station and a nature center with exhibits for bird watchers. I wondered if, far below the ground, it might also be a key entrance to the water supply. Windows originally open to the elements for the weather instruments were now closed and sealed during the latest security renovation of the structure.

However, soon I turned my attention to something else. Perhaps the clue was the presence of two DEP cars next to a small stone building, a structure that just might be what I was looking for. It wasn't like the unguarded open shoreline of the Pepacton, or even the visible barb wired stone fortress on the Rondout at the supply end of the world's largest city water system. I got as close as I could to observe the scene, but I stopped when I saw two DEP uniforms coming out of the front door and locking it securely. The last thing I needed was to be questioned for the second time near one of their prized pump houses. I was tired of walking, so I turned back towards the southbound subway to meet Parker at a café farther downtown on Bleecker Street.

Chapter 13

The Bleecker Street Café

T he Bleecker Street Café has a comfy eclectic feeling, an onsite bakery with fresh pastries and sandwiches, and an ambiance-plus environment filled with a collection of mismatched antique stuffed chairs, nineteenth century sewing machine tables, wrought iron ice cream tables, and royal purple paisley damask-covered couches. It is just comfortable enough to satisfy a happy crowd of haggard students, village residents, and star-struck tourists toting laptops, cell phones and tablets, and enjoying an atmosphere that could only exist on Bleecker Street in New York City.

I found Parker in a tall Windsor armchair covered in tattered red tapestry. His coal black lip goatee was a new addition that accented his modern beatnik look, complete with shiny black leather skinny jeans, a black Fab-Five tee shirt, a bright orange cardigan sweater with purple mag buttons, and four-inch raised-platform leather boots bound in stainless ringed straps. If he'd been carrying a silver flute, I'd have sworn Parker had transformed himself into the contemporary progeny of Jethro Tull, with his scary Pied Piper persona.

Two grande lattes sat waiting for us next to his laptop on the sewing machine table, and an original art deco kissing-lips love-seat in sexy rose-red suede stood across from him, empty and reserved only for moi. I stood next to the weird sofa, which made me feel strangely ill at ease, and totally out of my league in the intimidating environment of the big city. Still, Parker was completely in his element, looking like a student prince in charge of his life, ready to take on the world and the DEP. With his new look, Parker wasn't intimidated by anything. He was totally sure of himself in spite of destroying several basic rules of mountain masculinity. He exuded confidence like the peoples' pirate.

"Yo, wassup brother?" Parker stood to greet me. "Glad we could meet. This is my favorite place in the Village. Lots of cool people hang out here." I looked around to observe whom he would call "cool." Artists with paint-spattered jeans, young political rebels and intellectuals from NYU, international students from the Orient and the Near East, and dozens of eccentric personages from the newest beat generation populated the place. I felt like the newest nerd on the short bus, but the people and the décor together were so strange they almost made me feel close to normal.

The knuckle bump and the brother handshake made me feel a little less like biting my lip and checking my zipper. Maybe I shouldn't run for the door just yet. I pulled the video cam from my backpack, along with a notebook for the meeting.

"You're taking this seriously, with the notebook and all."

"I've thought a lot about this. I guess I fit in, no?" I shifted in my seat.

"Would you rather be in a gay bar? New York has plenty of those! You don't have to try to 'fit in.' The point here is that *nobody* 'fits in', but everybody who is here, belongs here. And nobody will give a shit about what we talk about."

"But...this place is like that weirdo bar in *Star Wars*. Do I look okay?" I removed my geeky Walmart glasses, straightened the pocket flaps on my plaid flannel shirt, pulled the shirttails out of my jeans, and mussed up my hair to that just-out-of-bed style in a vain attempt to be more like the disheveled young artist at the next table. People in this eclectic place had their own strange conformity. Almost every person was wearing skinny jeans and multiple rings, many of them piercing parts of their face, and other unlikely body parts.

As a true outsider, I had to say, "They're all different, but dumped out of the same can of paisley paint. I've never seen so many skinny jeans that weren't on a store rack. Everybody's pierced and inked. So much for individuality."

Parker laughed. "Of course. Okay, you're feeling like a mountain goat at the opera. But trust me, nobody cares. This is New York. This is Bleecker Street, spawning grounds for the weird and wonderful. Breathe it in. Enjoy the ride. Leave the gun in your pickup truck."

"You're not making me feel much better with comments like that. I didn't bring the truck or the freaking guns. Took the bus and the A-train. But I need a smoke."

"Relax. You can't smoke anywhere here. Maybe it's time to quit. I will if you will."

"Maybe later." I settled into the lipstick chair, still not sure whether it would molest me. "Okay. I'm okay. This fag chair is actually kind of comfortable."

"That kind of talk is not exactly acceptable in this neighborhood. You're sitting on a very famous love-seat, one of Dali's Lipstick Sofas."

"Dolly Parton's sleep sofa?"

He laughed at my naïveté. "*Salvador* Dali's surrealistic couch, bonehead."

I answered with mixed pronouns. "Yeah...well Dolly had best keep her lips to himself!"

"Come on, relax, and show me the video, tough guy."

94

I looked around to see if anyone could see my computer screen when it was turned towards Parker. There was a huge silver antique Russian samovar on a table against the wall, behind Parker. Great-really-great Grandma Van Rosendael brought one of those things from Holland, but this one looked like it belonged on the altar of a Russian cathedral. I should ignore my feeling that this place would harbor a costumed cop, listening in on our conversation. Bottom line, the only eyes on the video screen would be an occasional waiter drawing an espresso from one of its ornate silver spouts, me and Parker, and the artist stirring his chamomile tea with his multi-colored index finger across the aisle.

The camera spun out its story. First, the deer dying in complete agony on the shore of the Pepacton. A close-up of me shooting the deer, and the pained expression on my face. A shot of the coagulated white detergent toxin lumped up on the surface next to the shore, as if it was too cold to dissolve. Then, images of sign making at the protest party at Bonnie's house, protesters arguing over the issues, and a photo of the torrent of muddy water in the Esopus. Sounds of the Stones and Creedence Clearwater filled the room, and beer and box wine flowed like it came direct from an Esopus tributary. A group of Bonnie's friends from Woodstock chanted a slogan, their arms around Anthony and his buddies. Among them: the owner of a Woodstock souvenir shop, wearing most of his collection of political buttons. A wizened hippie couple, both working artists covered with recent traces of bold color choices on a canvas. A sculptor with a tattered kerchief around his head, spattered with bits of dried modeling clay. A man in a 70s double-breasted suit with a white silk ascot and a rainbow 'Marriage Equality' button, with unruly grey hat-hair looking like a radical gay cousin of Attorney William Kunstler. The owner of the local motorcycle store wearing everything Harley, his latest girl-fren on his arm trying to keep her pierced nose from tangling with elaborate art rings on her fingers. A pair of twenty-somethings arguing with their mother, who was busy trying to prevent her accidental toddler from trying on a super-sized bag of organic orange cheese doodles. And other eclectic wonders.

As the Beetles' "Revolution" blared in the background, the video revealed Anthony with his foot stuck in a can of paint, dragging a trail of Smoldering Red across the living room with his beret and his Frankenstein walk, commanding immediate attention that inflamed even the most sedate citizen into chants, cheers, and political action. Like Ché as the Pied Piper, he burst through the screen door to the porch, followed by fifty-some protesters out onto Tinker Street. He didn't get thirty feet before a reporter's flash blinded the neighborhood, not once, but five backup shots in order to pick the best one for tomorrow's headline photo. And New Yorkers think they've got the only license for weird on the planet? The film actually made me feel *more* comfortable sitting there in the Bleecker Street Café. There was safety among fanatics.

A film flicker and a moment of black segued into a pan across the *New York Times* and *The Daily News* cover photos the following morning. It wasn't hard to see how Anthony's arm splattered in dried red paint and raised in defiance had become an overnight symbol of the people's unrest. Anthony's computer screen sampled the Facebook calls to action. Another amateur film transition revealed the crowds of restless people the following morning: the lawyer with his bullhorn on the park bench. Candid shots showed the opposition on the other side of the square that really wasn't really square in the center of a small normal town that wasn't really normal and hadn't been the same since the concert on a farm close to Woodstock in 1969.

I sat there silently watching the looks of amazement on Parker's face. This was powerful.

The next sequence showed the source of the protest. The Esopus Creek, usually a gorgeous torrent of pure clear water full of fish taunting the fly fishermen who'd traveled from distant places, looked like a muddy river-born flash

, if ever there was such an ugly beast of nature. A continuous inundation of mucky brown water surged through the river channel, overwhelming it as it passed flood stage, sweeping away delicate spawning grounds for fish, carrying small saplings, bushes, and various creek-side architectural remnants with it. A flagpole from someone's flooded hunting cabin rushed by, with a shredded American flag struggling to stay aloft above the waves, reminiscent of the rubble of nine-eleven. An abandoned outhouse, still with the DEP condemnation notice ordering its immediate removal attached to the door, floated by and crashed into a huge uprooted willow tree stuck on a sand bar. Hundreds of fish lay dead on the banks. A small dog added pathos as he struggled against the current, his thirty-foot outdoor leash still attached to a stake that had ripped out of the ground. A woman waded a few feet into the water in a hopeless effort to rescue the pooch, while her two small children stood on the bank, scared and crying.

The camera panned high above to a clear blue sky with not a trace of wind or storm. The Catskills had lived through the melt, and the DEP exercised its right to control flooding by creating an even bigger flood, a deluge of water that hadn't been seen since Hurricane Irene spread eight vertical feet of raging water through the Catskills, the mega-storm that had leveled nine hundred seventy-three homes and the only shopping center with a grocery.

The camera panned across the peaceful waters of the Pepacton, showing just how massive almost 140 billion gallons looked like in a single reservoir. Next was a close-up of the fountains near Rockefeller Center and Central Park. Titus added two parting shots: first, a close-up of a drinking fountain in New York City, stuck in the "on" position and left abandoned until the next good citizen cared to drink or dutifully turn it off. A group of children ran through the torrent created by an open fire hydrant on a hot summer day, one of hundreds throughout the city showing the city's blatant disregard for water conservation. After the previous footage, this simple reminder of waste sanctioned by the City would affect any rational human being. My confusion was clearing as the issues confronted me.

Parker sat forward in his chair, commenting, "This is incredible. With the right editing and voiceover, this tells a story that no words could ever come close. Michael Moore would kill for this footage."

Our young waiter, a muscle toned student in a tight tee shirt and electric yellow hair sprayed into a permanent state of disarrayed statuary, had been hovering, and now saw fit to comment. "Damn. Was that a Mississippi flood? Looks treacherous."

Parker replied, "No, that's the Esopus Creek, where your drinking water comes from. Up in the Catskills."

"O-M-G—the Catskills? Like that's *our* water? I had no clue." He leaned over the top of my surrealistic Dali chair to get a better look. His breath on my neck made my hair stand up.

"Yep. And look what they're doing to it," Parker answered.

"You mean, that's not a natural flood?"

"No. This is what the Department of Environmental Protection calls 'protection.'"

He ran a hand through his steel yellow hair. "Damn. Look at that torrent. Makes you want to shower in Maine. Or not at all."

"Can't quite picture that," I said. "Usually, it's as clear and pure as it could be, the best water in any large city in America. And the best trout stream."

"Trout...huh?" he muttered. The waiter walked away, shaking his head. An immediate convert, he went from table to table in his section, clearing water glasses after a short explanation to each patron.

Parker shifted nervously in his chair. "See how panic begins. Just a seed of trouble starts a reaction that reverberates through a restaurant, and pretty soon it's on NBC Nightly News. We should never have told that waiter about the DEP. Dad would die if he heard about this."

I hid the phone in my backpack. "Do you see how weird this is for us? We've got video right in front of our eyes, but we both feel strangely guilty when we bring Dad into the picture. It makes my stomach queasy."

In a low voice, Parker said, "Just think what this would be like if they knew about the toxin. All hell would break loose."

"I've been thinking about that." I tried to whisper in the noisy atmosphere. "Parker, if you take away all the emotion for a minute, maybe...I mean, the terrorists might have the right reason...but the wrong method. What do you think?"

Parker jammed his finger on the table. "You've been talking to Anthony, haven't you? In other words, without some kind of radical action like a bomb or a toxin, the issue wouldn't get enough attention?"

"Well, yeah, I guess. But I also see how much—what do they call it? Collateral damage there is from the toxin."

"It's also a good lesson in how terrorism works. Forget about the toxin for a minute, and let's just look at the issue of the Esopus water release." He held up a water glass. "There's no muddy water in these glasses. Nobody in New York is showering in polluted water. Few people even know about the floods in the Esopus. In fact, that waiter, and very few New Yorkers have the slightest idea where their water comes from. But all it takes is the simple *fear* of a disaster to cause a panic." Parker drank from his water glass. "Terrorism is about fear, Titus. All they have to do is start with *a little* panic, maybe just kill *a few* people, and then spread the rumor that the whole population is at risk."

"Maybe that's why Dad hasn't reported it yet, and why the DEP hasn't announced anything," I said. "Think of the fear that would create."

"I don't know. It's been almost a week now. Has Dad said anything more about it?"

"Not much. He's waiting for something to grow in a Petri dish. But he's not the same. Something's not right. I know one thing, though. He's terribly afraid of his boss, and losing his job."

When Parker gets nervous, a twitch develops in his eyes. "Okay...but that doesn't seem like a reason to put all of New York City at risk. Surely he's done something."

"He says it will get diluted by the reservoirs and the aqueduct system. I don't know how he can be so sure. Parker, you saw the footage of that buck. I've never seen an animal suffer like that. It was...I don't know...terrifying."

"And if it was strong enough to kill a buck so fast, imagine what it could do here."

I didn't feel right about this. "Shouldn't we tell someone?"

"And violate Dad's trust? And maybe get him fired? I don't think so."

He leaned forward. "But if it's a real threat..."

"We don't *know* what Dad has done to address this. He may have already—"

"Seems like we're already on the inside. I *saw* the deer die. It's all on video that no one else has. What more proof do we need?"

The waiter brought bottles of spring water to replace the New York tap water throughout his section. I could tell he was proud to be able to do something for the crisis. After a long silence, Parker offered, "I know a guy who might help with this. One of my environmental studies professors, Dr. Jacoby, is an expert on the water system of New York. Yesterday I stopped in his office to turn in my term paper, and we talked—in general—about some of the issues. He knows I'm interested, and he volunteered to help me. I'll bet he has some connections we might need."

"But...can we trust him? How do you know where he stands on all this?"

"Trust isn't the issue. I know he'll be sympathetic. After he sees this video, there won't be any question." He pulled out his cell phone to arrange an appointment. After a short explanation of their mission, Parker had his answer.

"He's very interested. He says to drop in right now. Let's walk over to his office on West Fourth Street, near the park. We'll see what we can learn, and then we'll decide how to proceed."

"We've got some hot issues to think about. And we've got to do something about the toxin, fast."

"I know, Titus. But we're not going to panic. That's exactly what they want."

"What about all the protests? Anthony's so into himself that he's practically taken charge. He thinks he's the leader of some magical movement."

"Knowing him, he doesn't have a clue what he's yelling about."

"Right. He's like a tank running downhill with no brakes. He's liable to make trouble we can't even begin to control." I don't know why, but at this point I felt really grounded, with Parker there.

"Let's go. Professor Jacoby is our answer. He's waiting."

Chapter 14
Professor Jacoby

When Parker and I entered the wood paneled office, it was obvious we were in the domain of an academic giant. Dr. Lewis Jacoby was one of the world's authorities on municipal water systems. His office was cluttered with references and books, framed letters and commendations from Interior Secretary Ken Salazar, Presidents Reagan and Clinton, Robert F. Kennedy Jr., three past mayors of New York, and Governors Cuomo-the-First and Cuomo-the-Present. A picture of him on an anti-whaling mission with Greenpeace was blown up and placed in a prominent position next to photos of his grandchildren on the desk. His most recent book, *Water Supply: Safety or False Security?* was to be released in say, and the galleys from the publisher were waiting for his attention on a corner of his desk.

But it wasn't his own book he held in front of him. A tattered and bookmarked copy of *Liquid Assets: A History of New York City's Water System* was in his hands. He abandoned his thick bifocals, looked up and remarked, "Gentlemen, gentlemen, two of you! You must be brothers."

Parker said, "Yes, this is my brother, Titus."

"The Rose brothers! Come in. Come in. I have much to share with you." He gestured for us to sit in the two green leather chairs in front of a huge antique partners desk. "So, you're interested in the water supply, are you?"

Parker shook hands with his professor, and I followed his lead. I had never been in the presence of such a person.

Before us sat the distinguished Professor Emeritus, ready to help us define our mission. His eyebrows revealed the wizened age of a man nearly finished with his seventies, with errant whiskers emerging from his oversize ears, tangled grey eyebrows and a huge pockmarked nose. In spite of his wrinkles and turkey gobbler throat, he seemed as sharp as the best of his PhD students and still loved mentoring undergraduates interested in environmental studies.

"I read your paper, Parker. Very well researched...actually, quite insightful. You came to some marvelous conclusions. However, you missed one of the more important sources, instead of going to all that research. Not that your sources are bad, of course." He tapped the cover of the book he was holding. "Diane Galusha has many answers in her book, *Liquid Assets...*" He smiled when he handed the book across the table. "You'll enjoy this. And I think you should meet her. She lives near Margaretville. You keep it for a while. I left some bookmarks in there for you. And the bibliography in back is enlightening, duplicates some of the sources you cited in your paper." He coughed a deep raspy itch from his lungs as if a human hairball prevented natural breathing.

"Thank you, Dr. Jacoby."

"Galusha's book is a marvelous history. It doesn't pretend to answer some of the hypothetical and contemporary questions you raised in your paper. But you'll find much history that verifies some of your theories and premises.

"So! You have a story to tell me, I suppose. Let's have it, all of it. Don't hold back on me. I may be old, but I'll bet I can guess some of what you'll be telling me."

He was right. We spilled our guts, starting with great-really-great grandpa Rosendael, the bazillion-dollar trust fund, Dad's bewildering conflicts with his heritage and his DEP career, and the frightening terrorist attempt to poison the water supply with a mysterious toxic white powder. When Titus showed him the video of the deer at the Pepacton, Professor Jacoby sat up in his chair. His watery eyes and furrowed brow revealed his emotions.

"My young friends, it's always the animals that are innocent bystanders. The only thing that buck did wrong was to be thirsty at the wrong place at the wrong time. But his death proves how lethal this situation is. But you say the DEP removed most of the toxin before it dissolved?"

"I think so. Dad said the toxin had coagulated like wet globs of detergent when they removed it from the water."

"And the water was cold and hemmed in by ice," Parker added.

"Let me see the close-up of the toxin in the water." He replaced his glasses over his eyes, and I replayed the scene and froze the frame of the toxin on the boulder. Professor Jacoby sat for a moment, contemplating. He opened a reference book, looked at the index and turned to the pages he needed. He flipped back and forth between two sections. Next he opened a thick bound computer printout. I could read the label, "FBI Incident Report: NYC Watershed: Maximum Security." His expression amplified deep wrinkles high on his forehead, and his bushy eyebrows seemed to grow over the top of his reading glasses. Looking much like Bernie Sanders, his senior hair stood at attention in a wild array of fine white straw. He turned to his computer. I could see the screen obliquely as he tapped in his security code on a secure Homeland Security site then two more security codes. I assumed he had entered some sort of inner sanctum. I was astonished. Why would an NYU professor have privileged access to classified databases? Professor Jacoby noticed the look on my face. "Sir...how can you...I mean...how do you get access to these secure websites?"

"I have...some privileges based on my career before I joined the faculty at NYU and my classification as an expert in certain areas," he explained. He pushed a button on his intercom, saying, "Dotty, I need that large envelope that arrived this morning from the DHS."

From the picture frame behind him, Ronald Reagan smiled and shook his hand. In the next photo, a younger Professor Jacoby smiled as he posted a "No Hunting" sign at his country home with the ski trails at the Catskill's Hunter Mountain Ski Resort across the valley in the background, and President Clinton standing next to him. Parker discreetly pointed to the photo, and I acknowledged the discovery with a nod. Dotty entered with the envelope. I couldn't make out anything on the report, but the envelope had the label "CLASSIFIED: Department of Homeland Security" on the top line. Underneath, the letters "EMR-ISAC" were printed on the return address. I squinted hard and read the fine print below. "Emergency Management Response-Information Sharing and Analysis Center." Our government could never choose a simple acronym.

After a few moments, he said, "First, a little background. There have been several attempts to poison the water supply. I can tell you about some incidents in the past. There were threats as far back as the Civil War, attempts in both World Wars, and great concern during the Cold War. But up through yesterday, it's curious that there have been no reports filed to substantiate what you are telling me." His mouth wrinkled closed in a gesture of frustration. For the first time his demeanor changed. "Any idea of why that might be, young Master Rose?"

I stuttered a reply, "Uh...I think...I mean, I'm not really sure."

"Come on, son, let's have it. You're not telling me everything, and there simply isn't any more time to waste." A wry smile appeared on his face.

"We told you that our father is a DEP officer. Dad is...really afraid he might lose his job. His boss is a real assho—I mean, he's really hard on Dad. Maybe...well, I don't really know if and when Dad reported it."

"Ah! Classic. Intimidation always confuses and inhibits the flow of information. And progress is stopped like an eight-day clock. Meanwhile, the water flows southward to nineteen million thirsty people in metro New York. The question is, *is it still water we can drink?*" As a decision arrived, he pursed his lips and nodded his wise old head. "I'm glad you came here to tell me. I only wish you had come forth a few days earlier. Please, just sit outside in the waiting room for a few moments until I call for you." We exited the inner sanctum without any of our questions answered.

We heard the bolt lock to the inner office. Parker said, "He sure isn't acting like the professor I knew yesterday." The intercom buzzed on Dottie's desk, and he asked her to "pick up the private line". She squelched the speakerphone and listened to his instructions. "Yes, Doctor Jacoby. I'll take care of it."

Fifteen minutes went by. Was our report appreciated? Or misunderstood? Did he see us as the good guys or were we suspects? And how could the report of toxin in the Pepacton be omitted from the Homeland Security daily report? Or was it omitted? Parker and I looked at each other, both coming to the same conclusion. "He's not telling us everything," I whispered. Parker nodded his agreement.

****

After turning on a smooth jazz station for background noise, he dialed a number he'd committed to memory. "Myron, this is Dr. Jacoby, correspondent zero four eight six seven two one, dash F-B, clearance F eleven...Yes, NYU. Mother's name was Selma Andrews...died 1947, in Philly, U-PA Hospital. Thank you. I'm going to need some help. Highest security priority. Please contact—or, if you must, *send* out an APB for Officer Herbert Rose, stationed in the Downsville, New York office of the DEP in the Catskills...Right, 'Environmental Protection.' Treat him as a friendly witness...Right, I'm sure he'll have a beeper. When you reach him, let me know, and we'll do a video conference call to decide how to proceed...Thanks, Myron."

He pushed the intercom button. "Dotty, pick up the private line..." He switched off the intercom. "Dotty, we're going to need a conference call with FBI Bureau Chief Deforest, DEP Commissioner Calloway, NYPD Commissioner O'Riley, and the mayor on a secure line."

He settled back into his leather chair. "Also, call the DEP Testing Lab and find out more about what happened up there on the Pepacton last week and if they know of any other alerts. Actually, let's call the lab first. Call the one here and also the one in Downsville...and Dottie, get the boys something to drink. Don't let them leave, but don't let on what's going on. Do we still have those video games on the student computer in the lounge?...What about pizza in the frig? ...Might be an hour or so. Laurie can watch them there...Yes, turn the recorder on. We might need to know what they say...Cookies? Yes, of course. And some for me too, the tasty macaroons...I'm sure you'll be super nice. You're the best. That should do it. Oh, Dotty, perhaps you might stay a little late tonight...a bit of a crisis developing. That's my Dotty. You're the best."

Chapter 15

City Hall Beat

S tuart Novak had been covering the news from City Hall for four years and knew most of the regulars who frequented the steps to the main entrance of the beehive that governed New York City. He recognized the city councilmen, lawmakers and lawyers, commissioners, policemen, appointed officials, staff people and most of the lobbyists. He made a habit of hanging out by the hot dog stand on the corner and keeping a close eye on the people who walked hurriedly up the steps to the building. He could often match faces with the publicized meetings they attended. Stuart had become especially adept at spotting the people who weren't there on a regular basis but who showed up for an unscheduled meeting, a developing emergency, or to answer a call to the mayor's office in response to an unpublicized issue. His oversize jeans and nerdy red suspenders belied his powers of observation. He could recognize a crisis from a hundred yards away.

And so, he hung out at the hot dog stand in City Hall Park until at least 10:30 most mornings, and watched the people, imagining whom they might be seeing, and judging the urgency by their walk, their body language, and their facial expressions. As the resident geek Stuart was low down in the pecking order for the *Post* and seldom had specific assignments that mattered much, so he figured he could invest the time as an observer until one day he'd catch the big story that no one else had noticed. On certain days he had a feeling his break would come. He'd been in place since seven that morning, and it was already a three hot dog day with two Zantacs, three Tums and two cups of black coffee. He was psyched. As gas rose from his stomach he still had a good feeling today. And then he witnessed his story unfolding.

Emerging from a cab was DEP Commissioner Carter Calloway. On the steps he fell in pace with New York FBI Bureau Chief Joseph Deforest as they walked up the steps together. Stuart followed them discreetly all the way to the security metal detector inside, straining to hear the conversation between them.

"...and none of us want to take the risk that it works its way through the aqueducts," Deforest said.

Carter replied, "We can't be too cautious, Joe. But there's a chance we may be lucky on this one. When we get upstairs I've got some other factors that'll blow your mind."

"Look, there's O'Riley now. At least we can start on time."

"Who's that with him?"

"Professor Jacoby from NYU. Teaches environmental studies. He was in the conference last November. An expert on water terrorism."

"Clearance?"

"Top level. Used to be CIA, way back."

Stuart couldn't catch much more after they passed through the security line and entered an elevator. But he confirmed that the elevator carrying Police Commissioner O'Riley stopped at the same floor as the previous elevator carrying DEP commissioner Calloway and FBI Bureau Chief Deforest, and that floor was where the Mayor's office was located. So...the big wigs of the city's police force, the FBI chief of terrorist threats, the city's water supply czar and his ex-CIA environmental guru were meeting with the Mayor. The combination fascinated him. What is the only thing that would bring this particular combination of brass together at City Hall?

A water crisis event was unfolding. The only possible scenario. Deforest had talked about something "working its way through the aqueducts..." It had to involve the supply way up stream, possibly a reservoir in Westchester or even in the Catskills. If one of the reservoirs were compromised it would come directly to the city through the system of aqueducts, holding reservoirs, pumping stations, and purification plants. But what could be so toxic that it would "make it all the way through"? Ricin was a possibility. Maybe anthrax, like years ago in the post office. Or the dreaded E. Coli. But how much would it take to poison the water supply? What toxins are soluble in water? And would the system neutralize toxins that powerful? It didn't seem fair that all the experts were upstairs in the mayor's office probably sipping coffee and talking about the Yankees' latest trade until they hit on the crisis of the day. But Novak had other sources. Perhaps he could verify the threat by checking to see if there was any unusual activity in certain critical places along the path of the water supply.

First, he phoned his cousin Alan up in the Catskills town of Phoenicia and asked him to take a drive around the Pepacton and the Ashokan to observe any increased security activity from the DEP. Next, one of his contacts lived in Yonkers, near the transfer station at Van Cortlandt Park. A simple call could tell him whether there was increased police activity around the Hillview Reservoir or any of the strategic points nearby. And then there was his ace, his best friend from high school, who had just started a job in the new UV plant in Mount Pleasant in Westchester County. If he could get Stevie to share some inside information with him he'd have a story ready for the front page. This could be big—a career-maker if he played it right. And if he could scoop the boys at the other papers and news networks it could mean the coveted journalism Pulitzer. He tried not to project so far ahead. But inside, he knew he had a first-page breaking story.

He made the calls and waited for one of the terrorist gurus to emerge from the meeting at City Hall. After an hour he began to get restless, but when his cell phone starting ringing with a tidbit of information he knew he was onto a headline story. Shortly after, when Commissioner Calloway emerged with the professor, cub reporter Novak jumped at his opportunity.

"Commissioner Calloway, has New York City's water supply been threatened or compromised?"

"What? Are you crazy?"

"Sir, there is unusual police activity around the Hillview Reservoir. Can you explain what's going on up there?"

Calloway stopped in his tracks, turned to him, and scowled. "I have no idea. Probably a standard security drill. I'll...have to check the calendar..."

Stuart Novak dug deeper. "I believe you just came out of a meeting with the FBI and the mayor. Is there a terrorist event developing?"

"There's nothing to worry about just yet."

"...Not 'just yet'? And your meeting? Why were the Police Commissioner and the FBI Bureau Chief with you and the professor at this meeting? Sounds like a crisis brewing."

"Professor Jacoby is an expert in environmental affairs. The meeting was to confirm a strategic plan, in case the—"

"Has New York City's water already been poisoned?"

"I—have no further comment."

"Then why are the DEP cops swarming all over the reservoirs?"

"What? You are making things up. Reading things into this. There's no connection. It's just not true."

"'Not *true*,' Mr. Calloway? My sources have already confirmed the presence of four DEP cars at the pumping station on the Rondout, seven state and DEP patrol cars along the Pepacton, and several on both sides of the Ashokan. 'Not true,' Mr. Calloway? You don't look comfortable with your own answer."

"No comment, damn it."

For the first time the professor entered the fray. "Son, you don't understand what's going on here. Please! Let us sort this out. If you could just wait for the official press—"

Calloway cut him off, "There will be no press release, because there's no goddam problem."

Novak smiled. The professor had inadvertently confirmed his story. But he pressed on, mercilessly getting in Calloway's face. "And the troopers up in Yonkers, at the Hillview? I suppose they're 'just on patrol,' in groups of fifteen or twenty?"

"The Hillview always has extra patrols."

"And the Harlem River Bridge Aqueduct? The place looks like a police parking lot up there. And Jerome Park—"

"I've covered that already. And you'll have to ask the NYPD about the way they protect the reservoirs in the City. I don't have anything to do with their daily assignments."

"No problem, the Commissioner is just coming out now, from your meeting, I assume, with the —

"You *assume!*"

"—Mayor. Yes sir, from *your* meeting with the mayor. NOT an assumption. Comments sir?"

"NO comments. This interview is over."

As Stuart ran towards the top of the steps, and the men ran through City Hall Park towards a cab, the interview *was* truly over. But Novak's recorder had caught the entire conversation, the denials, the slip-ups, and all the innuendos between the lines. After the commissioner surrounded himself with uniformed escorts Stuart shot off a quick message to his boss on his iPhone and ran for the next cab to make it back to the office before the press deadline for tomorrow morning. He chattered out a story as fast as two thumbs could type.

Chapter 16

Satisfaction Guaranteed

"Look at this! Dude, we finally got noticed! It's on the front page of the *Post*. 'Terrorism Hits the NYC Water Supply.'"

"Nice headline, Michael. The feature article. We're famous!"

Michael danced around the room, "Listen to this: Reporter Stuart Novak says, quote, 'No one will confirm the presence of toxins in the water, however, there are battalions of New York State Police, FBI, and New York City Police surrounding key locations at the Hillview, Kensico, and Jerome Park reservoirs in Yonkers and the Bronx. DEP patrols have been sighted at all reservoirs in the Catskills. Officials would not comment, however the DEP Commissioner, Police Commissioner, and FBI New York Bureau Chief met at the mayor's office yesterday, presumably to discuss the danger and possible strategies to address the issue. The *Post* interviewed DEP Commissioner Carter Calloway, who introduced NYU Professor Lewis Jacoby, an environmental expert on water bioterrorism. After their meeting in the mayor's office, Professor Jacoby promised there would be an official press release forthcoming. The *Post* later interviewed a source who confirmed that results from laboratory tests were forthcoming to identify an 'unknown toxin' in water taken from the reservoirs. There have been no press releases from the mayor's office, no alerts from the DEP, the Environmental Protection Agency, or the Center for Disease Control in Atlanta. However, the *Post* can only assume that millions of residents may find that their drinking water is suddenly unsafe.'"

"Wow. This is incredible! The whole damn city will be scrambling for bottled water." He turned on CNN for the most recent update. In spite of the way he felt Bro was excited about the news. "'An unknown toxin,' they say. They don't know nothin' yet!"

Michael said, "They know. They're just not saying."

"Hell, WE don't even know what that stuff will do." Suddenly Bro felt a wave of uncertainty, like he had just figured something out.

Anderson Cooper announced that the mayor would soon begin a live press conference on the subject of bioterrorism in the New York City Water Supply. "Now, live at City Hall..."

The mayor stood at multiple microphones with an aide accompanying him. Reporters gathered in the pressroom at City Hall and welcomed him with applause. "Thank you for coming. I have an update on the news released in this morning's paper, which contained information mostly assumed and greatly exaggerated. There has been a minor incident along the shores of one of New York City's reservoirs in the Delaware watershed in the Catskill Mountains, where a small amount of toxin was introduced into the water. The substance has been confirmed as the Type A form of on botulinum toxin usually used in cosmetic and medical procedures. The vast majority of the toxin was removed from the water immediately after the incident. Fortunately the area was hemmed in by thick ice, and very little of the substance dissolved and entered the water system."

The mayor paused and looked directly into the camera. "There are many safeguards in New York's water supply already. There are three systems that supply water to the city: the original Croton system in Westchester County and the two Catskill mountain systems in the Delaware and the Catskill watersheds. These three systems supply over a billion gallons per day to metropolitan New York. The sheer volume of water insures that the relatively small amount of toxin introduced a hundred and forty miles upstream will be diluted to the point of becoming virtually harmless.

"The Delaware Aqueduct supplies almost fifty percent of the water used daily by New Yorkers. However, the recently finished facility at the junction of the Delaware and the Catskill aqueducts now allows us to pull either system off-line for inspection and repairs, or, in this case, to inspect one of the systems in order to insure that the water is rendered safe before it even leaves the mountains. In addition, the new UV treatment plant in Mount Pleasant is a vast improvement over natural filtration and in-line chlorination systems because it kills bacteria and other toxins by mutating their DNA. thus rendering them harmless. There are only a handful of cities in the world that have so many redundant safeguards in place. Our water supply is completely safe.

"We have tested our water at over forty different locations close to the user-end of the system. There was not a single positive testing result for any toxin that could be harmful. Therefore, we are confident that the toxin was introduced at only a single remote location far upstream. Fortunately, our DEP patrols caught the incident almost immediately and were able to mitigate the threat. I urge the public not to panic. Citizens can still trust the safest and most sophisticated water system in the world. I repeat: our water is safe."

The mayor held up a glass of water for the camera.

"However, we will be increasing security in the supply lines since it is now clear that an attempt was made to compromise the system. The DEP, the FBI, Homeland Security and the NYPD will be participating in providing the personnel necessary. Thank you for your confidence in our security system and our water supply. New York City is still the best city on the planet. And I am here to make sure it is also the safest city with the best drinking water anywhere!" The mayor nodded as if to toast the TV audience and drank heartily from the glass.

The applause was enthusiastic, but already there were hordes of questions from the press.

"Who do you think was responsible?"

The mayor replied, "We're working on that. There are several clues."

"Are there any suspects?"

His face seemed to tighten, and his eyes squinted slightly. "That's classified information at this time."

"Was it a foreign terrorist? ISIS or Al Qaeda?"

"We don't know yet."

"Where is the exact site? Where was the toxin dumped?"

"I cannot answer that...not at this time."

"Mr. Mayor, can you tell us how much was dumped?"

"As I said, a very small amount."

"Was it the Cannonsville, the Pepacton, or the Rondout that was poisoned?"

"At present, that's classified."

"Was it ISIS?"

He was clearly showing a little irritation. "Anything's possible at this point. Sorry. Next..."

"Sir, the muddy water was released in the Esopus Creek. But the Schoharie is part of the Catskill System. The water dump doesn't make sense if the Delaware System was the location of the incident."

"I'm afraid that's all I can tell you today."

"How do we know if they got it all?"

"That's it for today."

"If they can shut off the Delaware Aqueduct, why flush out a creek in the Catskill system? Sir? This is a critical question. Mr. Mayor, sir..." He shouted as the mayor moved across the stage. "I can only conclude, sir, that BOTH systems may already be compromised!"

In the analysis afterward, Anderson Cooper agreed. "I can't help but wonder, did they get it all? And if there are indications that both systems have been compromised, how can a brand-new switching system help if *both* the Catskill and the Delaware systems need to be shut down at the same time. The two systems together supply ninety per cent of the city's daily water needs. How can the antiquated Croton system suddenly increase its output from ten percent to one-hundred percent of the City's daily needs?"

There was no city official on the podium to answer Anderson's question. CNN quickly went to commercial break.

****

"They think we done *both* reservoirs already. They're gonna go to a hell of a lot of trouble, and we ain't even started yet!" Bro coughed hard, swallowing the phlegm this time. "How *you* feeling, Michael?'"

The boss was usually a macho man with illness, but he said, "I got the same flu you gave me. How *you* feelin'?"

"Me too. I can't breathe. I'm nauseated, and I feel like shit."

"Do you think that powder made us sick?"

"It better not have! We were careful...weren't we?"

"I thought so. Except when you lost your glove," Michael said.

"You'll never forget that, will you? I don't mean 'security' careful. I mean like 'were we exposed to that shit?'" Bro rose from the couch and began pacing around the room.

"I hope not. If we were, how the hell would we know?"

"I'm thinking we already know...and I didn't realize this could wipe out a whole city!"

"Come on! Don't tell me you didn't know..."

"You led me into this. I don't like it!" Bro scowled at the only person he could blame for this.

****

The commercial break was over. Police Commissioner O'Riley appeared at the microphone.

"I'd like to announce a few precautionary measures that will be put in place in regard to the reservoirs and streams. Beginning immediately there will be no access allowed to any of the reservoirs or streams in the Catskills or in Westchester County. All waterways are under an 'Imminent Threat' security alert. No citizen is allowed on property adjacent to these waters. In fact, all reservoirs are closed for recreational use: no boats, no shore or bridge fishing, no tubing, no fly fishing, and no swimming in any body of water that is part of the three watersheds: the Croton, the Catskill, or the Delaware, and its nineteen reservoirs and connecting rivers. Any person observed to be within fifty feet of the shoreline will be stopped and detained. Of course, this excludes homeowners who may own property immediately adjacent to a waterway. DEP officers will be visiting such households and issuing permits—much like special hunting licenses—to allow homeowners access limited to their own property. Some roadways will be closed indefinitely. There will be no stopping along open roadways that are within fifty feet of a stream or reservoir for any reason. This is a precautionary measure, but it must be declared immediately as an 'Imminent Threat.' This is the highest Homeland Security alert. Please observe these temporary restrictions or face immediate arrest and prosecution." The look on his face revealed how serious he was. "We will soon place temporary signs in these critical areas to keep the public away from the waterways. Please obey instructions from the NYPD, the DEP, state and local police, Homeland Security and the National Guard. Meanwhile, let me reiterate the mayor's statement. Until we announce anything different, New York City's water is, and shall remain, safe to drink, safe for bathing, and safe for cooking. That's all...no further comment." He turned away from the camera before reporters could utter a word.

****

Michael pranced across the small living room, celebrating by opening a beer that splattered fizz on the ceiling. He was sure of his own motivations, made stronger by the money he'd collected for dumping the toxin. His brother Billy was expelled with a disorderly discharge, Kevin left behind and never found, and Jerry paid with his life. And New York City was completely culpable. His only concern now was propping up Bro, answering his insecurities about what they had done. "Look at what WE did! Before long the whole city will be drinking nothing but Pepsi and Kentucky bourbon!" He stopped to cough a deep series of phlegm-hacking up-chucks. He spit a slimy brown glob into the garbage can.

"But, Michael...there's no fishing. No boating, and no rafting. No access, no recreation. Nobody can go near the water. This is martial law! Why'd we do this?"

"Cause we got paid good money, that's why. And we *said* we had to do *something*."

"But they're talking like we was terrorists. We're not terrorists, are we, boss? I don't like this. Shit, I feel like puking." On the way to the bathroom, he asked, "Who paid us, anyway?"

"You know I can't tell you that. I'd have to kill ya!" He pounded the kitchen table, coughing and choking. He tried to think fast, ahead of Bro's objections, but his head was clogged with phlegm.

"Come on, Michael, quit trying to con me. Where'd that money come from?"

"You're so damn stupid. Just trust that I know what I'm doing." Even Michael knew how desperate he sounded.

"But...we're hurting *ourselves*. We can't fish the Esopus or the Pepacton. What the hell?"

"WE didn't do that. The cops and Homeland Security did that. It isn't our fault they shut everything down."

"But...it's not just hurting New York like you said. We're killing people. And what...if...we poisoned ourselves?" Dry heaves morphed into a torrent of bloody phlegm. He flushed, and made it back to the couch.

"Our water is fine. It doesn't really hurt us; it hurts the city like we wanted. The frigging mayor lies."

"I don't know. I just know we both feel like shit. You said we'd hit the Schoharie next. Why do we have to do that, Michael?"

"The Schoharie is at the source of the other watershed you dumb ass. We nailed the Delaware system. Now we move to the Catskill system. Like Anderson said, they can't shut off both at once. Didn't you listen? They don't know we only got one of them. Damn shit-for-brains!" This was too much. He'd strained his lungs and they fought back with a series of gasps for breath and a low wheezing. He felt dizzy and that just made him boil over. He had already lost *family* because of New York City. But he didn't want to get into the personal reasons he hated New York City.

"You know, I don't like you calling me names like I'm some stupid country boy. And I don't know if I *want to* do this next one."

"YOU'LL DO WHAT I TELL YOU TO DO," Michael wheezed in a combination shout and throaty cough. This was trouble he didn't need.

"I don't think so this time. I'm...just sayin 'no.'"

"Dickhead. You don't even know trouble when it hits you on the head. And you have no idea what I'm capable of."

Bro loved working with Michael, being with him, feeling the anger that justified their actions. But his gut feeling had taken over. This was wrong on so many fronts.

"NO—means—NO. This is like, way too far. For once, Michael, I mean it." He could see the boss's temper rising. He guarded his face in case he had to defend himself.

"You can't cop out on me now you little prick."

The decision was made. "Oh yeah? WATCH ME!" He started for the door.

The attack came without warning. Michael clipped his face with a hard uppercut followed by a furious left that connected with his right eye and cut him across his face with Michael's skeleton-head ring. He didn't have a chance. His nose and eye spewed blood, and he stumbled. Michael punched him in the solar plexus. Bent over with his face exposed, Michael connected a karate chop with his front teeth. His face seemed to cave in, and he went down unconscious. He fell hard into the corner of the HDTV hitting his temple and landed on top of a pile of electronics on the floor. Blood erupted from his ear. He was never even close to a return punch. The Tevo blinked a warning, waiting for a command in a growing pool of blood.

"This just in. Police have identified two sets of prints on a beer can left at the toxic dump site that most likely belong to two persons involved in the poisoning of one of the reservoirs in New York City's water supply. The DEP now admits that—"

After an electronic fizzle the HDTV and the Anderson Cooper Show suddenly went black. Michael delivered a final furious kick in Bro's ribs and another to his face. He picked up his duffle bag, staggering and wheezing as he locked the door behind him. Cut by the other man's teeth, he dripped blood from his hand all the way down the stairs and out the door to his pickup truck on Main Street. "That one was for my brother Jerry. Two more to go...fucking New York City! Damn it! My lucky ring is all bloody."

Chapter 17

The Bun N' Cone

O ne of the most popular hangouts in Margaretville is The Bun N' Cone, a local favorite for nearly seventy years. An original fifties Art Deco diner, "The Bun" is filled with classic tin advertising signage ranging from Betty Boop, Marilyn Monroe and James Dean to '56 Chevys, Harley Davidsons and green and yellow John Deere signs. They serve sandwiches, homemade soup, and ice cream, and I would hang out after school almost every day during high school and even now when I come home from college.

That afternoon, Anthony and I moved from the booths by the window to the lunch bar where we could see the television mounted on the wall. Our attention turned to Anderson Cooper's report on the situation in the Catskills. A crowd of other locals gathered for the update.

"This just in. Police have identified two sets of prints on a beer can left at the toxic dumpsite that most likely belongs to two persons involved in the poisoning of one of the reservoirs in New York City's water supply. The DEP now admits that it was the Pepacton Reservoir that was deliberately polluted by an unknown amount of botulism toxin released several days ago in an icy inlet near the shore. The exact location is believed to be closest to Margaretville, New York, somewhere along State Route Thirty on the way to Downsville. The prints found on the beer can are those of Michael Capo, twenty-nine, and his accomplice, Paul Guarini, twenty-one, known as 'Bro'. Both left prints on a beer can found under a bush at the site."

Anthony said, "Shit! That's my cousin! Paul Guarini."

"Really? Are you sure?"

"Sure I'm sure. My last name is also Guarini. I can't believe...Damn!"

A large man in farmer's overalls said, "Come on, boys. Shut the hell up."

The waitress turned the volume up, and Anderson continued, "Both are already suspects in a theft of dangerous chemicals in 2008 from a DuPont plant in Delaware, and a more recent theft of explosives and blasting components from Enviro-Ore in Clearfield, Pennsylvania. Both men have arrest records from trouble during radical student uprisings at NYU." A set of their mug shots appeared on the screen. "If you see either of these men, likely to be armed and dangerous, please contact your local police."

It suddenly dawned on me, the resemblance. I whispered, "Jesus, Anthony! Paul looks almost exactly like *you*. More than just cousins!"

"Ugly mother, isn't he?" he joked. Nobody laughed, but the farmer turned around and stared.

"No, I mean it. You could almost be twins." I motioned for both of us to move to a table, away from the crowd.

"Shut up and listen, there's more," the farmer said.

"Police still claim that the amount of toxin dumped in the Pepacton was, quote, 'negligible,' with no measurable effect on the water supply by the time it was diluted in several reservoirs and passed through a hundred and forty miles of aqueduct, and the new UV and chlorination plants north of New York City. But other experts dispute this, claiming that even the amount believed to be still in the water supply could be dangerous.

"After this message, Chief Medical Correspondent Doctor Sanjay Gupta will comment on the threat and tell us how you can keep your children safe."

Chapter 18

Hero Herb

Herb put the phone back in its cradle, an amazed look on his face. He sat in his chair, speechless, shaking his head to clear the blur of disbelief. Mo stopped his work momentarily, noticing Herb's mood. "What? What happened? Who was that?"

"It was Carter Calloway, the commissioner. I thought I was going to get fired for holding back the toxin report. But instead—he complimented me on the work we did on the Pepacton incident and applauded me for using good judgment not to panic the public. He said a letter of commendation was forthcoming, and a promotion. I can't believe it!"

"Looks like the press leak actually helped him to see we were right." But Mo still paced back and forth in place, scratching in nervous places.

"Absolutely. He was pretty upset about that reporter from the *Post*. Called him a 'loose cannon' and talked about how the rumor mill is already out of control. Geek reporter Stuart Novak gets all the blame and I get a frigging promotion!"

Mo sat in the lab chair across the room. "We did the right thing. So...Mr. Toxin-Hero, who do we have for suspects? Not me, I hope!" He smiled like the Cheshire Cat.

"You have a weird sense of humor. Commissioner O'Riley gave me a list. He's looking at a suspect named Gerry Rainwater, a Native American activist from New Jersey, who was a member of CAN—Campus Antiwar Network—also a member of Greenpeace, and a radical environmental group at SUNY Albany. Even though he's been in Albany for many years, Special Agent Fitzgibbons intercepted e-mails that confirm his interest in watershed issues. I've seen some of the messages. They don't really even hint at anything close to terrorism, but we're keeping an eye on him."

"Sounds a little far-fetched. Living in Albany, he would have very little vested interest in the Catskills or even in New York City. Who else have we got?"

"Rahzid al Jaharhi, an NYU student radical from 2009 takeover of the student union by the group called Solidarity. They fought for the end to Israeli occupation of Gaza and support of Palestinian students, among other things. Al Jaharhi spent thirty days in Rikers for disturbing the peace, but he didn't spill anything after extensive interrogation. FBI Commissioner Deforest has him on a 'watch list.'"

"So he could even be al Qaeda or ISIS. But why is he on the 'watch list?'" Mo folded his fingers together to crack his knuckles one by one.

"Because he's taken out several books from the NYU library that indicate his interest in the watershed, toxins, *and* explosives. He's enrolled in Professor Jacoby's seminars on environmental science. The professor doesn't have any evidence, just a feeling about him based on a paper he turned in a few weeks back, and a certain 'weird vibe' he gives off."

"So? He checked out books so he could write a paper. Taking a class doesn't make him a terrorist. Neither does a kid's interest in bombs, unless, of course, he places an order for components..." But Mo didn't look entirely convinced.

"Apparently the Professor feels it's an unhealthy interest, with solutions hinting of violence. The term-paper called for radical action to fight the DEP—that's us, Mo."

"Okay. You've got my attention. You know, my childhood roots have gotten me in trouble because of certain racial profiling, even though I've been here for decades. After Nine-Eleven, they bugged my phone and followed me around for months. Now I just try to blend in."

"I know. Commissioner Deforest asked me about you. He knows your background, but he's very fair and reasonable."

He practically jumped out of this chair. "Holy Mo! Am I on the 'watch list?'"

Herb smiled at Mo's discomfort. "They looked into the possibility. And, with your jokes about it, you amplify their suspicion. But, no, I think you're clear. After all, we trusted you with the lab tests. You were the one who suspected botulism." Herb also left his chair, and cocked his head sideways to look at Mo. If it worked for Vincent D'Onofrio on *Criminal Intent...*

"You don't think I—?" Herb shook his head, and Mo was relieved. "So...who else?"

"We've all seen the broadcasts and the photos of Michael Capo and Paul Guarini. Their fingerprints are confirmed, but I don't see them as the brains behind it all. I think they're just small-time criminals for hire. Amateurs making stupid mistakes, leaving a lot of evidence behind, I don't think they'd know where to obtain that much botulism. If they're involved, there is someone else above them. *That's* who we need to catch."

"The fingerprints confirm they were at the site." The knuckle crack this time sounded like it hurt.

"I agree with you. But in court, it would still be pretty iffy with a good lawyer. The prints only confirm they shared a beer and littered Route Thirty with the can." Herb began pacing around the lab table, almost bumping into a test tube rack.

"Right. But it was a can found at the toxin dumpsite. Are there any connections that *have* been confirmed?"

"Well...my son Parker happens to be in the same Environmental Studies seminar as Al Jaharhi, with Professor Jacoby at NYU. But Jacoby called me. He thought I should have filed a report with the DHS. He knows about Al Jaharhi. Jacoby says that Al Jaharhi was in class the day of the incident. And Professor Jacoby is personally familiar with Parker. He doesn't believe Parker has anything to do with this."

"I hope not. That would compromise trust with the DEP forever."

"I know. You with your Muslim roots, and me with a borderline radical son with a big mouth, and a relative who tried to poison the Pepacton...but I think Parker's motivated to be smarter than that. I sure as hell hope so." Herb stopped and took time to put the test tubes safely on a high shelf.

"So...he *is* interested in the environment, but he *isn't* the guy who poisoned the Pepacton."

"Right."

"How can you be sure? Parker has been known to be a little impulsive. Remember when he was with that kid who blew up a cat with M-80s?"

"That was my other son, Titus. He was with *Anthony Guarini*, Paul's cousin. And he will never...not over my dead body... Please, just trust me. Parker will definitely be politically active someday, but he wouldn't do that."

Mo looked at Herb closely. He had to speak his mind. "Come on, Herb, there are too many connections, too many coincidences. Parker and Titus are brothers. Paul and

Anthony Guarini are cousins. There was a cat blown up, now a reservoir poisoned...they're all mixed together..." Herb scowled and looked at him severely. Mo knew he should change the subject. "I know you're close to them, but it just doesn't look good. There must be a money trail..."

"Not that we've found yet. We need to find out where these guys have been staying."

"New York is a huge city. That's a challenge."

"They could be up here too. The Catskills have nearly two thousand square miles to hide in." He gestured at the map on the wall with a broad sweep of his arm.

"We'll find them."

"I know we will. But it's got to be quick."

Chapter 19
Back at the Bun N' Cone

I sat there arguing with Anthony in a more private booth at the back of the Bun N' Cone. The issues were clear. The tactics were not. A young mother trying to teach her two kids some public manners sat in the next booth. She lectured him about his use of the ketchup bottle as a launching pad for sliming Betty Boop on the wall. Most of the Anderson Cooper crowd had left after the broadcast. The new minister at the local Church sat at a nearby table. He stood out in our little town because he was Korean and didn't speak much English. L's and R's were not his forte. He'd become the brunt of local humor when he promised to teach "Ressons in Lerigion, rike the stoly of the clucifiction and the less-erection." But little did I know that the minister was equally confused when he was eavesdropping on Anthony and me. What he overheard had a much different meaning to him.

I was saying to Anthony, "Parker says the flatlanders always think they have it right. Some of them don't even get that water is what we have in common."

"I still think we need to send them a freakin' message. Damn New Yorkers. But what can we do?"

"The toxin has already done it, Anthony." How in the hell was I going to control my friend? He was cocked and loaded, itching for trouble. And so naïve. Anthony would never be smart enough to become an effective radical.

"I'm not so sure. The poison hasn't shown up in the city yet." He scowled as he slurped down his chocolate shake. He pulled the pickles out of his burger, tossing them against

134

the window to see if the mayonnaise would serve as pickle glue.

I had to be careful with the next question, aware that Anthony knew nothing of the funding bestowed upon me and Parker. "So, if you had a bunch of money, how would you use it to get what we need?"

"Somebody should blow up the Pepacton dam in Downsville and change the Delaware back into a river. That would wake them up AND make a fucking statement."

"Anthony, please! Cool it. Besides, everybody knows they have security cameras at the dams. And it would take a hell of a blast to take out a dam that big. You're freakin' crazy."

"*You're* the one with the family grudge. I'd think you would *want* to send a message."

"Okay... But we've got to be smarter than that. Parker says we need to start a political movement, one that focuses on *changing* the DEP, not ruining our own environment."

"Parker says 'this,' Parker says 'that,'" Anthony whined with a big scowl on his face.

"You know those signs they have at the site of every town they destroyed when they made the reservoirs?"

"Yeah. 'The *former* site of Arena.' 'The *former* site of Shavertown.' And Boiceville, Gilboa, Union Grove, Shokan, Olive Bridge...there are dozens of towns now under water. So?"

"What if we replaced those signs with signs like, 'Entering Olive, graveyard of the DEP.' 'Entering Shavertown, under water since 1954.' Entering what's-its-name, swamped by the DEP. Thank you, N-Y-C!"

"You GO, Titus! And we could put up fake gravestones, with all the names of the former residents."

"I like it," I agreed. "There are hundreds of stories like my Great-Great Grandpa's. Then we could send press releases to increase awareness of why we're doing this, the issues."

Anthony replied, "I don't know. It's okay...but it won't result in change. We'd be arrested for vandalism. Radical action is the only thing that *really* works. The toxin in the Pepacton is already a done deal. I still think we should blow up the dam. You know, get some freaking dynamite, maybe a rocket launcher, something they can't forget."

Anthony was getting too loud. I shushed him with a hand gesture and answered in a low voice. "You're freakin' nuts. You're making it sound like poisoning the reservoir was a *good* idea. Jesus, Anthony! Let's call Parker. He'll have better ideas than that."

"My crazy mother comes from a long line of activists. Bonnie will know better than anyone. But I'll bet your brother will agree with *me. Somebody's* got to have the balls to do something that people will listen to."

"Dude, keep it down, will ya?"

The young Korean minister was new in town, but his English was better than people gave him credit for. He'd understood parts of the entire debate while he read his newspaper. He stared at the mug shot of Anthony's cousin on the front page and glanced at us with a strange look. I should have known something was going to happen when he left money on the table and exited the Bun N' Cone dialing his cell phone.

Within ten minutes, two Margaretville Police officers entered from the front door. They sat at a table near the door and glanced at us. While pretending to peruse the menu, they stared across the room. Alarms went off in my head.

Something was not right about two cops sitting on the same side of a table, positioned so they could both stare at us full front. Slowly, I sent a text message to Dad from my phone under the table, hoping I could keep the cops' eyes focused on my other hand on the table.

I warned Anthony, "Damn it. I knew this would happen. The police are here. They're looking at *us*." I shifted in my seat, but Anthony turned around in the booth to see the patrolmen. For the first time, police yes interlocked with Anthony's.

They stood up quickly, and Anthony reacted by running towards the emergency door at the back. After a brief struggle, he was pinned to the table with his hands wrenched painfully behind his back.

The big cop with the biggest gut said, "Paul Guarini, we need to ask you a few questions."

Anthony struggled to free himself. It was the wrong thing to do. "You've got the wrong guy. Let me go. Son of a—"

"Okay, if you can't come peacefully, we're going to have to do it the hard way." Suddenly his head was banged on the table, and he felt nylon zip-tie handcuffs applied to his wrists and tightened roughly.

The little cop with the bigger gun said, "Shut up, Guarini. We *know* who you are."

"Screw you. I'm not the right guy!" yelled Anthony.

Before they assaulted me, I glanced at the squeeze bottle mustard, the only possible defense on a restaurant table, but they outnumbered me and wrapped my wrists with a nylon tie faster than I could say, "Dijon." As they were preparing to haul us out of the Bun N' Cone, Dad walked in.

"Oh, for god's sake. Titus!"

"Dad, you've got to help us!"

"How in the hell did you get tangled up in this?" He threw up his arms in disgust.

"That isn't Paul, Dad. It's my friend, *Anthony*. His cousin—not the right Guarini!"

"Looks like Paul Guarini to me, son." He turned to the big Margaretville cop. "You've got my son, chief. Where are you taking them?"

"We're taking them in for questioning, county jail in Delhi. No arrest yet. But they wouldn't cooperate, so—"

Dad said, "I'm going to have to recuse myself from this. As for Guarini, we'll find out soon enough who he is." He looked at me with disdain. "We'll talk later—son." I'd never been arrested before, and I'd never been this afraid. But Dad did not do one thing to help. I was shocked to hear his reference to "Guarini" as if he didn't recognize Anthony immediately. Anthony had been over to the house; we'd been friends for years and been fishing with Dad on the Pepacton. But it was as if Dad had never seen him before. Was this what it would be like to see him play both sides of the fence? I noticed Dad making a call on his cell as he opened his car door outside. He swaggered alongside of the Margaretville cops. Happy they'd gotten their man, they all strutted around with chests blown up like beluga whales. Such bullshit.

Chapter 20
Booking

It might have brought on a bizarre new excitement to be on the receiving end of an arrest. But the hand on my head when they pushed us into the cop car violated my personal space. The smell of the drunks and unwashed convicts that had inhabited the back seat before me lingered like I was in a captured locker room. The sirens on the way to Delhi sounded more incarcerating from inside the car and the steel wire grid keeping me in the back seat became an animal cage, and I was the animal. The sound of the jail door closing and locking behind me carried a weird sense of finality. But as my entire life of minor infractions flashed before my eyes, no adrenaline rush arrived to elevate my sense of adventure. It was a dehumanizing nightmare, a complete bummer. They separated us, throwing Anthony into the drunk tank with a bunch of smelly alcoholics and addicts puking and detoxing on the floor. For some reason they put me directly into an interview room. Was that Dad's way of helping? Big whoop.

The interrogation lasted over two hours. The DEP cops asked the same questions over and over. I recognized the 'good cop/bad cop' routine from cop shows on TV. But it was entirely different when I was in a real suspect seat. At worst, they badgered me so intensely that I almost started to believe some of their shit. Even the little one, the 'good cop' had slowly tricked me into admitting things I knew might be used against me.

"Do you hang out around the Pepacton?"

"Yes. I *live* nearby." My defiant voice was obvious.

"Do you know Anthony Guarini or Paul Guarini?" His eyes carried an intense look.

"Yes. I just had lunch with Anthony..." I stared right back at him.

"Lunch, eh?" Like having lunch was a crime? "Do you ski?"

"Yes, both cross-country and downhill."

"Right. Did you leave tracks down along the Pepacton?" The big bad one leaned in close to my face.

"Hell no!"

"Do you drink beer?"

"Of course. Doesn't everyone?" I let a breath out so he could smell there was no alcohol.

"Don't be a wise ass. Where were you on the night of..."

"I think I was with Anthony."

"REALLY! Where did you go— 'with Anthony'?"

"We just...rode around..." I sighed and shook my head in disbelief.

"What roads did you take?" The little cop was back at me.

"Route Thirty..."

"Uh huh. And Route Thirty goes right around the Pepacton..." Big Cop said in his "gotcha" tone.

"We drove NORTH up to Roxbury, not south..."

"And north of Roxbury is the Schoharie reservoir—" He gestured over his shoulder with an angry thumb.

"—Which we didn't go anywhere near."

"How do you know Paul Guarini?"

"You people really don't understand the difference between two cousins, do you?" I raised a single finger on each hand.

"Shut the hell up, kid." Big Cop shook his head. "Unbelievable!"

"I have rights! So what are you going to do, stick my head in a bucket of water until you get the answer you want?" I wore my most defiant sneer.

"You're lucky you live in a free country, where unfortunately water-boarding is frowned upon!" He paused for close to a full minute before the big question and leaned in close to my face again. "Did you tell your buddy Paul that you wanted to blow up the dam on the Pepacton?"

"Hell no!" I pounded the table. I had to stick to my guns, but I needed time to think.

"And did you make this threat inside the Bun N' Cone Restaurant? With the Reverend Kim Su at the next table?"

Little cop chimed in, "He heard everything you said, you know."

"It wasn't in the context you think. And you're gonna believe a Korean who can barely speak English?" I needed a distraction. "Hey, officers, can I have a glass of water?"

"Now you *want* water!?" He looked at me like my request was a little ironic and shook his head. "I'll be back in a minute with a glass of *unpoisoned* water you can drink," Little cop said.

Big cop said, It'd be a good idea if you had some better answers ready. You're beginning to piss me off." They both left me alone in the room.

Looking back, I'm surprised they didn't just call the judge and throw away the key. Everything I had said only fed their suspicions. But I stuck to my insistence of innocence, and I knew Anthony was experiencing an even rougher ride in the room down the hall. How could they seriously mistake him for his cousin Paul? Right...they looked alike, but what about his IDs...fingerprints? Surely that would clear us.

Left in the room by myself for a few minutes, I thought about my predicament. I'd admitted to the discussions overheard by the Korean witness in the Bun N' Cone. But the fragments of sentences reported to the police could be interpreted in ways that were incriminating. They'd twisted my words every which way. The minister spoke imperfect English, and heard Anthony's bravado with entirely different ears, with damning connotations.

Big cop returned with my water and jumped right back into it. "So...you didn't say things like, 'Somebody should blow up the dam in Downsville, and make the Delaware back into a river.' And, 'Radical action is the only thing that *really* makes people notice'?"

"We were just joking around, not serious, for god's sake!"

Big cop leaned in again, close to my face. "You weren't serious when you said, 'The toxin in the Pepacton is already a done deal'? A 'done deal' matches what we found at the Pepacton, asshole. Like you knew about it already. Sounds pretty damn 'guilty' to me."

"That was Anthony who said that, and I strongly disagreed with him." I crossed my arms and threw a hate stare up at him.

By now, I'd said too much. The whole thing was an overheard plot and a nearly verifiable confession. I wished I'd lawyered up long before so much information was extracted and open for misinterpretation. I guess I thought Dad would show up and save me from the crocodiles. They hadn't formally charged me, and I guess I was naïve when I thought they would lay off, because, after all, we were innocent. Since we knew we were not the real terrorists, and there was a beer can with prints that were not ours, we agreed to be fingerprinted in order to clear ourselves. Finally, after another hour of badgering, the good cop returned and led me down the hall for my phone call. Dad obviously wasn't going to show up to help, so I dialed Parker's cell phone, even though I knew he was a hundred-fifty miles away in New York City.

Parker answered on the first ring. "Titus. Am I glad to hear your voice! Dad already called. I'm on my way. They haven't charged you yet, but if they do, I've got enough cash from our funds to bail you both out."

I was relieved. "I knew you wouldn't let me down. You know, I didn't have anything to do with—"

"I know, Titus. And even Dad knows you're both innocent. Anthony can't help that he looks so much like his cousin. We've always known his big mouth would get him in trouble. It's just...well, you know Dad can't be directly involved. He's got to keep his distance, and keep up the persona of a DEP cop. This is what it's going to be like, dealing with him. He'll only help behind the scenes. I'll get you both out as soon as I can."

"Got to go. The guard just entered the room. See ya, soon I hope."

"It's still a three-hour drive to Delhi from the City. Don't worry. I'll be there soon." What could happen in two and a half hours? A formal arrest maybe. Another grilling. Maybe the NYPD would show up. My imagination made me more paranoid. Christ New York! Just what I needed to support a claim of innocence.

Chapter 21
Escalation

Bonnie Guarini drove more than seventy miles at breakneck speeds from Woodstock to reach us. By the time she entered the detention center in Delhi, her temper was piqued, and her blood was boiling. She spit tobacco into the planter by the door, hitting the plastic plant dead on. She approached the officer at the front desk, looking like a frantic possessed witch from hell with last week's frizzed hair, scarlet sunglasses balanced on her nose mole, and a mouth full of rotten teeth. Before the desk sergeant could utter a single polite word, she screamed in a high-pitched decibel-breaker, "How dare you accuse my son! You've got the wrong man, for god's sake. I'm going to sue you. ALL of you. PIGS! You have no evidence. Messing with *my son*, damn you!"

"Ma'am, you're going to have to calm down, or you'll be in there with him," the Duty Officer said in his calmest voice. "Name of the accused, please?" And it went downhill from there, until Parker arrived. When he walked in, an extra guard was standing next to Bonnie, who was sitting in a chair, sulking, red-faced, and muttering to herself. She had her dusty jeans hiked up, so they could see the hair on her legs, and her eye makeup looked like a skid mark on Route 28. She pulled her corncob hash pipe out of her shirt pocket, and then thought better of lighting it in the police station lobby. I could tell when she saw Parker through the doors of the lobby. She screamed louder than that poor dying deer.

"I can't believe these pigs accused *my* son! Thank GOD you're here!"

"Calm down, Bonnie. I'll get them out." But after an hour, there was still no action forthcoming. I was still handcuffed to a frigging table by myself in a room that was like a sweat box, trapped with the stench of the last several losers they'd interrogated.

Soon, loud voices reached the front lobby, and we overheard the DEP arguing with the NY State Police. "I'm not doing anything until I hear from my Sergeant. He's on the phone with the commissioner right now."

"I don't care if he's with Moses. He ought to be on the phone with Homeland Security. This is a case of terrorism, and you're treating it like a jaywalking ticket, Sergeant."

Holy shit. Were they talking about us?

Another voice entered the fray. "Hold on, both of you. We got prints now, and they don't match the ones on the beer can. The kid was right. He's not Paul Guarini. We've got to let them go."

"But he's a dead ringer. Surely we have something else. What about the ski tracks?"

"Believe me, we got the wrong guys, both of them."

A door slammed. I had a sudden feeling that we were headed back to the freedom side of the jail bars. Parker stood opposite the Duty Officer, peering into the back hallway. After a long period of silence, with no news and no distant voices, an officer pulled us into the hallway, and two envelopes with our belongings were returned to us, even my pocket knife. A pathetic apology was offered, and they cut the nylon bands that bound us. I rubbed my sore wrists, and Anthony swore under his breath as we left the building with Bonnie and my brother.

****

"I need some coffee," I said. "Let's find a diner. I need to get rid of this stress."

Anthony said, "When I see my cousin Paul again, I'm gonna beat the crap out of him."

"And when I see my dad..."

We walked in silence until we found a small restaurant, a favorite hangout filled with SUNY Delhi students mixed with locals. When we were seated, we let out the emotions suppressed for the past several hours.

"What a bummer day."

"It was your big mouth again, Anthony. I can't believe they thought we poisoned the Pepacton." I brushed my hair back with my fingers.

Bonnie said, "I was so worried about you. Did they treat you okay?"

"Mom, believe me, that was no place for a hippie sorceress like you. The creeps in that cell would have laughed at me, after they had their way with my ass." Anthony sulked and tapped his fingers on the table.

Bonnie held an angry look on her face. "This is what I get for coming to rescue you!"

I had to ask, "Anthony, do you have any idea where your cousin is right now?"

"Fuck no. I haven't seen Paul since—"

"Anthony, I hate that word." She clenched her fists and nearly knocked over the salt.

"I was in fucking *jail*, Mom!"

"I don't give a...Don't use that word!"

"I can't help it. Can't I be a little fucking angry right now? *Fuck!*" The salt, catsup and mustard jumped when he pounded the table. Everyone in the place looked at us with frightened eyes.

"And quit shouting. You're free. I'd think you'd have learned about sounding off in public after this."

"Come on, everybody. We've got to talk. Get on the same page." Was Parker the only one with any sense around here? He clenched our wrists to calm us.

We ordered coffee and burgers. The silence at the table lasted while we all contemplated the facts and how they had all been lost in the confusion. Finally, Parker said, "I talked to Dad. He insists the best way to get the spotlight off us is to cooperate."

Anthony answered, "I already DID! I told the cops. It's *cousin* Paul Guarini and Michael Capo they should be after. Such arrogant snots. And I have no idea where they are. Last I heard they were sharing an apartment somewhere in the Catskills. But that, as you know, is a pretty big area, with a lot of places off the road. Mountain roads, campsites, hunting cabins, state parks, abandoned barns. Bigger than the whole state of Connecticut. They won't find anyone who doesn't want to be found."

Coffee arrived with the silverware. The waitress looked worried, but everyone seemed calm.

I said, "Do you have Paul's cell number?"

"Yep. I'll try again." But when he dialed, Anthony couldn't get an answer. "If I didn't look so much like Paul, we could have saved ourselves a lot of trouble." He paused for a minute, and finally admitted, "You, know, in a way I almost wish I *was* Paul. At least he did something heroic for the cause."

"Shut the hell up," I said. "Haven't you learned anything?"

Bonnie fingered a pendant around her neck that looked like a peace symbol over an upside down pentagram. "You don't mean that, Anthony. Come on. Poisoning the reservoir hurts everyone. It's not right, and against all the principles I've ever taught you. How could you even think you'd want to be involved? You may call me a hippie witch, but at least I know when to stop acting like an angry old fool."

"What would you do, Mom? You're the big Viet Nam protest veteran. And what the hell is that pendant? If a combination of peace and Satanism is a religion, then you're the only one in it."

"Have some respect, Anthony. And don't take my symbols lightly."

The burgers arrived. Anthony pulled off the pickles and stuck them on the wall, his favorite trick in a burger joint.

As the pickles slithered downward in a trail of mayonnaise, Bonnie said, "Protest is one thing. It's peaceful, and it's proactive enough to get things done...in the legislature, in the courts, increasing public opinion. But poisoning the water? Wrong, WRONG! Absolutely, totally over the top, Anthony."

"At least I don't try to put a hex on people I hate, like you do!"

"Bul-loney. Haven't you learned anything from me all these years? Think of how many innocent people could be killed. I'd expect that out of Paul. He's always been trouble. But you? *Think* about it! And take those pickles off the wall. Disgusting!"

As Anthony scraped pickles, Channel Seven News was on the television. Already there was a story on the mistaken identity of Anthony and Titus, and the two mug shots of

Michael Capo and Paul Guarini were substituted and displayed with renewed urgency.

Parker said, "Bonnie, we need your experience. Let me tell you something in confidence. We have tons of money for political action. I could have bailed both these guys out with cash, and I can finance just about anything we need to do. But please, tell us. How can we put this money to good use?" He squirted ketchup onto his burger and handed the squeeze bottle to me.

She was obviously surprised to learn of our resources. "Okay. I'll tell you what I think. My activism goes back to Viet Nam, then Nixon, Reagan, Iraq, Afghanistan, and so forth, as you know. The peace movement has had a lot of different faces. This is no different. Already you've got radicals like Paul and Michael, and you've got people with a little more control, a little more sense—like you guys. At least I *thought*, and now I *hope* to God..."

I couldn't help my suspicions. Bonnie made points tapping two fingers together, and talked about nonviolence, but her whole life had been devoted to radical causes and edgy tactics. Were radical tactics just for her? Whose side was she on, once her son was out of jail?

She fingered her pendant like it was a rosary. "Here's what you need to do. In my opinion. First you need a good liberal lawyer. someone who will find the right test case, and fight like hell in court. Then look for a sympathetic Congressman in the State legislature to lobby for issues that can be written into law. Align yourselves with Waterkeepers, started by Robert Kennedy, back when. Then publicize your side of the issues and organize peaceful protests to get your story into the press. Takes a lot of dedication, a lot of time, and the ability to focus on issues you can win and keep the fools who are out of control IN LINE!" She glared at Anthony.

Parker offered a challenge, "The DEP is controlled by the City, and the people at home don't have any say in their priorities. That'so why people call them 'water-Nazis.' They protect New York's water, but they can also write tickets, arrest anybody they want, flood the Esopus when they want, and all without any local supervision. They're sort of like an occupying army. But sometimes the things they do to protect the reservoirs also hurt the people who live there. We're ready. And we don't have to worry about money. We've got plenty."

Bonnie looked surprised; "I'd keep that to myself, if I were you. There are people who will want a piece of that action, and pretty soon you won't have any left if you make that public. Let your lawyer handle the checks. I learned that back in the Viet Nam protest days, when I...well, never mind..." She looked sheepish as she remembered things she wouldn't talk about.

"What about the lawyer?"

"I have a couple of friends in Woodstock, and there's an old rebel up in Margaretville who'd love to have a shot at this. He was at the Esopus protest." She wrote down three names. "The best advice I can offer is for you to stay in the shadows and surround yourself with the best people you can find. Don't try to be a hero, or put yourself in the news, like Julian what's-his-name from Wikileaks."

"Assange. Julian Assange."

Parker said, "Wow. I'm glad I talked to you. We're going to need you close by," But was I really convinced? Or was it like mother, like son with Anthony?

"You're a great guy, Parker Rose. I'll be there for you. Just keep my son out of trouble." She removed the crystal pendant around her neck and looked deep into the translucent gemstone as she mumbled a few words of magic. For the first time I noticed the pendant was carved out of a light collecting stone, like agate perhaps. I knew she was nuts, and maybe actually psychic, but this was more like hippie voodoo.

"He is a wild child. But we'll try." Parker looked across the table at Anthony. Anthony was very much like a younger Bonnie, unpredictable and often out of control. He smirked as if to tell me I would never get into his head while he was awake.

"I can handle Anthony," I offered. Anthony stuck his tongue out and delivered an armpit fart so loud that the waitress laughed from across the room. He'd be a challenge. And so, would his mad psychic hippie mother, if she could be trusted not to freak out. Stability is as stability does.

Chapter 22

Strange Alliance

The T-Bar is a popular bar and restaurant in Roxbury, located a few miles south of the hamlet, up on a steep hill overlooking the highway, and usually full of locals, as opposed to New York City weekenders. The T-Bar was so named after the old-style ski lifts that dragged skiers up the mountain on a spring-loaded upside down "T" that hooked behind your butt, a contraption seldom used now that chair lifts have long replaced them. But Roxbury's T-Bar Saloon has been there forever, a typical mountain tavern with pine paneling, a huge inviting fireplace, a collection of pinball machines and a pool table. Jonathan Biggs, a local plumber, sat on a barstool near the door, in his usual inebriated state six hours after work. His head rested on the bar precariously close to his beer, with his left arm nearly giving up conscious coordination and lying flopped downward towards the floor. Beside him sat Billy Walkerton, a corrupt city councilman-slash-contractor, also inebriated, bragging to Biggs about the money he'd conned out of a "damned flatlander." There was no one else in the place, and the waitress was dreaming about closing early.

When Anthony and Michael entered, they sat at the corner table in the restaurant section, where they could talk in private next to the roaring fire. The waitress delivered their orders for a dark stout and a mountain made amber. Anthony said, "Keep 'em coming, okay, Julie?"

"Like I was saying," Michael said, "Paul told me you were a hit in Woodstock, with your beret and red paint in a color photo on the *Times* front page. You're crazy brilliant, man!"

"At least I got the crowd all worked up. But Parker and Titus couldn't take it. They were acting like a couple of jealous pansies, telling me I was out of control."

"They're wrong. I thought it was fantastic what you did," Michael replied. "So what? It was over the top! You got great publicity for all the right issues. A little theatrical, but totally cool." He laughed at the top of his lungs and slapped Anthony on his back.

Anthony felt his ego being stroked, and that was okay by him. "The only thing that will work is being over the top. All those petitions and peaceful demonstrations are just a flash, and immediately forgotten after a few days. I wish we could do something they'd remember. Even though I got arrested for saying it, I still think if we blew up the dam, the city would have to take notice." This time, he looked around, but they were alone.

"The reservoirs are really vulnerable," Michael said as he coughed. He wished he could leave now, the way he was feeling, but he had to take this opportunity with Anthony.

"What if we dumped some sort of poison in them? Maybe...what's that stuff they poisoned the post office with? That would do it!"

"Anthrax. You know, you've got balls. That's what I've been looking for—a guy like you. Anthony, that's why we need to talk tonight. I'm already involved in something like that. But it's more complicated than it looks," Michael said quietly. This was the key bait; the opener he'd planned. He leaned forward towards Anthony's face.

Anthony said, "But the shores are wide open. The DEP can't possibly patrol everywhere. It would be a piece of cake to take out any one of them."

"That's what I thought too, but there's a volume issue." He grabbed a glass of water and a water pitcher from another table, left from a previous customer. After adjusting them so that the glass had only half an ounce, and the pitcher was full, he poured a drop of stout in each glass. "See how the water turns a little darker in the glass, but if you add a drop to the pitcher, it doesn't change color at all. Think of these glasses as a small pond, and a reservoir. You'd need a hundred trailer-truck tanks-full, like thousands of gallons of toxin, and that probably wouldn't even come close to the proportions you'd need to make a mixture strong enough to affect people in the City. And then, where would we get that much toxin? Impossible!"

Anthony put his hand on Michael's arm. "Michael, were you involved in that toxin in the Pepacton?" He waited and looked into Michael's eyes. "You did it. I *know* you did it. Talk about balls!" But he had raised his voice, too loud.

Michael coughed and tried to clear the congestion from his throat. With a modest look, he smiled. "Yeah, I guess I could take credit. But I learned a lesson about volume. It's not easy to make a dent in a reservoir that big. Dumping a hundred pounds in the water scared them, but there are more effective ways."

Anthony said, "I can't believe you did the Pepacton! Oh, man! You're a freakin hero!"

"Shhhh! We tried. But like I said, it just didn't work." But he could tell that Anthony was already intrigued. This would be easier than he'd thought.

154

"So...you must have reasons..." Anthony's hero worship was only beginning.

"I do. I've lost three brothers in the wars in Iraq and Afghanistan. Kevin was killed by friendly fire, by his own Sergeant in Operation Anaconda in Iraq. The fucking Sarge used to work for New York City. Then my brother Jerry was taken prisoner in Afghanistan, left behind by two guys from New York City. When the marines counterattacked, they destroyed the prison instead of rescuing him. Five Americans were struggling to get out after being bombed by their own troops. Jerry was one of them. He didn't make it, but the bastards from New York walked out without a scratch. And my brother Billy went into Leavenworth on a trumped-up charge, and where was the prosecutor from? You guessed it! And do you think any of my three brothers made it on to the war memorial wall in New York City? Shit no!" Michael took a deep breath, clenched his fist, and stood up, glaring at Anthony. Three great reasons for revenge, don't you think?" He hockered loudly in his throat, then spit the whole brown gob into the pitcher.

"Damn right! I never realized your family almost got wiped out." Anthony managed to say.

"Bitch of a cold. So, my man, we've got to find a better way than a hundred pounds of Botox." Michael paced around the table, with angry resolve on his face. He felt dizzy and weak. Paul had been right about the powder. It was lethal.

Anthony finally got the point. The reasons were clear and completely justified. He was starting to get into this and realized that his clown antics with paint were nothing compared to the commitment and dedication to the cause that Michael must have. He asked, "What about explosives? Would that work?"

"Depends. The dam is a half-mile long reinforced earthen structure that isn't going anywhere with anything less than a huge bomb, bigger than we could ever launch ourselves. Better to target the aqueduct itself, like maybe blow up the aqueduct intake location. That would take a much smaller charge to do the job. And if it stops the flow to the city, it's much more effective than trying to blow up an earthen dam. Problem is, they guard the dam and the aqueducts. We're gonna have to be really clever to get near them." He was starting to sweat in buckets. He grabbed his amber, and swigged half of it down in one gulp. But Anthony seemed not to notice.

"I've been blowing up birds and cats with my shotgun forever, and my dad got me a job at the firing range. Dad uses all kinds of charges in his construction. I can get all the stuff we'd need," Anthony said.

"Up til now, I've had my own sources, But...cool. You're really into this stuff. We should get together, be partners, and get something done that they can't ignore."

"We could work together on this?" Anthony said. He could hardly contain himself, and nearly spilled his beer.

"Sure. But you'll have to go underground with me. Disappear, and you can't tell anyone what you're doing. Especially Titus and Parker. Their dad is a DEP-geek."

"I just got arrested for looking like cousin Paul after I shot my mouth off in the Bun N' Cone. Parker was there to bail me out the other day. He's a great guy, and I'm tight with Titus. But I know they aren't into that kind of thing. I mean, that's way over the top for them!"

"It takes more than one person to pull off the kinds of things we need to get done. Why don't we take a ride, where no one can hear us? We'll talk while I run you home to Woodstock."

"Cool." They finished their drinks and left the T-Bar, still busy with two drunks and a waitress waiting for a late night patron.

****

In Michael's old Jeep, they continued as they drove through thick fog on Dimmick Mountain Road to Little Redkill Road, the shortcut over the mountains. The two men were getting closer, discovering they had much in common. Soon fantasies about effective radical methods became their focus and only priority. They discussed the ins and outs of using e-coli, ricin, generic rat poison, anthrax, and botulism. Anthony told him about his love for explosions and weaponry, since he was a kid. "I learned how to make an IED on the Internet," Anthony explained. "My mom was freaked. Dad thought it was cool. He was in the Rangers in Iraq. He helped me learn it all. He blows up mountain rock to make basements for his construction projects."

Michael admitted, "The toxin we used was botulism, just like they use for women's facelifts. Stole it from a lab down in Delaware, and we thought a hundred fifty pounds would do it. But it didn't work. Paul and I learned the hard way. It was a big disappointment."

"What happened to Paul, anyway? I haven't seen him for a month." Anthony asked, turning to face Michael.

"He and I had a...disagreement. Turns out, he doesn't have the stomach for this." He looked at the floor. "Paul just...left...took off somewhere. He has people out west someplace. Like, I don't know. Really." There was a silence as Anthony tried to read his face in the dark car. Michael rolled down the window again, and spit a gob of bloody phlegm out the window.

Michael cleared his throat. "Now that we've talked, I'm pretty sure *you* could fill that spot. We'd make a great team, Anthony. 'Course, if you don't want to..."

"Get out! Sure, man, I'm in! All the way."

"Plus, there's good money in it. We get paid for every job, every phase of the battle." He rubbed two fingers together to emphasize the word. He turned on the A-C, even though it was below freezing outside.

Anthony rose up off the seat. "Get out! Really? Who pays you?"

"I can't tell you...not yet. But I'll pay you a couple grand or so for every job you do with me."

"Wow! I can quit my job at the rifle range." Anthony was so ready to jump on command.

"Don't quit your day job. If anybody asks questions, it's better if you have a real job..." Michael turned on the Roxbury radio station, the only one that reached them on the mountain road. They turned off a windy road next to a creek, cutting through the tiny hamlet of Fleishmanns. Michael shot through Fleishmanns like it had no speed limit and skidded onto Route 28 South towards Woodstock. He turned to face Anthony so he could see his eyes. He pulled over to the side of the road for a minute. "Let me ask you—would your mom freak if you disappeared for a while?"

"She'd complain and call around looking for me. But I did it before when I had a wild hair that I was going to get married. THAT didn't last longer than our trip to Vegas. Gina was an ace at blackjack, but I lost four hundred dollars. After that we couldn't afford the wedding chapel, and she didn't want to settle for anything less. So, we broke up. Dad laughed, and Mom had a purple cow. She thought Gina would change me."

"Why don't you plan on spending the next week with me at my trailer up on Wildcat Mountain? We'd be training for the next mission. You'd have to call in sick for a week…"

"Okay. But I it looks like you're the one who is sick." He turned off the air, turned on some heat. "I was going to meet my dad tomorrow to try out our new miniature boat on the Pepacton. It's like, remote controlled."

"Really? Remember what I told you in the bar?"

"Yeah, cool. I'm in. I was just…looking forward to running that boat."

"You will. But I've got a mission, a really important mission that only you can run. And you can buy a whole fleet of boats with the money you'll make."

"Yeah? Cool." Anthony turned up the radio.

"What we do will bring real change to these issues." Michael scratched his stomach, a little nervous.

"So, where do we start? What are we going to do first?"

He stopped the jeep a few doors from Anthony's house on Tinker Street. "Just trust me. We'll get into it…soon. I'll pick you up tomorrow afternoon. Bring that little boat, and some clothes. Meet me in Joshua's here in Woodstock, about five. Right now, I've got to get going."

"Right. I'm totally with you. See you tomorrow." Anthony was full of excitement about the mission with his new ally. This would be much cooler than painting signs at his mom's house. He wouldn't make headlines with a photo, but he would make some cash. Anonymity was much smarter than being a red-paint celebrity on the front page. They'd get a lot more done that way, and they'd be politically correct. He was stoked.

Chapter 23

Return to the Scene

Michael needed a break to regroup. He felt a little better, but he still blamed Paul for giving him the illness that came from the powder they had handled. But at least he'd found a new partner to replace the little prick and finding Anthony would boost the confidence his employer had in him. Next priority, he needed to get back to the apartment and clean up the mess he'd made battling Paul before the police discovered the evidence. By now he figured Paul had stumbled out of the apartment, was tending to his wounds, and Michael would never have to deal with him again.

He circled back to Margaretville and drove past the apartment a couple of times, trying to decide whether he could enter without being seen. There were too many people left on the street even in the hour before midnight. It was Friday night, and even sleepy Margaretville had people coming and going from the bars and restaurants close by.

The second approach left him spooked when he crossed the bridge near the car wash, turned on Main Street and found he was blocked by a DEP truck towing a motorboat and stopped in front of Margaretville Central School. Ironic how the only one allowed to leak gas and oil into the reservoir was the DEP in their big motorboats. The DEP patrolman blocked the road in a double yellow-line no-passing lane. He seemed to be checking the tires on his boat trailer, standing behind the boat and directly in the way of Michael's jeep. If he stopped, the patrolman might recognize him. If he kept going and went around, he could get a ticket, no matter that the cop blocked the road. He tugged the string on his hoodie to hide his face, pulled his baseball cap lower, flipped the visor down and sat way up in the seat to cover his face in shadow of the visor. The patrolman looked up, but he was too wrapped up in the problem with his boat trailer, and waved him past, over the yellow lines to safety and anonymity. He would have to be more careful. But the close call was strangely exciting, and he felt a swell of adrenaline in his veins. He turned up a side street and waited another hour before returning. He sat in the driver's seat, boiling of thoughts of revenge for the loss of his brothers.

After two o'clock, he parked on Church Street, parallel to Main Street, and walked carefully through the back yards until he could cross the street and access the apartment building from the back stairs. The rickety old fire escape had practically been ripped off the building in the flood after Hurricane Irene and was still blocked off with tattered yellow police tape and a sawhorse. When he was half way up, the stairs lurched as if they were ripping themselves off the back of the building. With wide eyes, he glared at the treacherous boulders in Binnekill Creek directly below. But when he got to the top, it was no problem to reach through the broken glass in the door and let himself in to his old digs. In less than an hour, he would finish the cleanup and be out of there forever.

When he opened the apartment door, a horrible stench made him nauseous, reminding him of the illness he'd been battling all week. A dim glow from a small lamp lit his way as he crept across the living room. The mess was almost exactly as he'd left it. Almost.

Only one other person knew he and Paul were living together. Not even the landlord knew their real names. But suddenly, he felt something soft brush against the back of his ankle. He looked behind him, and for the first time the stench in the room made sense. Paul had not left the apartment after their fight. Instead, he had succumbed to his wounds, and lay dead on the floor. His eyes had turned a dark grey, but still made direct contact with anyone standing over him. Michael shuddered at the sight. How could this have happened?

The panic of reality hit him hard. He was a tough character, not usually squeamish. But to see the results of the battle before his eyes made him wince with regret over what he had done. But his emotions hardened, and he felt anger that Paul had dared to inconvenience him by dying from his wounds. He sat down to ward off a momentary breakdown, shaking from every bone in his body. "It was just a disagreement! Why the fuck did you have to die and leave me with this mess? Damn you, Paul." If he had returned earlier, he might have saved Paul's life before he bled out. Probably not. Paul couldn't stomach the things they had done anyway. Freaking coward!

But now, a new problem loomed over him. What to do with Paul's body? He couldn't risk hauling it down the rickety back stairs over the creek. The front stairway was risky too, with people on the street sure to notice. The risk of breaking the glass in the front door on the street, and trying to fit the body through was just plain stupid. He sat and stared at the body, contemplating, shaking his head. No. There was no alternative. Clean up the place, and leave Paul where he was, to be discovered by someone else. 'Later' was the operating word.

He paced nervously around the kitchen until he found a bottle of bleach, using an old tee shirt to wipe down the apartment. After cleaning every item he could find, he washed down the walls, windows, doors, appliances, sinks, and furniture. Even though he left streaks everywhere, he was satisfied there was no trace of lingering fingerprints. He filled a trash bag with small items that might incriminate him. He stuffed his favorite US Army coffee mug, his pocketknife, the TV remote, a toothbrush, and beer cans and bottles in a trash bag. Each damning print added to the evidence that could put him behind bars. His guilt made him shake nervously, but he had to be the tough one, even if nobody else saw his tears.

The one thing he couldn't do anything about haunted him. DNA. It had to be everywhere. He looked again at the streaks left after his cleanup. He would have to come back with something stronger, he decided.

He looked down at the body on the floor. Coagulated blood had turned black on the side of Paul's head and across his face. Two teeth lay beside him on the floor, and he looked like something from a B-rated Goth movie. But Michael could only look at Paul's death as unplanned collateral damage, like the Army Rangers would in Afghanistan. He'd already found a replacement, and he nursed a gut feeling that Anthony would be twice as effective and more committed to the mission than Paul ever was. And with the resemblance the two cousins had, it would be hard to determine whether Paul or Anthony had been involved in past or future missions. A small bonus to confuse the authorities. And why should he care which cousin was sacrificed first?

He still felt nauseated and weak, so he opened the front window to let in some fresh air. Most important, he opened the narrow built-in ironing closet in the kitchen, pulled down the hinged ironing board and popped open his secret panel in the wall, where his stash of explosives and powder was hidden. He carefully removed several packs of C-4, but suddenly there was noise from the front, someone approaching on the stairs. There were two apartments on the second floor, and he didn't know which door might open at any second. Noting that he only had seconds to escape, he took a quick look around and closed the panel in the closet. He slung the garbage bag over his shoulder, ran to the back window, and descended the fire escape in back as fast as he could. When he was almost to the bottom, the loose stairway groaned and teetered precariously, and suddenly broke free, starting at the top near the window to his apartment. It made a metallic ripping sound that promised structural failure. He scurried down the last five steps as the steel ripped away from the outside wall, bolt by bolt. He nearly dropped the garbage bag full of evidence. When he reached the bottom, his last leap to the ground caused the entire staircase to pull off its broken brackets and bolts, and tumble into the Binnekill Creek with a prolonged crash that almost flung him into the water along with tons of rusty metal. A gash opened up from his shoulder to his wrist, and blood dripped into the edge of the Binnekill Creek. He fought the feeling of passing out. There was nobody around in the back of the building. Nausea won the battle, and he threw up on the ground. This was now worse than any flu he could imagine. He lay on the ground for ten minutes while blurred visuals of Paul's bloody face spun in front of his eyes like a drug hallucination.

The fallen fire escape cut off any possible return to the apartment. Paul's body and whatever DNA was left would have to stay there until it was discovered. Michael struggled to his feet, knowing he was still vulnerable. Limping from the fall, he dragged the trash bag around to the front of the building. Perhaps he could bury the evidence quickly and safely in the forested mountains surrounding the town. Seeing only a couple of teenagers passionately kissing in a doorway, he hobbled across Main Street, hoping he could reach his Jeep without discovery.

Chapter 24

WaterForce

As we walked up the stairs and passed several NYU professors' offices on the way to Dr. Jacoby's, I asked, "I don't get it. Why do we have to be here again?"

"Because our new lawyer told us to come back. We're putting together a team," Parker answered.

"I just remember the last time we came here—I ended up getting arrested."

"And remember who came to help you?"

"Well, it certainly wasn't Dad," I complained. I guess I had a healthy dose of cynicism and mistrust of most adults over forty, after our last experience. And Dad? We hadn't spoken since the arrest. He wouldn't let me in, and I certainly didn't trust him in my head.

"Come on, Titus. Watch your 'dad' attitude. Here comes the prof."

Professor Jacoby emerged from his office and gave us a warm greeting. This time, when we settled into the green leather chairs, Dotty entered with a bottle of Chianti and four wine glasses.

As he poured, Professor Jacoby said, "Gentlemen, I trust my accommodations are more comfortable than the interview room in the Delhi County Jail. I can offer a more luxurious libation than the bread and water they have there." He laughed heartily at his own humor and poured Chianti expertly into each glass. "Of course, this is not a school project, so I can spoil you with premium wine.

"So! We've lived through a few new chapters since I saw you last. Your father got a promotion and a letter from the mayor—you must send my congratulations."

I groaned, but the professor raised his glass to a toast. He looked at me with eyebrows lowered. "Remember that your dad has his job to protect. And never forget he has released your grandfather's trust fund—a considerable amount—so that you two can do something worthwhile." His look lingered, then melted into a friendly expression. "The press is now involved, selling millions of newspapers by spreading their version of a crisis, in which they've misquoted me and stretched the truth around the next block. And fingerprints of two terrorists were identified on a beer can at the site." His eyebrows emphasized his amazement. "Well, Dotty, we've got two concerned citizens here again. Tell us, what can we do for you today?"

Parker began with his usual directness. "Well, first, maybe you can tell us if the reporter was right. Are you really a former CIA agent?"

"Yes, I confess, I am. 'Former' is the operating word. And that means I have security clearances even today, if I choose to use them. But since I'm retired, it also means I'm allowed to have certain opinions of my own. That, I hope, is what makes me a fairly decent teacher."

Dotty chimed in, "Right. Professor-of-the-Year Award for three years running. 'A fairly decent teacher', I should hope! The students voted for him."

"Now, Dotty. You're lucky to work for me, but you don't have to brag about it." They all had a good laugh. The atmosphere was comfortable, and I must admit, I felt more at ease.

"Professor Jacoby," Parker began.

"Why don't we start by calling me what only my PhD students are allowed—Professor Jac. Spelled J-A-C, pronounced like 'Jacque,' in French. You've earned it." His whole face smiled like a wise old grandfather.

"Right. Thank you, sir. I mean, Professor Jac. We told you just about everything when we were here before. You already know our father, and his issues with Great-great grandfather Rosendael, and you've seen the video with the deer and the poison in the reservoir, and the protest gathering in Woodstock. But the reason we wanted to see you is because we've talked to Bonnie, Anthony Guarini's mother. She's an old radical activist...I mean, she has lots of experience organizing for different causes."

"I know all about her, boys. She's a piece of work. A mixture of hippie that forgot to grow up, activist for current liberal causes, and modern sorceress who can scare the pants off most macho men." He wagged his hand back and forth showing we was more than a little off the charts.

I couldn't help myself. "Right. And she's so ugly she could make a freight train take a dirt road." A joke to replace my cynicism.

Parker smiled but tried to move things along. "Well, she suggested we find a good lawyer, and invite certain key people to be on our team. We think we can put all this money to good use if we have the right partners, as she said."

"A very smart strategy. Very good. I'm impressed with your thinking," Professor Jac said. "And what would you like to accomplish with your key players?"

"We're still considering all that. But we know that the people of the watershed still don't have a united voice. The DEP works for the City. The City buys much of the land and is able to influence or even set land prices because they're the biggest buyer. We used to have a decent economy back when we could sell milk to New York City, but now they take our water for free. We've always been told that the City will protect the mountains and," I used two fingers to make quotation marks—"'maintain its rural character,' as they promised. But often that means the region is perpetually kept in economic recession." Parker paused and looked down at the floor. "I'm sorry. Am I on a soap box?"

Professor Jac said, "That's okay, son. You understand this very well. Go on..."

"They flood our creeks—like the Esopus last week—which wreaks havoc on the fish and their delicate spawning grounds. They create beautiful reservoirs

we can look at, but we can't do any boating, swimming, or get too close to their dams because of the toxin crisis. This new security alert means we can't walk within fifty feet of *any* body of water in the Catskills."

Professor Jac leaned forward in his chair, clasping his fingers together, and said, "Now that brings up very interesting theoretical question: Who owns the water?"

I said, "We've asked that question ourselves. The laws are unclear. When the water flows through our property, it's our water. But when it flows into the reservoir, it becomes the City's water, and we have to play by their rules governing water that isn't ours anymore."

Professor Jac said, "It's difficult to draw a property line through flowing liquid, isn't it?"

Parker said, "Because of this new threat, the people who live next to the water now need permits to go on their own land. The DEP treats everyone like trespassers, and the reservoirs that used to be open for boating—like the

Cannonsville and the Pepacton—are now closed. We need a voice that's heard by the public, especially down the city."

I strained to get in a word. "Most people in New York don't even know where their water comes from. We'd like to help organize and create a new voice to represent the people."

Professor Jac leaned back in his chair, placing his hands folded behind his head. A smile on his face blossomed like old Saint Nick as he spoke. "My boys, you are the right people for this. You have far more potential power than you think. You can make this into a legitimate movement, one that is long overdue, and needs to be brought into the spotlight."

I asked, "The right people, you say. Would...*you* be interested, Professor Jac? After all, you teach environmental studies, and you have that background with the C-I-A"

"We will not mention my past affiliations, even in three-letter abbreviations, and even though the press seems to have embellished some of my credentials."

I sat down again, afraid that we were losing him. "Right. Sorry. But, with your background, you could be very helpful if you would be—"

"Yes. And I will be."

"...on our team?!" Parker and I looked at each other in complete amazement.

"It took you long enough to ask! So let's get started."

****

That Professor Jac would support us was huge, and even more amazing that he would actively participate in our cause. I sat forward in my seat, and as we shared a sigh of relief.

Parker added, "We need powerful people from both the City and the Catskills."

"You'll have to take Dotty as well. I simply can't do anything without her. And she's an old rabble-rouser from way back in the women's movement," Professor Jac said.

"Let's begin with a list of potential allies. We'll brainstorm that together. We need power-helpers, media, and politicians. But even more important, we need volunteers—grass roots power—a wakeup call to ordinary people."

I remembered the rally in Woodstock. "Do you know how we got like nearly three thousand people to come to Woodstock last week? Social media. The word went viral on Facebook and Twitter."

Professor Jac said, "We need *real* people-power, spontaneous and energetic, but Woodstock's demonstration was unfortunately lacking strong leadership. You see, the media got the details wrong on the Esopus River. Unfortunately, sometimes the press resorts to sensationalism without checking their facts."

I asked, "So our mobbing in Woodstock was like bogus?"

Professor Jac answered, "The Woodstock protest turned out to be an uprising without leadership or facts. CNN will retract the misinformation that a toxin compromised both systems. But, from now on, our new organization can provide a better link and help to verify information released to the press."

Parker was excited. "I hope so. We need to start a website and an active blog, one that will attract followers who participate and who can be there in person when a call goes out for action. And we need to use that video. Make a voiceover."

Professor Jac said, "Yes. Edit it for YouTube, Twitter and Facebook and later a paid ad on television. You've already got some great footage. Add a few outtakes from interviews, and you'll have a powerful tool for change." Professor Jac smiled and wagged his eyebrows up and down in his excitement.

"We've already got a ton of material to start with. I'm pumped!" Parker said.

I said, "Anthony's mom was in the Weathermen in the sixties. Maybe we should call it 'The WaterMen.' Like, it would be a whole new movement."

Dotty said, "WaterMen is too sexist. Too male. How about simply, 'WaterForce.'"

I said. "That's a thing. 'WaterForce.' It implies a powerful people's force that has influence."

Professor Jac said, "WaterForce is like the power of a waterfall, the thrust of moving water, and the influence of a positive brand of water politics. And it could even refer to the force necessary to protect the reservoirs without being so one-sided. It's a wonderful metaphor." He wrote the word on his legal pad in large letters.

Parker added, "And it could extend a physical presence too. A human WaterForce will help the DEP to guard the reservoirs like the Guardian Angels here in the City. But when we need it to voice an opinion, or even contradict the DEP, it can also be the force and the voice of the people in the Catskills. It will be the organized 'force' that creates change."

Professor Jac said, "We've got a name, and our name defines our mission. Now we need a blog and a website. We need some good footage with a convincing voiceover. I'll bring in the power players we need and help create the message. You guys will recruit and organize a force of citizens to help protect the water and to get the City to listen to reason. Guarding the reservoirs must be our primary mission. And we have plenty of money to back it. I think we've just launched a very important movement, my friends."

Parker said, "Our lawyer says we need a test case in the courts. Something that will challenge our lack of a voice in the management of the DEP."

Professor Jac said, "That will come in time. Your term paper had some good ideas, Parker. As I recall, you called for joint authority of the DEP by both the City and people who live in the watershed."

"Yes, I wrote about that, but I realize it's probably never going to happen."

"It's not a new idea, Parker, but your paper had a very contemporary argument. The idea of having five commissioners instead of one would allow democratic representation from the City, the Croton system, the Catskill, and Delaware systems, and a citizen representative, with a majority vote required on all decisions. Maybe it's time has come. The DEP will rally against joint authority with a citizen vote. Maybe we can begin with a non-voting representative from the Catskills on the board."

I objected, "Non-voting? That's lame. We'd still have no power."

Professor Jac answered, "Let's keep that in our future strategy book. It will all come together in time. Maybe it's best to focus on the immediate issues first. Like educating New Yorkers where their water comes from, why it's important to work together. One step at a time. You guys seem to know what you want..."

I started with, "Preserving our trout streams."

Parker said, "*Preventing* terrorism by patrolling the reservoirs." His fist raised into the air.

Professor Jac followed with his finger raised. "Channeling loose cannons like Anthony into a more productive path."

Dotty chimed in, "Defining priorities that help both the city and the Catskills."

"Avoiding public panic," Professor Jac reminded us.

Parker, "—but getting our message across."

"—and giving the locals a voice," I added.

Professor Jac, "Right. Giving *everyone* a voice." He wrote one-word goals furiously.

Dotty. "Including women in the cause."

"Not just the City and the water-Nazis." Parker clenched his fist. I thought of Dad.

The professor said, "Your father is anything but a water-Nazi, but as a DEP officer, he's in a delicate position...let's not use inflammatory language!"

I asked, "You've talked to him?"

"Yes, my boy, I think I'm getting to like him. He can help from the inside. He promised to do anything he could to help, although he may not always be able to be as visible as you guys are. Consider him 'invisibly' on the team."

Parker, "DAD said that? I'm so excited."

I had to admit, "I guess I've misjudged him. Maybe."

Dotty, "Here's to WaterForce!"

Glasses raised. Chianti was consumed. Smiles showed determination all around.

"To WaterForce!"

Jack Bell Stewart

Chapter 25

Going Viral

Within a week we'd launched the WaterForce website and blog and had spread the word through an email campaign to attract attention. Professor Jac got us on the NPR 1A program, and the response was immediate and overwhelming. We had computer geeks lining up to answer inquiries and maintain the volunteer lists, outdoorsmen wanting to man our new WaterForce patrols around the reservoirs, activists volunteering for demonstrations, and lawyers interested in lobbying for support in Congress and the State Legislature.

Professor Jac met with the mayor's office and received sanction for "watch patrols" around the waterways from the Pepacton, Cannonsville, and Schoharie reservoirs all the way south to Central Park. Dad heard about our patrols from the DEP Commissioner. He didn't really like the idea, but he couldn't disagree with the fact that the DEP was completely understaffed and couldn't guarantee the safety of the entire water supply and its tremendous vulnerability. Given the poisoning of the Pepacton, the public was more than ready to approve of our help. When the longtime leader of the New York City Guardian Angels supported WaterForce and dubbed the watch patrols the "WaterForce Angels," the mayor and NYPD Chief O'Riley were convinced we were a welcome addition to help guard the water supply. And leave it to Anderson Cooper to plug us and lend official media support. All this, and we really hadn't done a thing of note to establish a track record.

Dad and I were headed to the Cheese Barrel in Margaretville for some coffee. "Dad, we're so proud of you for helping us. I can't tell you how cool this is."

"I was amazed at how easily Commissioner Calloway agreed to this."

"He knows he needs help and with the waterways threatened, he couldn't refuse," I agreed. "I just wanted to tell you how much it means to us." Dad parked the DEP patrol car on Main Street in front of the liquor store and walked north towards the Catskill Watershed building.

As we passed a door leading upstairs, I retched. "Damn, what is that stench? Smells like a dead skunk."

"I don't think so. That is no skunk, son."

"Everybody lights up on the street. Maybe that's it."

Dad looked concerned. "No, Titus, but it does smell like something died." There was an open window in the apartment above. Dad looked up curiously. He dialed the Margaretville Police on his cell. "Ed, it's Herb Rose. I'm on the street across from the gun shop. You need to get down here right away. There's a terrible stench, smells like a possible ten-fifty-four." He exited outside and walked up and down the street. "I can't tell, Ed...Possibly from one of those apartments upstairs. Jeez. Makes me sick, and I've got a stomach of iron...Yep, I'll meet you here. Hurry." The owner of the gun shop across the street approached him.

"Herb, do you smell that? Been looking for a dead animal all week. What the hell do you suppose?" A siren interrupted their conversation. The police car skidded to a stop in front.

Herb and Officer Ed paced up and down Main Street. I followed closely behind.

I asked, "Dad, do you think someone dumped poison in the creek out back?"

"No, it's closer than that," said Herb.

Officer Ed said, "I called the landlord of the apartments upstairs. He should be here soon." He walked to the door of a building close by. The door was still covered with police tape from the flood. He peered up the stairway leading to the apartment on the second level. "This has got to be it," he said.

Soon, the landlord arrived with keys to the front door and the upstairs apartment. A long time Margaretville resident, Al Bristow was one of the last to repair the apartments over the stores on the street after the hurricane. "I haven't even entered the upstairs apartments since I rented to those two young guys," he said.

When the door was opened, the carnage was revealed.

****

I was the first to see it. "O-M-G. This is way nuts. What happened?" There was a pool of dried blood on the floor and bloody streaks where the victim had dragged himself across the floor, finally turning himself over to die staring at the ceiling.

There had been a brutal struggle. The young male had a gash at his temple indicating he'd had a collision with the large flat screen TV that had toppled next to him. Teeth were knocked out and he'd bled profusely from the mouth and nose. His nose was broken and crooked, and the side of his head looked smashed inward.

Herb said, "Wait downstairs, son. This is too much for you."

"Dad, I'm not a dweeb. I can handle this." But I had to admit; my color was turning the same shade as the dirty white walls.

Dad's face turned ashen at the sight. I didn't try to point out which one of us couldn't take the sight of death, but I glared at him as I walked ahead into the crime scene.

Small town police protocol was apparently less defined than crime scene rules in a larger city. I really shouldn't be there. None of us should be tramping through the apartment with body parts and blood on the floor. But I was glad to be on the front lines.

Herb said, "Jesus, Mother of—it's Anthony."

I corrected him, "No, this is twisted. It's Paul, Anthony's cousin."

Officer Ed eyed me suspiciously. "Just how well do you know these guys?"

"Like, well," I admitted. Two words too much.

Dad motioned for me to 'shush up' and wait for him downstairs like I was a nine-year-old kid or something. I wasn't used to this role yet. I ignored him and deliberately strolled across the room with the officer.

Officer Ed took a few pictures, but his hands wouldn't stop shaking. Paul's eyes were still open and frozen in fear as if surprised by whatever fatal blow had overcome him. Officer Ed walked around the small apartment, finding a pair of muddy jeans and a tee shirt full of blood and dirt, signs that someone had attempted to clean up the place. "There was a hell of a fight. Hmmm. A beer can left under the cabinet. The same label as the one at the reservoir. *Brooklyn Black Ops*. I'd try that myself if it didn't sound so much like a terrorist label."

I knew the label from my visit with Parker down the city. "It's a Russian black stout, but it's made in Brooklyn. A limited edition each year. I've had it myself. It's awesome." Dad looked at me like I'd just confessed to a murder.

Officer Ed smiled and looked cryptically. "Your favorite beer, eh? A frickin *Russian* label! You're a real patriot, aren't you?"

"It's brewed in America. There are hundreds of micro breweries now 'Ops' is a take-off on 'hops'. Get it?" I protested.

"Yeah, well, how did it get up here, both at the reservoir and now at a murder site? And it happens to be your favorite brew?" He rolled his eyes at Dad and strolled into the bedroom. "Two beds, one in the living room, one in the bedroom...two guys lived here."

"That had to be Michael Capo," I said.

Officer Ed gave me that look again. He felt under the couch, "Something is stuffed way under here." He pulled it out with his nightstick. "A plastic grocery bag with—don't touch that! There's a black glove in there—" He opened the bag slightly. "—with powder on it. We've been looking for the other glove."

Dad said, "We need a crime lab team in here. We can't disturb this too much."

I had to get out from under the accusing stares coming my way, so I walked into the kitchen, inspecting a narrow closet door. "What's this?" I asked.

"Might be a broom closet or a small pantry," said Dad.

I opened the door and pulled the hinged ironing board down. "I found something!"

"Don't touch that! Might have prints," said Officer Ed.

Too late. I was already fiddling with a panel that seemed loose in the back wall. Suddenly it fell open. "Jeez! Look at what I found. There's a container with...white powder and two packages...looks like packages of modeling clay inside. Tina used that in her art class."

Dad crossed the room to inspect the new evidence. "That's not art class clay, son. That's C-4 explosive. This is what the military uses to blow up bridges. It's like clay and can be molded into tight spaces and take any shape." He put on a pair of gloves and inspected the packages more closely. "Whoa! There are at least ten pounds of C-4 in here, some blasting caps, and a bag of white powder. This is the mother-lode."

I said, "Maybe they weren't done with the reservoirs yet."

Dad said, "Maybe. This is unbelievable! Ed, maybe we should stake out this place and see if Capo comes back for this." Again, he motioned for me to leave. I was getting real good at ignoring him. What was it about the word "adult" that Dad didn't get after I turned twenty?

Officer Ed said, "We really need to get Guarini's body out of here. Looks like this happened over a week ago. The windows and furniture are clean, streaked like they've been recently wiped down. But why would he leave the C-4 and the toxin behind? Surely he wouldn't forget this stuff."

Dad said, "Doesn't make sense. Maybe it's too risky to come back here."

Officer Ed said, "Yeah, with his photo on the evening news." He radioed for the Medical Examiner, Doctor Dan, a local man who was also a well-known veterinarian, to examine the body and remove it.

I asked, "There's something weird. They dumped the toxin directly into the water in the Pepacton. So why do they need explosives to deliver another batch?"

"I'm guessing they learned from the first one that the stuff doesn't dissolve that easily without help," Officer Ed said.

Dad disagreed. "No. Blowing it up would send it all over the woods. That's not it. It wouldn't be the best way to dissolve a powder, and the noise would attract immediate attention. I think the C-4 is for something specific." He examined the packages again. "These packs came wrapped in cellophane. Thing is, they're partially opened. There were at least a dozen units in this one. Now there are only three left in the first pack and five in the other. Whatever plan they have for the C-4 is already in motion. This is just the leftovers."

"Dad—I hate to rat him out—he was my ace buddy, but...Anthony rapped about blowing up the dam at Downsville. I really think he was just being a braggadocio, talking with his usual fat mouth. But that's why he was mistaken for Paul in the Bun N' Cone."

Officer Ed replied, "We'll pick him up in Woodstock and find out."

I walked to the back window. "Get outta here! I see why he didn't come back. Look, down there, in the creek." Dad and Officer Ed joined me. The back-fire escape lay smashed and broken in the shallow water of the Binnekill Creek. The torn shred of a lightweight jacket hung off the bottom banister as if part of the incident when the staircase fell. "I think he fell into the water with the staircase, and he couldn't get back up here."

Officer Ed turned to Dad and said the most awesome thing I'd heard all afternoon. "You're right, that's what happened, for sure. You know, Herb, this kid is a smart one. You ought to keep him around. He'd make a great investigator."

Hearing that made me just about bust out of my skin. Maybe he didn't mistrust me after all. But I had more to add. "Anthony's father buys him firearms. I've seen him plink at signs, trees, and birds just for fun. It drives his mother crazy. He killed a stray cat once and blew it up with a chain of M-80s. Like totally sadistic. We watched the buzzards eat what was left, and I saw an eagle circling above, just waiting."

"*Now* you tell me," Dad said. "That's sick. Kids like that grow up to be killers."

"It was summer before last. I'm not sure he'd do that now. And, you know, I was, like, just along for the ride. I would never have—"

"Right. Maybe you'd better take a big dose of 'shut the hell up' son, before you get you *and* your friends in trouble...again."

Amazing how he could cut me down so fast. Dad was so acey-ducey. I loved him, but I sure as hell didn't like him at times.

Officer Ed was skeptical. "I don't know. C-4 is powerful, but you'd need a hell of a load to blow that dam. And I don't think a terrorist could get near it without detection. The DEP has a bunch of eyes on it twenty-four seven."

Dad said, "Michael Capo and Paul Guarini were said to be very close. Worked together a long time. But this doesn't look like friendship. I wonder what happened between them?"

Officer Ed said, "Whoever did this left a lot of evidence."

"Maybe there's a third guy involved. Capo is M.I.A. Some of the C-4 is still here and another batch of toxin—I assume it's botulinum bacteria like the other—but this time it was left with a dead body."

Officer Ed said, "This is the first murder around here since Officer Brinkerhoff was killed, years ago. I wonder what the motive is…"

I answered, "Anthony told me Michael lost three brothers. Maybe that's part of it."

Dad said, "The apartment has been cleaned, but it's still a sloppy crime scene, just like the reservoir." He looked at me. "Let's go downstairs. We'll wait for the crime lab, then we'll figure out what's next."

Dad actually said "we" when he talked about the crime. Maybe "we" were a real team, my dad and I, even when he dissed me. And this all started when I put my big paws on a flip-down ironing board.

Chapter 26

The Commissioner

Dad and I sat on the bench outside of the bar on Main St. A pungent collection of months-old cigarette butts littered the sidewalk and created a stale ashtray aroma, but it was like fresh gardenias compared to the repulsive odor of death we'd left behind.

This was the first time we'd been alone together since the arrest, and I could tell I was in for his brand of a lecture.

"Son, this thing has gotten entirely too close to us. First, you and your best friend manage to get tangled up in a manhunt, and then arrested. And now we've got a dead body upstairs, and you're shooting off your mouth to police without realizing how much trouble you could be making for yourself."

"Dad, no way! Can't you see what went down? Anthony and his cousin Paul are like twins—you can hardly tell which is which. Especially with all that bruising and blood."

"I realize that, son. Okay, they'll sort out the identities from fingerprints, but you're tied to both of them now. You've been with Anthony, the loose cannon on the front page of the *Times*, shooting his mouth off and getting you both in hot water, and now you've identified his cousin. Don't you think they'll notice your associations? And what about that Russian beer we found? *Russian*, Titus! Christ! I thought you had better sense than that. If you weren't my son, I'd suspect you were guilty by association in a heartbeat."

"Officer Ed seemed to appreciate my input. I was the one who identified the body, and I was the one who found the broken staircase. A minute ago, you were talking about "we." But now, YOU'RE the only one who's paranoid about Anthony and me. And all over a Russkie *beer?*"

"Just stay away from the Guarinis...let them all hang themselves, especially that lesbian hippie witch in Woodstock."

"Anthony's mom?" I groaned. "You've got to be kidding me! She's no threat. Bonnie is on *our* side. And she's like *not* a lesbyterian."

But Dad didn't laugh. "Yeah—just the ally you need. Bonnie Guarini has a peacenik rap sheet that goes all the way back to the sixties. She's been hauled off from more sit-ins and demonstrations than I can count. I remember her in Occupy Wall Street in New York, when she fought like a scalded cat before they hauled her ass off to jail. She used her magic crystal pendant to put a hex on the arresting cop, and he had a car accident the next weekend that left him paranoid even today. Come on, Titus, wise up to this old witch!"

"At least she has principles she believes in. She's not a fucking hypocrite like you." I thought Dad was going to take a swing at me. I probably deserved it. If looks could kill...

"Just shut the hell up and let us solve the crime the way the professionals know how. And don't you go calling me a hypocrite. You don't know half the story."

"How do you do it, Dad? First, you tell us how the City took Grandpa's land, and left our family with squat. A deep dark family grudge from seventy years ago. Then you pull out this trust fund for us to fight the DEP and the city, but you won't bail me out when I get involved in the battle. Did we piss you off, Dad? Or are you just afraid to stand up? I mean, is that a *thing?*" I stood up and paced back and forth across the sidewalk, fuming and staring at him like he was my mortal enemy. "What's your mixed thing today, *Daddy?*" I could see his ears get red, then his whole face. Out of habit, he actually placed his hand on his revolver. Big threat!

As if on cue, Dad's phone rang, and I could hear the commissioner's obnoxious raspy voice from six feet away. "Herb, I just got your message about Paul Guarini..." They went on for five minutes about finding Paul's body in the apartment. I felt relieved that the anger between us had been interrupted before it got too far out of hand. Dad held his hands up in a kind of surrender mode. He formed the V-shaped peace symbol with his right hand and smiled. I tried, but I couldn't do anything but feel the anger melt away. I smiled back at him, partially because I did love him, but also because I knew I'd scored some big points that he didn't have to answer if he stayed on the phone. When he hung up, I let the silence permeate the air between us until he had one last shot at me.

"Titus, you have to understand. I've got a job to do. And you and Parker are much better off with me on the inside. But when I give you a sign to tone it down, trust me that it needs to happen. Trust me that I'd never do anything to hurt you guys. And I have confidence that you both will do the right thing. But you've got to learn to play the game in order to protect both of us. Notice who is in the room before you open your big mouth."

Age and wisdom struck me hard. "Dat's legit, Dad."

"And don't call me 'Daddy'. Now, as it happens, the commissioner is on his way. He wants to talk to both of us...not sure why. But you'd better treat him with respect. He's my boss."

"I think I know a little about his rap..." It had to be about WaterForce. So I took the opportunity to tell him more about what we'd been doing for the past ten days. He'd already talked to Professor Jacoby, and knew we were on the Internet. But Dad wasn't that savvy about websites. He'd learned how to use Mapquest until I got him a GPS for Christmas, and even then, he didn't seem to care about anything on a computer. When I told him we had over seven thousand names collected in less than a week, he was blown away. "Dad, we're going viral. Parker and I. We've had thousands of people hitting on our website. Like major hashtag. We've got people busy answering e-mails, and hundreds volunteering to go to demonstrations when we give the go. We even have a few like edgy activists willing to pitch in, nearly three hundred contributions, and a hundred and fifty people willing to patrol the reservoirs. We're going to call it—"

"WHAT? Patrol the...Titus, that's up to the DEP. That's MY job!"

"Dad, please, no offense, but we *know* you guys are understaffed. Like there's no way you can cover all nineteen reservoirs and every inch of shoreline. That's how they were able to poison the Pepacton. And even though it wasn't successful, there could be a next time."

"Jesus, Titus! This isn't going to go over well with the commissioner." He paced back and forth, and spit on the sidewalk in disgust.

"We'll see," I said with the sweet smile of 'inexperienced youth'.

Professor Jac told us he would handle all the big wigs down the city. When Commissioner Calloway pulled up and motioned us both into the back seat of his black Lincoln Town Car, I knew this could be the moment. The driver closed the security window to give us privacy.

"This must be your son. Titus, is it?" the commissioner said. "Glad you're here; you both need to hear the same thing. Professor Jacoby called me about your organization. I think it comes along at just the right time."

"WaterForce. I was just telling Dad." I looked over at him. Dad was in shock, simply speechless. I don't think he ever expected to have a meeting inside Calloway's Town Car, let alone with me there, and now realizing that I was three steps ahead of him, and Calloway actually approved.

"Good. That's why I'm here," Calloway said. "Okay, so you probably know about the website and the response they've received. There are a lot of good things that can come from this, as long as there is close communication and some controls put in place. You know, it took years for the NYPD to come to trust the Guardian Angels when they formed in 1979, and even longer for them to start to work together. But since then they've proven themselves to be an effective citizen force, and they've expanded internationally. With the Guardian Angels as a model, I think the WaterForce Angels can help us keep eyes on the reservoirs."

Dad said, *"Angels?* More like 'Vigilantes'. Commissioner, this goes against the policies we've had in place for over thirty years."

"Yes, perhaps. But we're living in a different world today, with new threats, and unknown terrorists. There are many ways they could gain the upper hand. And it's true that we are extremely understaffed."

"You talked to Professor Jacoby, right?" I said.

The commissioner nodded his head. "Professor Jacoby already talked to the mayor, to my office, and the governor. He's very convincing. We've linked up with the Guardian Angels. He suggested your citizen patrols be called the WaterForce Angels, and be charged with patrolling the rivers and reservoirs in the watershed in conjunction with the DEP. A DEP assistant will be assigned exclusively to train the patrols. And I understand you already have volunteers for reservoir duty."

"How in the hell did this all happen so fast? And are you sure we're not opening up ourselves to some horrible disaster? This is a whole new vigilante world. Good God! This is worse than I ever thought. Titus, how *could* you?"

"Keep your hair on, Dad. Professor Jac spoke with the mayor and the commissioner."

"So...you guys got instant trust because of some damn *college teacher*? This is way over the top." Dad had never been to college, except to arrest a druggie in a dorm at SUNY Delhi.

"He's more than a 'damn college teacher', Dad. *Professor* Jac used to be a major player in our country's security."

Commissioner Calloway said, "Thanks for your discretion, son. Professor Jacoby has the country's highest security clearance. After the NYPD has interviewed your Angels, we'll approve a limited force, with no weapons, just cell phones that can only be used within the police network. They'll have blue berets and sashes, and a special ID issued by the DEP. In other words, no authority to shoot or arrest anyone. You'll have ten of his guys, one to head up each patrol, with your local volunteers who know the territory. It's a good match of skills. We even got an anonymous donation to cover all the costs. I don't know where it came from, but as soon as I brought up the expense and quoted some numbers, we got a check the next afternoon from a lawyer in the Catskills, and a pledge to cover all future costs. This thing has come together very fast. But, under the circumstances, it really needed to. A miracle, if I ever saw one."

When Calloway mentioned the anonymous check, Dad smiled slightly, and bumped my knee with his. Just then the sun came out from behind a cloud. It was totally eerie, as if Great-Great Grandpa's spirit was smiling like the angel Clarence in *It's a Wonderful Life*. It would take a few more weeks for all of this to get organized, but I was busting out that WaterForce was gaining acceptance by the people who counted the most.

Commissioner Calloway had one more surprise. "As for your website, I think you've made a great effort to stay neutral, and not criticize the DEP like we were some kind of bumbling idiots. So let me give you a piece of news you can publicize. You know that we opened up the Pepacton for small boating a few summers ago, but we had to tighten security again last week. I hope we can reverse our crisis shutdown and go ahead with this program. Just canoes, rowboats, sailboats and kayaks, but I think this will go a long way towards creating good will for the public. Of course, I'm assuming the present threat may be over by then. We still have to catch the bad guys, but you can consider it a very hopeful possibility."

Before we got out of the car, Commissioner Calloway saluted to Dad, and said, "By the way—nice job up here, Herb. Congratulations on your promotion." How could Dad object to that dose of stroking? By the time the Town Car pulled away to return to the City, we were riding on a cloud of optimism.

Dad said simply, "As you would say, son, I'm blown away. I'm...so proud of you boys. You've really started something outstanding with that money."

I hadn't hugged my dad in at least three years. But I did it now, right there on Main Street in Margaretville, in view of the macho gun shop owner across the street. A full bear hug that he returned and held on for at least ten seconds of manly embrace. I felt his tear touch my cheek. That wasn't so lame, was it?

****

From the fingerprints and mug shots taken at his previous arrests, they verified what I already knew: the corpse upstairs was definitely Paul Guarini. They found traces of botulism on his glove, his coat, and his boots in the closet, and matched the glove with the stuff found at the site on the Pepacton. I was sure that Michael Capo's fingerprints would be found all over the apartment and the body, but I was wrong. Even though there were two guys living there, there were few fingerprints. Except on the cellophane wrappings of the C-4, Michael Capo had wiped everything else into blurry streaks.

There was something wrong, something I wasn't quite getting. They hadn't paid much attention when I'd shot off my mouth about Anthony. We had defended his jive in the Bun N' Cone and thought he was full of himself with his stupid violent ideas. But I knew how close to Paul he'd always been. Was Anthony involved? If he was, how long had he been lying to Parker and me? Somehow, I didn't trust my own instincts. No, he couldn't be...he would never...

Dad said the autopsy revealed Paul Guarini had been very sick with botulism poisoning. The M.E. found green and black phlegm deep in his lungs which would have eventually suffocated him and led to a horrible and painful death. I'd never liked him, especially when he'd influenced Anthony with loaded guns, shooting at anything that moved, and too often dangerously close to houses and roads. No respect for bullets. But nobody deserved to die that way, even though it might seem like justice in Paul's case. Having seen what the toxin did to that poor deer, I knew it was far less painful that the fight killed him first.

But what about Anthony? When I called his mother, she was frantic. He had called, and said he was going hunting up north for a week. But hunting season was over for deer. It just didn't sit right with Bonnie, or with me. I had this feeling that he was up to something, something bad.

Chapter 27
Training Anthony

M ichael and Anthony arrived at Michael's trailer at the end of a mile-long dirt driveway off a snowy road high up on a ridge between Wildcat and Table Mountains. They had a view below to the valley, where the Neversink River meandered towards the reservoir of the same name. If necessary, they could see approaching headlights on the driveway, and use a trail off to the south that only a four-wheel drive vehicle could navigate to escape capture. The tattered old Four Winds RV Camper was isolated with not a neighbor within a mile on any side and had the basic supplies they needed to survive for several days. The camper had been a low-end RV when it was new in 1976. By now, the engine was blown, the exterior was rusted and dented, and it had been parked permanently in the same place for over fifteen years.

Poison snakeberry bushes and small saplings captured it as if to reclaim the parking area for the wilderness and provided a perfect natural camouflage for the inhabitants. A sturdy clump of sumac had taken root and gnarled its way through the left side tires, tethering the once mobile residence to its spot on the mountain. Michael slept in the bedroom in the back. The bed over the cab in the front was stuffed with boxes and junk. Anthony converted the two-seat lunch booth by day into a cramped bed by night.

Michael spent the first two days communicating with his new recruit, making sure Anthony was successfully inducted as a partner with as much confidence as he could expect. Michael knew he couldn't do without committed help, at least for the next phase in the plan. He'd been trained in Iraq ten years ago and knew the survival techniques he would need in order to stay hidden in the Catskills.

"I'll bet you were pissed when they arrested you instead of Paul," Michael said, sliding into the bench seat opposite Anthony.

"I was furious. I still am. There's gonna be payback one of these days," Anthony said.

"I don't blame you. Maybe you'll have a chance for payback sooner than you think."

"You think?"

"I know we both feel the same way."

It was easy to bring Anthony over to the dark side. They talked in depth about certain radical notions on water politics. He could tell Anthony was excited, yet still had a lot to learn about the techniques of surviving as a successful subversive. After a few days, Anthony seemed more like a trusted associate, and he was starting to become useful when he supplied names and details about what had happened in Margaretville and Woodstock.

"Titus and Parker are into this big time, but they're doing it all wrong," Anthony said. They've got some ancient professor down at the university, and they made a web site. Like that's gonna make a difference! I'll bet their dad is just laughing at them, with their bogus so-called 'action plan!' and this thing called 'WaterForce Angels.'"

Michael replied, "Yeah, like double-you, double-you, double-you, we is makin' trouble-you! Ha ha!"

"Yeah, and they're gonna post signs like, 'The former site of Shavertown, land of the DEP'. Like, the big bad wolf, like."

"Whuppie! That'll scare people. If you and I did it, it'd be more like, 'the former site of the *reservoir*. What *was* its name?' Ha ha!"

"Or, 'The former water supply of New York.'" Anthony slapped him on the knee. Good buddies. He looked at Michael in admiration. They opened the first of a couple dozen beers. It was starting to click. "So...do you go by 'Michael, Mike'— what do you...?"

"Well, asshole Paul used to call me 'boss.'

"Ah, dude! I'll call you 'Michael.' Ain't no dweeb. Awesome!" He clinked his bottle so hard with Michael's that the glass nearly broke.

"I don't care, long as we get the job done."

"You can count on me. I'm not gonna mess you up, like Paul did."

"We got to get you trained. I've got some equipment and supplies you need to learn about."

"Awesome. This is like, what I've been hoping!"

"Read this manual. It'll save us some time. I was a munitions officer in Iraq. I lost my brother Kevin to fucking "friendly" fire in Iraq, and my brother Jerry in Afghanistan, and another brother..." A tear fell down his cheek as he stopped himself from further details.

"I really want you to study, this, like *memorize* it. Tomorrow we'll get some practice in. Right now, I'm going out for a walk." He left the book on Anthony's chair, opened a beer, and walked out of the trailer and into the night with his phone.

Anthony read about seven chapters and fell asleep at the lunch table. When he woke up, the moon was shining through the window of the trailer. He sat mesmerized by the light and found himself deep in thought about the path he was choosing. His mother's lectures from the Delhi lockup came back to him. Pangs of conscience and projected guilt about future transgressions haunted him. He knew this path was dangerous and over the top. He felt like a fly buzzing around a candle, mindlessly drawn into an irresistible flame, a fire that would scorch him until he and the candle were snuffed out. Could he—should he—would he resist the temptation?

But then, he remembered that Bonnie had been a Weatherman in her Viet Nam protest days, hanging out with the likes of Angela Davis when Davis spoke out against the "prison industrial complex". She'd broken into an ROTC building at SUNY Purchase, participated in demonstrations and ended up in handcuffs more than once. Her friends were involved in the Patricia Hearst kidnapping on the west coast. She wouldn't even talk about some of the activities she'd participated in, but her eyes revealed how proud she was of the excitement and accomplishments that resulted from years of radical action.

So, why shouldn't Anthony walk on a similar path? It was a good cause, just as valid as being against the war back in the late 60s. So how could his mother get so conservative now, and advise him against radical actions that she would have embraced back then? Hypocritical, he decided. He read another chapter in the munitions handbook, then drifted off and slept soundly. He dreamt about cell phones hooked up with wireless radio transmitters and blasting caps, followed by massive explosions. When he again awakened, dream visions of IEDs and faceless black-clad associates floated in his head, armed with explosives destined for an unknown target. He'd never done anything like this, but he was about to find out what it was like to be a real subversive, just like the Blackwater outfit, only much smaller, and much more lethal.

****

Five days of intensive training, repetitive practice, and endless lecturing, questioning, and scolding had produced results. Anthony began to feel the committed determination of stealth with elusive attack tactics employed by special forces, adapted to an untold subversive purpose. He now sported a black and khaki camouflage outfit that Michael had appropriated from an army store up in Grand Gorge. On Michael's property, he practiced repelling, launching ropes and grappling hooks from a special rifle, and climbing a completely vertical forty-foot cliff using an ascender that gripped the rope and slid upward as he climbed. In the evenings, Michael gave him more manuals to study, and they trained with weights, calisthenics, and running in the field outside the small trailer. The crash course in terrorism was a combo platter of rushed basic training and selected special skills, along with brutal physical conditioning.

Anthony knew better than to ask what they were training for, but he knew it was far more dangerous than stepping in a bucket of red paint or dumping powder into the Pepacton. Finally, on the fourth day, he successfully climbed forty feet up the cliff, planted a dummy explosive in a crevice under a bird's nest, and wired it with a radio transmitter in less than three minutes. Michael finally yelled some positive feedback. "Way to go, partner! You're nearly ready."

Anthony repelled efficiently down his climbing rope to the ground. Michael had called him 'partner'! It was time to ask, "So, Michael. What's our first mission? Something exciting, I hope."

"We were scheduled to hit the Schoharie, but they're watching too closely right now. And the botulism thing didn't really work very well. I guess it was too far from the city. Too much water to dilute it, and Paul fucked us up by leaving clues with his fingerprints all over. If they hadn't discovered the toxin and gathered most of it up the next day, it might have done some damage. But now we've got another way to bust the reservoirs."

"You mean...my toy boat?"

"Exactly."

"Awesome! So, like what's the payload?"

"Only about a hundred pounds or so. Until it explodes. Then...nothing but pay*back*!"

"Rad! It won't go very fast, but my little boat can handle it."

"How would you like to do a special mission with that thing? Say...Friday night."

"Oh man, that's fucking twisted. YAAAS."

Chapter 28
Small Craft Warnings

The miniature remote-controlled high-speed boat, a twin engine model favored by teenagers everywhere, was built to slam, cut and dive through the waves. If it had been a full sized speedboat, it might be called something like a "cigarette boat," named for its long sleek shape, and respected for its incredible speed and agile ability to cut through the water with almost no splash. But this toy was put to a different task near the southwest shore of the Ashokan Reservoir. The Ashokan was nearly five hundred feet lower in elevation than the other reservoirs, and the surface had already melted to navigable water. At six o'clock on a wintery Friday afternoon, the sun was already down below the mountains, and visibility was flat with no shadows on the dark black water. Clad in a full body black hooded wetsuit, Anthony moored his rowboat in the cattail weeds, and stood in four-foot deep water in a small inlet on the south shore. He was only five hundred yards from the dam on the other side. He had named his miniature vessel the "Lucky Strike", with its double entendre imbedded in the name.

He would have preferred to put the Lucky Strike to a test to see how it could dodge left and right with the barge attached and test its ability to cut through waves like a hot knife through butter. There was no time for a practice run, but he was sure that the boat could complete its task with the extra weight it towed without a trial run. The thirty-eight-inch-long miniature was powered by a 12-volt 2300 micro-amp battery and could travel easily at twenty-eight miles per hour. Pulling a small Styrofoam and plywood barge with a capacity payload proved difficult and slow, straining its normal capabilities with its top-heavy payload. Although a small distance, it took nearly thirty minutes for the boat to struggle across the water. It was straining and groaning by the time it reached its destination near the northeast end of the reservoir.

Anthony could see three DEP cars and a truck with a boat trailer spread out across the dam and an eighteen-foot DEP twin-engine motorboat traversing the long reservoir in the water from the west. There was no chance they would hear the Lucky Strike at that distance, but he held his breath anyway. It would be such a sweet victory to sneak past them. He felt like he was playing with his toys on Christmas morning, only this was far more exciting with a real mission and real results.

Two officers used binoculars to search across the dark water surface and scan the opposite shore. But Anthony was well hidden in tall weeds, and only his head and hands could be seen above the water. He smiled at the knowledge of his advantage, and how easy it was for his boat to slip unnoticed under the noses of the water-Nazis on the dam. If his timing were right, he would pass a good thirty yards in front of the DEP boat unnoticed. Fortunately, the DEP craft was headed to patrol the opposite end of the reservoir and would be out of the way for a few minutes. Perfect timing.

When the attack boat Lucky Strike and its lethal payload nearly reached its destination, he took special joy in pushing a button to send a radio signal across the water. The signal should have caused a small mercury tilt switch taken from a household thermostat to connect with the explosive and set it off. For a moment, when nothing happened, he faced the thought of failure. He pushed the button again and cursed softly when it again failed to respond. Quickly he turned the craft before it crashed into the dam. He'd run past the perfect position, and the boat labored at making the sudden turnaround because of the barge it towed. As it swung around, he saw the cumbersome barge scrape against the dam. It teetered for a dangerous moment as if it were ready to capsize and dump its load, rendering it useless before detonation.

Had the wires become wet, or perhaps become unattached from the terminals? He checked his controller, opening the battery compartment. The boat slowly circled away from the dam. He blew air into the compartment to dry it out. Small droplets of water flew out of the compartment. How had he been so careless? At least he'd discovered the problem, at his end, where he could fix it. Carefully he removed each of eight AA batteries and dried them on his shirt collar protruding from the neck of his wetsuit. No small feat when he was nearly up to his shoulder blades in water. He snapped the batteries back in, and pushed the battery cover back on the controller. But the cover didn't seat well, and suddenly flew off into the water. He thought, of course, the transmitter would work regardless because the batteries were still in place and making contact. The boat was now circling about twenty feet away from the dam. He needed it to be closer and waited until he could guide it to a more ideal position. By now the water was disturbed and swirling, and there was a downward current from the aqueduct outtake valves below, making it hard to navigate. Why the hell did the rudder joystick work, but the trigger did not? The Lucky Strike struggled and was almost capsized by the turbulence. He turned it again, just in time to save it from disaster.

Another threat reared its ugly head. A small craft flew through the air, like a miniature helicopter circling the area where the boat swirled through the water. It suddenly became obvious that the dam was better protected than human eyes could ever provide. The four rotating propellers on top gave it a strange surreal presence unlike any flying machine he had ever seen.

He saw movement on the dam, and he knew that the drone had given away his location. One of the DEP officers had his binoculars locked on the Lucky Strike. The cop shouted to the others and pointed into the water. Another officer ran to the edge with a large pole and a fishing net he used to try to capture the boat as it circled. A quick radio call was made to the life-size DEP motorboat patrolling at the other end of the reservoir. Time was running out. Another officer drew his pistol and aimed at the boat, but his superior officer shouted to stop him. Not a good idea to shoot at a boat that might be full of explosives. But now Anthony worried that maybe the drone was armed.

He turned the controller over to reach the button, and pushed hard, willing the signal to travel to the boat. A long moment of nothing was his reward. He pushed again and again, finally erupting in frustration and anger as he threw the controller back over his shoulder onto the shore. It travelled in a long arc and crashed against the trunk of a large sycamore tree. A rain of batteries flew out of the device as he muttered obscenities. But when he glanced back across the water, he realized that the impact against the tree had been enough to loosen the jam in the trigger. A powerful explosion erupted next to the dam, sending a geyser thirty feet in the air, and propelling the toy boat and barge downward to a watery grave below. The drone flew straight up at the impact and produced its own explosion high over the dam. The officer with the fishing net fell flat on his butt a dozen feet away. Officer Trigger-Happy emptied his gun at unseen targets across the water on the opposite shore. The bullets pinged harmlessly on a boulder twenty yards away, then closer to his head. The duty officer barely had time to radio an urgent red alert, but Anthony was confident that a hundred and ten pounds of a new toxin were sucked into the aqueduct when the exploding barge delivered its payload.

"Gotcha baby! Fuck you, New York," he said under his breath. Strange that his comment mirrored Michael's motivation for revenge, and that Anthony was merely a paid patsy, enabled only by money, rhetoric and loyalty to Michael. But the experience was too exciting to let guilt get in the way.

Anthony submerged himself and swam under water twenty feet to the shore. Leaving the rowboat behind, he crawled out of the mud at the water's edge like a wet crocodile and slithered up the embankment until bushes and trees sheltered him. After a satisfying glance at the mayhem back across the reservoir, he crawled furtively through the bushes back to his car parked on Route 28A. He drove westward, past an oncoming DEP car rushing to help with the crisis at the dam with his lights and siren on, oblivious to the terrorist that got away in oncoming traffic.

Still in his wetsuit, Anthony continued at the legal speed limit until he could turn away from the reservoir. He smiled with satisfaction, after delivering his payload and outsmarting a troop of officers and their drone. He felt like a seasoned operative now, with a successful mission under his belt. But then he noticed the blood from a stray bullet seeping through a slice between the shoulder and the neckline of his brand-new wet suit. Suddenly he felt faint at the sight of his own blood. But he recovered after a rush of macho adrenaline that filled him with chemical courage. A scratch, but nevertheless, a proud little battle wound. No big deal. He dialed Michael on his cell.

"Dude. The soap is out of the shower." If he had not been successful, the code would have been, 'The pickle is stuck on the wall.' He filled in the details of the battle, the explosion, the delivery of the payload, the threat of the drone, and a heroic account of his battle wound.

Michael replied, "Cool. I'm proud of you. You really came through, passed the test. But they know about it now. It'll rattle their asses, but if they can stop it, the payload may not make it to the city."

"Get out! The load is already on its way, inside the aqueduct. But, boss, there's no way they could stop it now—is there?"

"Well...there's a new switching station in Gardiner, just finished. They can switch off either aqueduct for servicing."

"That's a huge part of the water supply. So, what did we accomplish?"

"If it gets all the way through, we hit the jackpot. Even it doesn't, we're proving that we can hit the reservoirs anytime we want, no matter how many guards they have. It's possible to shut it down between the aqueducts if they can react quickly. But also, you proved that their drones don't always work!"

"Right...but where in Gardiner is the switching station?"

"I'm ahead of you, dude. Drove past it earlier today." There was a long pause while they both thought about the new challenge. Finally, Michael said, "I've got a plan. We'll talk when you get back. And, awesome work today, dude. And you shed some blood for the cause. Come on home!"

Chapter 29

The SEALS

"Herb. Commissioner Calloway here. They hit us again, at the Ashokan."

"Oh my god!" Herb tried to wake up quickly. It was late, and he'd only had a few hours' sleep. He wiped the sleep out of his eyes on the sheet.

"They sent a miniature radio-controlled boat towing a barge, across the reservoir with a C-4 charge. It blew up right next to the intake, and the stuff got sucked into the aqueduct within seconds."

"Botulism again?" Herb said.

"We don't really know. The charge was just big enough to sink the boat. Our men fired across the lake, but we couldn't really see the operator, and...unfortunately, we lost the drone in the explosion. He got away clean."

"Damn! You shut the aqueduct down, I hope." Herb sat on the edge of the bed, now fully awake.

" The new Stanford sensors detected the explosive immediately, and it automatically shut down the system farther downstream at the Gardiner junction."

"That's the good news."

"Also, I should add, we picked up the end of a phone call that sounds suspicious. Some guy said, 'I've got a plan... awesome work today, dude. You shed some blood for the cause. Come on home!' Tells me we might have injured the perp. That's all we got, but we're trying to trace the phone number.

"Keep on that. So, protocol, you probably called the SEALs." Herb started to pull on his uniform pants and searched for his gun in the drawer.

"On their way with three divers."

"And it's nearly twenty miles between the Ashokan and the new switching station."

"Yes. That's a hell of a lot of territory to cover in an underground aqueduct."

"What about the sensors inside, and the ones in Gardiner?"

"That's what's so strange. None of the sensors have picked up anything. No toxins, no explosives, nothing inside the aqueduct. Nothing."

Herb said, "That should be a *good* sign."

"Herb, come on! This time the explosion was clearly a delivery method. Something is in there. But it could be set to empty out later."

"How long can we keep the Catskill system off line?"

"Probably several days. But it's never been tested with the valves all the way off. We've already slowed down the spillway at the Schoharie to almost nothing. But there's heavy rain predicted later this week, and all that water will have to go someplace."

"So, no threat to the supply to the City...but, the Schoharie spillway is going to flood the Esopus before long. Christ!" Herb strapped his gun on and grabbed his keys.

"Right. It could be a major crisis by next week. Herb, I need you down there."

"I'm on my way. Where do you want me?"

"The Ashokan facility. I'm already on my way from the City. About an hour?"

"I'll be there before you. I'm still on my land line."

"I've got to stop in Gardiner. We need to talk through our strategy."

Herb jumped in his car and began the journey to the Ashokan barracks. "Where are you now?"

"I just got on the Taconic Expressway, near the Kensico dam. Everything's okay here."

"I've been trying to think of how we'd handle the flood threat if we need to keep the Catskill system shut off. I mean, what if we can't find the toxin?"

"It's got to be in there. There's no other place it could go. But the sensors haven't gone off at all."

"That means it's in a sealed container. But if the divers can't detect anything, we'll have to drain twenty miles of aqueduct, and flush it out before we can restore the flow."

"That's damn near impossible, Herb. The aqueduct is over fifteen feet in diameter, times twenty miles."

"I know. Where the hell are we going to put that much poisonous water? We'd have to have several fleets of tanker trucks. And then where would we dump it?"

"Everything depends on the SEALs. They've got to find *something*."

"What if they don't?"

"I think we'll be in big trouble, Herb. Hang on...No, I'll call you back. The mayor's office is calling in. I've got a conference call with Homeland Security. Later..."

****

Herb arrived at the same time as the Navy SEALs dive team. Shortly after, an anti-terrorist team from NYPD arrived. Between the Navy, the DEP, and NYPD, there were more than thirty officers standing on the dam. After a five-minute briefing, the SEALs donned their gear, and discussed a communication plan with the DEP officers above ground.

They planted a transmitter near the entrance to relay communication from inside the aqueduct. Signals would be airborne to a drone, then transmitted to the City. Three divers entered the water with high-powered floodlights attached to their helmets and an array of equipment to test the water for any one of ten different toxins, pollutants, or explosives. A DEP electric motorboat had been moored inside the aqueduct just for emergencies and would be occupying the air space above the water line in the tunnel to provide a way for the divers to take periodic breaks. Corporal Meyers would stay in the boat and relay information from the divers to the technician above ground.

The light was eerie inside the aqueduct, bouncing off the tubular tunnel and creating moving reflections all around. The water filled almost two-thirds of the fifteen-foot height of the tunnel, but the divers had to be submerged in the lower section to find anything under water level. Dive master PFC Rick Lanphear had run a complete array of tests with a device that analyzed the chemical composition almost immediately. A variation of the same hand-held device was used at airports everywhere to scan for toxins in passengers' luggage. This model was able to function under water and was more sophisticated in its ability to deliver results. Each diver had a tester, but they also had to search thoroughly for any physical sign of explosives or other suspected pollutants. Lanphear sent the two other divers ahead. They didn't have a lot of time to find the toxin. He surfaced and hung on the side of the small boat and pushed the "save" button to record the latest test. Corporal Meyers radioed in his findings.

"Captain...Meyers here. Nothing yet. There's only some natural debris that got through the filters, caught near the section junctions. We're about two miles in, and we've tested all along. There's nothing but clear water in here so far with eighteen miles to go."

"Roger that."

"Lanphear sent Gilford and Hayes ahead to look for anything caught in the debris. Maybe it's in some sort of sealed delivery container."

The captain said, "That's what I'm thinking. Maybe it was planned to dissolve over time, or perhaps it's in a second timed explosion, and that's why we can't find it."

"How fast did you say the water flow was shut off?"

Herb stepped up to the mike. "Herb Rose, here, Meyers. The Stanford sensors immediately detected the explosion at the dam and initiated a shutdown. Probably took less than five minutes to take effect down in Gardiner."

"Okay. If that's the case, I doubt if any container full of toxin could get past there."

Herb said, "You're right. But you're already two miles in."

The captain said, "You sent two guys ahead. So why don't you send Lanphear to circle back to the entrance and see if you missed something."

"Roger that. I'll check back in thirty minutes." The light bounced off the curved ceiling of the aqueduct when he turned around. He surfaced briefly. The smell in the aqueduct was stale like a huge pile of seriously moldy towels. After blowing the air out of his nose he seated his breathing tube back over his face and swam to the tunnel entrance.

Lacking big city lights, the stars overhead provided a cloudless celestial blanket in patterns of showy display across the sky. If there was no crisis, the black moonless sky would offer an aura of spectacular heavenly peace. But tonight, the DEP had set up a battery of floodlights in two parallel lines along the road over the dam and the bridge over the Ashokan. DEP officers walked along the shore with little else to do. The action was completely underground in the aqueduct, and everything depended on the Navy SEALs. Each officer was no doubt thinking of his family, and how close to the Ashokan and the Esopus they all lived. How long could the Gardiner valves last? Would the entire Catskill region be flooded when the water in the Schoharie was released, or worse, if the dam broke? Under strict vows of security silence, could they still get their families out on time? And what about an evacuation of the residents spread in small hamlets across the valleys between the mountains? The sparkling stars across a deep cosmic sky belied the threat that hung over the mountains like an ominous monster just beginning to wake up.

Herb Rose and Commissioner Calloway huddled together to talk through the possibilities and ramifications. No one seemed to know who was in charge yet—the DEP, Homeland Security, or the NYPD terrorist response team? There would be a difference in methods and priorities, depending on who was in command. It was DEP territory. They would be more sensitive to the residents in the mountains. NYPD would concentrate on priorities of New York City first. And Homeland Security would be hell bent to capture the terrorists and protect the United States of America. All were critical.

Commissioner Calloway seemed to be the highest-ranking official present. He took charge and assigned the DEP to prepare for an evacuation of people who lived in the lowlands along the Esopus valley and along the edge of the reservoirs in case the floodgates at the Schoharie and Ashokan reservoirs needed to be opened.

The DEP launched their motorboats to search the opposite shore of the Ashokan. The NYPD team began an investigation to find the terrorists, canvassing the immediate area with the DEP to search every house, trailer, cabin, and campsite within five miles of the south shore of the Ashokan. A fleet of drones was launched to canvas two thousand square miles of mountain territory in the Catskills.

The Homeland Security team was small at first and argued for authority with the commissioner. Their technicians set up a satellite transmitter to Washington for enhanced communication from officers' phones, radios, and the drones. The mountains had always been a problem for cellphone reception, leaving dead zones in valleys and low lying areas, much to the frustration of residents. Some locals fought the idea of additional cell towers, convinced that it would cause a flood of flatlanders migrating to the newly communication-rich mountains, ruining the rural character of the area. But no matter who voiced an opinion the temporary transmitter was a welcome necessity in a crisis and would be much needed in the coming days.

It was close to six in the morning, and the predawn sky glowed with the first signs of daylight. There was seldom a sunrise or sunset in the mountains because the sun disappeared behind the highest slope long before it merged with the horizon. But the bank of storm clouds stretching diagonally to the southeast reflected salmon and amber colors that would normally exude waves of hope and optimism. Today could only be a false reading of such a beautiful dawn.

Hours later the radio came alive again. Meyers' voice sounded tired and frustrated. "Captain, they've been through the entire aqueduct all the way to Gardiner. There is nothing they could find. The water tests clear and pure all the way through. And there is no sign of a container bigger than a fisherman's bobber. The men need a rest, and they're getting very cold, sir. I'm sorry."

The commissioner came on the line. "You've earned a break. We'll have to send you back down again, but we've got to discuss some alternatives first."

The captain said, "Return to base, Meyers."

"Ten-four, captain." The divers swam the last hundred yards back to the open waters of the Ashokan. After securing the filter entrance hatch, Meyers turned to signal the others. His floodlight illuminated a small stream of bubbles coming from the reservoir bottom, deeper than the entrance to the aqueduct tunnel. He swam towards whatever was leaking air. His light revealed the obvious. Two metal containers the size of ten-gallon drums lay on the bottom in the mud. He immediately radioed to the shore group standing less than thirty feet above him.

"Captain, I found something. There are two cylinder-shaped canisters on the bottom. They're both leaking air bubbles."

"That's got to be it. But why did you miss it before?"

"We were looking inside the aqueduct and the water was too murky to see down to the bottom. We'll bring them up immediately." He signaled to the others to help lift them. They struggled under the weight as it got heavier near the surface, but by then two other officers had jumped into the water to help secure them with ropes attached to a winch on the boat trailer parked on the dam.

Herb was excited. In his gut, he knew they had recovered the toxin containers. It now made sense that they had sunk as dead weight after the explosion and never entered the aqueduct. The shore crew struggled to pull up the canisters. A munitions specialist examined them carefully, popping off a pressure lid from the flat end of the canister. Inside, a timing device would blow the lid off the canister on command, and the toxin would dissolve quickly in the water. After deactivating the charge and removing a small radio transmitter the contents were revealed. Two men with HAZMAT suits examined the contents and tested the white powder inside.

"Sir, there's no doubt. It's another batch of omnibotulism powder, probably about fifty pounds in each canister. One could be activated at any time, but there was a double timer, the second one automatically set seven days ahead at eleven minutes after nine. I guess that's about when they could be sure it had arrived in the City."

Herb said, "Nine-eleven, again. Bastards! They used a much more sophisticated delivery method this time."

The commissioner agreed. "If the canisters had entered the aqueduct without a sighting of the toy boat we might never have detected this until it was too late."

Corporal Meyers said, "The important thing is that we *did* detect it and we stopped it. Before it reached its target."

"But how can we be sure there were only two canisters?" Herb said.

"We'll go back down. If the first two didn't make it in the tunnel, I doubt if any others could," said Meyers.

Herb said, "I doubt if that barge could have hauled more than a hundred pounds. You're sure there was only one toy boat?"

"Yes sir, we had more than a few eyes on that thing, and the drone sent photos. There was only one boat."

"You'd better be sure. Looks like the critical time is looming."

"Yes, sir. Going back down immediately, sir."

The commissioner seemed satisfied after the divers checked the bottom of the reservoir in a thousand-foot perimeter around the aqueduct entrance. The Catskill system would remain off-line for a few days to make sure there were no more canisters discovered.

But only the terrorists knew when they'd push the button.

****

Fateen beamed with satisfaction after hearing from Michael. Two reservoirs had been attacked, and only Americans were implicated. No one had a clue that there was a new organization behind it all, a new group that would prove more threatening and far more lethal than anything before it on U.S. soil. America hadn't seen anything yet.

Chapter 30

The WaterForce Angels

Just when I was worried that they wouldn't take us seriously, the Commissioner called. I was so excited I nearly spilled my coffee. He didn't waste words. "Titus, how soon can you be fully mobilized?"

"We can totally be ready and in place in less than six hours. All I have to do is activate the telephone and e-mail networks. We'll have twelve-man patrols on each of the large reservoirs, and a six-man patrol at the smaller locations."

"And which ones do you see as large and small?"

"The Cannonsville, Pepacton, Schoharie, Rondout, and Ashokan are classified as 'large,' and the rest will have smaller patrols, each with a Guardian Angel or a DEP officer along with us."

"Can you cover the Esopus River basin as well?"

"I hope so, Sir. I'm not sure how many guys we can add on short notice, but I'm sure we can cover the Esopus and all the Catskill reservoirs by tomorrow or the next day."

"That's terrific. And how many volunteers do you have?"

"About a hundred signed up, but not all have signed the papers, and been cleared through the background check."

"Surely you haven't had time to vet them all through security yet…"

"No sir, there's no time to check all of them now, but I'll try to speed up the process, Sir. We're honored to be of help."

"Good. And Titus, we've got to keep this as quiet as possible."

"Yes, Sir, I'll do my best to keep it all confidential." I knew that would be next to impossible, so I finished the call in short order. "I've got your number, Sir. I'll phone in a report in a few hours. Thank you, Sir, for your trust, and the opportunity to help."

When the connection went dead, I busied myself putting the team on high alert, which would mobilize the WaterForce Angels to patrol every reservoir in the Catskill and Delaware watersheds. The DEP would cover the dams and aqueducts from land, but WaterForce Angel eyes would be employed along the shores and along the major rivers and passages connecting the reservoirs above ground. Each patrol would cruise along the shoreline in canoes and kayaks, take photos of anything they found that was the slightest bit suspect, and report anyone or anything they found near the water.

Dad already knew about the mobilization, but I called Parker with the news. Parker had his own plan of action to mobilize down the City, working with the NYPD and the DEP. WaterForce volunteers would gather water samples directly from taps at more than two hundred locations in all five boroughs, and deliver them to testing locations throughout the city, a redundant system that would verify the automatic sensors already installed in the pipelines. WaterForce would be activated from Delaware County all the way to Staten Island!

At noon, I got a call from one of my biggest patrols. "Titus, this is Frankie, Patrol number four on the Ashokan. We're on the south shore. There's some kind of device at the bottom of a sycamore tree, all smashed to pieces. Looks like a standard TV remote control, I think. It hasn't been here very long. It's too clean—"

I said, "Maybe it was the remote that caused the boat to explode. Take lots of photos and flag the spots where the pieces were found. Then bag it and bring it back to base at the barracks. Don't touch it with your fingers. This could be really important."

Someone else joined the call. "Hey Ti, this is George Paterson. I found some tracks along the shoreline. Probably mucking boots, from someone who waded into the water near where we found the remote."

I said, "The DEP sergeant will know how to plaster-cast a footprint."

"Yeah, he's doing it now. There are several good prints. We think there was only one person, but it's the perfect location to launch a remotely controlled boat."

"Roger that. Let me know what else you find." Titus no sooner put the phone back in its cradle than his cell phone rang with another report.

"Titus, Joey Ashton Junior, reporting in from the Pepacton. Patrol twenty-two, with shit to report, y'know?"

"Like, go ahead, dude-bro."

"We've found a couple of hunting blinds on the south shore. No real evidence of bombs or anything, but they need to be removed. Like, it's illegal to hunt that close to the water." At fourteen, Joey was the youngest WaterForce Angel. At his age, he was so excited to be involved in a real operation, but he sounded more like it was a paintball game between friends. He was so official and stern, but very teenage "cute."

"That's fetch, Joey. Take pictures, and mark down the coordinates from your GPS."

"Done already, bossman. There's more. My squad found like basic kayaks moored on overhanging branches, stuck in the ice, like covered with camouflage material. Suspicious fishing gear."

"Fishing gear, suspicious? Probably nothing. It's still much too early for fishing yet. But record its twenty."

"We're looking at other boats. There's a mess of them on the shores. Can't get our kayaks out yet, but there's some open water." I could sense his pride and sense of duty. He'd make a good cop, like my dad, someday.

"That only means the enemy can't get across the water either," I said.

I was beginning to enjoy this new role. It was more fun than any video game, even though I didn't get the pleasure of simulated battle on the screen. This was much more exciting and gave us all an incredible feeling of something Dad called "civic responsibility," something none of us had ever been a part of. To us, it unified our mountain pride with the power of collective protection of...oh my god! We were doing this to protect our beloved watersheds, but we were also doing it to protect the City! I never thought I would feel like this. Proud to help, energized in an action that tied us to the City in the exact opposite way we had all complained about for so many years. Could this be the thing that bound us together instead of tore us apart? I was amazed at myself, like I'd awakened a strange hidden feeling inside. Parker knew about this already, living down the city. But suddenly I felt something that New Yorkers perhaps had not let loose since nine-eleven in 2001. Widespread unity. Intense patriotism. Combined anger. Group motivation. Personal adventure. Protection for all Americans. I had to admit—it was way off the charts.

Later I drove down Route 28 and turned off to meet my team on the Rondout. They were vastly understaffed for the size reservoir they patrolled, with two volunteers waiting for others to join them. I thought maybe they could use my help for a few hours, since they had only been able to cover part of the area, and the Rondout was a key strategic component of the Delaware system, where two major tunnels entered at the northwest end, and an 82-mile underground aqueduct exited at the southeast end. When I arrived, Scooter Wilson waved at me from a kayak a few hundred yards from the shore. His girl Marlene—we called her Gnarly Marley—peered through a large pair of binoculars from the shore.

Gnarly Marley turned to me. "I'm so glad you're here. We're just about wasted, and we're still shorthanded. Some of the neighbors are helping us by walking the shore, but it's too big to cover it all very well."

"Why don't you call Scooter in, maybe go chill for a few hours. I'm transferring some of the team from the Hillview down in Westchester. They should be here in an hour. Meanwhile, I'll take a kayak out and cover you while you take a break."

"No argument there. I'm whipped. I could use a chill." She signaled to Scooter and sat on a rock on the shore to wait for him. What a woman.

I called Timmy, who manned the computer and the phone-bank back in Margaretville. He would be able to call more volunteers for the second twelve-hour shift and help fill in the gaps. By tomorrow, maybe we'd have enough volunteers to support three eight-hour shifts. But for now, it was all we could do to try to cover a vast amount of territory on the five big reservoirs and numerous tributaries in the mountains, over six hundred miles of shoreline spread over three thousand square miles.

****

"Be careful. You're alone out there. You probably can't do this alone," said Gnarly Marley as they left.

I realized I was about to violate one of the basic rules of the WaterForce Angels: never patrol alone, always take a buddy along. But I *was* alone, with no one to notice, but I had never kayaked on a reservoir before. A few minutes later, I was paddling silently across the water, avoiding small icebergs still melting. My kayak sliced across the reservoir smoothly. It was a profoundly serene experience, almost Zen-like, that made me enjoy my assignment. I wondered how, in their infinite wisdom, could the DEP have denied this peaceful god-like pleasure to local people for almost sixty years, when they finally opened the waters to motorless boats. I looked up into the cerulean sky, and took a deep breath of pure unsullied air, and drifted my eyes reverently to the mountaintops surrounding me. This was the indescribable joy of life in the Catskills.

The automatic motions of paddling across glass-smooth water had made me almost forget my task. Scolding myself, my eyes returned to the shore on both sides. There were more trees and marshy water plants along one shore than the other. I paddled closer so I could make a thorough inspection.

The late afternoon sun was sending bright reflections back to my eyes as I glided through the weeds near the shore. I followed a path of water plants that looked a little disturbed, like some were broken or bent over. They were thickest near the shore, and nearly blocked a clear vision of the water. Suddenly the abrupt collision with something very hard stopped my kayak cold, and nearly knocked me overboard as the shock tipped my boat to one side. My paddle flew out of my hands when I grabbed onto a dead cattail, and I had to pull on the thick rooted stem to steady the kayak until I could get it upright and stable. My backpack slid across the floor, tipped over, and threw my cell phone skidding towards the wet puddle in the bottom of the boat. Still unsteady, I lurched forward barely in time to save the phone before it splashed into permanent disconnection.

My floppy fishing hat fell off in the water, the hat I'd filled with my collection of Mom's totally hoppin' political buttons since I was ten. I hadn't seen much of my mother since the divorce, but I knew that she was a close friend of Bonnie Guarini, and they had shared political beliefs through the years. That hat was like a history of Mom. My prized collector's headpiece floated away from the boat as I mentally bombed into space, and I watched it sink from the weight of fifteen prized collectibles into the shallow water. Buttons declaring Mom's allegiance to liberals of the past included *LBJ All the Way, Womens' Equality, Trusty Muskie, McCain=Bush, 2009-End of an Error, Dogs Against Romney, Got Romnesia-A Preexisting Condition, Dump Trump* and other classics.

The paddle floated farther out, now nearly fifteen feet from my kayak. I was destined to get wet. If Parker had been there, he would be totally mortified by my clumsy blunder. As it was, I embarrassed myself even though I was alone, and I was totally pissed at my blatant blunder.

It's not easy to get out of a kayak in the water without capsizing the damn thing. Somehow, I managed, and found myself in three feet of shallow water, my boots mired in thick black muck at the bottom. My wallet was already wet, so I had nothing to lose by swimming out to rescue my prized button collection. The water was frigid and below forty degrees, and I knew I couldn't stay there very long. But I had to get my hat.

After a cold swim back to the kayak, I used the paddle to search the bottom for my prized hat. No luck after several long swipes along the bottom. When I reached the bow of the kayak, I suddenly saw what had caused my embarrassing spill. A small rowboat, no more than five feet long, was tied to an overhanging branch, and I had broadsided it so hard that the disaster hit me like a series of shaking dominoes. I grabbed my bowline and tied the kayak to the rowboat. Fortunately, my camera was safe in my backpack, and I was able to get some photos after I hauled my salty-ass out of the water—without my awesome hat, damn it.

I was so cold and wet I thought that hypothermia would soon set in, even though I was sitting safely on shore. I stripped off my wet clothes, down to my boxers, and let the afternoon sun warm my bare skin while I wrung the water out of my clothes. I'd have given anything for a blanket or a warm fire, a dry pair of jeans, a sweatshirt, or even some dirty but dry socks. Since I let Scooter and Gnarly Marley take a break, I was without help. There were a couple of houses across the road next to the reservoir, but with my luck, they'd all be weekenders from the City, locked up tight with nobody home right now. What a dummy I was to break the partner rule! All I could do was shiver from the cold and work up the courage to squeeze into my damp threads again. I tried to wring more water out of them before I had to endure the cold cloth on my skin.

And then I saw it. A black felt beret lay wadded up under the single bench of the rowboat. I stared at it for a whole minute until I realized why it looked so familiar. A streak of red paint was splattered across the top and front of it in a random pattern. I'd seen that before, in person, and on the front page of the *New York Times* in a photo from Woodstock. I took some close-up photos to record the evidence. In search of my own treasured hat, instead I'd found Anthony's hat, in Anthony's boat. I was amped because I knew exactly what he had been doing.

I called Bonnie first with the news. It was evidence, and I was violating any reasonable police protocol by calling her first. But didn't Anthony's mother deserve to know? But she was anything but grateful.

"I simply don't believe it," she snapped. "That could be anyone's hat, even with paint on it. Anthony wouldn't be involved in terrorism! You're wrong, Titus. Absolutely, dead wrong. And your Watershed *Devils*—whatever! I'll get you for this, in ways you'll never see coming."

"Bonnie, I just wanted to let you know that Anthony might be involved in something. I called you before I turned this evidence in to the—"

"The *police?* You can go screw yourself."

"Yeah well, just stay in your lane, Bonnie."

So much for support from Woodstock. I was beginning to understand why people called her a self-centered evil old witch.

Chapter 31

The Rondout

I warmed up at home after a hot bath and a big cup of hot Kentucky bourbon, laced with a small shot of Tension-Tamers tea. Dad got a call a little after two in the morning. I crept down the hall and listened from outside his room. From the first words, I knew something was terribly wrong. Dad put the phone on speaker while he searched for his clothes, and I heard both sides of the conversation. "Officer Rose, sorry to bother you."

"That's okay. I've already heard about the boat Titus found, with Anthony's hat."

"Yes Sir. But there's something new. We've had trespassers at the Rondout southeast intake building."

"Go ahead."

"An infrared detector alerted us to a trespasser. Both camera systems showed a human image in the secured area, but it was compromised soon after the alarm."

"You couldn't see faces?" Dad asked. I could hear him pacing the room. I was afraid he'd open the bedroom door and discover me eavesdropping.

"Actually, sir, the video cams were redirected towards the ground by the intruder, and, as you know, infrared images cannot identify facial features, only a heat record of two possibly male figures after we lost the video."

"What about the drone?"

"Too many trees. Blocked from the air."

"Damn! So, what happened? Did you get there in time?"

"No sir, unfortunately, we didn't. It was probably an hour before we realized at the Ashokan barracks that something was wrong." The reception crackled as he seemed to panic and talk louder.

"Damn. So, what happened? Did they get inside?" Dad stomped around the room.

"Unfortunately, yes. They blew the door off the building and had about an hour to mess with the pumps. They shut off the main valve, set some explosive charges on the computer system, and left just before we got there. We've got a demolition team on site now to diffuse the charges, and there are four cars patrolling the area. No trace of the intruders, sir."

"And why in the hell is that? How the hell could you NOT catch them at the beginning of their visit? It isn't THAT far from the barracks to the Rondout. Where was the twenty-four hour watch I ordered after Anthony Guarini's rowboat was recovered?"

"Sir, there was an explosion across the reservoir, and the patrol car responded because he was the closest to it. Turns out, it was just a cherry bomb. A red herring. We found the remnants," the officer admitted.

"And he couldn't figure out it was a damn decoy?"

"He didn't realize—

"— set off to draw his attention away from his main job? JEE-SUS KEE-RIST!" Dad yelled.

"I'm sorry, Sir," he said in a very small voice.

Something was familiar about this, and I didn't like the feeling that was creeping into my head like a horrible nightmare. I felt like some sort of weird voyeur, invisible and not allowed to speak, but seething with paranoia out in the hall.

"And you sent four cars out chasing cherry bombs, and found nothing?"

"No sir, not yet."

"Did you send a patrol boat out on the water after Titus found the boat with Anthony Guarini's hat?"

"No, sir. But the DEP boat is on the way from the Ashokan. We don't keep one on the Rondout twenty-four-seven."

I could hear Dad fiddling with his belt, and the clunk of shoes being dropped as he one-handed them onto his feet. "Well, maybe we should. Damn it! If they'd fund us properly, maybe we could get our goddam jobs done right."

"I'm glad you mentioned that, Sir."

"We've got cameras, infrared, drones, and motion detectors all over the place. And those Stanford devices! Titus Rose found solid evidence, and you've ignored it. How could you let this happen?" There he was again, accusing people. Sometimes Dad had the diplomacy of a gorilla with a toothache.

"I don't know, sir. It's a stormy night, and the power went out for a while. We've got all available vehicles out patrolling a wide area around the perimeter. We're doing everything we can. We do know they drove a four-wheeler—an old Jeep—it was on the infrared. But they disappeared very quickly. We think they might be off-road, maybe even nearby. But there are hundreds of long windy driveways that could make a vehicle disappear quickly." The officer's explanation sounded like a weak rationalization, even to me.

"Did you call the bomb squad?"

"Well sir, Officer Rhinehardt has training in IEDs in Afghanistan. He disarmed the C-4 at the site. Rhinhardt said the rig was very professional, probably military style."

"How much exactly?"

"Enough to blow the door off the bunker, and another two pounds of C-4 in place at critical places inside the pump house, waiting for a signal to detonate. We got it disarmed."

"Well, I'll be damned if I'm gonna scare all of New York City just for an incident we were able to catch and diffuse." I could hear the clunk of his shoes pacing the room.

"You're right, Herb."

"Thanks for the call. Sorry about my bad temper. You did the best you could. I'll be down there in about an hour. I've got to call New York, report this immediately." Dad hung up the phone and dialed Commissioner Calloway at his home in Manhattan. Standing there on the other side of his bedroom door, I realized how weird it felt to be in the middle of a terrorist attack, but still be stuck where I wasn't supposed to know anything and couldn't do shit about it. I'm not sure I could have taken the abuse Dad had handed out. At least he thanked me when I found the explosives in the apartment, and Anthony's boat with the paint-streaked hat. But shouldn't that have promoted me to the A-team? I wanted to shake him, and scream into his face, 'Let me into your head. I'm not a damn kid anymore!'

But Dad did what Dad had to do. He explained the security breach to Commissioner Calloway and must have been ready for an explosion of anger. Instead, another surprise seemed to elevate the threat in the Catskills.

Calloway explained, "Herb, it's too late to keep this quiet. Turn on CNN, right now. They're reporting an ultimatum letter from the terrorists. And they're not just domestic. I got the call from the mayor a few moments ago. Apparently, the letter was addressed to the mayor, the governor, the president, the *Times*, and also copied to the

National Enquirer, of all the damn places. It's now a major national security threat. I've talked to Washington and was just about to call you."

"Credible?" Dad was leaning on the other side of the door from where I stood.

"You're damn right. But at least now we've got more to go on."

"But they disarmed the charges already. I hoped we could squash this and keep it out of the press." Herb coughed loudly, and I almost jumped out of my skin. I bumped into the door, and I was lucky Dad didn't hear me.

"Too late to put a lid on it. Don't you see? There's not much time before the alarm will spread in the city." Calloway's voice was rising to a panic pitch.

"I realize that, sir. I'm on my way there now to personally supervise a thorough search. We've already got leads from the Pepacton incident, and we've got evidence of C-4 in the apartment in Margaretville. Do you think they're connected?"

"I don't know. It's two different M-Os. We haven't found Michael Capo or Anthony Guarini yet. But the answer is yes. They're obviously connected."

"Titus found a boat and Anthony's hat hidden in the weeds on the shore of the Rondout, not long before the explosions." Herb walked away from the door. I could hear him fiddling with his keys.

"Yes, and they're raising hell in a lot of different ways."

"You know I'll do the best I can."

The commissioner's voice filled the room. "Doing your best isn't enough. You've got to *win* this one. I'll make some calls, put out a high security alert to all stations in the system. I want every man on duty for this. Red Alert. No excuses. The president is getting impatient. Call me immediately when you find something."

The line went dead before Herb could respond, "Yes, Sir."

I didn't just feel sorry for Dad. I was shaking, wondering if he could take the pressure, and how I could take it...trying to figure out how the WaterForce Angels could help. Somehow, there was a flaw in all this. The charges at the Rondout were in plain sight. Why would anyone go to all that risk, using a method that was sure to be noticed? It had to be *intended* as a warning shot, sure to get into the press at the same time the note arrived. My gut told me it had to be Michael and Anthony. Could Anthony really already be into it this deep? But in spite of his bravado, I couldn't quite believe it, even though I had found his hat splashed with paint. Anthony was careless, impressionable, and impulsive, and sometimes stupid. He could have been duped into this plot, but he wasn't evil. Or was he?

Chapter 32
Press Release

Mr. President, Mr. Governor, Mr. Mayor, The New York Times and The National Enquirer:

The Brotherhood of International Islamic Jihad is responsible for the poisoning of the Pepacton Reservoir with deadly botulism toxin. Two other attacks under the nose of your so-called security at the Ashoken and Rondout Reservoirs were launched within the last twenty-four hours, with more to come. The United States must meet all of our demands, or there will be more attacks throughout the entire New York City water supply. We will bring unprecedented catastrophe and destruction to metropolitan New York. Massive permanent damage will leave several hundred square miles totally without water and unlivable. Twenty million citizens will be without a drop of drinkable water. More will live in fear that their water is polluted and unsafe.

The United States has ISIS, Taliban, al Qaeda, Hezbollah, Boko Haram, Al Shabaab and other Islamic prisoners at Guantanamo Bay, international prisons and on floating Navy brigs. **The United States must release all of our brothers immediately and provide safe air transport to destinations according to our instructions.** The deadline is approaching within days. Your usual arrogant reaction will be to "refuse to give in to terrorism," but if you refuse, YOUR GOVERNMENT *will be responsible for killing your own people and destroying your largest city. Follow our instructions, or New York City will be crippled for decades.*

B.I.I.J — Brotherhood of International Islamic Jihad

****

DEP Commissioner Calloway, NYPD Commissioner O'Riley, Mayor of New York City, the Governor of New York, CIA and FBI Directors, and the President and Vice President of the United States sat in offices in six different locations and connected via secured conference call.

The president asked, "And I'm supposed to be intimidated by the fucking *New York Times'* fake news? Unbelievable! Are we any closer to capturing these guys?"

"Unfortunately, no, Sir," said the Mayor. "We have suspects, but so far the suspects are not foreigners. They are one hundred percent Americans, young men in their twenties."

"So how do we know these kids aren't protesters playing some kind of sick game with the media and the government?" asked the FBI Director.

The CIA Director said, "We have names, but we can't find them. Americans are involved, obviously working for foreign operatives, I'm sad to say. We've got enough evidence to know that this is serious. Between the Pepacton, Ashokan and Rondout incidents and the toxin found in the apartment in Margaretville, there are over two hundred pounds of botulism already discovered. I can't imagine where they gathered up that much. That's one hell of lot of toxin. This is no kid prank." They could hear him expelling the breath of a seasoned smoker.

Commissioner O'Riley said, "Let's not forget the C4 that we now know was stolen from a US military site."

The President was in no mood for this. "But what is the connection? This fake news came from a new Islamic terrorist organization, and you have no idea *who they are*?"

Commissioner Calloway said, "It's not fake, Sir. It looks like they have Americans on board to do their dirty work. Makes it look like a partnership with domestic terrorism, which gets to our citizens in a whole different way. People are angry enough that someone poisoned the water, but now they find out it was Americans working for foreign terrorists. Bottom line, their 'divide and conquer' technique is quite effective to split public opinion and cause a lot of panic."

The president promised, "They're not gonna live another week, believe me!"

The CIA Director said, "This is the first time anyone has claimed to represent a *united* Islamic front. We've never experienced them all screaming with one voice. If it turns out to be credible, this could be the worst threat this country has ever experienced."

"Worse than Iran's nuclear threat and the attacks in Paris?" asked the Vice President.

Commissioner Calloway said, "This one is on our own turf. This could shut down or even destroy our largest city, home of the world's financial center. Home of a major portion of our economy. And twenty million of our citizens. New York could suddenly be wiped out for a long time, without water. No disrespect, Sir, but I can't think of a more critical situation since nine-eleven. This makes suicide bombings look like mosquitos."

The entire conference call spoke up; all participants chorused, "He's right, Mr. President." "Uh huh!" "You got that right, Calloway." "Absolutely!"

The President made his kind of decision. "Gentlemen, this is bad, bad, and *cannot* continue. You do what you have to do to find these guys, and fast. Either we attack or we don't attack!" he said, quoting himself. "But I won't be in a position of bowing to their next ultimatum."

"Police Commissioner O'Riley said, "No disrespect, Mr. President, but this *is* the ultimatum. I don't think the tradeoff is a bad choice, Sir. If we release a few prisoners, our largest city will be saved."

"There's no guarantee of that," said the mayor. "We cannot be intimidated by terrorists, domestic OR foreign!"

"Right, but if we refuse to respond..." said the Secretary of Defense. "I can have planes over those countries within hours."

The VP answered, "That's JUST what we need again. Send planes to start wars in six or eight different countries, while our own homegrown terrorists blow things up at home. Come ON, you guys!"

"We don't even know what countries we're dealing with. What countries do we have prisoners that they want released?" O'Riley asked.

"Iran, Yemen, Somalia, Syria, Sudan, Libya, and others I'm sure," answered the CIA Director, coughing. "They haven't given us details yet. I say kill them before they have a chance to take their next breath," he said, straining what might be close to his own last breath.

"They've clearly demonstrated they have the knowledge and the capabilities to destroy the water system," said Calloway. "They've shown they can be a step ahead of us. And the system has many vulnerable points. They've hit three reservoirs already."

"Damn it! How could this have happened? We have so many safeguards in place." asked the Secretary of Homeland Security.

The President pounded his desk. "You mean, how could YOU have let this happen!? This is bad, bad, very bad. Stupid moron losers!"

Homeland said, "We've done everything to prevent it..."

Calloway interrupted, "You're right. We have infrared cameras, video surveillance, Stanford sensors, drones, a trained DEP security force on the reservoirs, and redundant systems throughout the entire water supply. We have discussed this many times. But, somehow, it isn't enough to combat a well-informed enemy, an enemy who may even have inside information, for all we know."

"WHAT inside information?" demanded the President in a voice louder than he intended. "I'M the only one that needs 'inside information.' These are very, very, bad dudes! Believe me!"

"There must be vulnerabilities through inside sources, or they made deductions from sources in our free-market, information society."

"I can have planes over those countries within hours," repeated the Secretary of Defense, coughing into his elbow. "Actually, within one hour. Just say the..."

"Oh, for Christ sake, let's not start World War III," said the Mayor.

The President was adamant. "I don't care how you think this leaked, or how they got a hold of our balls. I want it stopped, immediately. My promise is to Make America Great Again, not to give in to a bunch of snot nosed losers and an unknown enemy. I'm giving you forty-eight hours to get tough before I kick some ass."

"You're right, Mr. President, Sir! By God, I'd blow them all out of the water! The nerve!" Answered the Secretary of Defense.

The President stopped the escalation. "Shut the hell up, *all of you*! You are out of control and have NO common sense! These are bad, bad dudes—losers— and I'M the only one who can do this! We've GOT to protect our people first and get a plan to win for a goddam change. I want the National Guard out to protect the Croton in Westchester and the Catskill/Delaware systems. New York, Connecticut, New Jersey—all code red. I want every man you've got on this. Damn morons!" The slam of his fist on the solid cherry desk was loud enough to melt eardrums.

The FBI Director was the only one who dared to speak up. "Sir, it is likely that their attack strategy is already in place. The incidents were just warning shots, shots across the bow, if you will, for publicity, so we'd know they *could* do it, timed with a news release that we couldn't cover up. Of course, we have to take this seriously, but I think we can find a strategy that won't cause panic and won't escalate this into an international crisis. And sending the Guard out won't be effec—"

"The Guard is ready to report to stations all over the—"

"*DON'T* TELL ME HOW TO BE COMMANDER-IN-CHIEF! Mobilize the Guard immediately! Get every man on duty and every drone in the air. Hopefully, we HAVE forty-eight goddam hours before we lose New York! DAMN it. BELIEVE ME! This is *MY* NAME! CATCH the bastards. Make

Me...Make AMERICA White Ag—uh—*Great* Again. GET ON THIS—or you're all *FIRED!*"

The solid cherry desk sounded like it split open when the phone slammed onto it. The President's line fizzled out, but the conference call continued for two more hours while they debated a workable strategy that the alpha dog might accept.

Later, the President's tweet made it clear what he thought of the press release.

<I'm not going to tolerate these loser ragheads thumping their Qurans for one more minute. If these Johnny Jihads think they can intimidate Americans, they'd better be ready for a real war. Believe me. It will be huge!>

Chapter 33

Panic in the City

I finally reached Parker on his cell phone. He was dancing without a care in some dance club, half looped, and totally oblivious to the imminent threat facing the Catskills, New York City, and probably...the world. The music was deafening, drowning out our cell phone conversation.

"Parker! We've got to talk."

"Can't hear you. I'm danshin wit Tina. She's so hot!"

"I can tell. So how could you answer the phone if you can't hear?"

"...What?" The pulsating drone of house music seemed to control his mind. "Are you *there?* Ha Ha!"

I heard the phone crash on the floor when he dropped it, and loud crunch as if someone stepped on it. When he returned, the reception was still loud, but now it was loud *and* full of static. "Where *are* you?" This was not going to be easy.

"I'm at *Cielo* on Twelfth. Takin' four hours off. Totally aweshome!" Parker crowed.

"*Cielo!* Damn! Any famous people there?

"Yup. It's not every day you get to see Dom Diablo AND Afrojack."

"You're smashed, Dude!"

"Just a little mixture of elixshir. Ha! Get it?"

"Aw, man! Just when we need you!" How was I going to reach his pea-sized little brain? "CHRIST NEW YORK,

Parker! I have important news. About the water supply, el jerk-off!"

"Okay, okay. So. I'll go outside. I got a hand-shtamp—they'll have to letch me back in." After a minute, I heard a dull rustling and the music got a little less strident. And then, nothing. The call was cut off.

Outside, a young man shadowed Parker when he staggered outside. He lit a cigarette and leaned against the wall within earshot of Parker. He gloated at the progress the chaos was making in the world around him. This was an excellent chance to find out if Parker suspected the truth. When I called back, I got his message. All I could do was wait, and hope he remembered he was talking to his brother when he pocket-killed the call.

I knew a lot more than I could let on according to the rules, but I had to tell him how I'd listened in on the conversation between the commissioner and Dad, and Calloway's mobilization call after the President's meeting, Parker was the point man for WaterForce in the City. Shouting into the phone, now he was almost useless. Soon the City would be in a huge panic. I waited ten minutes before he called back as if *he* had news.

"Something's going on, Titus! There are all these air sirens going off," Parker said. "And cops and fire trucks rushing around everywhere. What the hell?"

"Ah! Earth to Parker! You *are* alert. A radical Islamic group has taken claim for the botulism poisoning. They're going to attack the water supply, in fact, shut it completely down for ten years, they say, unless the U.S. releases all the Islamic prisoners in Guantanamo and a bunch of prison brigs."

"Oh, my god! You know, Dude, I'm kinda shaky..."

"Bro, you've *got* to get your shit together. Get some coffee, or a Red Bull. Make it a six-pack. This is already in the *Times* and the *Enquirer.* Let me talk to Tina."

"She's not too well at the moment. I'll call the Angels. They'll be mobilizing, probably watching the key points at the Kensico, and Shentral Parch." I heard a loud belch when he held the phone away from his head. My confidence was waning. "And they might need help if there is mash panic, or traffic at the britches and tunnels. We have a plan...I know we do."

Keep it simple, I reminded myself. "Parker, you need to have your guys test the water every two hours and leave all the rest to the police and fire. THAT was the plan..."

"Okay. But you should see this. I was just inside a supermarket. There are people carrying cases of water out of the shtore. And beer, wine, drinks, energy drinks. You should see this. And you wouldn't believe the exit out of New York. I'm on Sheventh Avenue now, and there are southbound cars backed all the way up to Fourteenth Street in line for the tunnel."

"Panic already. You'd better stock up a little for yourself."

Parker said, "We've got to get over to Tina's house and warn her friends."

"What? Jesus, Parker, do you even *know* where you are?"

There was a pause while he found a brain cell. "Twelfth Shtreet I think. I'm just a little bent."

"Right! It's a *little* hard to be a *little* pregnant, too. Why this, of all days?"

"Last I checked, a woman can't be a *little* preggers," he said with an inebriated laugh. "But I can be totally bent."

"Damn. Send the boy to the big city, and what happens?" But really, how could I fault my big brother for a little fun out on the town? It's just...it was the worst timing.

"Parker, get a grip. Go mobilize the troops. *Be* a leader. This is the real deal!"

****

Parker felt like a stumble-fuck as useless as a pair of rollerblades on a gravel road. He could see the threat was imminent. People were scurrying about on Seventh Avenue, some carrying groceries, others with backpacks and overnight bags, hustling to pass slower pedestrians on the sidewalk. An army jeep led a convoy of trucks on a cross-town street, and police cars in full cherry-top mode struggled past the traffic jam. The Empire State Building, usually in a celebratory color to honor a different group nearly every day, was lit in bright red, and blinking on and off to warn New Yorkers of the impending city-wide emergency. News trucks mobilized for panic scurried from one location to the next, and drones competed with helicopters for command of the airways overhead.

Parker was battling a heavy dose of remorse for his indiscretion and hoped he could make up for lost time. He called his WaterForce captains from his cell phone. Most of them had already heard the news broadcast and phoned their teammates while waiting for Parker's leadership. He sobered up fast after downing three Red Bulls, two large black coffees, and a half package of double chocolate Oreos he bought after standing in a long line at a midnight deli. He made each call into a chain call, assigning each captain to call five others on the list in order to spread the word as fast as possible. He felt guilty, but a little more sober after the caffeine jolt.

"Hugh, this is Parker Rose, from WaterForce. This is a red alert, just like we talked about. Code word is "flagrant." The water supply is under a bomb threat and possibly more toxin poisonings. If you turn on the TV, you'll see the letter sent by the Islamic terrorists, and the President's response. Captains, please call your teams, and also call the next five people after your name on the list and repeat this information. We'll need water samples from your testing devices every two hours for at least the next forty-eight hours, with results phoned in to the DEP number on your contact list. Report to your emergency locations immediately, and help the authorities to maintain order, direct traffic, and do whatever else you can to assist. Please remember, we are NOT policemen. Please call nine-one-one rather than get involved in violence. Call the police and call me on my cell if there is any suspected terrorist action. This is Parker Rose. Good luck, Angels. Code word 'flagrant.' This is our ultimate test."

****

Captain José Hernandez stood at a window overlooking Lexington Avenue at the Sixty-Ninth Regiment National Guard Armory. His Lieutenants would soon be arriving along with their companies ready for deployment to various locations in Manhattan and parts of the boroughs of Brooklyn, Bronx, Queens and Staten Island. A famous Beaux Arts landmark, the Armory had been home of the New York Knicks until they moved to New Jersey in 1967. More recently, the Armory was the center of post nine-eleven counseling for victims' families for the past eighteen years. The old building was mostly ceremonial now, and the troops would generally be assembled at the armories in Brooklyn and Jamaica to cover the five boroughs, and upstate in the cities of New Windsor, Utica and Amsterdam to cover the reservoirs.

Captain Hernandez was perturbed that it was taking so long to call the men to duty. How could the WaterForce and Guardian Angel volunteers get their act together in a matter of hours when the country's National Guard needed most of a full twenty-four? Should the public compare the two, there would be embarrassing moments for him on the news. His challenge was to man seventy-two locations throughout the five boroughs, be on strict orders to stop and search any suspicious persons, and to guard the water supply with red-alert instructions. And he wasn't even sure this would be effective. Should people be exiting the city, or holding fast with bottled water and bathtubs full of water? It seemed that panic was already spreading. He needed someone higher up to make this call.

Chapter 34

Gardiner Junction

Michael and Anthony bumped along in the old four-wheel-drive jeep, both apprehensive about the task ahead. "I'm told this is the most important target so far. If we nail it, both mountain systems will be shut down, and New York will be thirsty for a long fucking time."

"I am so ready. I can't wait to scale that building," Anthony said.

"This will be easier than the stone cliff you practiced on."

At the end of a long gravel road with a twenty-degree incline, a series of gates and barbed wire fences seemed to grow like weeds every five hundred feet. A concrete bunker rose up over the tree line in the middle of a dense forest. Had the public been aware of it, the edifice would be seen as a grand architectural icon of the triumph and power of the New York City Water System. Although it was a public project widely covered in the media, its location was hidden from view and closely guarded by a series of redundant security systems. Such was the importance of the new junction.

The Catskill and Delaware aqueducts were designed to cross over each other near Gardiner, the former supplying forty percent and the latter fifty per cent of the total daily water consumption of New York City. Until the completion of the merger between the two systems, one aqueduct passed only a few dozen yards below the other, but the two may as well have been a hundred miles apart. Engineers envisioned a vertical connection between the two huge aqueducts when they built the Delaware system in the 1940s. The two were connected by an underground system of valves, pipes, and pumps that allowed the DEP to shut off one entire aqueduct in order to inspect, clean or repair its components. Meanwhile, the other aqueduct would take on double duty for the short duration of the shutdown. At a cost of over twenty-one million, the new connection provided great flexibility and yet another safeguard to New York's water supply.

Michael cut off the jeep lights, pulled off the gravel road, and bushwhacked over thick undergrowth of poison snakeberry bushes and small saplings until they were hidden well in the forest. They climbed over each security fence far from the road, so they wouldn't be noticed by unknown sentries.

Anthony used a long pole to redirect security cameras towards the ground and disabled an infrared camera on a telephone pole by disconnecting the wires at the junction box. In the back of his mind, his thought was *this is it, this is exciting, this is cool.* But his conscience was beginning to interfere. That little voice inside again…

After crawling more than five hundred yards past several fences, they unpacked a duffel bag and prepared for the assault. Michael fired a 22-caliber rifle with a rope and climbing harness up to the roof, which towered over the top of the nearest oak tree. Anthony expertly scaled the rope, and soon disappeared over the top ledge onto the roof. Two blinks from his red LED laser pen signaled his safe arrival to Michael on the ground. He hauled up the canvas bag with cordless drills and saws and dropped the rope and grappling hook to the ground. In minutes, he cut through the ventilation door on top of the roof, entered the building and dropped to the floor. Meanwhile, Michael packed up the rope, and waited for spider-man Anthony to disable the security alarm and open the front door at ground level.

A miner's light strapped to his head was the illumination of choice and provided a blinding glare to unseen cameras that would disguise his face even if he stared directly into a lens. Soon he ran across a night guard who turned in surprise and tried to pull a gun. But Anthony was ready. He quickly maced the guard with pepper spray and tied him securely to an eight-inch vertical pipe in the hallway. Another DEP officer in the guardroom was sitting behind a desk facing a wall full of monitors. In a split second, Spider-Man threw a burlap sack over his head and secured his wrists and ankles with nylon bands. The two guards were injected with a potent drug to keep them sleeping for several hours.

He texted Michael, *I'm in. 2 guards down. Be at front door in a sec.* But he had to stop for a minute to get over the shakes. He realized how deep he was into this, far beyond what he'd anticipated. He knew he couldn't show fear to Michael. But he'd just attacked and disabled two cops. It was too late to get out of this. He had to get a grip. *Shut the hell up, voice!*

He trashed the security alarm and opened the front door to let his partner in. Soon they descended by elevator to the switching system a hundred feet below the surface. A chain of C-4 explosives was set into various crevices. The clay-like C-4 modules easily molded to the equipment, as if they were just another bumpy component in the complex system. Blasting caps and small micro wires served as detonators, attached with care to avoid an early explosion. Long-range telephone receivers with remote electronic relays were hidden along the way. Wires and C-4 module were carefully disguised or hidden, but they worked fast. It was obvious they had practiced the procedures many times. Anthony's hands trembled. His mother's warning came back to him, and the voice of retreat started sending messages to his conscience. But he had to go on. It was now a matter of sheer masculine pride and guile. Michael didn't seem shaken, so why should he?

Two more pumping systems received the same treatment on different sub-basement levels. On the opposite wall on each level, the entire system was duplicated, but this time wired together with a series of redundant micro radio transmitters, each one capable of setting off the second set of C-4 charges. Redundancy would increase the margin of success.

With military precision, the two men finished in less than two and a half hours. Anthony untied the sleeping guards. It would still be several hours before they woke up.

After reconnecting the security alarm, Anthony said, "Let's get out of here. Mission accomplished

But Michael had one more thing to do. "You go ahead and focus the security cameras, so they can't tell we were here. I'll catch up when you get to the first security fence."

"You got it, Boss." But when he got outside, he heard two muffled gunshots. Maybe Michael had shot the locks off the door. But it didn't make sense—why execute two guards after they had been carefully drugged and kept alive? His sense of right and wrong went ballistic, but now he felt trapped in something that was far too big for him. He couldn't tell himself if he could escape the game or join it in earnest. He had to find out more details.

Soon they were on their way in the old jeep, with no one the wiser.

"So, Boss, how'd we do?"

"Fantastic. We got in and out just like clockwork. Good thing we drilled this thing. You did good!"

"Awesome. So, what now?

"We wait. We'll get instructions soon. The next one will be awesome. Just wait!"

"Come on, man. Don't you trust me yet? Who are we working for?"

"Soon enough, Anthony, my man. We've been away from a television for almost a week. We're almost there. You'll know. Soon enough."

Chapter 35

This Just In

"This just in. A letter from a previously unknown terrorist group known as the 'Brotherhood of International Islamic Jihad' has been sent to the *New York Times*, the *National Enquirer,* the mayor and governor of New York, and the President of the United States. The letter describes a serious threat to the water supply of New York City unless all al Qaeda, ISIS other Muslim prisoners are released from Guantanamo and various floating brigs around the world. The Brotherhood of International Islamic Jihad is previously unknown, but it seems that several international terrorist groups may have united together, which has never happened in the history of the war on terror. The B.I.I.J. claims responsibility for the recent toxic poisoning of New York's Pepacton Reservoir and attempts on the Ashokan and the Rondout reservoirs.

A so-called "catastrophic" attack on New York's water supply is threatened, an attack so serious that it would cripple the city for decades. World officials seem puzzled. The B.I.I.J. has no history and no single country of origin. Therefore, the questions arise, 'Who do we attack? How do we defend the United States against an international group with no known geographical center?' At least the leaders of any one of the groups can be identified and geographically located. But where is the B.I.I.J.? There are prisoners of war from more than six different countries. Who is to blame?

"The United States has never caved in to terrorist demands. However, now, against the threat of crippling New

York City by destroying its water supply, who can predict how the President will respond to this imminent threat? Anderson Cooper reporting."

****

Anthony sat on the floor of the trailer with his back up against the bench seat that became his bed at night. He tried to remain calm. He had never been so confused and befuddled in his entire life. But he had finally realized what he had done.

He watched Michael smile when Anderson Cooper read the letter. He could hardly believe what he was hearing. He thought back to the day he had joined with the "boss", the con man named Michael. He realized that the *New York Times* photo of him in a red painted beret had catapulted him to a perceived leadership role in a movement he thought was entirely domestic, completely justified, and not at all lethal. But now, to discover that a *foreign* terrorist organization was behind all this, millions of New Yorkers were potentially threatened with a horrible future—and HE, Anthony Guarini, had laid the groundwork, it was all too much.

It was an American "friend" who had deceived him, and Anthony had taken money for it, and allowed himself to be led like a blind soldier into a battle he would never have supported if only he had known the true motive. And now accessory to the murder of two guards was added to terrorism, and Anthony was trapped squarely in the middle. And in this moment, in this trailer on a remote Catskill mountain, he felt as if he'd torn his own heart out.

How could he stop it all? He asked the obvious. "Michael, did you...did you know we were working for some Islamic terrorist group?" He fidgeted in his seat.

"Anthony, let me explain this to you. Turn off the television."

Anthony said, "No, Michael, I don't think so. The President is coming on."

"The President is an asshole."

"Maybe so, but he's *our* asshole, but I'm thinking that maybe someone *else* is the leading asshole around here."

Michael rose from the old leather chair and turned off the television. "Come on. Walk with me, down the trail. We've got to have a talk."

There was something in his eyes...

****

I was panicked. After ten attempts, Anthony's voice message box was full, and I couldn't even update him with the latest news from the City. But before I could continue with my own preparation, my cell phone rang, and Parker was finally geared up to high speed.

"Titus, we are ready in the City. We're everywhere. I'm so proud of the WaterForce Angels!"

"That's fantastic. We're ready in the mountains too. Dad says that all DEP officers were called to duty. Armed units have been dispatched to every reservoir. DEP boats and kayaks manned by WaterForce Angels have been launched on the reservoirs in both systems in the Catskills, and all strategic points in the Croton system in Westchester."

Parker said, "Helicopters are all over the City. Roadblocks are up at all the entrance points, the bridges and tunnels. I've never seen anything like it! And WaterForce Angels are taking water samples everywhere."

A ring of security had enveloped the Catskills. Cars were being stopped on the roads from Kingston to Oneonta, from Albany to Binghamton and down to Liberty. Local radio stations broadcast a warning for locals to report suspicious strangers, stay away from the waterways, and give the DEP and local police a wide berth on the highways. Finally, Hunter, Windham, Plattekill, and Belleayre Mountain ski resorts were closed, and their ski lodges commandeered for emergency barracks and food stations for troops patrolling the Catskills.

Parker continued, "There is far more panic than I ever imagined. Nobody was prepared for this to happen so fast. People down here are buying up all bottled liquids; and there is traffic backed up on all the bridges and tunnels from people fleeing the city. And it's only eight-thirty in the morning."

"Any more response from our website?"

"Incredible! In only a few days, we've had eighty-three thousand hits, with nearly a hundred percent positive support, and we've gathered over three hundred names of volunteers who want to be actively involved. And money coming in every hour."

"Social media. It's amazing how fast people can be mobilized for a good cause," I said.

"Right. But we're still untested. We don't have the notoriety of the Guardian Angels, who've been around for decades. The blue berets and sashes we ordered just arrived, and we're already mobilized to help. The amazing thing is that we're getting political support from both the left and the right. This is a threat to America, and everybody is on board."

"What is Professor Jac doing?"

"I talked to him a few moments ago. He's planning to appear on all the major networks with the Mayor in an hour and represent us."

"That's fantastic. He'll be far more credible than any of us could possibly be," I said.

"What about Anthony? Have you talked to him this morning?"

"Parker, we've got a problem. He's disappeared, and I have no idea where he is, or even if he's heard about the crisis. I've been trying to reach him all week. Bonnie hasn't even seen him since we got out of jail, and she's his mom. She says he took off with those guns his dad gave him. She hates guns. She said to check up at his cousin's trailer on Wildcat, and then she told me to 'fuck off'. She doesn't believe her little angel could be a terrorist."

"Michael's trailer? That's the wrong side of the tracks for him to be making friends. What the hell is he thinking? And with guns..." Parker saw trouble everywhere.

Finally, I said, "My next task will be to find Anthony...keep him out of trouble."

"Do you know where Michael's place is?"

"Not exactly...near Wildcat Mountain, up a mile-long driveway."

"Oh, Titus, be careful. I have a weird feeling about this. Call me later."

I always assumed half the stuff Anthony said was just sounding off, far from serious. But what if he believed his own bull? Some of it was way too similar to the threats from that Islamic group, even if he wasn't trying to play vigilante. As if on cue, his mother called me from Woodstock. She didn't even start with a "hello" or small talk.

"Homeland Security and a DEP officer are here with all kinds of questions. I don't know where he is, Titus," Bonnie fumed. "But if you guys have drawn him into some kind of plot, you're going to be sorry. You'd think we were at war. What the hell is going on?"

Did it have to be me to break the news about the Islamic threat? "Bonnie, just turn on CNN. You'll see what's going on. We need to find Anthony, and make sure he hasn't gotten himself in trouble. Look into your psychic crystal ball, maybe you'll see him someplace." Oh boy. I knew that was a mistake as soon as I said it. I heard a shriek, and I heard the phone hit the wall across the room. It took a whole minute before the swearing stopped, but she picked up the phone again and was a little calmer.

"Now don't you go blaming my Anthony. He may be a radical—he takes after me, you know—but he's *not* a criminal. There's a difference."

"I know, Bonnie. But they might *believe* he's involved. We need to find him."

"The cops just told me exactly what they think. And they're wrong, *wrong* again. All I know is he went somewhere to do some hunting. He was pretty rattled after that ridiculous arrest and everything. He just wanted to get away."

She should know where he would go. Of course she knew!

"Bonnie, do you know where that trailer is?" I said into the phone, "The one owned by Anthony's cousin Michael?" Now I was shaking.

"Not really...I'm not sure...I think it's in the Adirondacks, I think." *Was she being evasive because there were cops present?* "It's his *father* that gave him all those guns. But he likes his friend's place up near...Utica, much better. Closer. Lots more deer." *Right Bonnie! Utica is not even*

close to the Adirondacks. Anthony's never even been to Utica.
"Maybe he's up there…I think so," she said.

"I'm going to find out," I said. Bonnie was about as good a liar as Casey Anthony.

"Titus, please just stay out of it. I'm serious." I could feel her voice faltering.

"Yeah. I'll try not to. But if you hear from him, please! You need to *get* involved enough to call me." I gave her my number again. I could tell her pen wasn't working. Her brain was probably on the same crash course.

****

I joined a group of locals gathered in the Bun N' Cone around the television mounted on the wall. An announcer on CNN made the simple introduction. "And now, broadcasting from City Hall in lower Manhattan, the President of the United States."

I hoped he would be rational instead of spouting his usual biased rhetoric, and use real facts…

"The attack ten days ago in the Pepacton Reservoir was bad, bad, but there is absolutely no threat to the city of New York. The huge amount of water in the system diluted the small concentration of toxin. Believe me! The toxin dump was less than a hundred pounds. Added to over 140 *billion* gallons of water in the Pepacton, and billions in several other reservoirs, it ends up diluted so much that there is zero threat by the time it travels south through natural filtration, a chlorination plant and the new ultraviolet treatment plant in Westchester County, and finally into the distribution system in New York City. Zero chance to get out of control. Zero bad toxin in the City. This attack on New York City's water system was completely bogus. Unsuccessful. Zero threat. Believe me.

"However, there have been new attempts. But we found them before they could become a disaster. The fake news released to the press promises even more attacks. But we found the explosive charges—bad, bad—and disarmed them. Police tell me that the charges were very small, and not nearly bad enough to be totally out of control."

The waitress turned up the volume in the Bun N' Cone, and the entire restaurant moved to the counter to listen. A man in khaki pants and shirt raised his glass to the President.

"These tough guys claim responsibility for all the recent attacks on our water supply and issued an ultimatum to the United States. Let me be really clear. We will never bow to terrorist threats. We will never give in to these morons. They're not even legit. They're probably illegals, let me tell you! The B.I.I.J. has no history, no track record, no known leaders, and no known presence in any Islamic nation. The governments of Iran, Iraq, Yemen, Saudi Arabia, and other Arab nations have never heard of these losers. Putin has never heard of them. Why in God's name would the United States surrender to an enemy without a country or territory, and lacking any proof of existence from all international agencies? I don't care what their threats are. The United States of America—will—NOT—give in to their demands!"

****

Fateen Bushahma smiled to himself. It was so easy to rattle a president who was so clueless. He called Michael and gloated. "That idiot doesn't recognize a real threat when it hits him on the head!"

****

The patrons at the Bun N' Cone cheered and applauded. The waitress began to refill all drinks on the house. And the man from the White House continued...

"People of New York! Your water is safe. Your city is safe. Do not let these bums send you running for cover. Our armed forces are the strongest they've ever been, the best in the world. There is no enemy who can defeat us. Do not let reckless fake news frighten and threaten you. Go about your business. Return to your homes and your jobs. The success of terrorism depends on the spread of fear. If we refuse to be afraid, there will be no panic. And if there is no panic, these tough guys cannot scare us."

The cameras zoomed back slightly to show the President drawing a glass of water from a cold-water faucet. The skyline of New York City as seen from City Hall was majestic through the window behind him. Borrowing one of Obama's most theatrical moments, he raised his glass, and said, "This is New York City water, the finest and purest city water in the nation. Join me in a toast: to peace, to your health, and to your safety. Lastly, to the United States of America! Let's make America great again!" With that, he drank the entire glass.

The crowd at the Bun N' Cone reached for their glasses. Applause filled the pressroom at City Hall as thirty-five members of the press drank their water, obviously impressed with the President's performance. Shortly after the prolonged applause abated, the Mayor of New York broadcast his strategy for safety.

"This is the appropriate time to announce the formation of a new citizens' watch group, Associated with the Guardian Angels of New York City. The WaterForce Angels have already been helping to patrol the reservoirs, test water samples, and assisting the excellent security now provided by the DEP in the Catskills and the City. As long as this and other citizens' groups remain in an observation and reporting role only, I highly approve and welcome their help.

"I admonish you to be observant and to be vigilant. Watch over our reservoirs, our waterways. Report any and all suspicious activity. Keep the phone numbers on your screen close at hand, and call Homeland, the DEP, or your local police if there is any indication of trouble. Above all, trust in your government to protect you from harm. God Bless America!"

Citizens in the local Margaretville pub were moved by the speech. But I wasn't as confident as the politicians on the television. In spite of the President's show of patriotism, I knew more than the press had revealed, and I couldn't delay any longer. My search for Anthony had only begun. I was sure he was in Michael's trailer near Wildcat Mountain, a long ridge that runs between two winding mountain roads. The territory was large, with many cabins and trailers far off the road. With no certain address, it would be a challenge to find. I hurried outside to begin the search.

Chapter 36
Wildcat Mountain

I had just about exhausted all the known hangouts of Anthony Guarini. I stopped by his favorite watering hole in Roxbury, with no sign of him. When I arrived in Woodstock, I argued with Bonnie Guarini, who still refused to believe her son had any part in a terrorist plot. She didn't mention the Adirondacks or Utica this time, obviously a fabrication from her earlier rant. But now she was starting to worry, and she let me use her computer to search Facebook and Twitter for any sign of him. His screen name was Magneto, originally an evil comic book villain with occasional worthy environmental causes taken from a popular classic Marvel series. I had known about Anthony's fascination with comic book villains but had never thought he would actually emulate Marvel's Magneto and his radical actions. I guess I was wrong to assume that it was merely the leftovers from Anthony's cheeky teenage bravado.

No answers there. Magneto existed in Marvel's world, but nowhere did I find any evidence of Anthony or Magneto beyond his Facebook page and the pictures of his red-paint caper in the press. But then, if he'd had time to work on Facebook fiction, perhaps he wouldn't be hiding in a remote trailer planning his next audacious antic.

The evening dusk was less than two hours away. A cold mountain fog was creeping down the slopes. I wasn't looking forward to searching along the valley next to Wildcat Mountain in such weather, but I'd eliminated all other possibilities. Michael's trailer was the most likely place according to Bonnie's theory, and it was also the most difficult to find. Highway 28 was populated with regular signs of civilization—houses, businesses, and an occasional town—but as soon as I turned off the main highway, it seemed desolate, with only a sparse collection of small mountain homes, and steep driveways that were typically unpaved gravel or dirt paths that ended at secured houses owned by weekenders or summer residents not present in late March.

I had a six-battery mag light with a strong beam that would illuminate anything off the road within a few hundred feet. It was difficult work, trying to stay on the slippery road, and searching both sides off into the woods with my light. Twice I almost skidded into the ditch, and nearly got stuck trying to spin my wheels back onto the road. My windshield was dirty with mud and snow, and the washer solution was spurting its last. I was almost to Frost Valley, where there was a large vacant encampment run by the YMCA, with over a hundred cabins waiting for summer visitors. Surely I'd find signs of life before I reached Frost Valley. I decided to double back when I got to the YMCA property. The road was getting dangerous, and I lectured myself again that I shouldn't be alone on this search. This was the time I could use Dad's or Parker's help. But Dad would insist on rules I couldn't live with, and he'd insist I stayed out of the circle of danger. No way. After all, Dad was Officer Herb—the DEP—who would arrest him, and I needed to approach Anthony alone, where I could reason with him.

I slowed to a stop when I saw a deer running across the road five hundred feet ahead. The deer was far enough away that my Jeep couldn't have spooked it. There had to be something else. I killed my headlights and waited in a narrow shoulder off the road. I could feel the danger. I opened my door quietly and armed myself with my mag light and my rifle. Slowly I picked my way up the road to the place where the deer had crossed. The desolate night seemed to weigh in on me, and I was beginning to feel very alone and vulnerable as I walked along the edge of the road. Something had to have scared that deer. Perhaps a coyote, a black bear or a rare mountain lion hiding in the frigid mist creeping down the mountain. Or maybe a human.

The night was eerie, with a bright moon trying to sneak through thick snow clouds and overhead branches, but providing only a creepy uneven glow on the snow. An occasional errant ray seemed to flash across the ghostly branches like a searchlight as the clouds traveled swiftly across the sky.

I stopped, listening for sounds of life, and was rewarded only with the sounds of howling wind on top of the mountain. I continued up the incline to the next driveway. As I approached, I noticed a garbage can turned over, with its contents spilled and scattered through the woods. Someone was home at the top end of that driveway. Perhaps a noise from the garbage can had scared that deer. If I drove up the driveway, I would be noticed. But if I walked carefully, I could discover more and perhaps find the answers I was seeking.

I turned up the private driveway, a long and narrow winding path with car tracks from traffic earlier in the day. I blinked my mag light briefly to examine the tracks. It was clear that the same vehicle had left the house, and then returned after another few inches of snow had fallen. It seemed safe to walk up the drive out of sight of the house. I continued to walk up the road before I heard a low growl off my left side. Again, I blinked the light on, only to discover I was less than thirty feet from a beautiful bobcat, feasting on a garbage bag she'd dragged from the can by the road. She had to be over thirty pounds, fast and sleek, and able to attack in seconds. A long tuft of spiked hair accented her pointed ears, with a white triangle framed by an outline of black. Her bobbed tail stood out against markings that almost mimicked a jaguar, and she looked as if she could compete in a race with a speedy leopard.

Do bobcats attack? I wasn't sure. Suddenly I realized my stupidity. I wanted to kick myself. Because I was already spooked, I'd never loaded the rifle before retrieving it from the back window, and now I was way too far to go back for the ammo in the Jeep. I was certain I would never want to shoot Anthony, but really, it was just foolhardy to leave myself unprotected, particularly after dark. Idiot! I just didn't have the mind of a foot soldier or a hunter, like my dad. I'd have given anything for him to be with me.

The growl increased in intensity, and she snarled in a high whining voice as I froze on the driveway. It is not good to run from a wild animal, but I didn't think she would attack unless there was food involved, or kittens threatened. The bobcat could easily outrun me, and I now had several hundred feet to travel before I could jump into my Jeep. I didn't have much of a choice. I waited silently for several minutes without moving, and the big cat held its ground, still tearing through the garbage bag with hungry enthusiasm. Finally, I moved slowly, step-by-step down the driveway. The sounds of a bobcat delighted with the taste of people-food replaced the warning growls as I put some distance between myself and a furry creature that only wanted to protect her dinner.

I watched her rummage through the smell of hops in a beer bottle and then toss it aside and tear through a pizza box. The box tore open easily and flew a few feet in the air to catch a stray slice of moonlight. A familiar label on the box caught my attention. "Catskill Mountain Pizza," a place I had been with Anthony many times. The best pizza in Woodstock! Beer and pizza—Anthony's diet food. Coincidence? I stopped to consider, with one eye on the temperamental cat. I had a feeling, getting stronger each minute. Yes, Anthony probably would be the one to run out during a snowstorm to his favorite pizza joint. Hence, the double tracks in the snow. The box was big enough for two. I could imagine him eating his half in the car on the way back.

Convinced I was close to Michael and Anthony but stuck on the downhill side of a gnarly bobcat, I carefully made my way back to the safety of my Jeep. When I got within twenty feet, I could sense her tracking me and traveling downhill. Another low growl made me glance over my shoulder. What could I do, hit her with the barrel of my unloaded gun? Dive into the underbrush? But soon she stopped near the garbage can, and I realized that the furry beast was merely after a second helping of pizza with pepperoni and extra cheese. Once back inside the safety of my Jeep, I slammed my door several times to scare the creature away. Again, I felt stupid for making noise that might give away my location to the inhabitants of the trailer on the driveway above. If I was lucky, it was probably too far out of hearing range in the noise of the wind. I would make a lousy detective and an even worse soldier. I could do nothing but wait until the cat meandered off for other treasures after she picked the pepperoni off the top of frozen dough.

I abandoned the idea of walking back up a driveway littered with food. Instead, with my lights off, I drove slowly up the highway to see how wide the property was. Land parcels in the mountains still had the old stonewall borders used for three centuries in the days before accurate surveying tools. Sure enough, about a half a mile from the driveway was an old broken down stonewall that wound uphill. To my surprise, there was a second driveway on the same property and not far from the wall that was snow covered and showed no signs of traffic. Perhaps this was a back entrance to the residence on top, where Michael and Anthony might be staying.

The secondary route would be safer. With headlights off, I made my way up the steep driveway, hoping I could reach the top without being seen and without getting stuck in the snow. My engine struggled with an icy uphill section, and my wheels spun gravel and dead weeds before it leveled off to an easier climb. Moonlight revealed an old decrepit trailer with a television illuminating the interior. I stopped just before a sharp curve, a good distance short of the clearing that was still a hundred feet higher than my location. I turned off the engine and settled in for surveillance. It was unlikely anyone would see my Jeep through the trees, but I could observe the trailer without much risk. I reached behind the seat to retrieve my rifle. This time I loaded it and checked it twice.

Before I opened the door, I felt a wave of fear overtake me. It was too cold. It was too dark. It was too dangerous. It was too icy. The bobcat might return. Michael might have a gun. And his mother said Anthony had his entire collection of guns with him. Would they shoot at me? I had witnessed Anthony pick off a crow on a fence post at a hundred feet, and I knew I wasn't the marksman I should be. It was two against one. Is this the way I was forced to confront Anthony, with Michael there beside him? What was I thinking? He was a good friend, but now he had changed. I had to consider him a soldier of the enemy. I had to forget our friendship and take care not to assume any part of our former relationship still existed.

But the situation suddenly changed when I heard a shout from inside the trailer. It was definitely Anthony's voice, and he was angry. But what if he heard my engine coming up the driveway, and they were merely getting ready for a rain of bullets? Someone turned the outside light on, and the door opened. No one would turn on a light if they knew I was outside with a gun. I assumed I was still unseen. Anthony stood in the doorway, with three rifles under his arm, a hank of climbing rope over one shoulder, and a duffle bag strapped over the other. He turned and shouted something back into the trailer. He seemed angry. I heard the words, "You don't give me any choice!" Anthony slammed the trailer door and loaded everything into his pickup truck. I realized I had witnessed the last barrage of a serious argument, and he was as angry as a wet cat. But instead of turning his truck around in the clearing, he lurched forward as he put it into gear and proceeded down the auxiliary drive, only a hundred yards from my jeep, and headed straight towards where I was hiding around the first curve.

What should I do? Should I get out of the Jeep and wave my arms for him to stop? The man was obviously furious. Would he stop? If the rage was directed at Michael, maybe it was an opportune time to stop him and reason with him. I had only a few seconds to decide. I realized that, no matter what I did, the narrow driveway would never accommodate two passing vehicles without a head-on collision. I started my engine, and blinked my headlights frantically to warn Anthony, but there was very little room between my right side and a large stand of trees next to the driveway. I pulled off as far as I dared and hoped that Anthony would see me in time.

When he was ten feet from me, he slammed on his brakes, sending him into a downhill skid as he sideswiped trees on his right, barely avoiding a head-on collision, and finally slowing to a stop with less than an inch of clearance between our doors. His window slid down, and the barrel of a rifle emerged and touched the glass of my window. Terrified, I turned on my inside lights so he could see me clearly and placed my hands on the steering wheel in a gesture of complete submission.

"Jesus, it's YOU. *Following* me! What the hell? Titus, what do you think you're doing?" The gun slid back into his truck.

At least he knew it was me, and I knew I was going to live another minute. A sweet breath of air entered my lungs as I inhaled. I rolled my window down to confront Anthony with my plea. "I found you! Thank God I found you! Everybody is worried. I'm your FRIEND, Anthony. What's going on with you?" But already there was another threat when the light from the open door of the trailer was shadowed by Michael emerging on the run.

Anthony said, "Let's get out of here! Michael's packing a gun!"

As he glanced in the rearview mirror, Anthony gunned his engine. I heard a metallic ripping sound. Our side mirrors were history. If he'd been any closer, he would have skinned the paint off my Jeep. Michael raced down the narrow driveway on foot, with his shotgun across his left wrist and his right hand on the trigger. If he stepped in a rut, the gun would explode. I followed Anthony in a crazy backwards skid to stay out of Michael's fire and prevent myself from careening into the trees. I had seconds before he had a clear shot at me, but fortunately I could drive faster going in reverse than he could run after me. He finally got off a shot as he rounded the bend near the top. A splatter of buckshot broke through the rider's side of my aging windshield and blew glass everywhere. My face was grazed from the fragments, but I kept on moving down the curvy driveway, at least eight hundred feet to the bottom. When I swerved onto the pavement, I saw Anthony standing on the road next to his truck, with his shotgun aimed uphill, in case Michael dared to appear. I jumped out of my Jeep and stood there with him with my Remington XCR II cocked and ready. My eyes confirmed how fast he changed sides to defend me against his former accomplice.

"He's on foot," I said. "He'll never catch us if we leave now. Let's head up to the Y at Frost Valley. We can lose him there."

"Let's roll Dude." It wasn't the detailed explanation I was looking for, but it was enough for the moment. Before Michael could round the last curve in the driveway, we were gone.

Chapter 37

Fateen

Fateen paced next to a bench in Central Park. He wasn't supposed to meet his handler face-to-face in public. But circumstances had changed, and he was frustrated that his attempts had failed to seriously threaten the City. Dumping botulism in the Pepacton was ineffective. Even though Anthony's exploding toy boat was a fascinating theatrical stunt, it wasn't effective either. Delivering toxin by blowing up an aqueduct had proven risky, like a shot over the bow without hitting the ship. What had he been thinking? Michael's new recruit was unproven and inexperienced. And now Fateen was feeling the frustration of failure. Time for a change in strategy. He needed to stop depending on incompetent Americans and take a more active role. He prayed for inspiration.

He could feel the hatred in his gut. It was a lifelong vengeance against America. Images of his family massacred by American troops in Iraq still smoldered with memories of his home in ashes. He was here not to emigrate, but to retaliate. He was joined by serious militants who supported his crusade for revenge. Members of the B.I.I.J. transcended national borders and unified jihadists with the single goal of striking the United States with a united effort and a hall of fame roster. Al Qaeda contributed members from eighteen countries, all devout servants of Allah. Hezbollah was rooted in seven countries, seven more from the Taliban, eight from HAMAS. Terrorists from the Kurdish Workers Party in ten nations. All were united to defeat the United States. America would never be able to identify a common target for all of them. Who would they bomb? Certainly not all forty countries. It would be much easier to simply release Islamic prisoners. Finally, a plan with teeth.

Fateen's handler was a seasoned Jihadist who commanded a hidden network of zealous Islamic patriots from all over the world. So why was this so hard? Why couldn't he succeed with an attack effective enough to bring results? What was he doing wrong?

He had valuable experience from the USS Cole in Yemen to lesser attacks on American Jews and violence in four US cities. Since he was never a primary suspect, he was never detained. He seethed and simmered on the sidelines with American militants doing the actual work. But now he needed a moment in the spotlight. The vision of his mother's bloodied face was always in his consciousness, and often was vindicated with gratuitous acts of violence. A brutal beating of a teenager who dared to wear a "Fuck Islam" tee shirt was his latest act of vengeance. He glared at the memory and spat out the consonants like bullets through his teeth. "Bokonamet! Mawt Amerik!" *Fuck You. Death to America!*

By 2015, when membership in the B.I.I.J. had slowly grown to over two thousand dedicated extremists, no one was aware of a connection to a united jihadist movement after attacks in San Bernardino, Columbus Ohio, and New York City made the news. The B.I.I.J. made public demands that the US release political prisoners from Guantanamo and US brigs. Some of their most talented members were long time prisoners on board US Navy ships. The B.I.I.J. wanted them back. And Fateen was eager to shed blood to accomplish that goal. He would bring the enemy to its knees. But the method was still elusive and frustrating.

Today he needed another dose of revenge to fuel his hate. He stalked a small stray dog in the park and coaxed it over to his side. Slowly he reached down until he could touch the poor starving animal. But instead of offering affection, he grabbed it by the neck and strangled it and slammed it on the bench until it was motionless. It felt great when he threw it in the bushes. A woman on the path ran away quickly. He smiled at his power and spat on the ground. It fed his sense of control and domination and stoked his anger with pure adrenaline in preparation for his meeting. The smell of blood was in the air. But he still lacked the big idea to attain his goal. He clutched a copy of the Qur'an and said a short prayer, begging for inspiration. *"Allah huh akbar,"* he muttered. *Allah is good.*

Soon he noticed Abdul approaching. He had shaved his head and grown a month-old beard since they last met in Aleppo. With his Yankees jersey, Danner hiking boots, and Nike backpack, no one would ever guess he wasn't American. He looked around to verify their lone command of the area and sat next to Fateen.

"I've been waiting," Fateen said in Farsi.

"You know the rules. We're in public. English, not Farsi. Keep it neutral. Be careful." He stretched and placed his backpack on the bench between them. He looked around for trouble. Minutes passed before he asked, "So tell me what you've accomplished."

The request was more like a criticism, a veiled challenge as if nothing was ever enough. "I *told* you in my email. But the code we have doesn't begin to translate into what happened..." Fateen said.

"I have other sources. I already know. The mission at the Pepacton didn't work. Too much water–not good." He tapped the backpack on the bench. "I brought something else. This time we won't have to worry about the volume. The water simply carries it to the victim. It's self-contained inside tiny capsules that dissolve in the human body. It's ten times more effective. I tested it on a man who is *very* dead. You'll like it."

Fateen was curious. And his anger subsided when he realized Abdul wasn't going to berate him for the failure of the recent attacks. "So, how does it work...the delivery, I mean?" Could this be the new plan he needed?

"It's more personal, more direct. You can target individuals, or groups, maybe a whole building full of people who will make the news. It travels in liquids, and dissolves in the warmth of the stomach. Guaranteed results! All you need is access to their local water supply, or in tea, coffee. If you choose the right targets, the president will have to listen, and release our men. Stop praying to Allah and use your head this time!"

Fateen was amazed. "Damn! I could have used it on that dog a few minutes ago."

"Yes. I saw that. You are a cold-blooded sadist, Fateen. You must learn to channel your passion. Think about this weapon, and how to focus on the right group."

"Like maybe a Christian church, or..."

"No, not a church. Something more political, higher up. Something that leaves the President no choice." Abdul shifted to look Fateen straight in the eyes. "This will get you started. I'll send more to your man on the inside. Remember our ultimate goals. Unless the U.S. is really stupid, we will get our people released. Unless *you* screw it up, this is guaranteed to work. Remember that."

Abdul stood and walked away quickly, leaving the backpack on the bench.

Chapter 38

Frost Valley

We drove several miles until we reached Frost Valley. A truck and a jeep traveling at night with no headlights are an eerie and dangerous procession on a desolate winter mountain road covered in snow. The complex at the Frost Valley YMCA was completely uninhabited in winter this late at night, and there was a maze of curving roads ending in cul-de-sacs layered up the slope of the mountain, filled with empty cabins. I worried about the tracks our vehicles made in the snow on the gravel road, but I hoped the wind would quickly cover our trail. We parked behind a small cabin on a blind alley high up on the mountain. It was easy to jimmy open a window and retreat to safety in a dark cabin. We found a supply of blankets and wrapped ourselves in warmth. As long as we didn't light a fire or turn on a light, Michael would still have a hard time finding us off the road. At least now I could talk to Anthony in relative quiet.

I didn't know how to start with him. Somehow it still seemed tenuous, like a ceasefire in Syria. Finally, I found words of truth with approachable tones. "I guess friendship is still alive with us...at least you didn't shoot me. Thanks for that."

"Are you kidding? Titus, I would never threaten you. You're my friend for life. You know that."

Did I? Anthony looked at me with deep brown eyes, as if he didn't quite know what to say. We had barely escaped a treacherous situation. We had come out of it on the same team, a small miracle born from a battle in which Anthony had switched sides so fast he amazed himself with logic even he could not comprehend.

"But why, Anthony? What were you *thinking*?"

"I...don't even understand how this all happened." He looked sheepish, as if wishing perhaps I might understand without a long explanation. But I kept my silence, waiting an eternal minute before he spoke again. "I didn't understand why people were running around carrying protest signs, and how it could possibly matter. I guess I was stoked when they ran my photo in the *Times,* you know—with the paint."

"You became an overnight celebrity..." I said. *Right! Stroke his ego...*

He smiled like a jackal. "Yeah. It was cool. But when Michael approached me, I wanted to do something with balls that would really matter. I thought change could only happen if we...well, if there was severe...radical action. He convinced me that we would make our mark if we showed how vulnerable the reservoirs are. Real incidents became a like, wakeup call. And he paid me, *good* money, to join him. But today I figured out who is really behind all this, and I...I just couldn't...do it any..." He shivered in the cold, not able to finish the sentence. We huddled together under blankets, as close as two friends could be.

I didn't know where to start. The poor boy had been so misinformed, so gullible, so confused. He'd sold himself to an Islamic devil without checking for credentials and the creed behind the mission.

I had trouble comprehending his naiveté, his inability to make good decisions, and his lousy choice of allies. I needed to make him confide in me. I needed to help him find a way back up a steep one-way street. I hugged him and felt him shaking to his core. He was my lifelong friend, but he had really screwed up, big time. Although I would ultimately forgive him, would my father do the same? Would my brother give him the break he needed? What about Professor Jac, and the DEP, the Mayor, and the feds? Friendship wouldn't be worth spit in a true case of domestic terrorism. There was no one I knew who was in deeper trouble. We sat in the dark, huddled together. Anthony was shaking. I wondered if the dynamic duo was responsible for everything that had happened. But was this the time to ask him? I didn't have much choice.

After a few moments of silence, I ventured forth, one step at a time. "How long have you been hanging out with Michael?"

"Maybe, two weeks."

"And you joined him—followed his lead, I guess, when he tried to blow up the aqueducts at the Ashokan?"

"Jeez! Damn it, you think that was *me?*"

This had to stop. First, he nearly admits he participated, and now he's in denial, and he lies to me? "Anthony, you're the only one I know who owns five different models of remote control miniature boats. I've seen you race them and make them do elaborate tricks. Eye-witnesses said the toxin in the Ashokan was delivered by a miniature toy boat. I know your handiwork. This has signs of *you* written all over it!"

Anthony stood up and paced back and forth in the dark cabin. I could empathize with his discomfort, but I had to keep the pressure on to get him to tell the truth. I asked, "Have you seen a news broadcast lately?"

"Yes. That's what finally proved I was in deep shit. I'd been talked into doing things that hurt my own country."

"You realize that if they are paying you, they don't consider you a real ally. You're just a hired gun."

I didn't realize...I don't know. I'm *sorry*." He broke down sobbing, shaking from his very core, and couldn't stop for several minutes. This was a real psychotic break, but I had to let him work through this. Finally, he sat on the bed across the room, and lowered his head.

"I only wanted to do something that nobody else had the balls to do." His voice was small and whiney, and his shoulders compressed into a rounded silhouette.

"Go on..." I said heartlessly. *He talks about 'balls'?*

"The demonstrations just seemed so useless, so...ineffective. That's what Mom said about some of the protests in the past. It's good energy, but it never brings about real change."

"I know. She hasn't stopped organizing for the right causes, but she hasn't gone all postal with bombs and lethal toxins...like YOU did."

"Okay, maybe you're right...but Michael is the leader, and I didn't realize he would go there. I'M TRYING TO DUMP HIM, DAMN IT."

"Yeah, but not before you attacked the Ashokan aqueduct, and tried to blow up the pumping station at the Rondout. What else have you been involved in, Anthony? Are there more bombs? There's a whole list, isn't there? And you say you're just the pawn in somebody else's game? I don't *think* so." I felt like a police interrogator, not Anthony's best friend. Reality is a harsh road in an intervention. I had to do it that way. But I felt terrible about it. At times I was my father's son, with police tactics in my genes.

"YOU THINK I DON'T REALIZE THAT? I'm trying to get away. I'm SORRY if you think I KNEW who paid us." He looked up at me like I was the enemy. "I need to get away and think. I just need you to..."

If I didn't back off a little, I would lose him. "Listen, my friend. You and I had better learn to trust each other. We need to stay close. You NEED me. You'd better find some way to redeem yourself, because you are an inch away from finding yourself in prison for the rest of your life."

Anthony blurted out a protective truth. "You can't stay with me, Titus. You'd put yourself in deep shit if we're found together."

"Yeah, well, thanks for that, partner. But I'm not leaving. You need me, and we need to get back to the front lines, and this time on the *right* side of the battle." There was a long silence while we both considered our options. Finally, he stood up and looked towards the cabin door. I thought I had lost him to another foolish choice. As he opened the door, I tried one last time.

"Anthony, *please*, don't leave; and don't do anything stupid. You only have one good choice besides turning yourself in." And I only had one good offer left for him. He hesitated slightly, perhaps ready to listen. I gave it my best shot. "Join us in WaterForce. Maybe you can prove that you've changed. You may not have any sense, but you've got balls. We can use someone like you. Maybe you can prove where your heart really is, before they catch up with you."

"The trouble is, we've set some other explosives in places that—Oh crap! He's here!"

His confession was interrupted by the flash of headlights turning into the cul-de-sac. Anthony closed the door, and we both crawled to the window to observe the sudden intrusion. We occupied one out of a hundred cabins. How could Michael have found us already?

WaterForce

Chapter 39

Bad Odds

Would Anthony run back to Michael's side, in spite of the argument they'd had? Would Michael take him back, or would he violently dispose of poor Anthony, as he had done with Paul? Was Anthony rational enough to accept the solution I was offering him? In spite of the danger approaching, I needed to connect with him, and for him to join me on the right team.

Neither of us could move. I used his Facebook name; taken from his favorite comic book villain, as I whispered, "Stay with me, Magneto. We need you." Somehow, that hit home, and he smiled at me, like the old days, and I thought maybe I'd won him back. But there was a new threat.

We heard the vehicle stop, and a door opened outside the cabin. The shadow of a rifle or shotgun crossed the curtain over the window, and we heard footsteps moving around back to investigate our tracks. It wouldn't be long now. WaterForce was sworn not to employ violence. If we fought him with guns, we would be equally culpable, but if we could fight in self-defense... I motioned for Anthony to arm himself with a stick of kindling from the fireplace. We would be two men with clubs against a man with a long-barreled gun. We moved silently through the kitchen and waited on either side of the back door. I pointed to my head and motioned for Anthony to strike high. I positioned my crude stick weapon and pantomimed my own assignment. Anthony nodded to me, and we had a simple plan of attack. Surprise was our only advantage.

We could hear the intruder turning the latch, and slowly opening the door. The barrel of the gun appeared first. The door opened against my side, which prevented me from seeing the intruder, but it also hid me from discovery. I raised the stick and hit the gun barrel sharply. I heard the snap of Anthony's stick against the bone of his forehead. As he fell backwards, the gun exploded into the floor with a single blast from his twelve-gage. At the same time, we both raised our clubs and hit him again on the back of his head and the small of his back as he went down. He didn't move after he hit the floor.

Panic rushed through my mind like a lightning bolt. What if we'd killed him with our sticks? We'd have no evidence to convict him, let alone verify the many questions the police would have about the things he had done and the things Anthony had done. We would have to justify the murder of a man who had not attacked us directly. And what good would our choice of weapons be then? I flipped him over to identify him, but his grey stocking cap had filled with blood from the blow to his face. He was unrecognizable in the dark cabin. What if it wasn't Michael? Had we murdered a night watchman in the middle of his rounds? Or a stranger who had nothing to do with any of this?

Anthony seemed to harbor the same questions. He crouched down to get a better look. He pulled off the stocking cap and used it to mop up the blood on the guy's face. "It's Michael, for sure," he announced. He spit. "I can't think of anyone who deserves this more."

"Yeah, well, let's hope the jury agrees with us. Is he alive?"

"I don't know." He checked for a pulse. "I think he's okay. He's like, breathing a little." Anthony stood up and turned on the kitchen light.

"Anthony, no, not the light. Someone heard that shot. Turn it off."

"Right."

"Christ! What are we going to do now?" Here we were with Michael unconscious and wounded, and Anthony was still seen to be on the devil's team. I grabbed a kitchen towel and tried to stop Michael's bleeding. We needed him alive and ready for arrest. He moaned, but still was not fully alert. I checked his body for wounds. Blood was flowing from his forehead. Head wounds always bleed profusely. Perhaps it wasn't as bad as it looked.

Anthony said, "I've got an idea. Maybe we can save ourselves."

"I think you've had enough bright ideas lately. We've got to call the police. Damn it. We're totally fucked. They'll never trust me or WaterForce again."

"But hear me out. You're looking for some miracle to save my ass, right? We'll tie him up, and I'll call it in, using my own name, so they can drive over here and capture their main suspect. I won't mention you at all. This could be the only thing to keep me out of trouble."

"You can't be..." I started. But maybe...I ripped my flannel shirt into strips to bandage Michael's wounds. If I didn't stop his bleeding, he would die. I tied the flannel strips around his head and leg. As I worked, I realized there was something in Anthony's plan that just might be crazy enough to work. Anthony could prove he was on the right side, and they could capture their suspect. Anthony and I would disappear and rejoin the defense of New York. Perhaps he could prove himself there. A long shot, perhaps. But what other choice was there? With Michael out of commission, the Islamic terrorists behind all this would have to regroup and find someone else to do their dirty work. Perhaps this could slow them down long enough for the police to catch up to them. The issue, after all, was saving New York.

I began to believe that he might make it through alive. There was little time to think. We couldn't just leave him there on the floor. The plan could work if we handled it the right way. A thousand thoughts crossed my mind, and I fought hard not to panic.

My phone was unresponsive. Cell phone reception was nonexistent on this side of the mountain. We would have to leave the scene for the police to find it, and drive somewhere else to call it in. I needed to talk to Parker. He had to be in the loop. I felt totally alone, stuck in a wilderness on a mountain that could be ten thousand miles from New York City, instead of just over a hundred. Suddenly, I remembered the temporary communications center they set up at the Ashokan. We were already close to the top of the east slope of Doubletop Mountain. If we could reach the top, maybe my cell could connect through the new cell tower. It was worth a try.

Chapter 40

The Summit

It was tough to justify tying up an injured man with a head wound that could easily open at any moment. We left Michael tied up with a blue nylon rope I had in my Jeep. We used his belt to attach his tied wrists to the bed in the cabin. I felt sort of sorry for him: a small amount of blood was still seeping from the flannel bandages I had fashioned. He looked like a bloody pork roast trussed up for the oven. He was weakened, but not unconscious. We took his keys, so he couldn't get far even if he did manage to free himself.

"We've got to find the summit, make the calls, and get back..." The climb was difficult on a snowy night with the wind and fast-moving clouds under a Stephen King moon. We wound our way through thick underbrush and fields of massive boulders for nearly a mile until we reached a small clearing at the summit of Doubletop Mountain, high above the Frost Valley cabins. The icy fog was nearly impenetrable on the way up, and we had no reference point for a long time until the sky opened up to thousands of bright stars above. We could see past Wildcat and Slide Mountain directly to the East, with a partial view of houses in the valley near Phoenicia along the highway. The Ashokan reflected moonlight to our position on Doubletop. I hoped we could connect to the tower near the aqueduct. I dialed Parker's number. I thought of the ad, "Can you hear me now?" If Verizon delivered on their promise tonight when we most needed them, I'd be a customer for life. The one-bar connection was crackly and weak, but he finally answered down the city.

Instead of the usual niceties and small talk to begin a conversation, Parker answered with, "Where the hell have you been? There's stuff happening down here, like all over. I need you to stay in touch with me, Bro!"

I wasn't ready to put up with his big brother scold, especially after all that had happened. "Cool your jets, big-ass bro! We just climbed a mountain to get a signal. I'm with Anthony. He's cool, back on our side...and we captured Michael. He's tied up in a cabin at Frost Valley. But Parker, we've got to keep Anthony out of the limelight for a while, until we can figure something out for him." I gave him just enough to pique his curiosity, and maybe lay off the bully-style leadership he could get into when he got excited. By now we knew how to play each other. Actually, we were a damn good team because of that. I brought him up to date, and he listened, for a while at least.

But Parker was Parker, still nervous. "I can't believe you found Michael and Anthony! That part is great. But Titus, do you realize how you've jeopardized us? WaterForce Angels aren't supposed to act as cops! We're supposed to *call* the cops and stand on the sidelines. Why the hell didn't you call Dad, at least? And Anthony is still guilty as hell of the Ashokan and Rondout incidents, no matter how you try to paint him as a crossover hero."

"Did I mention there was NO cell service there? What was I supposed to do—ask him to wait at the door while I call Daddy? No other way, Bro!"

"Okay, my bad!" Parker said. "You did what you had to do. But you cannot let him get into even the slightest bit of trouble from now on." There was background conversation that interrupted him. "Hold on a sec—"

During the pause, I could hear him directing a WaterForce team to patrol the Kensico Reservoir in Westchester County near the Bronx. He was speaking to a DEP patrolman. I heard him ask whether they had heard from Sergeant Rose lately—Dad. When the group left on their new mission, Parker could talk.

I explained as best I could. "I was thrown into this. I wanted to find Anthony, but I didn't think I'd be walking into an argument, with guns drawn, and with Michael chasing us all the way to Frost Valley. Give me a break, here!"

Parker said, "It won't be long until Michael and Anthony are replaced with some other sucker—somebody we can't even trace."

I replied, "I know. We still have to be smart here, even with Michael tied up and almost in custody."

"Their goal is still to threaten the water supply, *any way they can.* And they will keep trying with different methods until they find something that really works. But they haven't always played it smart. First, they dump a hundred pounds of powder in a nearly frozen reservoir, a hundred pounds that barely dissolved, and was easily filtered on the way to the city. Then they blow off a couple of bombs so weak they couldn't blow the door off an outhouse. They're getting closer to the city, and their next move—I'm guessing—like maybe the Kensico or the Jerome Park reservoirs. And they've got to find a way to *localize* it and prove they can kill. Their strategy for the Pepacton was ridiculous, like peeing in the Atlantic to poison some dude in London."

"I agree with you, Parker, but we can't just ignore these threats. We have to protect the *entire* water supply. And we need to start outsmarting them. They're always three steps ahead. We're like a slow train half way over the cliff."

"Yes, and they're attacking closer and closer to the City. The only thing they've accomplished so far is to spread fear. But isn't that what terrorism is all about? *Fear*, Titus! *Mass hysteria.* But they need some dead bodies to ramp it up. Really, *one death* is all they would need with the right press, even though they'd probably be happy to kill hundreds."

I asked, "What do you think their new strategy is?"

"I just talked to Professor Jac. He says the initial poisoning and the explosions served to get media attention. The President responded, but refuses to give in. The media is in a feeding frenzy over this crap. And now that the terrorists have our attention, all they have to do is prove they can actually kill us. They need real victims followed by news releases and more threats. A rash of fatalities would be like, perfect for them, far more effective to create widespread panic."

"How do you figure they're gonna do that?

"Professor Jac already has proof of their new tactics. He told me not to discuss details on an open line. But he knows, Titus. He's CIA. Like he already *knows* how they'll do it."

It was cold, and I really needed to get him to shut up. "Is it...still through the water supply?"

"You got that, Sherlock. The water supply still reaches every single person in the city, okay? But this is like, a new method...Now, let's move on and do what we can do effectively. We've got a lot to accomplish, and not a lot of time. I *need* you, little brother. You've gotta stop hunting bobcats and bad guys and come back to the City."

Parker was still acting like an arrogant ass, but at least he was sober, and at least we were communicating. I responded, "So you want me to drop everything, when our major suspect lays bleeding in a cabin at Frost Valley, and become your batboy in the City? But this right here is important too. We've got to get some medical attention for him, and fast. The last thing we need is for Michael to die before we get him into a courtroom."

"Right," Parker agreed. "But you've got to keep Anthony out of this, that is, if he really did change sides. We need to bring Dad into it. Let him call the ambulance. This is his chance to help us from the inside, like he promised. It's become very complicated. We're going to need him. If you want, I'll talk to him..."

"No, Parker, I'm not an idiot! I can take care of this. You have enough to do down the City. I'll call you after I reach him."

I hung up. The wind was raging over the summit of Doubletop, and a new storm front was approaching from the west. My battery was getting weak. I dialed Dad, and left an urgent message, telling him how and where to find Michael. I painted a hero's story for Anthony's role, and said we would leave the lights on in the cabin, with Michael tied up inside. I told him we had to split, and I would explain later. "Please, Dad, just tell them you got an anonymous tip so we can get out of here. I've got other problems, and I need to get back to my team." I was worried that he might not see it the same as I did. I worried even more that Michael's head wound was more than superficiel. We had to get back to the cabin. The last thing we needed was to be forced to explain why there was a corpse instead of a live suspect waiting for the police.

We flew down the mountain. Sliding straight down the steep slope was faster than winding our way around the summit. But soon we realized it was far more dangerous. Small rocks and loosened soil cascaded ahead of us as we grabbed on to saplings and roots on the way down. We were back in that frozen cloud of mist again when we doubled back around an outcropping of huge boulders. We nearly missed the location of the cabin because of our shortcut. Finally, we could barely make out the eerie glow from the porch light through the mist and the trees.

As we got closer, I could see the back of the cabin. It was then that I realized we wouldn't have to worry about a corpse. There was another crisis, far worse than my fears for his bleeding. Michael's truck was still parked in front of the cabin on the road below. But Anthony's truck was gone. When we checked inside, we discovered he had broken free from his restraints, using a steak knife to cut the rope around his wrists. We had carefully locked Michael's truck and taken the keys but forgotten that Anthony's old pickup could easily be hot-wired. And now, Michael not only had an escape vehicle, but also, everything he did in that truck would be traced to Anthony. And the worst, I had left a message on Dad's phone that would surely send him on a worthless chase to nowhere when he found Michael missing. He would be totally pissed, and I felt completely inept. Like Dad used to scream at me, I could screw up a one-car funeral.

Chapter 41

Herb and Mo

There was no cell service along the reservoir road until Herb arrived at the DEP office in Deposit, at the west end of the Cannonsville. There was a good chance he could use his cell with signals from towers in nearby Walton. He needed to find Mo and check the results from new test samples taken from the Pepacton and the other Catskill reservoirs. But the office was dark, with no clue of where Mo had gone. Perhaps he was still in the field, returning from his daylong mission, but he was long overdue. Herb's job was to coordinate the teams patrolling the six largest New York reservoirs, and collect water samples for the lab from WaterForce patrols. Mo would then test them for toxins. Herb was also concerned about Titus, who'd been missing all night. What could have happened to him?

The weather had cleared by seven in the morning, leaving the mountains glistening with fresh snow, and the air frozen with crystal clear freshness under an intense blue sky. The sun was just above the mountains, leaving the hidden horizon still glowing with golden light spilling over pristine peaks to the East. But in spite of the perfect winter day, Herb was uneasy.

He listened to the message from Titus twice before he began to understand the terrible position his son was in. It was great news that they had captured Michael. But the last few words were telling indeed. "Dad, you've got to help us. This is your chance to help WaterForce, like you promised. Please! Just trust me for once."

Herb settled heavily into the desk chair in the dark office. Titus had explained that they had captured Michael Capo, and that Anthony was "on our side now." In other words, Dad, 'Do me a favor and *don't arrest Anthony*.' Surely Titus didn't believe the police would agree to abandon a search for a suspect just because he had "changed sides." As if that wasn't strange enough, Titus said he couldn't stay and wait for the police to arrive. How could Herb justify this cockamamie story after the crimes Anthony had committed? And why couldn't Titus wait? Obviously, he didn't trust his dad. But what was the big secret?

He wanted to trust his sons. He wanted to help them. But special favors were always against police protocol and came back to bite him in the ass. He could lose his job and ruin his entire career with a bad decision during a terrorist incident. And this would prove favoritism. Worse, he feared making a decision that would facilitate a terrorist attack on his country. How could he balance the needs of law and order against his sons' risky demands?

Great Grandfather Rosendael's suicide in the wake of the formation of the Pepacton made him consider the opposite side as he weighed the consequences. He'd silently supported his sons with Great Grandpa's trust fund, yet Herb worked for the DEP. Reality hit him between the eyes as he realized his actions had made him into a duplicitous double agent. The whole set of opposing values was like a hungry man swallowing poison ivy, and it was sure to haunt him no matter what he did.

He paced back and forth in the DEP office, feeling a wave of nausea. The smell from the wood-burning stove was usually comforting, but tonight the place smelled like a dead rat burning. Was protecting Anthony worth forsaking the vows he had taken as a DEP officer? Or was it part of a larger issue, one that would mean something for the defense of his country? He removed his badge, trying to decide whether to throw it in the stove, or pin it back on his shirt. He paced into the bathroom and looked into the mirror, which was cracked in a jagged line down the middle. He was startled to find that even his reflection seemed to have a double image, split just like his divided loyalties. The significance of the double image created a jarring surreal feeling. He felt a strange presence, as if his Great Grandfather was there, reminding him of a promise made nearly seventy years ago. With his badge back on his shirt, he shook his head, knowing that his choices would send him traveling on a narrow and treacherous tightrope.

He slammed the mirrored door of the medicine cabinet, as if to erase the crossroad he saw in it. Shards of glass hit the floor when the left side fell, leaving a single image staring back at him. Strangely, it helped him make the decision. The effect on his family through four generations could no longer be ignored. He would find a way to make this work. He would have to trust that his sons had made the right decisions. He resolved to ignore the dichotomy of Anthony's reappearance, and let him join the activists united in WaterForce, in spite of his base instincts as a cop. Never before had he ignored his sworn duties. He'd never thought he would let a proven threat to the reservoirs sneak through the network of justice. But as a father, he realized that the boys were old enough to make good decisions, and he had promised to trust them.

It was a tenuous situation; with consequences he could only accept reluctantly. Worst of all would be the path he would have to travel with Commissioner O'Riley of the

NYPD, the man who not only had disapproved of the WaterForce Angels but had belittled and bullied Herb at every turn.

He could only concentrate on one thing, and that was arresting Michael Capo. When he was just about to leave, Mo arrived. "Boss, sorry I'm so late. I had to check the team on the Ashokan. They were all out on the reservoir, and one boat got a little lost."

"That's okay, Mo. But I need you to go with me to arrest Michael Capo. My son managed to capture him, and he needs us, immediately. I'll explain in the car. Let's go." Mo left with him, satisfying the protocol for backup. They took off from Deposit and took the back-mountain roads to be the first to reach the cabin on Wildcat Mountain. It should be an easy arrest, considering Michael was already tied up and injured.

Mo's aversion to violence made him as nervous as a cat in a bathtub. He brought Mo into the loop, explaining that Titus had captured him and left him tethered to a chair in a cabin not far from them. He decided to leave out the information about Anthony's role. The double images in the bathroom mirror came screaming back like a bad nightmare. He felt a twinge of guilt in the first of many lies to facilitate his sons. He had started across the tightrope, with no safety net below.

Turning into the Frost Valley YMCA, they could see the lights in a single cabin high on the slope. They followed faint sets of tire tracks on the snow-covered road. Two cars had recently arrived and departed the scene. A vehicle registered to Michael Capo was locked and sat in front of the lit cabin. When they entered, they were shocked to find it completely empty. Michael was gone. A blue nylon rope lay in a pile on the driveway in a small pool of blood. They had come to arrest an important terrorist, and all they found was that the suspect had escaped. Herb sat on a mountain rock, trying to recapture his resolve, and justify his double role. Mo seemed strangely relieved. Herb decided that his own son would never mislead him, waste his time, or deceive him on purpose. But still. How could he explain this? What would he write in the report?

****

Michael's vision was blurry, and the seat of Anthony's stolen truck was soiled with his own blood. He still felt nauseated and weak from exposure to the toxin. The road through the narrow river valley was treacherous with ice. He took a direct route north, through Big Indian and Shandaken, then through Deep Notch to reach the only place he could go for help. He almost drove off the road and down a steep embankment when the dizziness returned. He pulled off the road and drank some half-frozen Gatorade he found in a bottle on the floor of the truck. He rested before continuing on the dangerous journey. Blood was still seeping through the flannel strips on his head. His wrists throbbed from rope burns, but he pushed onward.

His resolve was still strong because of the loss of his brothers many years before. He clenched his teeth as he remembered that New York City was to blame. Determined, he would follow through with his plans. His blood tasted like the revenge he sought.

When he finally reached Prattsville, he had trouble remembering the location of the emergency rendezvous set by his handler. He drove through the town until, finally, he turned down a dead-end street and pulled into the driveway of a small ramshackle wreck of a house along the river.

Canted at a dangerous angle off its foundation, the house was still abandoned after the floods following Hurricane Irene many years before. The stain from the floodwater line was two feet over the windowsill. A broken venetian blind hung out of a shattered window, flapping in the March wind against a downspout hanging from the half-shingled roof.

New inhabitants now used the dilapidated structure as a safe house, Michael's only link to his employers and his only hope for survival as blood continued to dribble down his face. He felt like he was ready to pass out and couldn't stop the vehicle before it bumped into the collapsed carport sagging off the left side of the house. The noise from the collision raised the attention of the occupants. They carried him into the house. After a short time, two men emerged from the house, jumped into Anthony's truck, and drove it quickly away.

Chapter 42

Gardiner Junction

The two men travelled carefully along the road near Minnewaska State Park and followed the long ridge of Millbrook Mountain on the way to the small town of Gardiner. They had been there before to set the charges, but it was still a challenge to find. They turned off the road and studied a hand-drawn map showing the unmarked junction of the Catskill and the Delaware aqueducts. With no working heat in Anthony's truck, the cold air was brutal. They finally recognized the landmark scribbled on the map, an old barn with double silos, one painted half way up in faded red, the other torn open by the weather and in complete disrepair. An abandoned tractor sat rusting on the ground between the silos. They turned on a dirt driveway ending in a field high above the town and hid the truck behind the barn.

"There is no need for us to come closer. We are already in the range. I know where is the target." The man wore faded blue jeans with a cloth belt, a dirty tee shirt with a Yankees logo, and a backwards baseball hat, but his dark olive skin hinted at foreign origin. His friend looked even more American the way he dressed but could have been a brother by the way he talked. The driver turned off the ignition and waited until the appointed time. Both men mumbled a prayer in Arabic and repeated it fervently. A pair of skunks crossed in front of the truck, causing them to freeze with wide-eyed looks. But the search for food was on the minds of the furry creatures, and there was no interest in spraying a truck that smelled only of dirty oil and worn tires.

****

A second email was sent at 6:35 PM to CNN, the New York Times, the Mayor of New York City, the Governor in Albany, and the President in Washington:

The Brotherhood of International Islamic Jihad will launch another attack on New York City's water supply within the hour. Others will follow using different methods of delivery. You have no choice but to comply with our demands to release all Islamic political prisoners NOW. Remember, WE set the deadlines, and WE control the results. B.I.I.J

****

At exactly 9:11 PM, the driver dialed a number and pushed the send button on a cell phone he'd removed from his jacket. The men yelled in unison, "Mawt Amerik! Allah hu akbar!" *Death to America! Allah is good!* As the truck skidded on to the highway, an underground explosion rumbled through the earth, and echoed off nearby peaks. There was no flash, no flying debris, but the ground rumbled like a small earthquake had suddenly altered the Catskill landscape deep below the surface.

In Gardiner, lights blinked on as citizens wondered why an episode of *Criminal Minds* had been so rudely interrupted with severe static. Men exited to their porches with shotguns and cell phones in hand. Dogs howled, and cats dove to safety under the nearest piece of furniture. The power blinked off and on repeatedly while teenage students groaned when their unsaved homework was lost after their computers crashed. The sound seemed to echo for a full minute with muffled secondary explosions.

A DEP car rushed to the scene. Soon the area was alive with DEP, National Guard, and NYPD vehicles. Water bubbled out of the ground while an acid smelling steam mixed with toxic smoke rose from Shaft Number Four of the crossroad of the Delaware and Catskill aqueducts.

Across the Hudson River, at a manned station along the aqueduct route in Yonkers, a DEP attendant gasped as he stared at gauges registering a sharp drop in water pressure, and the reading for the Catskill Aqueduct suddenly dropped to zero. When he called his supervisor, the Delaware Aqueduct gage was faltering, as if some unknown phantom was squeezing the huge pipeline like a limp hose. Commissioner Calloway was contacted at 9:23 PM in Manhattan. He tested the faucet in his kitchen, making sure the pressure was still good in the City.

"Don't ask ME what to do," he yelled into the phone. "That's what you guys in Gardiner are FOR, to control situations like this between the two systems!"

"The water is flooding and backing up into the aqueducts and rising up the shaft. We won't be able to repair it quickly," the sergeant said.

Calloway wasn't ready to deal with another emergency today. It seemed like the terrorists were watching his every move and setting off booby traps like landmines wherever he went. His voice was riddled with irritation. "Divert the supply from the Delaware channel...a hundred percent. Damn it! They keep figuring out different ways to bust our balls."

"How do they know?"

"I don't KNOW how! This is the first real test of the new switching station. Call Herb Rose and ask him to schedule an emergency team and a mucking crew in Gardiner immediately, like TONIGHT. We have to fix this, and FAST."

"You see, sir, we can't even get access to the lower shaft. It's filling up with water at a very rapid pace."

"You can't get IN? Well, then, DIG your way into that shaft. Get the emergency sump pumps going. Why do you have to ASK? You've still got two giant backhoes on site, and mucking equipment we used in the excavation." He took a deep breath to calm down. "How bad is the flooding?"

"Well, sir, the water is starting to come out the top of the shaft. It's like, the entire upstate water supply is gushing out. Wait! It looks like... Jesus! Two bodies just flew up five feet in the air, like a shotgun. They just blasted out the shaft with the water surge. Oh my god! I think it's the guards! I don't think they're—they can't be alive, Sir."

"Okay. Try to recover the bodies and call me back. But man, you're in charge up there! Don't ASK my permission. You make the big bucks. Use your fucking head. Call the crews upstream at all stations; tell them to slow down the flow as much as they can. And don't let anybody talk to the press, or we'll have a major panic on our hands down the city. What the hell! I'll call Herb myself. You GO. Get on it! NOW!"

"Sir, looks like we're getting some help. Herb Rose and his assistant just got out of a truck. Do you want to talk to them?"

"No. If he's there, he'll figure out how to deal with it, and recover the bodies. Have him call me when he can." After he disconnected, Commissioner Calloway tried his water tap again. He was relieved that he still had enough water to mix with two shots of bourbon. And a Xanax or two.

****

Parker dialed Tina to check in. He'd neglected her for several days, and he owed her some quality girlfriend attention.

"Parker boy, you've got to come home soon. I'm sick with a bad flu. My whole body aches, and I can hardly breathe. PLEASE!"

"What have you had to eat?" he asked cautiously.

"Just some rice, and two cups of Tummy-Soother tea."

"Tea is good for the flu. Have you called your doctor?"

"Not yet. But I can't drink any more tea."

"Jeez, Tina, you aren't...pregnant, are you?"

"No way. I'm sick to my stomach, honey-dew. And there's this funny taste left, sort of like...tastes like metal," she said.

His face turned to worry. "Did you finish the rice and tea?"

"Yeah, I ate the rice, but I left the tea next to the sink."

Parker's intuition kicked in like a five-alarm fire. "You used tap water to make both, right? Listen to me and do exactly as I say. Pour the tea into a clean glass jar. All of it. Don't drink any more. I'm sending someone over to test it."

"Aren't you being a little paranoid? Just because you're in charge of the water samples, doesn't mean everybody you know is going to die! Besides, I don't have a clean glass jar."

Parker tried to maintain a calm voice. "Sweetie, just wash out that jar of strawberry jelly in the frig."

"But...it's your favorite...and they're home-made preserves...by my mom!"

"Forget about that. Throw the damn jelly away and use the jar! I've got a WaterForce team in Central Park, near your apartment. Just let me keep you safe. We've had botulism, and that makes people very sick. I've got to meet Professor Jac, and I can't get there as fast as one of my guys can. When José rings the bell, just let him in and tell him to put a rush on this. Promise me. Do it now, okay?"

"Parker love, you're making me nervous." But there was no arguing with him. Control was his mode of operation these days. But afterwards, she ran to the bathroom. Her face in the mirror looked jaundiced. The porcelain throne beckoned, and she threw up the entire contents of her stomach. She felt weak, but she couldn't face the thought of bottling up her vomit, so she flushed it down. She didn't want Parker to worry. He had enough on his mind. Maybe she *was* pregnant. Perhaps José would be a gentleman and take her to the clinic when he came to collect the tea sample. Her life with Parker would change drastically if she were with child. She poured the tea into the jar, and dialed Dr. Angelica. She had to find out.

Chapter 43

A New Threat

Professor Jacoby felt old and foolish sitting on the surrealistic lipstick couch in the Bleecker Street Café, waiting for Parker to arrive. He checked out the eclectic furniture and artwork that adorned the walls and surveyed the student population from various New York universities hanging out after classes. Their trendy hair and fashion styles told a story of millennials' quest for individualism and freedom of expression. Jacoby remembered his own college days at Columbia, when beatniks like Jack Kerouac, Allen Ginsburg, and William S. Burroughs blazed new pathways similar to the youth of today. Of course, his straight and narrow path in the CIA had kept the empathy towards such liberals hidden deep in his heart. As a professor, he could finally feel comfortable among these young students finding their way like carrier pigeons on a jagged journey through multicolored clouds.

A young orange-haired waiter approached him and ushered him into a room in the back where they would have the privacy they would need tonight. Professor Jac had a serious agenda to discuss. The information he had received that afternoon was disconcerting at best. He'd shared frustrations with law enforcement agencies, the mayor, and the President. As a former CIA agent, the professor knew the United States would never give up on the search for those responsible. But at what cost? There was a serious gusher in Gardiner. Would they be able to stop the assaults while New York's water supply was catapulted thirty feet into the air, before there was no drinkable water left for millions of people in the Northeast, and before people would abandon the City in a panic?

The devastation from nine-eleven in 2001 had left lower Manhattan broken and rebuilding for many years. But the new threat was a thousand times worse. If the entire New York metropolitan area was left without safe drinking water, the economy of the entire country would be crippled for the next several decades even if the terrorists were defeated.

And so far, they had proven several times they could pull off multiple acts of water terrorism with impunity. The implied threat of a *united* Islamic organization was previously thought impossible due to the innumerable divisions between factions of al Qaeda, ISIS, Hamas, Taliban, Hezbollah, and dozens of other groups active in more than thirty-five countries. Each group had its individual issues and goals, and, except for the far-reaching hand of ISIS, there had been virtually no unity across borders since the death of Osama bin Laden, if even then. Yet it seemed real, and so far had proven effective.

Parker entered the private back room in the café to join Professor Jac.

"Parker, my boy. You picked an interesting place to meet. I haven't been here in years. How are you? How are the WaterForce Angels doing? What do you have to report?

"Well, Sir—I mean, Professor Jac—we've got over six hundred volunteers now. The reservoirs are being patrolled just about every minute of the day, and our people are collecting water samples all over the City. We're everywhere, just about. I hope the DEP and the NYPD appreciate our help."

"Good. Very good. People feel a great affinity for all of you and appreciate your help. And your people are wearing the blue berets and WaterForce sashes, I see. Very good."

"Thank you. We've got instant recognition with the public, and everybody is proud to wear them." He placed his beret on the table when the waiter served two glasses of Argentine Malbec. They toasted, and Parker asked, "You seem...troubled today. Is there something new?"

Jac tented his hands together. "My boy, as you may have heard from your father, they've attacked the aqueduct junction in Gardiner, and they are just as devious as ever. We don't have a single lead. The explosives were preset and very cleverly hidden. And I'm afraid there may be other locations with hidden explosives."

"That's terrible," Parker replied as his eyes widened.

"It's frustrating. Fortunately, however, not all of the explosives went off. But only the Catskill system is completely offline. The Delaware system was damaged, but some of the water has been routed through bypass tunnels that will deliver a reduced volume for several weeks. Meanwhile, we might be able to repair the damage before the Pepacton reaches dangerously low levels. If it had been a bigger bomb, we'd be in a horrible situation."

"As you know, we were not allowed inside the perimeter fences at Gardiner. Too high a risk for even the Angels." Parker showed his frustration with a frown. "I just don't understand. With all the safeguards in place, how can they keep getting closer and more dangerous? I get how the volume of water would be a safeguard for toxins. But what about the new UV filtration plant, the cameras and drones, the new chlorination plant—and the patrols? How can they be so successful with all those safeguards?"

Jac frowned, and said, "It is frustrating. We thought it was adequate until now. But they attack the water system differently every time. No one is blaming WaterForce. Unfortunately, the water supply may not ever be completely safe from terrorism. It seems as if the master plan is to focus attacks closer to the City and ever more serious."

Parker said, "What would happen if a dirty bomb, a homemade atomic bomb with nuclear fallout, was employed instead?"

Again, Professor Jac wrinkled his brows. "New York City would become an American Fukushima, unlivable for many decades. Ultimately, America could be next on history's list of fallen empires, a fate that Americans have never even considered."

"I never thought of it that way. What do you think is their next move?"

"We've learned of another situation that could be their next method of attack. Perhaps this time we can stay ahead of it."

"Tell me, please. We'll be extra vigilant. We've got to stop this."

"Parker boy, you're doing a fine job as it is. This new thing is a completely different monster. A company down in Delaware suffered a security breach the other night. They've developed a new product, intended to thwart the abuse of prescription drugs by locking the drug in a tiny capsule, smaller than a kernel of rice."

Parker looked confused. "Okay...but I don't get it. How would a kernel for prescription drugs affect the water supply?"

"It doesn't poison the entire water supply. It only uses the water system as a delivery method to get to where it does its real damage. You see, the capsule itself is small enough to pass through filtration systems without harm. The capsule is made of a hard-skinned, heat-sensitive polymer that will only dissolve when it reaches a certain temperature. It's loaded by a special machine with an individual dose that is protected until it is ingested. Quite ingenious. Once swallowed, the capsule dissolves from the heat of human body temperature and releases its contents." Jac's bushy eyebrows raised up to acknowledge Parker's mouth gaping wide open.

"But, the water supply...?"

"The water supply acts only as the conduit and is not directly poisoned in the way they've attempted before. Unfortunately, it is not detectable before it dissolves. The capsules will flow through the system and directly out of a water spigot. The kernel is nearly clear colored, barely visible, and the toxin inside isn't released until it dissolves when it hits the warmth of the stomach. If it goes into a coffee urn, it dissolves from the heat and poisons the entire contents. If it's used in cooking, say a homemade stew or soup, it poisons the entire batch. Ninety-four degree heat is all that is necessary to dissolve the kernel."

"Oh—my—god! But a grain of rice is tiny. Surely it can't carry much poison." Parker was hopeful.

"My friend, it doesn't take but one one-thousandth of a milliliter to be an effective dose to kill a human being with several known toxins. The issue of being dissolved and ineffective in billions of gallons is no longer a deterrent. Unlike the Pepacton poison, this delivery method is by individual dose. It is most likely delivered randomly, but it could also target specific individuals or groups."

"Jesus! That means we're guarding the reservoirs for nothing!"

"No, it only means they may have found an effective way to use the water supply as a vehicle to attack people. They can still compromise any part of the system with munitions. But all it would take to create widespread panic is a few dozen deaths from these capsules." Professor Jac leaned forward as he delivered the main point. "It's an attack on individuals instead of the entire system. This is more personal, instead of a broad stroke affecting masses of people. But it only takes a few deaths to create widespread panic. Fear is their most effective tool, Parker."

"Oh...my God! My girlfriend went to the hospital today after drinking tea and eating rice made with tap water. She had severe stomach pain, vomiting, diarrhea, and respiratory congestion. Do you think it's already starting? Jesus, how did they *find* her?"

"No. No, Parker. The theft at the plant in Delaware happened just the other night. Your gal probably has the flu. But the symptoms may be very similar, and impossible to distinguish without a medical examination."

"I sent out the tea to have it tested." The thoughts of losing Tina haunted him. Why did this crisis have to get so personal?

"Good. You're always a step ahead. That's my boy. The reason I told you is that we need to be extra vigilant at any place close to the City where someone could introduce these tiny capsules. Unfortunately, there are thousands of vulnerable entrance points in the pipes of New York."

"It sounds like almost impossible to prevent." Parker's worried expression turned very dark.

"It could be, unless we can catch up with the terrorists before they figure out how to load the capsules with whatever the toxin is."

"How do you load them?" Parker was surprised that the professor was sharing this new threat. Was it because he finally trusted Parker?

"It's not easy. It takes a special machine, two of which were also stolen along with the capsules. These events are *all* connected."

Parker said, "This sounds terrible. But I don't understand. How do you know the theft of these capsules in Delaware is connected to the terrorists in New York?"

"There is an awful lot of coincidental evidence and one very clear link." Jac's eyebrows lowered and his face changed to his CIA demeanor. "My boy, do you know where Anthony is? His mother can't find him, and he's been off the radar for several days."

"Wait a minute! I know for a fact that Anthony couldn't have been three hundred miles away in Delaware."

He leaned across the table and stared into Parker's eyes. "And you're so sure because..."

"I just know. That's all. Don't you trust me, Professor Jac?"

"I have always trusted you, Parker, but you're not telling me everything, my friend. And we need to be completely honest with each other if WaterForce is to be trusted in the future."

Parker had been sworn to secrecy after a long discussion with his brother. They already knew Anthony used his tiny speedboats to deliver explosives and botulism at the Ashokan. Only his father knew about his liaison with Titus on Wildcat Mountain, but Anthony would have to stay hidden for a while longer. Titus was in charge of keeping Anthony safe from harm and away from any more trouble. Parker could feel the conflict within. He wanted to tell

Professor Jac, but feared Jac would lose trust in the WaterForce Angels, and worse, it would divide him from his brother. Both Parker and Titus could be arrested for obstructing justice. He knew he was no match for Professor Jac's razor sharp intuition and his CIA style of interrogation. "Professor Jac, just give us a chance. We'll find Anthony. But I *know* he was not in Delaware last night."

The professor's face darkened when he delivered the key evidence. "You see, Anthony's truck was used in Delaware for the burglary. His license tag appeared on the security camera at the loading dock."

"They took it all the way to Delaware? I'm telling you, Anthony was *not* driving that truck!"

"So, Anthony was not in possession of his own truck? Don't you think that might be a little hard to believe?" Jac's entire face wrinkled into doubt.

Parker sighed when he knew he could not win. "Anthony's truck was stolen the day before yesterday from the Frost Valley YMCA in the Catskills. Titus and Anthony captured Michael and took his keys away from him, but he stole Anthony's truck and escaped."

"Aha! So it only *appears* that Anthony was responsible for the burglary in Delaware because they used his truck. I hope there is a police report forthcoming." The professor paused to think this over. "Okay. That's possible. I believe you. Where is Anthony now, this minute?"

Parker said, "Okay! I'm sorry. All this *just* happened. Anthony is truly, truly on our side now. When he found out he was working for an Islamic jihad group, he had some kind of epiphany with his conscience, and he jumped ship. Anthony helped Titus when they captured Michael Capo at Frost Valley. Michael was injured, but when they climbed to the top of Doubletop Mountain to get cell phone service, Michael broke out of his constraints and got away with Anthony's truck."

Professor Jac said, "Now I see. So, it looks as if Anthony is in the hot seat. They're placing the blame for the industrial burglary on him. Very smart of the terrorists, when you think of it. And Anthony is afraid of arrest, so you and Titus are hiding him somewhere, right, my friend?" He leaned forward at the moment of revelation.

There was little Parker could say. "I know it looks bad, but Anthony is my friend. He would not have done those things if he knew who he was really working for."

"It doesn't matter. The explosion and toxin at the Ashoken is still illegal. And trying to protect him doesn't look good for you. The legal system doesn't forgive without due process, a trial in a court of law." Professor Jac scowled as his bushy eyebrows shaded his eyes.

Parker hoped that Professor Jac wanted to be on his side in spite of the interrogation. Parker needed to find out immediately. He stood up, walked to the door, and turned to say one last thing. "I'm leaving now, because I don't think you want to be wasting your time arresting me when you know damn well we both have important things to do for the City. Professor Jac, you *know* you can still trust me. As for our methods...well, Titus and Anthony didn't have much choice. Please, just trust us. I'll check in with you later." With that, he was gone before Professor Jac could retrieve the cell phone from his pocket. Jac felt helpless in his eighty-some years. When his fingers reached the keyboard to dial, he felt nothing but guilt and sorrow for a decision he didn't want on his conscience. After a pause, his fingers made him dial Herb's cell phone instead.

WaterForce

Chapter 44

A Mole?

Parker stood leaning against the wall of the NYPD station at the south end of Times Square when I called. The news ticker across the CNN building across the street said ...*New York holds its breath after water botulism scare...Mayor declares water safe...President toasts the city, drinking Catskill water...Terrorism suspects elude police...*Parker knew the news ticker wasn't telling the whole story. After his meeting with Professor Jac, Parker realized there had to be some major strategy changes. Funny how those feelings landed simultaneously in my mind and Parker's. I told him what the local rumor mill added to the news of the explosions at Gardiner—news travels faster than you'd think in the mountains—and he told me about the misinformation on the CNN ticker broadcasting from the crossroads of the world.

"The thing is, Parker, we've all known about the project to link the two aqueducts at Gardiner, but nobody knew the exact location of the new junction."

"That's what I've gotten from Professor Jac. So...how did the terrorists find it?"

"There HAD to be leak. An informant who is feeding information to them," I said.

"Right. And you know who they are sure to blame?"

"Right—Anthony. He's been on both sides and would be immediately suspected of being one of the only people to be in a position to leak information. Problem is, Anthony was never close to anyone on our side who knew anything of value."

"Maybe you're right, Parker. But if they find out I'm protecting Anthony, they will immediately think you and I are in on it, by association. And they'll never trust us again."

Parker finished my thought. "And WaterForce will be finished."

"What are we gonna do?"

"Damn it! We started something so good—for the protection of the water, and now...because of Anthony, it could be ruined. But he can't possibly have insider information without an informant higher up."

Parker paused for a minute, then almost whispered through the phone. "Titus, who knows about Anthony up there?"

"You and I, his Mom, our Dad, and Mo."

"Where is Anthony?"

"Safe. I'm not gonna say where. But he's off the map," I replied.

"You and I haven't told a soul. So that makes only a few people who might have yapped to someone else."

Parker answered. "I just talked to Professor Jac. He squeezed the information out of me about you and Anthony, and Michael's escape."

"Oh, man! How'd he do that? Shit!"

"I guess I caved after his CIA interrogation. But if he wanted to act on the information about us hiding Anthony, I'm pretty sure he would have detained me. But he didn't."

"Wow...maybe he actually trusts us," I said.

"I hope so. Well, I sort of walked out on him."

"Rad! But in spite of everything, Dad's not going to give up his sons, and neither is his top assistant."

"I agree. We've known Mo since we were five years old. He would never betray us," Parker said.

"Mo was the one who tested and discovered the botulism in the water from the Pepacton."

"He's the guy Dad trusts most of all...but no, not Mo. But how did they find the exact place in Gardiner?"

I began to pace back and forth as my nerves began to fall apart. "We haven't considered the other people in the DEP who know about Gardiner: Commissioner Calloway, the guys on the mucking crew, the DEP officers who man that station. Anyone one of them could be a mole. We don't know how much any one of them knows. But this isn't a thing we can answer. Our job is to protect the reservoirs and protect Anthony until the real terrorists are found."

"I think we need a shift in strategy, Ti. Let's look at this again. The threats are getting closer to the city. We still have to patrol the Catskill reservoirs, but I think the threat is getting more serious down in Manhattan. I need you in the City, and soon. We're a great team. We could keep much better control over Anthony if he was in the City, where they are NOT looking for him."

"I get your message, bro. Now that WaterForce is fully staffed, I can delegate my role, so I can get to the City. Let me make some calls. Can you be ready to hide Anthony in a safe place by tomorrow morning?"

"You bet. Meet me at that place where the party was last summer. Bring him to the super's apartment in the basement. The super is one my best guys in WaterForce, completely trustworthy, and the apartment is secure."

"Let's meet about four, before dawn. This is weird harboring a fugitive, and still thinking he's my best friend.

But maybe he'll have a chance to prove his innocence..." A ray of hope entered my mind.

"Don't count on it, Titus. As soon as you have him out in public, he'll get caught, and we'll be in deep shit. For now, let's just keep him out of the limelight. The mission comes first. No big macho tricks to prove that Anthony's a saint, okay?"

"Right." But inside, I knew Anthony. And I knew it would take a miracle.

Chapter 45

Getting to the Source

T he men at the meeting in the oval office had been mired in a dour mood the entire morning. The President paced around the room, trying to put together all the information provided by his key national defense team. It was now clear that there was a mole that was feeding information to the terrorists. There were simply too many breaches in confidential information. The fact that Americans were clearly involved on a subordinate level to do the dirty work of foreign terrorists was alarming. Emotions overflowed into anger, and the President feared that plans of retaliation would soon reach the boiling point and erupt against the countries that had been named as destinations for the prisoners they demanded to be released.

The Secretary of State commented, "We've reached out diplomatically to Yemen, Syria, Somalia, Iran, Qatar, and Pakistan. You know how hard that is with all the other issues we're dealing with. Nobody is cooperating, not even an admission of knowledge of a terrorist organization called the Brotherhood of International Islamic Jihad. So far it's a phantom."

The Mayor said, "And maybe it isn't even real. Maybe it's a complete hoax. There is no proof that the B.I.I.J. is real."

The FBI Director said, " I think the toxin and the explosions are real enough proof!"

The Secretary of Defense said, "But we have to take this seriously. The clock is ticking, and we could lose New

York for decades. A squadron of bombers over each of those so-called countries will get some information quickly."

"If you don't find them soon I'm gonna bomb every country in that news release, believe me," said the President. He smiled closed mouthed at his hawkish secretary.

"Come on, guys! Let's cool our jets!" said the mayor.

The Secretary of State said, "We've tried to work through intermediaries. Going through tribal leaders instead of the government. Talking to Iran and Yemen through links in Jordan. Pakistani officials close to some higher-ups in al Qaeda and ISIS. And our man in Kenya is friendly with leaders in Somalia. But nobody admits knowledge of the B.I.I.J. I'm beginning to suspect it's just a front for an existing group..."

The President answered, "And how would that make a difference when they blow up another part of our water supply? We'd be better off concentrating on finding the losers here at home. And especially that mole. He's done more damage than a room full of rats. What do we know about *that*?"

O'Riley spoke up. "Mister President, Sir, if I may say, we now believe that the information was most likely leaked from the DEP itself." He looked over to Commissioner Calloway of the DEP, who shifted uncomfortably in his chair. "We've been discussing ways of trapping the mole, but events are happening so fast, it's hard to launch a realistic plan. Usually we place an agent for months to gather evidence and information before an arrest can be made. But now we've got only days at the most—maybe hours!"

"Okay...what *have* you got?" said the President.

"Sergeant Herb Rose has four officers and a biochemist in his office, and he has a network of the

WaterForce Angels. If we could feed some false information through individual channels, a little at a time, just to selected coworkers of Officer Rose, we might be able to identify who is responsible," said Commissioner Calloway. "And I've put a tail on Officer Rose, just to verify what he tells us. We can't be too careful. He knows something about one of the domestic suspects that has gone missing. Both of his sons are leaders in the new WaterForce Angels. Titus in the Catskills, and Parker down the City."

O'Riley saw his chance to let out his hate and mistrust. "I *told* you guys that WaterForce group would be a menace! We had to give them security clearances so fast, and they're all just kids for Chrissake."

The President said, "How can we trust a bunch of snot nosed kids with national secrets and security? You'd better start believing me!"

"What about Officer Rose? If you think he is withholding information, and his sons are both involved in WaterForce, let's question him," said the FBI Director.

"Damn it, I just promoted him a few weeks ago!" said Calloway. "Herb Rose was the one who discovered the toxin in the Pepacton. He's the best we've got!"

O'Riley said, "This is just like the arson case last year. The fireman who played the big freaking hero was the one who set the fire. Personally, I think Rose is an idiot! You'd better question him real good. Actually, let ME at him. I can get that two-faced shithead to talk."

Ironically, now it was the Secretary of Homeland Security who said, "You'd best stay in your own jurisdiction. Cool your jets, O'Riley!"

"We've got National Guard everywhere in the metropolitan New York area. We've got the Angels in the

Catskills, and the DEP guarding every critical junction of the aqueducts and the reservoirs. But we need a break. We need something to point to that needle in the haystack. A word from someone..."

****

(Front page. *New York Times*)

The Editor in Chief of the *Times* received a copy of a message sent from the Brotherhood of International Islamic Jihad. A copy was also sent to the President at noon today. The B.I.I.J. has finally placed an ultimate deadline for the U.S. government to release all political prisoners held in Guantanamo and various Navy brigs across the world. The deadline is now set for Friday noon, ten days from now. A spokesman from the Department of Defense claimed that the fact that the U.S. has not responded has finally resulted in the terrorists setting a real deadline.

This move may mean they are now more willing to respond favorably to negotiation instead of brinksmanship. Still, there is no indication that the U.S. has made any successful attempt to reach the so-called 'Brotherhood', or that any real negotiations are in progress since the explosions last night in Gardiner, which is sending a geyser of water skyward that so far cannot be stopped. The Secretary of Homeland Security has sent detailed instructions to all communities in the New York City watershed on how to face the reality of losing our supply of water.

Some areas will be evacuated. Other areas are believed to be safe as long as they find alternative water sources during this temporary crisis. Safe fresh water is being transported to neighborhoods throughout the city in tanker trucks that will temporarily serve our needs until the crisis has been resolved. However, for the foreseeable future, water from the tankers will be limited to a ration of one gallon per family member per day.

Chapter 46

Got to See Mom

'No big macho tricks', Parker had said. But Anthony had a right to see his mom before we hustled him into hiding someplace in the City, right? I drove past the storefronts in Woodstock and turned into an alley behind one of the stores. We entered through the back and waited in the storeroom for Bonnie to join us. When she showed up after closing around eleven, we related the unfortunate tale of Anthony's escape from Michael's clutches, and Michael's escape from capture. She already knew about the explosion in Gardiner from friends who lived nearby. I could have predicted how she'd react.

Her whole body shook with anxiety. Her beaded necklaces, multiple bracelets, flamboyant knuckle rings, eight-inch earrings that could run a grandfather clock, and the bodacious hair jewelry seemed to rattle and jangle as her face beamed like a Christmas tree. Finally, she spoke. "I'm so proud of you. You made the right decisions. But, Jesus, Anthony! The police have been here almost every day, looking for you, asking questions, accusing me of raising a 'dangerous stoned-out dissident', as they say. We've got to be careful! You're a fugitive, and we'll never be able to prove you've changed. I'm so angry at Michael for putting you in danger." As she shook her head for emphasis, her dangling earrings nearly struck midnight as they threatened to tear through her lobes.

"I'm sorry, Mom. I'm in an impossible position."

I said, "Bonnie, we've got to protect Anthony until he can prove he's really on our side. I'm taking him to the City late tonight, for his own protection."

She answered, "You can't stay in Woodstock, son. I know they're watching the house, just like the Viet Nam days. I even recognize the cop, with his phony long-haired frigging wig and all that fake jewelry and temporary tattoos." As soon as she said it, she looked at the collection of jewelry on her own body. Her nose ring twitched as she laughed in her witch's cackle at the irony of her jewelry critique.

Anthony laughed, and said, "Mom, you're so paranoid of the pigs. This isn't nineteen sixty-nine!"

"Honey, it's the same thing, all over again. We've got evidence of terrorism, now, and YOU are a prime suspect. But I wish I'd been WITH you when you sent that boat across the Ashokan—you DID that, didn't you?" Her eyes bulged out, the black eyeliner made her look like a YouTube parody.

"Well, yeah, Mom, I kinda did, but..."

"I KNEW it! As soon as I heard about that miniature boat! I'm gonna put a goddam hex on those cops, if it's the last thing I do. I'm so proud o' you."

"Mom, will you stop with the witch's crap, already! You KNOW that never works."

"Yeah, ask Freda Levine about my hexes. And Angel Tohicken...like she ever WAS a frigging angel! And George W. Bush. I fixed him good, and now he's off in Texas making dog paintings! I'll show YOU what works." When she flipped him off, her prized rattlesnake ring flew off and damn near parted my hair.

Anthony screamed, "Mom, will you stop? You almost killed him with that ring! You're scaring him...and me too!"

"You are my son, all the way!" she said. "Christ New York! I miss the old days, when we could get something done without a bunch of rag-heads hijacking our issues!"

"MOM, you can't call them 'rag-heads'! That's language the president uses!"

"It isn't like that, Mrs. Guarini. Anthony left when he found out who he was really working for."

"I know, honey. The worst part is the risks my boy had to take." When her nostrils flared, I imagined that flames would appear.

"Mom, you don't know how bad we feel about letting Michael escape."

"You've got to concentrate on capturing him again. Do you know where he might be?" she asked. "If they weren't watching me, I'd join your magic Angels!"

"And you'd stick out like a shotgun in a Chase Bank," Anthony said.

I was laughing, but I had to get this scene back to reality. "Actually, there's only one possibility. Michael said there was a safe house in Prattsville, where his contact hangs out. That's where he gets paid. I don't know exactly where it is, but I think that's the only place he could be right now."

"Oh my God! If you could capture him again, that would completely exonerate you!" she said.

"It would help...but we don't have a single idea where in Prattsville, or nearby, he could be. Grand Gorge, Gilboa, Prattsville...and any number of little villages and mountain roads around there. Plus, the Schoharie Reservoir is nearby, and the DEP is patrolling everywhere, not to mention our own patrols from WaterForce. I've discussed this with Parker, and we both agree. Even though it would be great to capture him, it's not in the best interest of our main mission.

And it's not the best use of our time to go looking up every tree in the forest for him," I offered.

I turned to Anthony. "You and I need to get to New York City. Parker has a safe place for you there, and there are new developments every day. Let somebody else go chasing after Michael."

Bonnie said, "Still, if the WaterForce patrols could look for him, you might get their gun sights off my son."

"I've already put that into motion, Mrs. Guarini. We just stopped so you could spend a little time with your son before we leave for the City tonight.

Bonnie said, "I talked to friends down the city today. Everybody is in a panic. Water pressure is low. There will be severe rationing in all five boroughs, and they're trucking in water in big tankers, from god knows where. You'd think the goddam world was ending, starting with New York City. A hell of a nice place to visit, before all this!"

I hadn't known how serious it was. "You mean, the Gardiner explosion...?"

"I'm afraid so. Because of the attack in Gardiner, the Catskill aqueduct is completely off line, and the supply from the Delaware system will only last a couple of weeks. After that, it's going to be very difficult. Everybody up here is talking about it. Gardiner will become as notorious as nine-eleven."

I was shocked. I was so sure that WaterForce could prevent incidents like this. But the NYPD had forbidden us to patrol the Gardiner junction facility and refused to reveal its exact location. How had the terrorists gained access so easily? There had to be someone on the inside, a mole that we thought was on our team, but had been feeding them critical information from the beginning.

I turned my attention back to her explanation. "The networks said the details of the rationing plan would be announced tomorrow morning."

She pulled out several quarts of Poland Spring bottled water for us, and we left for the city that never sleeps.

Chapter 47
A City Without

At three-thirty in the morning, Anthony and I drove on I-684, one of many routes into the City. We drove past the large Kensico Reservoir. But as we cruised near the shore, I could see the place was crawling with NYPD and DEP cars. There was no way anyone could get within a hundred yards of the place without a badge. Directly to the East, it looked like Westchester County Airport was also in lock-down. We passed a couple of army tanker trucks, big ones carrying nearly ten thousand gallons. And then it hit me. As we went around a curve, I could see an almost endless line of tanker trucks headed towards the city. It looked like an armed invasion, and proof of an imminent threat. Now caught in slow traffic, I switched on the radio, and learned that two hundred more trucks each crossed over the George Washington Bridge, the Triborough Bridge, through the Lincoln and Holland Tunnels, and over the Outerbridge Crossing to the South. Each truck held ninety-two-hundred gallons of water that would be distributed at stations on every other block in all of Manhattan, Queens, Brooklyn, Bronx, and Staten Island, for an undetermined time until the Gardiner aqueduct junction could be repaired. The City's daily requirement was normally almost one point four billion gallons. The newscaster reported that much of the water was shipped from Lake Ontario in the Great Lakes, a supply with hundreds of trillions of gallons, practically inexhaustible.

I changed the radio channel to catch two of my favorite all-night deejays as they covered some of the challenges facing the city.

Like the two brothers on CarTalk, Rosco Rossini and sidekick Zeke Rothburg were commenting with their usual ribald sense of humor in the face of tragedy. Rosco said, "The water coming in is raw untreated water from the Great Lakes, with all the pollution from Chicago, Detroit, Cleveland, and Buffalo. I wouldn't put that stuff in my mouth if it were the last water on earth. It's full of rusty autos, slime and oil...and God knows how much raw sewage...from places like Cleveland, land of the Cleves! Bleck!"

"Yeah, but they're purifying it with mammoth doses of chlorine dissolved in each truckload. We don't have any choice, Rosco. Fact is, we're totally spoiled with unlimited pure water from the Catskills. But what's so 'great' about drinking water from the Great Lakes?"

"Nuttin! Do you realize, Zeke, in order to meet the daily consumption in the five boroughs–do you realize how many truckloads of water has to be shipped in ...*every freakin day*? And we only get a gallon each, not enough for a decent shower. The trip from Oswego to Manhattan is five and a half hours one-way. They can only make two round trips per twenty-four-hour period for each truck. Why don't they just build a damn pipeline?"

"Yeah! They do it for oil!"

"And where do they get all those trucks?"

"When I talked to our City Hall reporter, Stuart Novak, he said they had a hard time finding enough tanker trucks. Milk, gasoline, oil, and chemicals have commonly been carried by liquid tanker truck. Some of the trucks have recently carried petroleum or chemical products, and had to be thoroughly sanitized before they could be filled with potable water. Rosco, this is a BIG DEAL!"

"Right, Zeke. We'll be drinking Hess Oil cocktails, seasoned with Great Lakes grunge. Why don't we all just suck on a bus pipe? And this doesn't just affect the need to drink water. Water—our most basic need. But think of all those trucks diverted from the flow of materials to construction, food, manufacturing, and the petroleum industries along the entire East coast. Industries will soon be in a panic to keep their doors open and be forced to swallow increased shipping charges from sources far up and down the East coast."

"Ha! You said 'swallow' the shipping! After the show, my wife and I are going up to the Catskills to our camp in Woodstock. That'll be two less mouths drinking Lake Ontario toxic soup. What a mess, Rosco."

"And isn't it ironic. First, they poison the water up there. Turns out, our mountain water poses no real threat, but the Gardiner explosions squeezed off the supply. And everybody who *can* is fleeing the city and going *back* to the Catskills to get some of our own pure mountain nectar, the very stuff we can't get anymore in the City! Talk about irony! So you're gonna leave us with our thirst, Zeke?"

"Damn right, Rosco, my man. Nobody trusts their own faucets. It's only going to get worse, since the supply is down to a trickle."

"So, what does a chlorine tablet taste like in Lake Ontario water?"

"Like, 'drop, drop, fizz, fizz, what a freackin mess it is...'"

"I drank my own pee when I was in the Marines in Nam, Zeke, but that's no reason I'm gonna do it now."

"So, which is worse, drinking water from Lake Ontario, or drinking your own pee?"

"To each his own, Zeke. Each to his own. But if I drink my own pee, at least I know what's in there. It's probably half Budweiser." They laughed at the crisis, sounding like clones of 'Car-Talk'.

"I gotta say, I'm not usually in a panic when these things happen. But retailers are pulling bottled water from their back rooms and warehouses to restock their shelves. I got a series of tweets from my girlfriend in Manhattan. She says they're gouging prices by over four hundred per cent in Times Square. Long lines reach around the block when a retailer is found to have a stock of water, soft drinks, beer— just about any liquid at any price. And here's a comment from Sam Dyson, on Facebook, about trucking Lake Ontario water: he says. 'with a couple o' shots of chlorine in trucks that carried *fertilizer* last week? What's the big deal? Maybe it'll make my little green willy grow into a jolly green giant!'"

"I think it'd be safer to siphon the East River, boil it, have a nice long drink, and watch your skin turn green."

"We better get off the air, Zeke, before the Mayor finds out we're not voting for him until we get safer liquids around here."

"You're right, Rosco-Bosco, and just wait until water is more expensive than gasoline!"

"Knock it off! You're scaring me, water-boy."

"Damn right you're scared, Rosco. So am I! Even though we make jokes, this is a serious situation. It's just that, in any crisis, if you meet it with humor, it seems easier to get through it. This is the Zeke and Rosco Show. Until tomorrow, when those tanker trucks show up on your block: stick with imported alcoholic beverages, and drink water at your own risk! Cheers, Rosco."

"And rethink that New Year's resolution to lay off the Jack Daniels. G'night, Zeke." *Burp!*

****

I had to laugh as they signed off the air. I pulled up to the building on W. 83 St., where Anthony would be staying. I parked around the corner on Central Park West, and we walked on the deserted street to the middle of the block. The Belvedere Castle was nearby, on the 79th St. Transverse Road in Central Park, and I recalled how I had strolled through the park not too many weeks before, in search of signs of the maze of water valves and pipes I knew were nearby, hidden by the cloak of peace on Strawberry Fields in the park.

We were fifteen minutes early, but Parker buzzed me in on the first ring. When we entered the two-bedroom superintendent's apartment, Parker explained that the super had recently returned to Puerto Rico, and his friend Romondo was staying for the duration.

"Romondo leads one of our best patrols. They cover the North half of Central Park and collect water samples from the Columbia University campus nearby.

"Can I join his team?" asked Anthony.

"Sorry, it's too risky for you right now. But you can listen to the chatter on the police band receiver. You'll learn a lot, and, when we can risk it, we'll hook you up with Romondo's team."

Anthony looked disappointed, but he knew it was for the best.

Chapter 48

Death in the City

P arker stood against a lamppost at his usual urban command center at the south end of Times Square. From where he stood outside of the NYPD station, he could see the corner of 45th and Broadway, where a Pakistani terrorist had attempted to ignite a bomb in 2010. This was exactly the kind of event that he hoped the WaterForce Angels could prevent. His eyes were a little more seasoned now, and he noticed every foreigner, every suspicious American, and noted the license plate of any vehicle that slowed down in the crossroads of the world. The electronic news tickertape from CNN broadcast updates. But the usual pulse of humanity in Times Square had dwindled to a trickle. The tourist trade was all but dead. Theaters and many businesses were closed. Hospitals, essential services and utilities were protected by armed National Guard or police. The ten-day warning from the terrorists was rapidly coming to a head. Scenarios of the next supposed attack were exaggerated by the press and the public rumor mill. Fake news only confused the public. Every mistaken arrest was blown out of proportion.

Some New Yorkers left the City in fear of what might happen. Others fashioned a way of collecting or importing water, or standing in line at a neighborhood tanker truck, staying home to wait for the crisis to end. A dwindling minority believed the threat was unsubstantiated and drank water from the tap as if nothing was ever wrong. Citizens who ventured out carried a plastic bottle in a backpack, purse or briefcase in case breaking news elevated the crisis. Psychologically, everyone was thirsty, all the time.

Parker's phone rang with one of his water patrol commanders reporting in. Parker was afraid that his patrols were getting bored, and possibly becoming careless. Jévon reported, "I don't know if there is a connection yet, but I think you should know that an Israeli woman on First Avenue was taken to the Bellevue ER with severe respiratory problems and internal bleeding. She'd made some oatmeal, and almost immediately got very sick. I took the remaining food and a sample of tap water to the lab, and they said both contained Ricin. She died shortly after they tried to administer intravenous fluids."

"They switched to Ricin! Jesus! It's finally happened. Professor Jac predicted this. He knows how this happened. Who was this woman?"

"An Israeli woman, whose husband made a big speech about terrorism yesterday at the UN."

"The UN. This is not good," Parker said. He moved towards a subway entrance.

"They've taken most of the residents of her building to Bellevue for testing and possible treatment, and they've quarantined several other buildings in the neighborhood until further tests can be conducted. All of them have high populations of UN personnel."

****

Parker hurried downtown on an express A-Train to visit Professor Jac. The good professor would know more than anyone on the street. When he arrived, he was greeted in the hall, and ushered quickly into Professor Jac's inner office.

Professor Jac said, "I've heard the details, Parker. This is very serious. It escalates the crisis in many ways. The specific attack on UN personnel is disturbing and will cause international pressure on the President from the entire free world."

"We've GOT to capture these guys now. I'll call my team..."

"Yes, Parker, but we need a new plan. The Mayor is calling an emergency meeting in City Hall. The rationing plan is scaring everyone, and people are leaving the city in droves."

"We all feel so helpless," Parker said. "Professor Jac, I hate to sound dumb, but what exactly is Ricin?"

"Ricin is a toxic protein, a byproduct from the castor oil plant, *ricinus communis*, and is highly poisonous even in tiny quantities. As little as five hundred micrograms is enough to kill an adult, in a quantity barely the size of a grain of salt. The frightening thing is, Ricin was found in substantial quantities in terrorist sites in Afghanistan only a few years ago and was also used in Iraq's war against Iran years ago. Its use here is not surprising. The link to terrorist organizations substantiates what we have surmised from the evidence so far." He leaned forward in his chair. His bushy eyebrows waved up and down.

"How does it work?"

"It attacks all major organs. Basically, it prevents cells in the body from making protein, leading to internal bleeding in the stomach and intestines, severe problems breathing due to fluid in the lungs, and muscular pain and cramps. In less than forty-eight hours, the liver, spleen, kidneys, and lymph nodes simply shut down, and a very painful death is the result."

"Jesus! Is there any test for it? And what about an antidote or treatment?" This seemed worse than botulism. He squirmed in his seat as he tried to see some hope.

"There is no reliable test for Ricin poisoning, and no antidote. Treatment is sometimes effective, and is usually done by administering intravenous fluids, helping the patient to breathe, and prescribing certain medications. People who manage to survive for more than four or five days are said to have a good chance of recovery, though they may suffer permanent organ damage that will create problems later on."

"Sounds like it's almost always fatal."

"It's terrible, Parker. Ricin poisoning is lethal."

Parker said, "So, the tiny capsule you told me about... was that the *way* it got into that specific building?"

"Probably. Like many buildings in the City there is a water tower on the roof that serves as a reservoir for the building. These water towers are often vulnerable. Ricin-loaded capsules were inserted there and went through the pipes serving all one-hundred-sixty apartments. They've inspected the pipes and water in the top five floors already and found over a hundred undissolved capsules." As he spoke, he drew the water tower on a pad of paper, and connected squares with scribbled lines.

"How did they know how many people from the UN live there?"

"It wasn't hard for them to find out. That building is over sixty percent UN personnel. Representatives from thirteen different countries, attachés, service personnel, secretaries and assistants."

"A deliberate, targeted attack," Parker said.

"That's the obvious conclusion." His cell phone rang, and he answered it quickly, then walked to his window. "Yes,

Charles... I'm sorry to hear that. I've called the Red Cross, to find lodging for them. Don't let anyone in that building." As the call ended, he looked at Parker with sad eyes. "Another tragedy, in a building about three blocks from the first, with over a hundred UN personnel in residence. The delegates and their wives from France and the Netherlands have passed away, after morning coffee in their apartments."

When the call ended, he wiped a tear from his eye. "I knew them both well. The intent is now quite clear. We're gathering a list of addresses of all UN personnel. I'll need your WaterForce testing crews to concentrate on those buildings right away. This attack is directed towards the UN to retaliate against the speech yesterday, and in order to put pressure on our President. It won't be long until every nation puts pressure on us to release those prisoners. Gather your teams and prepare for deployment, mostly East side midtown. Don't let me down." He handed Parker a new phone. "Use this only to talk to me. It's completely secure. Call me when you have eight or ten testing teams in the streets near the UN. I'll provide a list of buildings that are high risk. Now go...quickly and gather up the Angels. We'll need test results by the end of the day."

Chapter 49

Frustration on High

H erb was perturbed. His key biochemist was not by his side when samples were arriving by the dozens from all nineteen reservoirs for testing. But just as he tried again to radio him or reach him on his cell, he saw Mo's car arriving in the parking lot. With one problem solved, he tried to calm down before the dreaded daily call to Commissioner O'Riley at NYPD headquarters, when typically, O'Riley took on a condescending attitude that was difficult at best. When he reached O'Riley's office on the phone, he had to be careful about the information he divulged in order to honor his promises to the boys. Walking the tightrope of truth was not easy.

"Commissioner, Herb Rose here. How are things going down there?"

"You had to ask? We've never had panic like this since nine-eleven. The whole goddam city is either evacuating on their own or chewing nails before the next threat surfaces. I've never seen such fear and chaos. So, what do *you* want?"

"I'm trying to track Michael Capo. I understand you've picked up cell phone signals."

"Not good enough. His phone is never on for long enough to triangulate. We haven't been able to get an accurate location. What else?"

"I remember you picked up his signal in Gardiner the day of the explosion," Herb said.

"Right, and after that, we've traced him to a block away from the Hillview Reservoir in the Bronx, and a few nights ago, near that chemical plant in Wilmington, Delaware. The security camera picked up photos of Anthony Guarini's license plate at the entrance. That's damn good proof Capo and Guarini were the ones who stole those capsules," O'Riley said.

"Maybe so," Herb said. But I've got reason to believe Michael Capo was injured up here in the mountains. I'm now sure that the foreign terrorists are using Guarini's truck and Michael Capo's phone to incriminate the American co-conspirators and get the heat off themselves." Herb hoped he had been careful enough.

"Interesting...a pretty wild-ass theory," the commissioner said. "There's something else. I think we've got a major leak coming from up your way, Herby. One of your staff, or maybe one of those Girl Scouts you have taking samples of the water." He laughed in disgust.

"Commissioner, those 'Girl Scouts' are the most dedicated group of volunteers you could have anywhere. Frankly, I resent the implication that one of my people, or one of the WaterForce Angels—who are headed by my own sons—are leaking information!" He began to pace and squeezed the phone hard.

"The presence of your son makes you blind and prejudiced. The President *wants* me to find the mole, damn it! And that's just what I'm going to do...whether it's your boys, their friends, or whether it's even YOU."

"Oh, come on, Commissioner O'Riley! I am working with my *own* boss, Commissioner Calloway, on that very problem, and we don't need interference from other agencies, and especially from YOU! When we have more facts, you'll be the first to know." He was happy the way that came out. It was forceful and stood up to the bullshit he was hearing.

"How about your staff?"

Herb looked at Mo, who was across the room testing samples. "I have coworkers, dedicated officers who each have a spotless record! And a biochemist lab tech who was the *first* to identify the first toxic dump of botulism in the Pepacton and was a key in preventing maximum damage at the Rondout and the Ashokan incidents. I've vetted every one of these people, and I'm still checking on the Angels." From across the room, Mo smiled at Herb.

O'Riley scowled with an expression of doubt, the eye of a seasoned skeptic. He let his New York superiority show through. "Hmpf! I don't know, Herb. Sounds like you're *fishing* for facts up there in those mountain streams. You trying to protect someone? Your stories don't always make a hell of a lot of sense."

"I am protecting no one, sir. But right now, the cell phone tracking and Anthony's truck are the best clues we've got." Herb bit his tongue. He didn't need the condescension and the attitude, even if it was from the top cop.

"I don't really care *who* is driving the truck or bleeping their phone. If it keeps up, it may be the only way to nail these guys before their next move."

Herb said, "The WaterForce Angels have done a fantastic job bringing in leads and some excellent evidence, Commissioner. We have water samples from every borough because of them. I wish you'd recognize how valuable they are." Herb braced himself for yet another onslaught.

"They still wearing those sissy bonnets?"

"*Berets*, not bonnets!"

"...and those Girl Scout merit badge sashes in baby blue? Please!" said O'Riley.

"Everybody likes them; and the berets and sashes are just like the Guardian Angels, only they're blue. An anonymous donation paid for them; and these uniforms help to identify WaterForce Angels to the public. They've performed an excellent service in this crisis! It's not right to make fun of people who are allies. I wish you would recognize their contributions."

"Right, Herby. I've got a drawer full o' merit badges just waiting for your teenie-boppers. See, by now, Michael Capo must be feeling a little better from his 'injuries', since his phone was picked up last night, headed north through Harlem and the Bronx, towards the Van Cortlandt Valve Chamber in the Jerome Park Reservoir. That's the biggest valve chamber in the distribution system, Sherlock!"

"But the Van Cortlandt is guarded like Fort Knox," Herb said. "He's not going to get anywhere near it."

"He may not know that, but it's the best magnet we've got to catch him."

"But that's only a theory, right, Commissioner?" Herb thought of the dozens of parts of the systems, literally over a hundred access shafts and gatehouses. Too many places to guard effectively. Just like the shoreline of the reservoirs, only this area included every borough of the city, spread out over hundreds of square miles. "Commissioner, about that signal from his cell phone. What if *he* is baiting *us*, instead of the other way around? He could be drawing our defenses towards the Van Cortlandt but planning an entirely different attack."

"Yes, Herby. But logic tells us where he's been, and we're following his path, even though the signals are infrequent. I'll be able to figure out real soon where he will attack next. Nothing for you to get all wet about, son. Ha!".

The man had the nerve to make water jokes at this critical moment! Herb cringed. First O'Riley called him "Herby", and then "son", and belittled the Angels with Girl Scout jokes. His sarcasm was nearly intolerable. Herb tried to ignore the put-downs. Still, he said respectfully, "You're making a lot of assumptions, Sir. I think he's scouting various places, looking for the weakest link. This is going to end soon, and maybe not very nicely if we start ignoring leads and belittling a whole army of valuable allies."

"Herby, you're quite the expert at both exaggeration and pessimism. Let's chat again when we're not talking about bonnets for sissy teenagers."

The line went dead. Herb was pissed. There was so much wrong with that conversation. If anything, O'Riley was the pessimist, he was exaggerating, and he had the nerve to insinuate that even Herb might be a mole passing information to the terrorists. Herb didn't feel free to share the information he actually did have, because of his promise to his boys, but that didn't make him a traitor. He knew that both Anthony and Michael had reappeared, had a falling out, and each had escaped to opposite sides. But there was no way he could get a word in with critical information when Commissioner O'Riley was acting like such a pompous ass.

O'Riley had only reluctantly approved the help of the WaterForce Angels, and did his best to belittle them at every turn. 'Sissy bonnets' and 'Girl Scout merit badges'! Between Mo's bad communication and O'Riley's big mouth, an attack that could be a fatal blow for the City was almost inevitable. Herb had his back against the wall. The best communication was with Commissioner Calloway, the only higher-up he could almost trust...or directly with his sons. And O'Riley made it so easy to make that choice.

There were only a few possibilities Herb could believe. Michael could be out of the picture. Perhaps the terrorists were setting Michael up for blame by using his phone, just as they were using Anthony's truck, which might account for the intermittent ability to track his phone signal. Or maybe Michael had recovered enough from his wounds to begin creating havoc in all these new places. The pattern had moved from the Catskills to New York City. The traced locations in the City made sense to Herb, and linked the Ricin attacks to the general terrorist war on the water supply. Of special concern was the guarded and heavily fortified Hillview Reservoir, which fed water lines to most of Manhattan, Queens, and Brooklyn.

Herb knew that a terrorist was unlikely to get within 200 feet of the Hillview without being noticed, if not questioned and detained. But if the terrorists had shifted their strategy to Ricin attacks on individual water towers in buildings inhabited by UN personnel, why would they need to scout reservoir locations in the Bronx? Had they not already "arrived" in Manhattan? Were they deliberately keeping attention on the reservoir security as a foil for their new Ricin strategy of selective kills of UN personnel in their own homes? Or were the two somehow linked?

The trail in the State of Delaware was less clear. There seemed to be no interest in obvious targets, like the Salem Nuclear Power Plant along the Delaware River, although the phone traces indicated he had travelled within sight of it as he drove down Interstate 95. However, he had stopped at a major biochemical manufacturer near Dover in the middle of the night. Short duration calls several hours apart were separated by blackouts when the phone was turned off. Police could have captured him there if only they had followed up on a rare and obvious opportunity when Michael stopped at the plant burglarized in Dover.

Chapter 50

People on the Street

"It's going to be one of those days, Bruce," Anderson said to his technician. "News feeds from all over the City. People are panicked."

Through his hidden earpiece, he heard, "Going live in five, four, three..."

"This is Anderson Cooper with a special update on the situation in New York City. There is little activity in the City this evening. All theaters and public places are closed due to the newest threats to the safety of the water. The UN and ten square blocks surrounding the UN building have been evacuated while teams check the water towers on every building, and inspect the water mains feeding the area. Many are leaving their homes in New York, but others are sticking it through, hoping that something will change to restore the safety of the largest city in America.

"We reported yesterday that water from Lake Ontario is being shipped by tanker truck into the City, but there is a limit to one gallon per person per day. Many people cannot carry gallons of water from the trucks to their homes. So, for those who are staying behind, there are some interesting solutions to the water crisis. New Yorkers have again proven how innovative they can be. First, we'll hear from Stuart Novak, an independent reporter from City Hall...Stuart..."

"Hello, Anderson. I'm here with Natalie Sanchez, who lives on the lower East Side with her four children. Natalie, tell us how you have solved the need for fresh water..."

"We tape off the faucets so the kids, they can't drink no water. Now we have water from the roof, where my husband, he make a cistern to collect the rain."

Stuart asked, "So you have to go to the roof for water?"

"No, Señor. My husband, he use plastic pipe to send the water down to each floor, we collect the water in big pots on the fire escape—for to drink. And my neighbor, he very smart. He use upside downward umbrella and collects on the fire escape, and drips into big big pasta pot."

"But can you get enough water for cooking and for all your children?"

"It rained this morning. I fill many pots, and take to the bathtub."

"And this is your sole source?"

"Yes, Señor, we not afford water in the store. Too much expensive. Can't carry enough from the trucks. And we not afford to leave. Where would we go?"

Anderson said, "And here's a shot of the backyards near Natalie's home. You can see dozens of makeshift ways to collect rainwater. Pots and pans on the fire escapes, cisterns crafted out of barrels, umbrellas, wastebaskets, anything they could find. Temporary plastic pipes to send the water down to apartments below. Bathing is by washcloth or sponge. Let's hear another story from Samantha Moyes, near the UN building...Samantha?"

"Anderson, this morning on my way to work, I witnessed people siphoning off puddles in the street after this morning's showers. The police are installing locks on every hydrant in the area, to prevent people from opening them. A lot of people are pouring tap water through coffee filters, boiling it, then adding a few drops of Clorox to make sure it's safe. I use that method for my own family."

"That's incredible, Samantha. So, you are purifying your own water! How do you know how much Clorox to add?"

"My son learned how to do it in Boy Scouts." Her face was glowing with pride.

"Amazing! A Boy Scout always learns to "be prepared", I guess. Let's now cut to Terrence McClelland, at a firehouse in the Village. "Terrence, tell us about our preparedness in case of fire. Will the firemen have access to enough water?"

"There isn't enough water in the hydrants, Anderson, so they've sent trucks to the Hudson and the East River to fill up in case of fire. But, honestly, if we were faced with a huge blaze, I'm not sure if there would be enough. The chief here is already prioritizing buildings not used as living quarters, buildings that stand alone, away from other structures. My guess is that some of those structures would simply be allowed to burn, in order to save water for more critical buildings with people living inside."

Anderson responded, "So there could be fires that we simply have to ignore until they burn themselves out." Live footage of an unnamed fire played in the background.

"I'm afraid so. Before the explosions in Gardiner, no one would have ever dreamed it could get this bad in New York City."

The camera showed short vignettes as he described other locations. "Meanwhile, the lines are long at local liquor stores, beverage stores, and Walmart and Target stores in New Jersey and Connecticut! Almost every cart is full of any drinkable liquid customers can find on the shelves. Reports of rushes on liquids are coming in from Pennsylvania and

West Virginia as well as throughout the tri-state area. Our correspondent in Paramus, New Jersey, has some alarming news...Reynard?"

"Anderson, it appears as if local mob organizations have already cashed in on the shortage, by quickly buying up supplies from Midwest sources much like the supply of liquor in prohibition days. Truckloads of bottled water are going for three times the normal price after shipment from Philadelphia, Pittsburgh, and as far away as Chicago. The price gouging is phenomenal, and highly illegal."

The camera returned to Anderson. The camera flashed to the Jacqueline Kennedy Onassis Reservoir in Central Park. "In spite of negative testing for toxins, New York tap water is now mistrusted and ostracized, yet, the people in the mountains enjoy unlimited supplies of pure, unfiltered water from wells, as long as they don't breach the security surrounding the reservoirs. Water that has flowed freely to most citizens only a month ago is now less than half of what normally comes from Gardiner, and remains yesterday's luxury."

The report continued, covering the suburbs, and the extent of the crisis north of the City. Still, the crisis of fear affected everyone. Instead of remaining the country's safest and best-tasting water in any big city, the water in New York had become the most maligned and outcast liquid in the country. The waiting was excruciating, and the lack of action frightening after officials on all levels admitted there were serious holes in their defense strategies.

When and where would the terrorists strike next? The weekly threats had ended, leaving citizens mired in the terror of silence. Which was worse, the next attack, or the fear of it? How long would this last?

WaterForce

Chapter 51
The Grand Plan

Still hurting from his wounds at the hands of Titus and Anthony, Michael prepared himself for the final attack on the City, one that would leave decades of destruction and fear in the metropolitan area. He walked east on 42nd Street, and soon into light crowds spilling in and out of Grand Central Terminal. He paid cash to check in to a luxury VIP Suite in the Grand Hyatt New York. He changed into a white silk shirt, black pants, and dark glasses, and rode the elevator down to the lower level for his rendezvous. The hotel had a clean contemporary style, and radiated expensive décor under a sloped glass atrium appealing to wealthy clientele. After a careful glance around the lobby, he strolled into The Market, a gourmet variety store primarily serving hotel guests.

He thought about his brothers, all victims he blamed on New York City. Kevin, left behind by two New Yorkers in Iraq. Jerry, taken prisoner in Afghanistan while five New Yorkers got away. And Billy, incarcerated by a New York judge. Add to that his radical politics, and New York was the major—no—the ONLY thing he could blame. New York stole Catksill water and profited by selling it down the city. New York hired Nazi DEP patrolmen who unfairly persecuted rural people in the mountains. New York polluted with impunity, and ruined the environment. New York persecuted his Islamic friends. A New York patrolman put the ugly scar on his arm. There was no end to his blame and his hate. And there would be no end to his vengeance. His Islamic allies offered a grand plan, too radical for Paul, too drastic for Anthony. But Michael needed no further justification. Violence was his nectar. Revenge his release. Destruction his solution, and water the vehicle for his weaponry. Waiting for his Islamic partner, he boiled with pent up anger.

He browsed through premium bottles of wine and champagne in The Market until he got a hold of himself again. Soon he felt the presence of someone approaching from behind. Glancing over his shoulder, Michael commented, "They don't build stores like this to sell cheap wine."

The correct answer came back in fake British English. "Quite right. I say, old fellow, if you like reds, try the J. Opi Argentine Malbec Reserve. They'll deliver it to your chamber."

"And it's only twenty-nine-fifty!" said Michael. "Not bad." With that, Michael paid for the bottle, strolled out of The Market, entered an elevator, and waited in VIP Suite 2950 to meet his contact.

The man who called himself 'Fateen Mujahid' was a renegade Saudi with a wiry thin physique, educated at Cambridge and Columbia before he returned to the Near East where he dropped out of sight. Fateen had developed a formidable network of operatives, all unknown to each other, but all crucial to the goals set by a few Islamic leaders higher up. The equivalent of the Islamic general, he was the key figure to implement the wave of violence around the world. His movements were quick and precise after years of training, and he was a deadly marksman, a trained explosive expert, and lethal with a knife. His big trustworthy brown eyes belied his terrorist experience with numerous violent missions against the United States and half a dozen foreign countries. He had been a young associate of Osama bin

Laden, and brought through the ranks in more recent years by radical Islamic cleric Abu Hamza al-Masri, head of the outlawed British terrorist group Al-Muhajiroun, a radical group that advocated the unification of all Muslims everywhere, by force if necessary, under a single fundamentalist theocratic government headed by Wahhabis clerics.

He had chosen his Islamic alias with care. 'Fateen al-Mujahid' literally translated from Arabic to English as 'cunning warrior'. The Boston Marathon bombers had followed Wahhabis teachings, and the group had drawn followers from radical Islamic sects all over the world. Even the Saudi royal family paid homage to the group, and respected their ability and power to recruit young male Muslim rebels for tasks not acknowledged in legitimate political circles. His links to the radical group ISIS were intertwined with all of his other notorious associations. But all of his former groups lacked the unity that the B.I.I.J could provide.

In room 2950, Fateen and Michael commiserated for hours, going over their plan of attack with all contingencies and emergencies considered. Since the beginning, Michael had never seen his face, even when he sought refuge in the safe house in Prattsville. Still, it was a face that exuded arrogance and confidence. Even the long scar from his ear downward to his neck told a story of brutal survival in an unnamed mêlée in the relentless jihad against America. Battle scars and hate were the primary thing the two men had in common.

Fateen stood in front of the white curvilinear luxury sofa with his arms crossed and feet wide in a military stance, choosing not to sit. Perhaps it was his training in the desert, or maybe the level of dominance he carried with him everywhere, ready for an attack from the CIA or the British Counter-Terrorism Police he had narrowly escaped more than once. He seemed not to desire any contact with the grandiose trappings of the hotel room.

Fateen said, "I thought you would have chosen a hotel that was a little less ostentatious, a bit less obvious. How do you expect us not to be noticed here?" His Cambridge-trained English belied the fact that he was one of the most dangerous terrorists on the planet.

Michael explained, "The Hyatt is right next to Grand Central Terminal, giving us an easy escape from the city on any number of trains in all directions, and we can blend in with thousands of people coming and going." He opened the rich red wine, and poured two glasses. "Let's concentrate on what we have to do, and enjoy my taste in wine, instead of my choice of hotels."

"Right. Maybe a high-profile hotel is the last place they would expect to find us. It's just that I didn't expect to have to personally participate in this. I thought you had a trained partner."

"Anthony. Yes, he was quite good, and he had skills no one else had. His remote-controlled boat was unique. But he didn't have the stomach for this. The Islamic link interfered with his loyalty," Michael said.

"Then we're better off without him. As you people say, keep it close to the vest. You and I have the best skills for this job." Fateen looked out the window at the view of Park Avenue and its grand display of American prosperity. "We won't have any trouble from him, will we?"

"I haven't seen him since our fight at the cabin in Frost Valley. I never told him of any plans beyond the immediate day. He has no clue. He didn't follow me to the safe house. And if I see him, I'm going to kill him." The anger showed as his face reddened.

"Best not to draw attention with an unnecessary corpse. Do you have outfits for both of us?"

Michael said, "Your clothes are in this duffel bag, along with a backpack for the C4 and the other stuff. We'll look like a couple of tourists. There are extra hats and scarves to change our look when we need to."

Fateen opened the duffle to inspect the clothes they would wear. He raised the black turtleneck against his chest to see if it fit. "And you still think this is the best target? From the looks of it, I would think it would be heavily fortified. Aren't there other shafts in the water system that would be easier?"

Michael answered with confidence, "I know this territory. You don't. Some of the original access shafts are now closed off. In the early twentieth century, they dug shafts all over New York, at Jerome Park and One Ninety-Sixth Street, Hundred Seventy-Ninth Street, Ninety-Ninth in Central Park, and so forth. The Van Cortlandt valve chamber in the Bronx is the biggest distribution center. If we could get inside at that point, it would be awesome! But there is an army of guards all over that area. Completely impenetrable."

Fateen asked, "So, why this place in Central Park?"

"The building already has tourist traffic inside during the day. There is a major weather center on the top, with weather scientists coming and going. This gives it more public access during the day, and more vulnerability. Other locations are exclusively guarded, with no public access. It stands over one of the most easily accessible shafts in terms of the length of time we can be protected, and allowing us a longer time we can work inside once we gain access. We don't need Van Cortlandt. This location is almost dead center in Manhattan, where we can create the biggest fear factor. Water is fed to three boroughs from there."

"Very well. I am...pleased." Fateen didn't usually get effusive with praise, but his face showed his approval.

Michael pulled out a detailed drawing of Central Park, pointing to red marked arrows and paths. "We'll enter the park from different directions. You'll camp out here in the dressing room for the Delacorte Theater, and hide in a basement stairwell around the corner from the guard station. Here's the key I got from my contact," Michael said.

"Is your contact reliable?" Fateen glanced at him with doubt on his face.

"Absolutely!"

"Who is he?"

"Someone high up in the DEP...someone they completely trust. Look, there's a lot you don't tell me. So why should I...? Let's just say, the key will work in the door." For once Michael was in control. He paced the floor with confidence. "I'll approach from the east by car on the Seventy-Ninth Street Transverse, in that Toyota van your guys got for me, at exactly three-fifteen AM. With the trailer attached, I can block traffic in both directions under the overpass a few hundred yards from the target. It will be easy at that hour. The diversion will grab the attention of the guards. I'll hide in the bushes near the south shore of Turtle Pond. When I send a text saying 'see you at the club', we'll take out the guards—both at once."

Fateen asked, "How many guards?"

Michael demonstrated with two fingers striking his other hand. "There are never more than two armed guards outside at night, and maybe one inside, and a DEP car patrolling every thirty minutes on Seventy-Ninth Street across the park. If we both attack at once, we can eliminate them before the next DEP patrol arrives. We must strike simultaneously, from the north side. A blade or a garrote...your choice. Michael folded his hands and sat on the bed, waiting for Fateen's approval.

Fateen seemed to relax as he sat in a chair. "You are a worthy partner. I shall use my own garrote. Your choice for the other. After they are eliminated, we use the keys you got from your man for the rest of my team. But I still have reservations."

"Don't worry so much. If we need to, we'll have some C-4 for the door at the top of the stairs on the north side, but only if the key does not work. My source has been embedded for years. Totally reliable. He also showed me how to turn off the power for the security lights inside, and provided a detailed drawing of the interior with all the valves and major junctions. Let me show you the places we need to hit." He stood and opened an inside diagram on the bed. The building had multiple levels underground and access points. He had marked specific places they could gain access to the water flow, and others where they would load explosives.

Fateen was impressed with the detail in the diagram. He seemed to trust Michael a little more. "Timing is critical. We want the capsules to get through the pipes before any explosions begin. That's why the timers need to be set for noon tomorrow, after the flow of water has delivered the capsules, set to precede the press conference scheduled for one o'clock."

Michael answered, "We'd better get started. We've got nearly ten thousand capsules to load." They put on rubber gloves, a facemask, and a protective shirt with a full-length apron, and set up two machines to load the tiny kernels that would spread through the pipes of New York.

"Ricin?"

"As you Americans would say, nothing but the best."

"Got it," Michael said. "And if they release the prisoners..."

"We might have some fun anyway! I mean, how can we resist if we're there already? *Mawt Amerik! Allah hu akbar!*"

Michael smiled and raised his fist with Fateen. "Right. Death to America! *Allah*...whatever."

"Allah is good, Michael. *Allah hu akbar*! Remember the words. We do this because Allah has directed us to take up the sword. After this, you must come for more training to my homeland. More language skills, and better attack methods. I still call it Arabistan, which refers to the entire Arabian Peninsula. Taken in a modern context, to me it's the closest thing to refer to a united Islamic brotherhood, and, in our battle, the Islamic Jihad. But, you know, the Saudis were terrorists from the best of traditions of our people, and liberated us all from the Turks. Maybe...after everything, it will change again, when all Muslims are united. Then you will learn the language AND even better methods, my friend. We will prevail! *Al Ukhuwwa Mujtama Islam Jihad!*"

"Yes! Here's to the B.I.I.J.!" Michael replied. To him, privately, the jihad was bullshit. Fateen's team of Islamic psychopaths was only a tool to bolster his own reasons to attack New York City. This way, no one would single out Michael Capo when there was a more hateful public enemy to blame.

After many hours of loading the capsules, they exited the room separately, and took different routes to the basement of the Hyatt, where they found their way to Grand Central Terminal.

His brothers deserved a well-planned revenge. Michael's older brother Kevin had been killed by "friendly fire" by his own platoon sergeant from New York, his body never retrieved after a battle in the first Iraq war. His brother Billy was incarcerated in Leavenworth by a New York prosecutor on a trumped-up charge. And Jerry had been left behind in Afghanistan by two New Yorkers who rescued the rest of his squadron but left him behind with his guts spilling out.

In Central Park, Michael muttered phrases he had learned in pigeon Arabic, *"A'ta habibi khoya!"* For my dear brothers! *"Allaenat'nat, Niu Yurk!"* Fuck you, New York!

Chapter 52

In Plain Sight

"Professor, our surveillance picked up an image of the suspect Michael Capo at the Hyatt New York near Grand Central Terminal. It looks like he contacted a Middle Eastern man in the hotel store called The Market. The man has a nasty scar on his face, tall, thin, with a partial scruffy beard covering the scar. Our facial recognition software positively identified him, no question. We picked up the image from about six hours ago on the surveillance tape, and traced it to a V.I.P. suite in the Hyatt. Officers have already raided the room, but the occupants were not present."

"This is great news," said Professor Jacoby. "What did they leave behind?"

"We found the two missing kernal-loading machines—the ones that were taken from the Delaware chemical lab—several bags of raw capsules, unloaded, and a dozen vials full of a powder—probably Ricin. There's a fair chance they may be returning later to retrieve their belongings."

"Great work! Anything else?"

"Two wine glasses with prints. Oh, there's a notepad with a few lines in Arabic, and something in French, or maybe Italian. I texted an image of his scribbles, and our translator thinks it says 'La Belle de Vue' in French." He spelled the words. "Not sure how to translate the Arabic." He spelled it, then tried to pronounce it. "'*Al-la-e-nat-nat, Niu Yurk!*' Maybe, something...cussing out New York..."

Professor Jacoby answered. "The French could almost mean, 'beautiful sight', although it's not exactly right."

"As in Bellevue Hospital, you think?" said the officer.

"A possibility, " Professor Jac answered. "You'd better send some cars down to Bellevue right away. And dust that room for prints. Confirm a match to Michael Capo. Compare the prints we lifted at that cabin, and down in Delaware. There are survivors of the Ricin poisoning at the UN recovering in Bellevue Hospital. Maybe they are after someone specific...someone who didn't die after the first try...we've got to protect those patients—better get moving!"

"Yes, sir. I'm on it. We'll talk soon." The officer left immediately, focused on his mission.

Jacoby called Parker right away. "My boy, we may have an important lead on where to find Michael Capo."

"Really!" Parker was with Anthony and Titus in the 83rd Street basement apartment. The professor updated them on the new information. This might be the most important lead so far. But there was a strange feeling they both shared. Parker said, "But why Bellevue Hospital? The survivors are very ill, and still extremely vulnerable. Why go after people who've already been hit, but are still barely alive? Doesn't make sense! After all, the main target is New York City. But the French seems important. I wonder if the Arabic means something."

The professor said, "Maybe they deliberately left a red herring to confuse us. And now we've got half the cops in New York rushing to a hospital at Twenty-eighth and First, when the main water valves are farther uptown, in the Bronx and in Central Park."

"Exactly. Their mission has been to attack the water supply, not a hospital with victims that may die anyway." said Parker.

While the professor stopped a moment to answer his cell phone, Parker said to Anthony and Titus, "Guys, the police are swarming all over Bellevue Hospital. But I studied Italian last semester. I think the translation is wrong. When you translate 'beautiful view' or 'La belle de vue' to Italian, you get something like 'la bella vista'. Or perhaps 'belvedere'."

The three recited different possibilities. "Bella vista…La belle vue… Bellevue…Belvedere."

Parker shouted ,"Belvedere Castle, guys! That's where they're going! To the park! Jesus! We can damn near see it from here."

Anthony said, "You're right, Parker. That's where there are valves and pipes in Central Park! I think it's time for a visit."

The professor had been listening. "I think you might need some backup. I may be in my eighties, but I've still got some old tricks that might come in handy. I'll meet you near the entrance of the Seventy-Ninth Street Transverse, at Eighty-First and Central Park West within the hour. Hurry!"

Professor Jac called the police commissioner for backup. When he explained the interpretation of 'beautiful view', the commissioner was skeptical. "Bellevue Hospital makes more sense, Professor. It's full of injured UN personnel. Seventy-three people poisoned with Ricin. In twenty minutes, we'll be evacuating the entire hospital. There are four other hospitals waiting to admit their patients. But I can't send swat teams all over the damn city. This is crazy. Make up your mind!"

"Commissioner, I think Bellevue is a false lead. Don't you have some men to send to the park? I'm convinced, and I'm going over there myself with WaterForce."

"Jesus! Are you crazy? You're too damn old to...and those kids are too young to... Never mind! Look, most of my teams are spread out at critical points from Times Square to the Kensico Reservoir. And Central Park is no small area. I can't handle them all."

"We're not talking about the entire park, just the castle. Belvedere Castle. 'Belvedere' is Italian for 'beautiful view', and 'Bellevue' is essentially the same thing. They left evidence and used the French spelling to mislead us. Can't you see the mistake you're making?"

"Okay, you win. But we're getting mighty thin. I'll send a car over to check it out," promised the commissioner.

"A car...one car! Thanks a lot." The professor hung up the phone, hoping he sent the appropriate message. Now, it would be up to the WaterForce Angels.

Chapter 53
Mole Trap

Herb paced back and forth in his office in Downsville, checking his watch again. Mo was two hours late, and his role was a major necessity to test the hundreds of samples turned in by the WaterForce volunteers. Herb worried about his sons, who were both in the city sticking their noses in places only the police should venture, and their best friend Anthony was now likely involved, trying to redeem himself from a host of bad choices. Herb had second thoughts about the whole WaterForce idea. It had put his boys and countless others into the middle of an international terrorist plot that was way beyond their ability to deal with the enemy, like asking children to guard the doors of Rikers, and only arming the inmates. WHAT could he have been thinking?

New York City was in grave danger with a water crisis that seemed to get worse every day. The various agencies were fighting amongst themselves, which only helped the enemy. And there was still the problem of the mole, the informant who seemed to foil every effort to capture the terrorists. Herb was deeply conflicted between his duties in the DEP and his complicity releasing Great Great Grandfather Rosenthael's money to a bunch of young vigilantes. At times he doubted if they had any minute chance to win the battle.

His pacing was interrupted by the Fedex man delivering a package addressed to Mo, from City Chemical Supply. Normally, Mo would open the deliveries, and inventory the supplies. Herb muttered to his tardy assistant, "Damn it, Mo, now I have to do your job, too?" He ripped open the package, finding twenty brown plastic bottles filled with tiny pills. The handwritten label on the bottle simply said, "R-72, #500" Herb had never been aware of a chemical called "R-72", but he could tell there were probably five hundred tiny capsules in each bottle, totaling ten thousand capsules in the delivery. But why was there no commercial label identifying City Chemical Supply as the supplier? No logo, no printed return address, no evidence that this business was legit. That alone violated FDA rules governing the handling of industrial chemicals. Herb Rose couldn't think of a single procedure in his remote testing lab that would require that much of any substance.

His policeman's cynicism kicked in. Before unpacking the bottles, he put on a pair of gloves. One of the bottles had a piece of paper folded and wrapped around it with a rubber band. Curiosity made him open the note with tweezers. Inside was a handwritten note:

Mo—

As we discussed, for the Ashoken—place 100 or more in each valve. It's small enough to get all the way through the system. In case we are discovered in C.P., get rid of this! Mawk Amerik! —Fateen.

Herb was completely shocked. He was not prepared for this. It was crystal clear. There wasn't any doubt now. Mo had worked for the DEP in Downsville for over twenty-five years. He had emigrated from Pakistan in the late 1980s, and brought up two children to be loyal American citizens, and eventually been entrusted with all of the water testing in the Catskill region. Had he been a friend of the enemy the entire time? What else had he compromised? Herb realized that Mo had access to every single one of the secret safeguards and security devices in the entire reservoir system, classified codes now also available to the terrorists who threatened the entire water supply of New York. The list grew longer as he considered the exposure. Mo had access to cameras, Stanford sensors, door keys to the aqueducts and tunnels under New York, and detailed maps of the entire water system. He could even access the drones flying over the reservoirs, and download surveillance photographs. He could control the drones remotely, and send them off to alternate places. He'd attended strategy meetings when security policies were reviewed and revised. He knew everything. Everything.

And at this very moment, Mo was walking through the front door.

"Sorry, very sorry, boss, I am late again. I wish our WaterForce youngsters would be more prompt with their reports." Mo settled into a lab chair next to the table. He glanced down at the brown bottles in plastic Ziploc bags. His eyes opened wide. "So...what is this?"

"It seems to be a delivery for you, Mo. I opened it by mistake. But what is this, 'R-72'? I'm not familiar with that chemical."

Mo took a moment to answer. His raised eyebrows exuded sincerity. "Oh! Yes. Of course. R-72 is a catalyst reactant needed to form the biosynthesis involved between the two chemicals we use to test the water. Absolutely essential. But very strong, very strong. Be careful. Don't touch." He put on a pair of rubber gloves, and gestured across the table. "Here, give it to me. I'll put it away."

After sliding the bags across the table, Herb opened the note and held it up for Mo to see. "Who is this 'Fateen', Mo? And what does this note mean?" He looked sadly into

Mo's eyes almost in a fatherly way. Mo was at a loss for words for several seconds. His brown eyes fluttered with hesitation. His eyes rested on Herb's feet.

"I...order this chemical from Saudi Arabia...it is not available any more in the States."

"So, you're saying, every single municipal water station in the state is dependent on Saudi Arabia to test their drinking water?"

His eyes seemed to flutter. "Right," he said. "Yes, of course, boss."

"And the source, the place called 'City Chemical Supply', with a handwritten address in Brooklyn, is actually in Saudi Arabia?"

"Well, yes...I don't...I guess..."

"And in case the 'thing' in Central Park doesn't work, you are to get rid of all this? How would you do that, Mo? And, the note gives you a dose of one hundred each for the testing valves, with an ultimate destination in the City. This sounds more like the capsules they used at the UN. A dangerous toxin, Mo-Bear—What are YOU doing with it?"

Mo didn't answer. He fiddled with his keys and looked at the front door.

Herb fingered his holster. "Then it says in Arabic, 'Mawk Amerik'. Couldn't be clearer. It means 'Death to America', the same language that was used in the letter to the *Times*. Come on, Mo. 'R-72' on the label is some kind of RICIN, isn't it?"

"If you say so, boss." Mo said as he folded his arms.

"I think I've heard enough." He walked around the counter and slammed Mo against the wall, pulling his arms up behind him. Mo didn't resist, but tears ran down his face.

"I'm sorry, boss. They threatened my wife, my children. I had to…"

"Bull shit. If that were true, you would have come to me a long time ago, when Fateen first approached you. Don't you think our CIA could have protected you? This was all about money. And you couldn't resist big money, could you? And, in the end, you were true to your roots in Pakistan. You've been feeding them information for years!" Herb closed the clasp on the left handcuff.

" It's not like that, boss…My children, they need…college, and…"

"And New York needs to be safe from people like YOU!" Herb put on the second handcuff, and slammed him down on a chair.

His wife had called him 'Mo-Bear'. But Herb now realized that Mo's name had more meaning than he'd ever imagined. "YOU are the goddam mole! YOU gave them classified information."

Herb pulled his phone out to call for local backup. "You're under arrest, Mohammed. You have the right to remain silent…although I wish you'd give me an excuse to blow your ass away."

Chapter 54

A Walk in the Park

I t was fairly quiet at the two o'clock hour, even for New York City. The bars had closed for the night, and most people had already returned home with or without an overnight companion to share their beds. A man in jeans and a pajama top waited patiently for his hyperactive terrier to pee on a lamppost. Two men emerged from Central Park and crossed the street to hail a passing cab. A rat the size of a Chihuahua competed with a scrawny stray cat foraging in an overturned trashcan. Tall buildings struggled to reveal themselves through meandering banks of thick fog. It was one of those nights when New York took on the quiet threat of a dangerous and lonely city where something bad could happen...and often did.

Parker, Anthony, and I waited on the corner of 81st Street. Soon an old nomadic figure approached, dressed in a long-tattered overcoat and a wrinkled rain hat, a pair of torn laceless boots, and three garbage bags slung over his shoulder. From his gaunt homeless appearance, we didn't recognize him until he was ten feet away. Underneath his overcoat, he was well armed, and surprisingly spry for a man in his eighties. He said he could get closer to the action in this disguise, and might serve as a communications relay. I was happy with his support, even though I worried that a man that old has no business being on the front lines at two AM in a treacherous city.

Professor Jac had toys we didn't even know we needed. He handed out tiny wrist radios to each of us. Normal communication was just between us, but a red panic button could call for help. After a short consultation, we decided to give his extra Glock to Anthony. Our lack of experience with firearms had been a major concern, and it might face the ultimate test tonight. The plan was to split into two teams of two each. Parker would go with Jac, and I would stick with Anthony. The promised NYPD car had not arrived. But we agreed that there was no time to waste.

We walked on a park trail parallel to the 79th Street Transverse, and split up so that Parker and the professor could approach from the east side near Turtle Pond, and walk along the north side of the Belvedere Castle. Anthony and I would walk along the south side. Shortly after they moved ahead, I heard a loud screech of brakes, but no collision. Perhaps a drunk had dozed off at the wheel, and recovered just in time. But in the overpass next to the Transverse, I could see a van with a trailer blocking both sides of the road, with its emergency blinkers on. I would normally think nothing of a skidding vehicle in New York City traffic, but I could see the van was abandoned. No driver, no passenger, no real accident.

The driver's door was left open, and there were already a couple of taxis showing their New York impatience with their horns. The motion detectors on top of Belvedere Castle switched extra floodlights on automatically to illuminate the immediate grounds. Not surprising, I thought, and perhaps it was a good thing, since it provided a layer of visibility around the castle. Nothing we could do...the floodlights would illuminate the good guys just as well as a terrorist. But I felt fear creeping into my bones, and I couldn't stop my knees from shaking. My tongue searched my mouth for a drop of moisture, and my breathing nearly stopped, with air half way up from my lungs. I studied our destination in the glare of the floodlights, and tried to stay next to the cover of bushes and tree trunks.

Belvedere Castle was impressive when lit up at night. Isolated by a thickly wooded section of Central Park, it dominated the landscape at the highest elevation in the park. With its imposing mix of Romanesque and Gothic styles, it was designed in the late 19th century by Frederick Law Olmstead and Calvert Vaux as a sort of Victorian fancy, and ridiculed by locals and critics as a strange albatross that the city spent too much money building, without a definite purpose for the structure. In other words, a perfect place to hide the underground water system. Originally built with open doorways and windows, it housed the New York Meteorological Observatory and later a U. S. Weather Bureau Station. Belvedere Castle was restored from ruin in 1983, and used as a location in movies like *The Bostonians, Alone in the Dark,* and *Sesame Street.* Today, it is a nature observatory and museum, and still houses weather-measuring equipment. Few people remember that the Jacqueline Kennedy Onassis Reservoir to the north was once the only reservoir for the water supply of New York. And tonight, the Park would play a major role in the future of the City.

The first person we saw was a bag-lady wheeling a rickety shopping cart across the grass, full of everything she owned on this earth. There is some sort of logic to homeless fashion. Under a tattered summer dress, she wore jeans and combat boots. I couldn't make out her face, except for the unusually large brown eyes that seemed to gleam out from under a bright floral scarf covering her head. She stood unexpectedly tall, and seemed to move as if she was late for work. At this hour? She had an ugly facial scar, and filth all over her face. She turned on the path towards the Delacorte Theater. There were no more signs of life as we carefully proceeded through the Shakespeare Gardens towards the Belvedere.

Parker and Professor Jac walked around the north side, between Turtle Pond and the castle. It was peaceful for nearly fifteen minutes until they came upon a dark shape barely in the water at the edge of the pond. Professor Jac was the first to see it, and sent Parker ahead to investigate.

The call came over the radio. "Ti, I've got trouble. There is a lit flashlight, still on the ground...and...a body, I think, partially in the water."

"Okay, Parker, check it out. I've got trouble here too," I replied.

Parker said, "Oh god! Help me turn him over, Professor...It's a DEP officer. For a minute I thought it was Dad! He's been strangled. There's a red line around his neck. Jesus, look at his face! This must have just happened, minutes ago. He's still warm. The look of fear is still on his face."

"Be careful, brother," I radioed back.

"What have you got there?" Parker asked.

"The south door to the castle is hanging open, unguarded, the interior lights are turned off. We're going in..."

"NO! Wait for us. You're going to need help," Parker replied. But Anthony was already inside. I was torn between following him in, or waiting for help. But the radio crackled with Anthony's fearless voice.

"Tyler, there's a trail of blood, and...there's a guy in here on the floor. He's been strangled, and it looks like he dragged himself back inside. His cell phone is still in his hand. Oh my god, it's another DEP guard. You'd better call for help. He's saying something...he says, 'four men...below...armed...careful...'"

"Professor Jac here. I'll call it in. You guys be careful. We've just reached the east end of the castle. Don't go any farther without backup. Keep the volume down if you can."

But Anthony was already on the stairs going down, and frantically motioning me to catch up with him. I couldn't believe how fast he moved down flights of narrow staircases with only the glow of scattered safety lights. I leaped two or three steps at a time, but the fool was soon several flights ahead of me. We had entered a deep shaft. The walls were covered with vertical pipes, junctions, valves, and control panels. Yellow numbers painted on the walls indicated how far underground we were. Soon it was eighty-four feet...seven flights if they were twelve feet each. We should be moving much more carefully, inspecting every corner and every junction. But Anthony forged ahead like a mad dog.

Chapter 55
The Tunnels

At ninety-six feet below the earth, I nearly caught up with Anthony at the entrance of a huge underground room, and I could tell from my flashlight that we were at the junction of an enormous tunnel, with a twelve-foot diameter aqueduct running from the north into the room, and splitting into three different directions downward to lower levels. There was a moving reflection that flickered ominously on the ceiling. How far was it to the bottom of the shaft?

Professor Jac radioed softly, "Help is on the way. We're in the elevator... be there shortly." I had no idea where the elevator door was, and not a clue where Anthony was. How long would it take for a century-old elevator full of counterweights and chains to travel over a hundred feet into the earth? But I could hear sounds of movement on a level below, as I carefully made my way down the stairs. When a wet cobweb dragged across my face I nearly cried out.

Suddenly I could hear a violent struggle, the clang of metal, and the echoes of two men's feet jockeying for position. A fearful whelp came from a voice that could only be a man receiving a serious injury. I was sure it was two people echoing through the huge underground chamber, but it sounded like several men in combat. A body crashed against something metal, and fell to the ground. Did it sound like Anthony? The silence held no clues. Why didn't he call on the radio, or yell to me?

I heard a soft but frantic command. "You two! Watch the elevator door. Abdul! And Jareed, with me. Continue with your jobs. There is not much time!"

A voice answered, "Fateen! Let's get it done!" Not just any voice. *Michael* was with them. I was glad we weren't still up in Prattsville trying to find him.

But no sign of Anthony...was he the victim on the floor? If only he had waited for me. As I thought about different possibilities, I'd never felt so afraid. I crept half way down the stairs, keeping my head below the railing. When I reached another stairway, I heard the unmistakable sound of the arrival of an elevator. Professor Jac and Parker would be walking into a trap. If I warned them, I'd give away both of our positions. I heard the door open, and sounds of a struggle reached my ears. The elevator door closed, and it moved upward. Sounds of ripping fabric, a blow that I was sure had cracked a bone, and a crash.

"Put him in the closet. There! Latch it...Let's go..."

Who was it? Why was there a reference to only one? Surely Professor Jac wasn't putting himself in danger. Someone had been incapacitated, and locked away. Was it Parker? The thought made me just about lose my cool. I squelched a shout in my throat.

I could hear the squeaking sound of a tool turning a valve open after several twists of a wrench. I descended down far enough to see Michael and Fateen opening a valve. The marker on the wall said, "Water Sampling. Manhattan 42nd St". Michael held a funnel while another guy prepared to pour from a gallon container full of tiny kernels.

This had to stop. This was my moment. This is what WaterForce was all about. Suddenly my reflexes took over. I jumped up on the wet railing, using it as a ski slope, and literally skated down a full flight of steps on the groove made by the heel on my boots. Thank god for the skateboard training I'd had on the streets of Margaretville. At the same time, I saw Anthony out of the corner of my eye, leaping out from behind a huge junction of pipes. But Michael was well trained. Fateen was equally prepared with jujitsu and karate moves. We would be no match for them. But as I slid down the last four feet of railing, I jumped off and hit him full force in the face with the heels of my hands, landing on my butt on the steel-plated floor.

I knew I had a lucky hit when he fell over the railing and sailed into the stairwell. Anthony hit Michael from behind, taking him down with a classic high school football tackle. But the jar full of kernels went flying, down through the open stairwell to another level below. We could hear the glass break and the capsules scatter across the floor until there was the splattering sound of tiny splashes. Helpless to follow the sound, we continued our assault on Michael. Michael counterattacked, sending me crashing into Anthony. We both went flying into the latched door where one of ours was imprisoned. I knocked the latch upward to release him. Anthony hit the stairs to find the other terrorists and continue the battle. The wind was knocked out of me, and I was almost down for the count.

When the door unlatched, Professor Jac was ready. I couldn't believe how fast he overcame a man a third of his age, and at least twice his strength. The way he took down Michael Capo was nothing short of amazing. Our man Jac delivered a feigned motion to the left that knocked him off guard and made him turn. A kick to the back of his knee took him down in one movement. A swift chop to the neck made him choke. When Michael raised both hands to his neck, a nylon handcuff was waiting to bind his wrists in one swift movement. In an instant, Michael was handcuffed by a locking nylon band, and quickly secured to the door handle of the closet that had just imprisoned Professor Jac. In less than three seconds, Jac had proven his career in the CIA was something to be reckoned with. Michael Capo was a prisoner again, taken by a man in his eighties. As I recovered and got up off the floor, the professor nodded to me, and promptly got on the elevator and disappeared upwards with a slight victory smile, like Santa up the chimney.

But where was Parker? I'd lost track of him during the struggle. He was not visible anywhere. There was blood on the floor. I guessed that he had gone ahead to catch up with other terrorists on levels below us. Fateen had a five-minute head start on us, if he'd survived the fall. I rushed down two flights of stairs to reach the bottom level. I arrived in a room full of valves, pipes, and junctions, on a small open steel grate, and almost crashed into a two-foot diameter aqueduct. This was the motherlode of connections to dozens of locations in New York City. The painted marker on the wall reported we were 196 feet below ground level. The junctions and valves made the previous level look like a practice field. But there was no sign of either Parker or Anthony.

I needed to think with a terrorists' mindset to find them. Above each pipe was a capped drip-valve. This must be how the DEP took samples from water pipes destined for many parts of the city. Each drip-valve had a marker like the one we had seen in the previous chamber, with a coded location identifier. The room held a major labyrinth of pipes heading off into six different directions, through tunnels full of smaller aqueducts. This could be the final interchange in the water's long journey.

The problem was finding Fateen. He could squeeze in between any one of the tunnels channeling off the room. If he had explosives, they would be hard to find. The capsules on the floor were from Michael's supply he'd spilled from the chamber above. I had to go with a conclusion based on the evidence in puddles on the floor. I carefully checked the drip-valves. Upon inspection, I discovered that each sampling valve had a keyed lock on it. I couldn't think how Michael and Fateen would be able to get keys to dozens of locks in order to drop capsules of ricin into each and every supply pipe. The mole had probably provided keys. It just didn't seem possible that there had been enough time to complete the job, even if they'd had a master. With us in pursuit, it was more efficient for them to set a single large explosion to blow up the pipes in the tunnel. But where? There was no sign of either friend or foe. With more than a dozen tunnels from which to choose, I had never felt so frustrated and without a clue.

I whispered into my radio to try to locate Professor Jac, Parker, or Anthony. No one seemed within range. Maybe all the metal and concrete was a block to communication. Or had they been taken out by the enemy? If only there was a sign, a footprint, or...anything to lead me the right way. And then I saw it. A tattered lady's scarf with a bright pink floral pattern lay on the floor only a few feet into one of the tunnels. I had seen it on the homeless lady in the park, the one I should have recognized as a terrorist in a well-conceived disguise. But underground, it was like a beacon in the dark...and a lucky pointer down the right path.

Chapter 56

The Fight

The rusty chains of the elevator scraped over the century-old steel pulleys. I dove under a five-foot diameter pipeline. Were the terrorists escaping? Or had someone above called the elevator, and help was on the way? Either way, it began to rise upward, and I crawled out to follow the clue from the scarf in the tunnel.

The light was full of high contrast and impenetrable shadows. There were bare light bulbs spaced about every twenty-five feet, and many were burnt out, leaving patches of near darkness along the way. Cobwebs hung from the ceiling, connecting the top layers of pipes, and continuing down to the narrow metal grid that served as a walkway on the right side of the pipeline. I never dreamed I would be called to duty in a place this creepy under Central Park in New York City. But I could not allow fear to control my thoughts. I had to pull myself together and proceed.

I was almost sure the cobwebs along the walkway had been disturbed. There was at least six inches of water under the gridded walkway, the source of a rancid smell I recognized from stale water standing for months or years. Perhaps there were junctions that weren't quite sealed, and leaked constantly onto the tunnel floor. I wondered how they kept the black mold on the tunnel walls out of the conduits carrying the water supply, a condition that would never reach the public's scrutiny. I came to a junction, where a pipe suddenly veered off into another tunnel smaller than the main passageway. Just past the junction, there was a steel ladder leading to the top. With the new headroom, I could walk along a catwalk on top of the aqueduct if I kept my head down. Also, I'd be able to stay in the brighter light near the ceiling.

Suddenly I tripped over something heavy that clattered along the catwalk and over the edge. I peered downward and saw the business end of a large pipe wrench below on the lower catwalk. Had the terrorists left it there...or perhaps a workman? At this point it didn't matter; I had already revealed my presence with the noise. I backtracked to the ladder and scrambled down to retrieve the wrench. When I returned to the top catwalk, I hoped I was on the right track. Soon, I would know. But the ceiling lights didn't hold much hope when I realized how they blended into a tiny vanishing point fading for what seemed like a straight-line mile in the distance.

I'd walked about fifty yards when I noticed what looked like a discarded brown medicine bottle containing hundreds of small kernels about the size of short-grained rice inside. Each had a tiny slit along the center, where I guessed they had been loaded with Ricin. Positive proof! Professor Jac had described the capsules exactly. I left my baseball cap on the grid to mark the spot, then capped and wrapped the bottle in a Hershey's wrapper I found in my backpack pocket. Not the tightest security, but a Hershey's foil wrapper would have to suffice. The farther I ventured on the endless catwalk, the thicker the putrid air was in my lungs.

Soon I began hearing strange echoes farther along in the tunnel, hollow echoes that were like an intruder in a large empty auditorium. I couldn't see anyone up ahead on the upper catwalk, so I assumed the voices came from the path below at the bottom of the tunnel. This could be my lucky break. I hurried ahead as fast as I could move quietly, and soon I was within twenty-five feet. There was another junction ahead, with pipes turning off left and right. I guessed there would be another ladder and a small landing platform just beyond the pipes branching off. I leaned over the edge to try to see them. But instead, something else caught my eye. Small gauge copper wires protruded from under one of the pipes, stuffed mostly out of sight. They were no doubt attached to explosives that could rip holes in the pipes and cause a major water spill through every manhole and shaft from Central Park to Battery Park. If the water was laced with Ricin, it would combine toxin with flooding, a lethal combination for all of Manhattan. How far back had they laid in the explosives?

I glanced ahead, trying to figure the odds of stopping them. How many were there? I'd heard at least two voices, maybe three. I wished I had my rifle. Should I rely on a plumber's wrench to attack two or more men alone? The odds were against me. Or should I try to move backwards fifty yards to the elevator, and call for reinforcements? Surely the police were on the scene by now. The second alternative was a guarantee that time would run out before help could arrive. The tunnel system could stretch as long as Manhattan itself.

Ahead of me, a ceiling light went out, then flickered back on, and out again. There was no sign of anyone, but when I looked behind me, I saw the answering signal. A light behind me was being screwed on and off manually by someone I could only see in silhouette as he reached to the ceiling. After a minute he did it again...off, on, off, only this time twenty-five feet closer. It felt creepy, like a signal of impending doom. And then it happened about fifty feet ahead of me...off, flicker on, and off. A sudden thought occurred to me. What if they were connecting the ignition wires for the explosives to the lights in the tunnels, perhaps screwing in a lead wire to the socket, which could then be used as an igniter for the C4 charges. And I was caught in between two of them.

I hit the floor and crawled slowly, but I could hear the guy in back of me moving swiftly forward. I rolled off the catwalk and hid between the two pipes below the walkway. Surprise was my only advantage. Perhaps I could trip him with the pipe wrench, send him flying, and create an escape route. As I waited balanced between the two pipes below the catwalk, I realized I had never been so vulnerable, so outnumbered, and so afraid as in this surreal place. My hands shook so much that I nearly dropped the wrench. Moreover, I was completely beyond the authority of WaterForce to engage. No matter what I did, it would be over the line. Which should I choose—keeping within my authority, or saving New York? Not a fair choice. I readied my arm with the pipe wrench, reaching up so that it could trip him.

He caught up with me very quickly, but before I could act he stopped, reached up, and fiddled with the light bulb until it blinked off, on, then off. I could see now. It was a signal, not a fuse. And there was something familiar about the shoe on the catwalk just over my head. It was a Skechers GoBionic orange athletic shoe, with yellow accents. Parker!

"Parker, it's me, down below you!" I whispered hoarsely.

He hit the deck, and found my eyes peering from below. "Titus! Damn! Just in time! Come up here. We've got them surrounded. Hurry!"

I scrambled over the pipes and up onto the catwalk. There was time for a brief brotherly hug before another signal came from the ceiling lights. I realized that the enemies below were covered in shadow and would not see the signal that was so clear on our level. The signals came from fifty feet away now, and I could finally see who it was. But there was no time for an explanation. Parker counted to ten as he ran forward. I ran behind, not knowing what the plan was, or what I could do to help. Suddenly, both men jumped off the catwalk and landed feet first on top of the men below. There was a struggle, sharp metallic noises, and finally four or five gunshots. A bullet ricocheted off the ceiling and hit one of the smaller pipes. A stream of water leaked out, and splashed onto the catwalk below. Another bullet ricocheted off the ceiling. Pain seared through the left side of my body just at the moment I was prepared to jump on top of one of the terrorists. I could feel the bone splintering my left shoulder. I aborted the jump, and scrambled to hold on to the outside pipe above the action with a precarious bear hug. I held tightly onto the wrench.

I could hear Parker moaning, and knew he'd been hit. There was an ongoing struggle below. I could hear Fateen's curt orders. When I looked over the edge, he was directly below me. Suddenly I saw Anthony's boot flying through the air and connecting with Fateen's face. I remembered the karate training Anthony had a few years before. He jabbed again at Fateen's neck, and the terrorist went down, but another man quickly moved in to replace him. That was when I jumped down into the melee. I connected with number two terrorist feet first, hitting him in the head and chest. But two more men jumped on Anthony, and I could see he was in real trouble. But he had a crazy and determined look on his face.

Chapter 57

Heroes and Rescuers

M y man Anthony was ready for them. I don't know how he did this, but within seconds he'd taken them both out, both unconscious on the floor. But a bottle of Ricin capsules rolled across the catwalk and landed in the water below. I knew we had to get that thing out before it contaminated the runoff trough. And Fateen was up and fighting again. Anthony could not have seen him behind. I knew I was the only one who could react in time. He went down when I swung the pipe wrench and hit him on the back of the head. I retrieved the bottle of capsules from the water. It was floating, and I hoped the capsules had not been touched by water. This time I did it bare-handed, fearing I would be contaminated with Ricin. In fact, I could feel a tingling in my fingers as I shoved the bottle into my jacket pocket, searching for the inner foil Hershey's wrapper. Was it imaginary, or was I going to die from the slightest contact with the treacherous poison?

I heard the sound of the elevator in the distance. It was a century-old industrial elevator with chains rattling like Marley's ghost, and an open wire cage that revealed the occupants. Should I run back and try to secure the door until I knew who was inside? Anthony would not appreciate being left with two attackers, but what if there were more in the elevator? I took off running along the lower catwalk, and arrived at the door seconds before the elevator car arrived. The lights were dim enough to leave questions, so I jammed the pipe wrench into the door handles and shouted, "Who are you? Who's inside there?"

"Reinforcements, my lad. Police and DEP officers!" It was Professor Jacoby's voice. Five officers and Professor Jac. The NYPD bomb squad experts were equipped to defuse the explosives left in the tunnels. The DEP officers were ready to handle toxins. After I turned over the two bottles to them, I guided the NYPD to my baseball hat marker at the junction, and we entered the dark chamber. My shoulder was bleeding and the pain nearly made me pass out, but I was the only one who knew where to lead them through the maze.

I could see Anthony at a distance with his two attackers. He'd come prepared with rope, and had already tied one securely to the metal catwalk grid. The other writhed in pain, holding his neck. By the time we caught up with him he had both tethered to the lower catwalk, and was standing guard over them. I was bursting with amazement. Anthony was a hero!

More police arrived in the second elevator trip, and fanned out to search the maze of tunnels and pipes. The explosives that had been hooked up to blasting caps were defused and rendered harmless. The gang of terrorists was arrested and taken away. Professor Jac shook our hands and smiled like a crescent moon. When we arrived on the top level, the *New York Post* was there to photograph Parker, Anthony, and me with Professor Jac. We looked like mud puppies, but we managed to straighten our WaterForce berets and sashes for the photo. From there we went directly to Bellevue Hospital, still full of police cars and DEP waiting for trouble.

The headline in the *New York Times* the next day shouted "WaterForce Heros Save New York". On page 2, there was a picture of Anthony, reunited with his paint-spattered beret, and a story about the information he provided to police, his days on the "Inside' with a terrorist leader, and the hero he became down in the tunnels under Central Park. Page 3 featured two columns about how Officer Herb Rose—my dad!—captured Mohammed Punjab, the Pakistani mole who had been embedded in the DEP for all those years, providing inside information to the terrorists that allowed them to attack vulnerable points in the system.

Meanwhile, several prisoners were transferred to mainland US prisons. The official reason was to manipulate space in the many US brigs and prisons. Fifteen remaining inmates staged a hunger strike at Guantanamo, but the President vowed to keep them in custody. There was a special report on the WaterForce Angels, with pictures of Professor Jac, the mayor, Dad, Anthony, Parker, and yours truly, all toasting each other with glasses of pristine Catskill water from a New York City tap; no champagne necessary. That photo was taken on the best day of my life.

The B.I.I.J. was thought to be an elaborate hoax created by a small core of international terrorists smart enough to rig the system and create widespread fear in New York by striking at strategic places along the secure route of drinking water into the City. Without the inside information from Mo, they quickly ceased to be a threat. There still was not a shred of evidence that they represented an existing international coalition.

After extensive tests, no traces of Ricin were found in my body. The scrapes on my arms did not come in contact with the sealed bottle of Ricin. But my left shoulder needed two operations and months of healing from the gunshot. The following week, Professor Jac awarded Parker and me a full scholarship to NYU, gratefully paid by the City of New York. Michael's guilty verdicts earned him ten to twenty years in a federal prison for terrorism, followed by life in a state prison for the murders of three men.

For months we were all celebrities. Anthony wore his blue beret and sash on the Stephen Colbert Show, and paraded around like a peacock, as if he needed another ego boost. And the WaterForce Angels, financed discretely and privately by the endowment left by Arnold Rosendael in 1954, continued to assist the DEP to patrol the nineteen reservoirs supplying New York City. Like their predecessors, The Guardian Angels, they perform a valuable function to patrol the nineteen reservoirs supplying water to New York City.

Life is back to normal in New York. The City people and the Catskill Mountain citizens tend to get along a little better, now that everyone understands what a symbiotic relationship they have with each other. But some habits never change: New Yorkers still pay over three bucks for a bottle of water that isn't nearly as pure as good old Catskill water, right out of the tap, and still the best water in any city in the country, if not the world.

ABOUT THE AUTHOR

Jack Bell Stewart, author/word artist

I grew up a curious eccentric in Cleveland, Ohio. With an MFA in Design from Indiana University, I designed sets and lights for several hundred theatre productions in New York and regional theater. Tempted by bigger budgets and fees I could actually live on, I migrated into trade show and special event design. I designed and directed design for exhibits and environments for Adidas, Merck, Mitsubishi, Comedy Central, SGI, Johnson & Johnson, GE Financial, Hewlett Packard, Acclaim, Astra Zeneca, and other major corporations, and worked on the 1980 Winter Olympics. I worked for big exhibit firms until I started my own design group in the mid 90s. For fourteen years, it was a blast to be my own boss and offer alternative thinking at Jack Stewart Design Inc. With projects throughout the world, I was honored with several awards over the years for marketing and design and taught seminars on design marketing and branding. I served on two college faculties.

But when it ceases to be fun anymore, it's time to move on. Find a new creative outlet. Reinvent yourself! After writing hundreds of creative design proposals, I got tired of answering to somebody else's marketing plan. I began to write fiction. My creative muse started to inspire me in new ways. SO, it was inevitable. I fired myself as a designer, and began to write fiction.

However, let's go back a few years. After living in New York City and several other major cities, I designed my own home in 2007 and moved to the Catskill Mountains. Porcupine, fox, black bear, deer, bald eagle, pheasant, wild turkey, coyote, and other critters shared our no-hunting zone.

The longer I lived in the Catskill Mountains, the more I became aware of the very real possibility of terrorism against the New York City water supply somewhere in the reservoir system located in the area in which I lived. *WaterForce* is the result of my research into this very real threat. The locations in this work of fiction are real. Many of the local attitudes, events, official policies, and possibilities are real. I have purposefully fictionalized some of the most vulnerable locations so as not to make this work of fiction into a recipe for disaster. For example, Although Belvedere Castle is a real location, I have no idea if there is a labyrinth of pipes and valves below it or not. Best to keep what is "too much information" in the fiction column. My hope is that someone will read this, and be motivated to help the severely understaffed DEP by forming a similar citizens' action group like the WaterForce Angels. Terrorism is now an all-too-real part of our lives. They will never stop discovering our vulnerabilities if we don't protect our way of life, and the necessities like our water supply, essential systems that perhaps we take too much for granted.

Thanks for reading. Send me a message if you have feedback or criticism. I need all the help I can get.

Jack Bell Stewart
jackbellstewart9@gmail.com

www.ingramcontent.com/pod-product-compliance
Lightning Source LLC
Chambersburg PA
CBHW061302170626
46817CB00001B/21

* 9 7 8 0 6 9 2 1 0 2 7 5 6 *